THE HUMAN STAIN

In 1998 Philip Roth won the Pulitzer Prize for *American Pastoral* and received the National Medal of Arts at the White House. In 2002 he received the highest award of the American Academy of Arts and Letters, the Gold Medal in Fiction, previously awarded to John Dos Passos, William Faulkner, and Saul Bellow, among others. He has twice won the National Book Award, the PEN/Faulkner Award, and the National Book Critics Circle Award.

In 2005 Philip Roth will become the third living American writer to have his work published in a comprehensive, definitive edition by the Library of America. The last of the eight volumes is scheduled for publication in 2013.

ALSO BY PHILIP ROTH

Zuckerman Books

The Ghost Writer
Zuckerman Unbound
The Anatomy Lesson
The Prague Orgy

The Counterlife

American Pastoral
I Married a Communist

Roth Books

The Facts
Deception
Patrimony
Operation Shylock
The Plot Against America

Kepesh Books

The Breast
The Professor of Desire
The Dying Animal

Miscellany

Reading Myself and Others
Shop Talk

Other Books

Goodbye, Columbus
Letting Go
When She Was Good
Portnoy's Complaint
Our Gang
The Great American Novel
My Life as a Man
Sabbath's Theater

Philip Roth

THE HUMAN STAIN

VINTAGE BOOKS
London

Published by Vintage 2005

6 8 10 9 7 5

Copyright © Philip Roth 2000

Philip Roth has asserted his right under the Copyright, Designs
and Patents Act 1988 to be identified as the author of this work

First published in Great Britain by
Jonathan Cape in 2000

First published by Vintage in 2001

Vintage
Random House, 20 Vauxhall Bridge Road,
London SW1V 2SA

www.vintage-books.co.uk

Addresses for companies within The Random House Group
Limited can be found at: www.randomhouse.co.uk/offices.htm

The Random House Group Limited Reg. No. 954009

The quotation from *Oedipus the King* is from the David Grene
translation (*Three Greek Tragedies in Translation*, University of
Chicago Press, 1942). The dictionary definitions on pp. 84 and
85 are from *The Random House Dictionary of the English
Language* (1973, p. 1375). The author wishes to acknowledge
as a primary source *Gouldtown, a Very Remarkable Settlement
of Ancient Date*, by William Steward and Theophilus G Steward
(JB Lippincot Co., 1913)

A CIP catalogue record for this book
is available from the British Library

ISBN 9780099282198

The Random House Group Limited supports The Forest
Stewardship Council (FSC), the leading international forest
certification organisation. All our titles that are printed on
Greenpeace approved FSC certified paper carry the FSC logo.
Our paper procurement policy can be found at:
www.rbooks.co.uk/environment

Printed in the UK by CPI Bookmarque, Croydon, CR0 4TD

For R. M.

OEDIPUS:
What is the rite
of purification? How shall it be done?

CREON:
By banishing a man, or expiation
of blood by blood . . .

—Sophocles, *Oedipus the King*

The Human Stain

1

Everyone Knows

IT WAS in the summer of 1998 that my neighbor Coleman Silk—
who, before retiring two years earlier, had been a classics professor
at nearby Athena College for some twenty-odd years as well as serving for sixteen more as the dean of faculty—confided to me that, at
the age of seventy-one, he was having an affair with a thirty-four-
year-old cleaning woman who worked down at the college. Twice a
week she also cleaned the rural post office, a small gray clapboard
shack that looked as if it might have sheltered an Okie family from
the winds of the Dust Bowl back in the 1930s and that, sitting alone
and forlorn across from the gas station and the general store, flies
its American flag at the junction of the two roads that mark the
commercial center of this mountainside town.

Coleman had first seen the woman mopping the post office floor
when he went around late one day, a few minutes before closing
time, to get his mail—a thin, tall, angular woman with graying
blond hair yanked back into a ponytail and the kind of severely
sculpted features customarily associated with the church-ruled,
hardworking goodwives who suffered through New England's
harsh beginnings, stern colonial women locked up within the reign-
ing morality and obedient to it. Her name was Faunia Farley, and
whatever miseries she endured she kept concealed behind one of
those inexpressive bone faces that hide nothing and bespeak an

immense loneliness. Faunia lived in a room at a local dairy farm
where she helped with the milking in order to pay her rent. She'd
had two years of high school education.

The summer that Coleman took me into his confidence about
Faunia Farley and their secret was the summer, fittingly enough,
that Bill Clinton's secret emerged in every last mortifying detail—
every last *lifelike* detail, the livingness, like the mortification, exuded by the pungency of the specific data. We hadn't had a season
like it since somebody stumbled upon the new Miss America nude
in an old issue of *Penthouse,* pictures of her elegantly posed on her
knees and on her back that forced the shamed young woman to relinquish her crown and go on to become a huge pop star. Ninety-
eight in New England was a summer of exquisite warmth and sunshine, in baseball a summer of mythical battle between a home-run
god who was white and a home-run god who was brown, and in
America the summer of an enormous piety binge, a purity binge,
when terrorism—which had replaced communism as the prevailing threat to the country's security—was succeeded by cocksuck-
ing, and a virile, youthful middle-aged president and a brash, smit-
ten twenty-one-year-old employee carrying on in the Oval Office
like two teenage kids in a parking lot revived America's oldest communal passion, historically perhaps its most treacherous and sub-
versive pleasure: the ecstasy of sanctimony. In the Congress, in the
press, and on the networks, the righteous grandstanding creeps,
crazy to blame, deplore, and punish, were everywhere out moraliz-
ing to beat the band: all of them in a calculated frenzy with what
Hawthorne (who, in the 1860s, lived not many miles from my door)
identified in the incipient country of long ago as "the persecut-
ing spirit"; all of them eager to enact the astringent rituals of purification that would excise the erection from the executive branch,
thereby making things cozy and safe enough for Senator Lieber-
man's ten-year-old daughter to watch TV with her embarrassed
daddy again. No, if you haven't lived through 1998, you don't know
what sanctimony is. The syndicated conservative newspaper col-
umnist William F. Buckley wrote, "When Abelard did it, it was

possible to prevent its happening again," insinuating that the president's malfeasance—what Buckley elsewhere called Clinton's "incontinent carnality"—might best be remedied with nothing so bloodless as impeachment but, rather, by the twelfth-century punishment meted out to Canon Abelard by the knife-wielding associates of Abelard's ecclesiastical colleague, Canon Fulbert, for Abelard's secret seduction of and marriage to Fulbert's niece, the virgin Heloise. Unlike Khomeini's fatwa condemning to death Salman Rushdie, Buckley's wistful longing for the corrective retribution of castration carried with it no financial incentive for any prospective perpetrator. It was prompted by a spirit no less exacting than the ayatollah's, however, and in behalf of no less exalted ideals.

It was the summer in America when the nausea returned, when the joking didn't stop, when the speculation and the theorizing and the hyperbole didn't stop, when the moral obligation to explain to one's children about adult life was abrogated in favor of maintaining in them every illusion about adult life, when the smallness of people was simply crushing, when some kind of demon had been unleashed in the nation and, on both sides, people wondered "Why are we so crazy?," when men and women alike, upon awakening in the morning, discovered that during the night, in a state of sleep that transported them beyond envy or loathing, they had dreamed of the brazenness of Bill Clinton. I myself dreamed of a mammoth banner, draped dadaistically like a Christo wrapping from one end of the White House to the other and bearing the legend A HUMAN BEING LIVES HERE. It was the summer when—for the billionth time—the jumble, the mayhem, the mess proved itself more subtle than this one's ideology and that one's morality. It was the summer when a president's penis was on everyone's mind, and life, in all its shameless impurity, once again confounded America.

Sometimes on a Saturday, Coleman Silk would give me a ring and invite me to drive over from my side of the mountain after dinner to listen to music, or to play, for a penny a point, a little gin rummy, or to sit in his living room for a couple of hours and sip some cognac and help him get through what was always for him the worst night of the week. By the summer of 1998, he had been alone up here—alone in the large old white clapboard house where he'd raised four children with his wife, Iris—for close to two years, ever since Iris suffered a stroke and died overnight while he was in the midst of battling with the college over a charge of racism brought against him by two students in one of his classes.

Coleman had by then been at Athena almost all his academic life, an outgoing, sharp-witted, forcefully smooth big-city charmer, something of a warrior, something of an operator, hardly the prototypical pedantic professor of Latin and Greek (as witness the Conversational Greek and Latin Club that he started, heretically, as a young instructor). His venerable survey course in ancient Greek literature in translation—known as GHM, for Gods, Heroes, and Myth—was popular with students precisely because of everything direct, frank, and unacademically forceful in his comportment. "You know how European literature begins?" he'd ask, after having taken the roll at the first class meeting. "With a quarrel. All of European literature springs from a fight." And then he picked up his copy of *The Iliad* and read to the class the opening lines. "'Divine Muse, sing of the ruinous wrath of Achilles . . . Begin where they first quarreled, Agamemnon the King of men, and great Achilles.' And what are they quarreling about, these two violent, mighty souls? It's as basic as a barroom brawl. They are quarreling over a woman. A girl, really. A girl stolen from her father. A girl abducted in a war. *Mia kouri*—that is how she is described in the poem. *Mia*, as in modern Greek, is the indefinite article 'a'; *kouri*, or girl, evolves in modern Greek into *kori*, meaning daughter. Now, Agamemnon much prefers this girl to his wife, Clytemnestra. 'Clytemnestra is not as good as she is,' he says, 'neither in face nor in figure.' That puts directly enough, does it not, why he doesn't want to give her up? When Achilles demands that Agamemnon return the girl to her father in order to assuage Apollo, the god who is murderously angry about the circumstances surrounding her abduction, Agamemnon refuses: he'll agree only if Achilles gives him *his* girl in exchange. Thus reigniting Achilles. Adrenal Achilles: the most highly flammable of explosive wildmen any writer has ever enjoyed portraying; especially where his prestige and his appetite are concerned, the most hypersensitive killing machine in the history of warfare. Celebrated Achilles: alienated and estranged by a slight to his honor. Great heroic Achilles, who, through the strength of his rage at an insult—the insult of not getting the girl—isolates himself, positions himself defiantly outside the very society whose glorious protector he is and whose need of him is enormous. A quarrel, then, a brutal quarrel over a young girl and her young body and the delights of sexual rapacity: there, for better or worse, in this offense against the phallic entitlement, the phallic *dignity*, of a powerhouse of a warrior prince, is how the great imaginative literature of Europe begins, and that is why, close to three thousand years later, we are going to begin there today . . ."

Coleman was one of a handful of Jews on the Athena faculty when he was hired and perhaps among the first of the Jews permitted to teach in a classics department anywhere in America; a few years earlier, Athena's solitary Jew had been E. I. Lonoff, the all-but-forgotten short story writer whom, back when I was myself a newly published apprentice in trouble and eagerly seeking the validation of a master, I had once paid a memorable visit to here. Through the eighties and into the nineties, Coleman was also the first and only Jew ever to serve at Athena as dean of faculty; then, in 1995, after retiring as dean in order to round out his career back in the classroom, he resumed teaching two of his courses under the aegis of the combined languages and literature program that had absorbed the Classics Department and that was run by Professor Delphine Roux. As dean, and with the full support of an ambitious new president, Coleman had taken an antiquated, backwater, Sleepy Hollowish college and, not without steamrolling, put an end to the place as a gentlemen's farm by aggressively encouraging the deadwood among the faculty's old guard to seek early retirement, recruiting ambitious young assistant professors, and revolutionizing the curriculum. It's almost a certainty that had he retired, without incident, in his own good time, there would have been the fest-schrift, there would have been the institution of the Coleman Silk Lecture Series, there would have been a classical studies chair established in his name, and perhaps—given his importance to the twentieth-century revitalization of the place—the humanities building or even North Hall, the college's landmark, would have been renamed in his honor after his death. In the small academic world where he had lived the bulk of his life, he would have long ceased to be resented or controversial or even feared, and, instead, officially glorified forever.

It was about midway into his second semester back as a full-time professor that Coleman spoke the self-incriminating word that would cause him voluntarily to sever all ties to the college—the single self-incriminating word of the many millions spoken aloud in his years of teaching and administering at Athena, and the word that, as Coleman understood things, directly led to his wife's death.

The class consisted of fourteen students. Coleman had taken attendance at the beginning of the first several lectures so as to learn their names. As there were still two names that failed to elicit a response by the fifth week into the semester, Coleman, in the sixth week, opened the session by asking, "Does anyone know these people? Do they exist or are they spooks?"

Later that day he was astonished to be called in by his successor, the new dean of faculty, to address the charge of racism brought against him by the two missing students, who turned out to be black, and who, though absent, had quickly learned of the locution in which he'd publicly raised the question of their absence. Coleman told the dean, "I was referring to their possibly ectoplasmic character. Isn't that obvious? These two students had not attended a single class. That's all I knew about them. I was using the word in its customary and primary meaning: 'spook' as a specter or a ghost. I had no idea what color these two students might be. I had known perhaps fifty years ago but had wholly forgotten that 'spooks' is an invidious term sometimes applied to blacks. Otherwise, since I am totally meticulous regarding student sensibilities, I would never

· 6 ·

have used that word. Consider the context: Do they exist *or* are they spooks? The charge of racism is spurious. It is preposterous. My colleagues know it is preposterous and my students know it is preposterous. The issue, the only issue, is the nonattendance of these two students and their flagrant and inexcusable neglect of work. What's galling is that the charge is not just false—it is spectacularly false." Having said altogether enough in his defense, considering the matter closed, he left for home.

Now, even ordinary deans, I am told, serving as they do in a no man's land between the faculty and the higher administration, invariably make enemies. They don't always grant the salary raises that are requested or the convenient parking places that are so coveted or the larger offices professors believe they are entitled to. Candidates for appointments or promotion, especially in weak departments, are routinely rejected. Departmental petitions for additional faculty positions and secretarial help are almost always turned down, as are requests for reduced teaching loads and for freedom from early morning classes. Funds for travel to academic conferences are regularly denied, et cetera, et cetera. But Coleman had been no ordinary dean, and who he got rid of and how he got rid of them, what he abolished and what he established, and how audaciously he performed his job into the teeth of tremendous resistance succeeded in more than merely slighting or offending a few odd ingrates and malcontents. Under the protection of Pierce Roberts, the handsome young hotshot president with all the hair who came in and appointed him to the deanship—and who told him, "Changes are going to be made, and anybody who's unhappy should just think about leaving or early retirement"—Coleman had overturned everything. When, eight years later, midway through Coleman's tenure, Roberts accepted a prestigious Big Ten presidency, it was on the strength of a reputation for all that had been achieved at Athena in record time—achieved, however, not by the glamorous president who was essentially a fund-raiser, who'd taken none of the hits and moved on from Athena heralded and unscathed, but by his determined dean of faculty.

In the very first month he was appointed dean, Coleman had invited every faculty member in for a talk, including several senior professors who were the scions of the old county families who'd founded and originally endowed the place and who themselves didn't really need the money but gladly accepted their salaries. Each of them was instructed beforehand to bring along his or her c.v., and if someone didn't bring it, because he or she was too grand, Coleman had it in front of him on his desk anyway. And for a full hour he kept them there, sometimes even longer, until, having so persuasively indicated that things at Athena had at long last changed, he had begun to make them sweat. Nor did he hesitate to open the interview by flipping through the c.v. and saying, "For the last eleven years, just what *have* you been doing?" And when they told him, as an overwhelming number of the faculty did, that they'd been publishing regularly in *Athena Notes*, when he'd heard one time too many about the philological, bibliographical, or archaeological scholarly oddment each of them annually culled from an ancient Ph.D. dissertation for "publication" in the mimeographed quarterly bound in gray cardboard that was cataloged nowhere on earth but in the college library, he was reputed to have dared to break the Athena civility code by saying, "In other words, you people recycle your own trash." Not only did he then shut down *Athena Notes* by returning the tiny bequest to the donor—the father-in-law of the editor—but, to encourage early retirement, he forced the deadest of the deadwood out of the courses they'd been delivering by rote for the last twenty or thirty years and into freshman English and the history survey and the new freshman orientation program held during the hot last days of the summer. He eliminated the ill-named Scholar of the Year Prize and assigned the thousand dollars elsewhere. For the first time in the college's history, he made people apply formally, with a detailed project description, for paid sabbatical leave, which was more often than not denied. He got rid of the clubby faculty lunchroom, which boasted the most exquisite of the paneled oak interiors on the campus, converted it back into the honors seminar room it was intended to be, and made the faculty eat in the cafeteria with the students. He insisted on faculty meetings—never holding them had made the previous dean enormously popular. Coleman had attendance taken by the faculty secretary so that even the eminences with the three-hour-a-week schedules were forced onto the campus to show up. He found a provision in the college constitution that said there were to be no executive committees, and arguing that those stodgy impediments to serious change had grown up only by convention and tradition, he abolished them and ruled these faculty meetings by fiat, using each as an occasion to announce what he was going to do next that was sure to stir up even more resentment. Under his leadership, promotion became difficult—and this, perhaps, was the greatest shock of all: people were no longer promoted through rank automatically on the basis of being popular teachers, and they didn't get salary increases that weren't tied to merit. In short, he brought in competition, he made the place competitive, which, as an early enemy noted, "is what Jews do." And whenever an angry ad hoc committee was formed to go and complain to Pierce Roberts, the president unfailingly backed Coleman.

In the Roberts years all the bright younger people he recruited loved Coleman because of the room he was making for them and because of the good people he began hiring out of graduate programs at Johns Hopkins and Yale and Cornell—"the revolution of quality," as they themselves liked to describe it. They prized him for taking the ruling elite out of their little club and threatening their self-presentation, which never fails to drive a pompous professor crazy. All the older guys who were the weakest part of the faculty had survived on the ways that they thought of themselves—the greatest scholar of the year 100 B.C., and so forth—and once those were challenged from above, their confidence eroded and, in a matter of a few years, they had nearly all disappeared. Heady times! But after Pierce Roberts moved on to the big job at Michigan, and Haines, the new president, came in with no particular loyalty to Coleman—and, unlike his predecessor, exhibiting no special tolerance for the brand of bulldozing vanity and autocratic ego that had cleaned the place out in so brief a period—and as the young people Coleman had kept on as well as those he'd recruited began to become the veteran faculty, a reaction against Dean Silk started to set in. How strong it was he had never entirely realized until he counted all the people, department by department, who seemed to be not at all displeased that the word the old dean had chosen to characterize his two seemingly nonexistent students was definable not only by the primary dictionary meaning that he maintained was obviously the one he'd intended but by the pejorative racial meaning that had sent his two black students to lodge their complaint.

I remember clearly that April day two years back when Iris Silk died and the insanity took hold of Coleman. Other than to offer a nod to one or the other of them whenever our paths crossed down at the general store or the post office, I had not really known the Silks or anything much about them before then. I hadn't even known that Coleman had grown up some four or five miles away from me in the tiny Essex County town of East Orange, New Jersey, and that, as a 1944 graduate of East Orange High, he had been some six years ahead of me in my neighboring Newark school. Coleman had made no effort to get to know me, nor had I left New York and moved into a two-room cabin set way back in a field on a rural road high in the Berkshires to meet new people or to join a new community. The invitations I received during my first months out here in 1993—to come to a dinner, to tea, to a cocktail party, to trek to the college down in the valley to deliver a public lecture or, if I preferred, to talk informally to a literature class—I politely declined, and after that both the neighbors and the college let me be to live and do my work on my own.

But then, on that afternoon two years back, having driven directly from making arrangements for Iris's burial, Coleman was at the side of my house, banging on the door and asking to be let in. Though he had something urgent to ask, he couldn't stay seated for more than thirty seconds to clarify what it was. He got up, sat down, got up again, roamed round and round my workroom, speaking loudly and in a rush, even menacingly shaking a fist in the air when—erroneously—he believed emphasis was needed. I had to write something for him—he all but ordered me to. If he wrote the story in all of its absurdity, altering nothing, nobody would believe it, nobody would take it seriously, people would say it was a ludicrous lie, a self-serving exaggeration, they would say that more than his having uttered the word "spooks" in a classroom had to lie behind his downfall. But if *I* wrote it, if a professional writer wrote it . . .

All the restraint had collapsed within him, and so watching him, listening to him—a man I did not know, but clearly someone accomplished and of consequence now completely unhinged—was like being present at a bad highway accident or a fire or a frightening explosion, at a public disaster that mesmerizes as much by its improbability as by its grotesqueness. The way he careened around the room made me think of those familiar chickens that keep on going after having been beheaded. His head had been lopped off, the head encasing the educated brain of the once unassailable faculty dean and classics professor, and what I was witnessing was the amputated rest of him spinning out of control.

I—whose house he had never before entered, whose very voice he had barely heard before—had to put aside whatever else I might be doing and write about how his enemies at Athena, in striking out at him, had instead felled her. Creating their false image of him, calling him everything that he wasn't and could never be, they had not merely misrepresented a professional career conducted with the utmost seriousness and dedication—they had killed his wife of over forty years. Killed her as if they'd taken aim and fired a bullet into her heart. I had to write about this "absurdity," that "absurdity"—I, who then knew nothing about his woes at the college and could not even begin to follow the chronology of the horror that, for five months now, had engulfed him and the late Iris

Silk: the punishing immersion in meetings, hearings, and interviews, the documents and letters submitted to college officials, to
faculty committees, to a pro bono black lawyer representing the
two students . . . the charges, denials, and countercharges, the obtuseness, ignorance, and cynicism, the gross and deliberate misin-
terpretations, the laborious, repetitious explanations, the prosecu-
torial questions—and always, perpetually, the pervasive sense of
unreality. "Her murder!" Coleman cried, leaning across my desk
and hammering on it with his fist. "These people *murdered* Iris!"

The face he showed me, the face he placed no more than a foot
from my own, was by now dented and lopsided and—for the face
of a well-groomed, youthfully handsome older man—strangely repellent, more than likely distorted from the toxic effect of all the
emotion coursing through him. It was, up close, bruised and ruined
like a piece of fruit that's been knocked from its stall in the mar-
ketplace and kicked to and fro along the ground by the passing
shoppers.

There is something fascinating about what moral suffering can
do to someone who is in no obvious way a weak or feeble person.
It's more insidious even than what physical illness can do, because
there is no morphine drip or spinal block or radical surgery to alle-
viate it. Once you're in its grip, it's as though it will have to kill you
for you to be free of it. Its raw realism is like nothing else.

Murdered. For Coleman that alone explained how, out of nowhere, the end could have come to an energetic sixty-four-year-old
woman of commanding presence and in perfect health, an abstract
painter whose canvases dominated the local art shows and who
herself autocratically administered the town artists' association, a
poet published in the county newspaper, in her day the college's
leading politically active opponent of bomb shelters, of strontium
90, eventually of the Vietnam War, opinionated, unyielding, impol-
itic, an imperious whirlwind of a woman recognizable a hundred
yards away by her great tangled wreath of wiry white hair; so strong
a person, apparently, that despite his own formidableness, the dean
who reputedly could steamroll anybody, the dean who had done

the academically impossible by bringing deliverance to Athena College, could best his own wife at nothing other than tennis.

Once Coleman had come under attack, however—once the racist charge had been taken up for investigation, not only by the new dean of faculty but by the college's small black student organization and by a black activist group from Pittsfield—the outright madness of it blotted out the million difficulties of the Silks' marriage, and that same imperiousness that had for four decades clashed with his own obstinate autonomy and resulted in the unending friction of their lives, Iris placed at the disposal of her husband's cause. Though for years they had not slept in the same bed or been able to endure very much of the other's conversation—or of the other's friends—the Silks were side by side again, waving their fists in the faces of people they hated more profoundly than, in their most insufferable moments, they could manage to hate each other. All they'd had in common as comradely lovers forty years earlier in Greenwich Village—when he was at NYU finishing up his Ph.D. and Iris was an escapee fresh from two nutty anarchist parents in Passaic and modeling for life drawing classes at the Art Students League, armed already with her thicket of important hair, big-featured and voluptuous, already then a theatrical-looking high priestess in folkloric jewelry, the biblical high priestess from before the time of the synagogue—all they'd had in common in those Village days (except for the erotic passion) once again broke wildly out into the open . . . until the morning when she awakened with a ferocious headache and no feeling in one of her arms. Coleman rushed her to the hospital, but by the next day she was dead.

"They meant to kill me and they got her instead." So Coleman told me more than once during that unannounced visit to my house, and then made sure to tell every single person at her funeral the following afternoon. And so he still believed. He was not susceptible to any other explanation. Ever since her death—and since he'd come to recognize that his ordeal wasn't a subject I wished to address in my fiction and he had accepted back from me all the documentation dumped on my desk that day—he had been at work on a book of his own about why he had resigned from Athena, a nonfiction book he was calling *Spooks*.

There's a small FM station over in Springfield that on Saturday nights, from six to midnight, takes a break from the regular classical programming and plays big-band music for the first few hours of the evening and then jazz later on. On my side of the mountain you get nothing but static tuning to that frequency, but on the slope where Coleman lives the reception's fine, and on the occasions when he'd invite me for a Saturday evening drink, all those sugary-sweet dance tunes that kids of our generation heard continuously over the radio and played on the jukeboxes back in the forties could be heard coming from Coleman's house as soon as I stepped out of my car in his driveway. Coleman had it going full blast not just on the living room stereo receiver but on the radio beside his bed, the radio beside the shower, and the radio beside the kitchen bread box. No matter what he might be doing around the house on a Saturday night, until the station signed off at midnight—following a ritual weekly half hour of Benny Goodman—he wasn't out of earshot for a minute.

Oddly, he said, none of the serious stuff he'd been listening to all his adult life put him into emotional motion the way that old swing music now did: "Everything stoical within me unclenches and the wish not to die, never to die, is almost too great to bear. And all this," he explained, "from listening to Vaughn Monroe." Some nights, every line of every song assumed a significance so bizarrely momentous that he'd wind up dancing by himself the shuffling, drifting, repetitious, uninspired, yet wonderfully serviceable, mood-making fox trot that he used to dance with the East Orange High girls on whom he pressed, through his trousers, his first meaningful erections; and while he danced, nothing he was feeling, he told me, was simulated, neither the terror (over extinction) nor the rapture (over "You sigh, the song begins. You speak, and I hear violins"). The teardrops were all spontaneously shed, however astonished he may have been by how little resistance he had to

Helen O'Connell and Bob Eberly alternately delivering the verses of
"Green Eyes," however much he might marvel at how Jimmy and
Tommy Dorsey were able to transform him into the kind of assail-
able old man he could never have expected to be. "But let anyone
born in 1926," he'd say, "try to stay alone at home on a Saturday
night in 1998 and listen to Dick Haymes singing 'Those Little White
Lies.' Just have them do that, and then let them tell me afterwards if
they have not understood at last the celebrated doctrine of the catharsis effected by tragedy."

Coleman was cleaning up his dinner dishes when I came through
a screen door at the side of the house leading into the kitchen. Because he was over the sink and the water was running, and because
the radio was loudly playing and he was singing along with the
young Frank Sinatra "Everything Happens to Me," he didn't hear
me come in. It was a hot night; Coleman wore a pair of denim
shorts and sneakers, and that was it. From behind, this man of seventy-one looked to be no more than forty—slender and fit and
forty. Coleman was not much over five eight, if that, he was not
heavily muscled, and yet there was a lot of strength in him, and a lot
of the bounce of the high school athlete was still visible, the quick-
ness, the urge to action that we used to call pep. His tightly coiled,
short-clipped hair had turned the color of oatmeal, and so head-
on, despite the boyish snub nose, he didn't look quite so youthful as
he might have if his hair were still dark. Also, there were crevices
carved deeply at either side of his mouth, and in the greenish hazel
eyes there was, since Iris's death and his resignation from the college, much, much weariness and spiritual depletion. Coleman had
the incongruous, almost puppetlike good looks that you confront
in the aging faces of movie actors who were famous on the screen
as sparkling children and on whom the juvenile star is indelibly
stamped.

All in all, he remained a neat, attractive package of a man even at
his age, the small-nosed Jewish type with the facial heft in the jaw,
one of those crimped-haired Jews of a light yellowish skin pigmen-
tation who possess something of the ambiguous aura of the pale

blacks who are sometimes taken for white. When Coleman Silk was a sailor at the Norfolk naval base down in Virginia at the close of World War II, because his name didn't give him away as a Jew—because it could as easily have been a Negro's name—he'd once been identified, in a brothel, as a nigger trying to pass and been thrown out. "Thrown out of a Norfolk whorehouse for being black, thrown out of Athena College for being white." I'd heard stuff like that from him frequently during these last two years, ravings about black anti-Semitism and about his treacherous, cowardly colleagues that were obviously being mainlined, unmodified, into his book.

"Thrown out of Athena," he told me, "for being a white Jew of the sort those ignorant bastards call the enemy. That's who's made their American misery. That's who stole them out of paradise. And that's who's been holding them back all these years. What is the major source of black suffering on this planet? They know the answer without having to come to class. They know without having to open a book. Without reading they know—without *thinking* they know. Who is responsible? The same evil Old Testament monsters responsible for the suffering of the Germans.

"They killed her, Nathan. And who would have thought that Iris couldn't take it? But strong as she was, *loud* as she was, Iris could *not*. Their brand of stupidity was too much even for a juggernaut like my wife. 'Spooks.' And who here would defend me? Herb Keble? As dean I brought Herb Keble into the college. Did it only months after taking the job. Brought him in not just as the first black in the social sciences but as the first black in anything other than a custodial position. But Herb too has been radicalized by the racism of Jews like me. 'I can't be with you on this, Coleman. I'm going to have to be with them.' This is what he told me when I went to ask for his support. To my face. *I'm going to have to be with them.* Them!

"You should have seen Herb at Iris's funeral. Crushed. Devastated. Somebody died? Herbert didn't intend for anybody to *die.*

These shenanigans were so much jockeying for power. To gain a bigger say in how the college is run. They were just exploiting a useful situation. It was a way to prod Haines and the administration into doing what they otherwise would never have done. More blacks on campus. More black students, more black professors. Representation—that was the issue. The only issue. God knows nobody was meant to *die*. Or to resign either. That too took Herbert by surprise. Why should Coleman Silk resign? Nobody was going to fire him. Nobody would dare to fire him. They were doing what they were doing just because they could do it. Their intention was to hold my feet over the flames just a little while longer—why couldn't I have been patient and waited? By the next semester who would have remembered any of it? The incident—*the incident!*—provided them with an 'organizing issue' of the sort that was needed at a racially retarded place like Athena. Why did I quit? By the time I quit it was essentially over. What the hell was I *quitting* for?"

On just my previous visit, Coleman had begun waving something in my face from the moment I'd come through the door, yet another document from the hundreds of documents filed in the boxes labeled "Spooks." "Here. One of my gifted colleagues. Writing about one of the two who brought the charges against me—a student who had never attended my class, flunked all but one of the other courses she was taking, and rarely attended *them*. I thought she flunked because she couldn't confront the material, let alone begin to master it, but it turned out that she flunked because she was too intimidated by the racism emanating from her white professors to work up the courage to go to class. The very racism that I had articulated. In one of those meetings, hearings, whatever they were, they asked me, 'What factors, in your judgment, led to this student's failure?' 'What *factors?*' I said. 'Indifference. Arrogance. Apathy. Personal distress. Who knows?' 'But,' they asked me, 'in light of these factors, what positive recommendations did you make to this student?' 'I didn't make any. I'd never laid eyes on her.

If I'd had the opportunity, I would have recommended that she leave school.' 'Why?' they asked me. 'Because she didn't belong in school.'

"Let me read from this document. Listen to this. Filed by a colleague of mine supporting Tracy Cummings as someone we should not be too harsh or too quick to judge, certainly not someone we should turn away and reject. Tracy we must nurture, Tracy we must understand—we have to know, this scholar tells us, 'where Tracy's coming from.' Let me read you the last sentences. 'Tracy is from a rather difficult background, in that she separated from her immediate family in tenth grade and lived with relatives. As a result, she was not particularly good at dealing with the realities of a situation. This defect I admit. But she is ready, willing, and able to change her approach to living. What I have seen coming to birth in her during these last weeks is a realization of the seriousness of her avoidance of reality.' Sentences composed by one Delphine Roux, chairman of Languages and Literature, who teaches, among other things, a course in French classicism. *A realization of the seriousness of her avoidance of reality.* Ah, enough. Enough. This is sickening. This is just too sickening."

That's what I witnessed, more often than not, when I came to keep Coleman company on a Saturday night: a humiliating disgrace that was still eating away at someone who was still fully vital. The great man brought low and suffering still the shame of failure. Something like what you might have seen had you dropped in on Nixon at San Clemente or on Jimmy Carter, down in Georgia, before he began doing penance for his defeat by becoming a carpenter. Something very sad. And yet, despite my sympathy for Coleman's ordeal and for all he had unjustly lost and for the near impossibility of his tearing himself free from his bitterness, there were evenings when, after having sipped only a few drops of his brandy, it required something like a feat of magic for me to stay awake.

But on the night I'm describing, when we had drifted onto the cool screened-in side porch that he used in the summertime as a study, he was as fond of the world as a man can be. He'd pulled a couple of bottles of beer from the refrigerator when we left the kitchen, and we were seated across from each other at either side of the long trestle table that was his desk out there and that was stacked at one end with composition books, some twenty or thirty of them, divided into three piles.

"Well, there it is," said Coleman, now this calm, unoppressed, entirely new being. "That's it. That's *Spooks*. Finished a first draft yesterday, spent all day today reading it through, and every page of it made me sick. The violence in the handwriting was enough to make me despise the author. That I should spend a single quarter of an hour at this, let alone two years . . . Iris died because of *them?* Who will believe it? I hardly believe it myself any longer. To turn this screed into a book, to bleach out the raging misery and turn it into something by a sane human being, would take two years more at least. And what would I then have, aside from two years more of thinking about 'them'? Not that I've given myself over to forgiveness. Don't get me wrong: I hate the bastards. I hate the fucking bastards the way Gulliver hates the whole human race after he goes and lives with those horses. I hate them with a real biological aversion. Though those horses I always found ridiculous. Didn't you? I used to think of them as the WASP establishment that ran this place when I first got here."

"You're in good form, Coleman—barely a glimmer of the old madness. Three weeks, a month ago, whenever it was I saw you last, you were still knee-deep in your own blood."

"Because of *this* thing. But I read it and it's shit and I'm over it. I can't do what the pros do. Writing about myself, I can't maneuver the creative remove. Page after page, it is still the raw thing. It's a parody of the self-justifying memoir. The hopelessness of explanation." Smiling, he said, "Kissinger can unload fourteen hundred pages of this stuff every other year, but it's defeated me. Blindly secure though I may seem to be in my narcissistic bubble, I'm no match for him. I quit."

Now, most writers who are brought to a standstill after rereading

two years' work—even one year's work, merely *half* a year's work—
and finding it hopelessly misguided and bringing down on it the
critical guillotine are reduced to a state of suicidal despair from
which it can take months to begin to recover. Yet Coleman, by
abandoning a draft of a book as bad as the draft he'd finished, had
somehow managed to swim free not only from the wreck of the
book but from the wreck of his life. Without the book he appeared
now to be without the slightest craving to set the record straight;
shed of the passion to clear his name and criminalize as murderers
his opponents, he was embalmed no longer in injustice. Aside from
watching Nelson Mandela, on TV, forgiving his jailers even as he
was leaving jail with his last miserable jail meal still being assimi-
lated into his system, I'd never before seen a change of heart transform a martyred being quite so swiftly. I couldn't understand it,
and I at first couldn't bring myself to believe in it either.

"Walking away like this, cheerfully saying, 'It's defeated me,'
walking away from all this work, from all this loathing—well, how
are you going to fill the outrage void?"

"I'm not." He got the cards and a notepad to keep score and we
pulled our chairs down to where the trestle table was clear of papers. He shuffled the cards and I cut them and he dealt. And then,
in this odd, serene state of contentment brought on by the seeming
emancipation from despising everyone at Athena who, deliberately
and in bad faith, had misjudged, misused, and besmirched him—
had plunged him, for two years, into a misanthropic exertion of
Swiftian proportions—he began to rhapsodize about the great by-
gone days when his cup ranneth over and his considerable talent
for conscientiousness was spent garnering and tendering pleasure.

Now that he was no longer grounded in his hate, we were going
to talk about women. This *was* a new Coleman. Or perhaps an
old Coleman, the oldest adult Coleman there was, the most satisfied Coleman there had ever been. Not Coleman pre-spooks and
unmaligned as a racist, but the Coleman contaminated by desire
alone.

"I came out of the navy, I got a place in the Village," he began to tell me as he assembled his hand, "and all I had to do was go down into the subway. It was like fishing down there. Go down into the subway and come up with a girl. And then"—he stopped to pick up my discard—"all at once, got my degree, got married, got my job, kids, and that was the end of the fishing."

"Never fished again."

"Almost never. True. Virtually never. As good as never. Hear these songs?" The four radios were playing in the house, and so even out on the road it would have been impossible not to hear them. "After the war, those were the songs," he said. "Four, five years of the songs, the girls, and that fulfilled my every ideal. I found a letter today. Cleaning out that *Spooks* stuff, found a letter from one of the girls. *The* girl. After I got my first appointment, out on Long Island, out at Adelphi, and Iris was pregnant with Jeff, this letter arrived. A girl nearly six feet tall. Iris was a big girl too. But not big like Steena. Iris was substantial. Steena was something else. Steena sent me this letter in 1954 and it turned up today while I was shoveling out the files."

From the back pocket of his shorts, Coleman pulled the original envelope holding Steena's letter. He was still without a T-shirt, which now that we were out of the kitchen and on the porch I couldn't help but take note of—it was a warm July night, but not that warm. He had never struck me before as a man whose considerable vanity extended also to his anatomy. But now there seemed to me to be something more than a mere at-homeness expressed in this exhibition of his body's suntanned surface. On display were the shoulders, arms, and chest of a smallish man still trim and attractive, a belly no longer flat, to be sure, but nothing that had gotten seriously out of hand—altogether the physique of someone who would seem to have been a cunning and wily competitor at sports rather than an overpowering one. And all this had previously been concealed from me, because he was always shirted and also because of his having been so drastically consumed by his rage.

Also previously concealed was the small, Popeye-ish, blue tattoo situated at the top of his right arm, just at the shoulder joining—

the words "U.S. Navy" inscribed between the hooklike arms of a shadowy little anchor and running along the hypotenuse of the deltoid muscle. A tiny symbol, if one were needed, of all the million circumstances of the other fellow's life, of that blizzard of details that constitute the confusion of a human biography—a tiny symbol to remind me why our understanding of people must always be at best slightly wrong.

"Kept it? The letter? Still got it?" I said. "Must've been some letter."

"A killing letter. Something had happened to me that I hadn't understood until that letter. I was married, responsibly employed, we were going to have a child, and yet I hadn't understood that the Steenas were over. Got this letter and I realized that the serious things had really begun, the serious life dedicated to serious things. My father owned a saloon off Grove Street in East Orange. You're a Weequahic boy, you don't know East Orange. It was the poor end of town. He was one of those Jewish saloon keepers, they were all over Jersey and, of course, they all had ties to the Reinfelds and to the Mob—they had to have, to survive the Mob. My father wasn't a roughneck but he was rough enough, and he wanted better for me. He dropped dead my last year of high school. I was the only child. The adored one. He wouldn't even let me work in his place when the types there began to entertain me. Everything in life, including the saloon—*beginning* with the saloon—was always pushing me to be a serious student, and, back in those days, studying my high school Latin, taking advanced Latin, taking Greek, which was still part of the old-fashioned curriculum, the saloon keeper's kid couldn't have tried harder to be any *more* serious."

There was some quick by-play between us and Coleman laid down his cards to show me his winning hand. As I started to deal, he resumed the story. I'd never heard it before. I'd never heard anything before other than how he'd come by his hatred for the college.

"Well," he said, "once I'd fulfilled my father's dream and become an ultra-respectable college professor, I thought, as my father did, that the serious life would now never end. That it *could* never end once you had the credentials. But it ended, Nathan. 'Or are they spooks?' and I'm out on my ass. When Roberts was here he liked to tell people that my success as a dean flowed from learning my manners in a saloon. President Roberts with his upper-class pedigree liked that he had this barroom brawler parked just across the hall from him. In front of the old guard particularly, Roberts pretended to enjoy me for my background, though, as we know, Gentiles actually hate those stories about the Jews and their remarkable rise from the slums. Yes, there was a certain amount of mockery in Pierce Roberts, and even then, yes, when I think about it, starting even *then* . . ." But here he reined himself in. Wouldn't go on with it. He was finished with the derangement of being the monarch deposed. The grievance that will never die is hereby declared dead.

Back to Steena. Remembering Steena helps enormously.

"Met her in '48," he said. "I was twenty-two, on the GI Bill at NYU, the navy behind me, and she was eighteen and only a few months in New York. Had some kind of job there and was going to college, too, but at night. Independent girl from Minnesota. Sure-of-herself girl, or seemed so. Danish on one side, Icelandic on the other. Quick. Smart. Pretty. Tall. Marvelously tall. That statuesque recumbency. Never forgotten it. With her for two years. Used to call her Voluptas. Psyche's daughter. The personification to the Romans of sensual pleasure."

Now he put down his cards, picked up the envelope from where he'd dropped it beside the discard pile, and pulled out the letter. A typewritten letter a couple of pages long. "We'd run into each other. I was in from Adelphi, in the city for the day, and there was Steena, about twenty-four, twenty-five by then. We stopped and spoke, and I told her my wife was pregnant, and she told me what she was doing, and then we kissed goodbye, and that was it. About a week later this letter came to me care of the college. It's dated. She dated it. Here—'August 18, 1954.' 'Dear Coleman,' she says, 'I was very happy to see you in New York. Brief as our meeting was, after I saw you I felt an autumnal sadness, perhaps because the six years since we first met make it wrenchingly obvious how many days of my life are "over." You look very good, and I'm glad you're happy. You were also very gentlemanly. You didn't swoop. Which is the one thing you did (or seemed to do) when I first met you and you rented the basement room on Sullivan Street. Do you remember yourself? You were incredibly good at swooping, almost like birds do when they fly over land or sea and spy something moving, something bursting with life, and dive down—or zero in—and seize upon it. I was astonished, when we met, by your flying energy. I remember being in your room the first time and, when I arrived, I sat in a chair, and you were walking around the room from place to place, occasionally stopping to perch on a stool or the couch. You had a ratty Salvation Army couch where you slept before we chipped in for The Mattress. You offered me a drink, which you handed to me while scrutinizing me with an air of incredible wonder and curiosity, as if it were some kind of miracle that I had hands and could hold a glass, or that I had a mouth which might drink from it, or that I had even materialized at all, in your room, a day after we'd met on the subway. You were talking, asking questions, sometimes answering questions, in a deadly serious and yet hilarious way, and I was trying very hard to talk also but conversation was not coming as easily to me. So there I was staring back at you, absorbing and understanding far more than I expected to understand. But I couldn't find words to speak to fill the space created by the fact that you seemed attracted to me and that I was attracted to you. I kept thinking, "I'm not ready. I just arrived in this city. Not now. But I will be, with a little more time, a few more exchanged notes of conversation, if I can think what I wish to say." ("Ready" for what, I don't know. Not just making love. Ready to *be*.) But then you "swooped," Coleman, nearly halfway across the room, to where I was sitting, and I was flabbergasted but delighted. It was too soon, but it wasn't.'"

He stopped reading when he heard, coming from the radio, the first bars of "Bewitched, Bothered, and Bewildered" being sung by Sinatra. "I've got to dance," Coleman said. "Want to dance?"

I laughed. No, this was not the savage, embittered, embattled avenger of *Spooks*, estranged from life and maddened by it—this was not even another man. This was another *soul*. A boyish soul at that. I got a strong picture then, both from Steena's letter and from Coleman, shirtless, as he was reading it, of what Coleman Silk had once been like. Before becoming a revolutionary dean, before becoming a serious classics professor—and long before becoming Athena's pariah—he had been not only a studious boy but a charming and seductive boy as well. Excited. Mischievous. A bit demonic even, a snub-nosed, goat-footed Pan. Once upon a time, before the serious things took over completely.

"After I hear the rest of the letter," I replied to the invitation to dance. "Read me the rest of Steena's letter."

"Three months out of Minnesota when we met. Just went down into the subway and brought her up with me. Well," he said, "that was 1948 for you," and he turned back to her letter. "'I was quite taken with you,'" he read, "'but I was concerned you might find me too young, an uninteresting midwestern bland sort of girl, and besides, you were dating someone "smart and nice and lovely" already, though you added, with a sly smile, "I don't believe she and I will get married." "Why not?" I asked. "I may be getting bored," you answered, thereby ensuring that I would do anything I could think of not to bore you, including dropping out of contact, if necessary, so as to avoid the risk of becoming boring. Well, that's it. That's enough. I shouldn't even bother you. I promise I won't ever again. Take care. Take care. Take care. Take care. Very fondly, Steena.'"

"Well," I said, "that *is* 1948 for you."

"Come. Let's dance."

"But you mustn't sing into my ear."

"Come on. Get up."

What the hell, I thought, we'll both be dead soon enough, and so I got up, and there on the porch Coleman Silk and I began to dance the fox trot together. He led, and, as best I could, I followed. I remembered that day he'd burst into my studio after making burial arrangements for Iris and, out of his mind with grief and rage, told me that I had to write for him the book about all the unbelievable absurdities of his case, culminating in the murder of his wife. One would have thought that never again would this man have a taste for the foolishness of life, that all that was playful in him and light-hearted had been destroyed and lost, right along with the career, the reputation, and the formidable wife. Maybe why it didn't even cross my mind to laugh and let him, if he wanted to, dance around the porch by himself, just laugh and enjoy myself watching him— maybe why I gave him my hand and let him place his arm around my back and push me dreamily around that old bluestone floor was because I had been there that day when her corpse was still warm and seen what he'd looked like.

"I hope nobody from the volunteer fire department drives by," I said.

"Yeah," he said. "We don't want anybody tapping me on the shoulder and asking, 'May I cut in?'"

On we danced. There was nothing overtly carnal in it, but because Coleman was wearing only his denim shorts and my hand rested easily on his warm back as if it were the back of a dog or a horse, it wasn't entirely a mocking act. There was a semi-serious sincerity in his guiding me about on the stone floor, not to mention a thoughtless delight in just being alive, accidentally and clownishly and for no reason alive—the kind of delight you take as a child when you first learn to play a tune with a comb and toilet paper.

It was when we sat down that Coleman told me about the woman. "I'm having an affair, Nathan. I'm having an affair with a thirty-four-year-old woman. I can't tell you what it's done to me."

"We just finished dancing—you don't have to."

"I thought I couldn't take any more of anything. But when this stuff comes back so late in life, out of nowhere, completely unex-pected, even unwanted, comes back at you and there's nothing to dilute it with, when you're no longer striving on twenty-two fronts, no longer deep in the daily disorder . . . when it's just *this* . . ."

"And when she's thirty-four."

"And ignitable. An ignitable woman. She's turned sex into a vice again."

"'La Belle Dame sans Merci hath thee in thrall.'"

"Seems so. I say, 'What is it like for you with somebody seventy-one?' and she tells me, 'It's perfect with somebody seventy-one. He's set in his ways and he can't change. You know what he is. No surprises.'"

"What's made her so wise?"

"Surprises. Thirty-four years of savage surprises have given her wisdom. But it's a very narrow, antisocial wisdom. It's savage, too. It's the wisdom of somebody who expects nothing. That's her wisdom, and that's her dignity, but it's negative wisdom, and that's not the kind that keeps you on course day to day. This is a woman whose life's been trying to grind her down almost for as long as she's had life. Whatever she's learned comes from that."

I thought, He's found somebody he can talk with . . . and then I thought, So have I. The moment a man starts to tell you about sex, he's telling you something about the two of you. Ninety percent of the time it doesn't happen, and probably it's as well it doesn't, though if you can't get a level of candor on sex and you choose to behave instead as if this isn't ever on your mind, the male friendship is incomplete. Most men never find such a friend. It's not common. But when it does happen, when two men find themselves in agreement about this essential part of being a man, unafraid of being judged, shamed, envied, or outdone, confident of not having the confidence betrayed, their human connection can be very strong and an unexpected intimacy results. This probably isn't usual for him, I was thinking, but because he'd come to me in his worst moment, full of the hatred that I'd watched poison him over the months, he feels the freedom of being with someone who's seen you through a terrible illness from the side of your bed. He feels not so much the urge to brag as the enormous relief of not having to keep something so bewilderingly new as his own rebirth totally to himself.

"Where did you find her?" I asked.

"I went to pick up my mail at the end of the day and there she was, mopping the floor. She's the skinny blonde who sometimes cleans out the post office. She's on the regular janitorial staff at Athena. She's a full-time janitor where I was once dean. The woman has nothing. Faunia Farley. That's her name. Faunia has absolutely nothing."

"Why has she nothing?"

"She had a husband. He beat her so badly she ended up in a coma. They had a dairy farm. He ran it so badly it went bankrupt. She had two children. A space heater tipped over, caught fire, and both children were asphyxiated. Aside from the ashes of the two children that she keeps in a canister under her bed, she owns nothing of value except an '83 Chevy. The only time I've seen her come close to crying was when she told me, 'I don't know what to do with the ashes.' Rural disaster has squeezed Faunia dry of even her tears. And she began life a rich, privileged kid. Brought up in a big sprawling house south of Boston. Fireplaces in the five bedrooms, the best antiques, heirloom china—everything old and the best, the family included. She can be surprisingly well spoken if she wants to be. But she's dropped so far down the social ladder from so far up that by now she's a pretty mixed bag of verbal beans. Faunia's been exiled from the entitlement that should have been hers. Declassed. There's a real democratization to her suffering."

"What undid her?"

"A stepfather undid her. Upper-bourgeois evil undid her. There was a divorce when she was five. The prosperous father caught the beautiful mother having an affair. The mother liked money, remarried money, and the rich stepfather wouldn't leave Faunia alone. Fondling her from the day he arrived. Couldn't stay away from her. This blond angelic child, fondling her, fingering her—it's when he tried fucking her that she ran away. She was fourteen. The mother refused to believe her. They took her to a psychiatrist. Faunia told the psychiatrist what happened, and after ten sessions the psychiatrist too sided with the stepfather. 'Takes the side of those who pay him,' Faunia says. 'Just like everyone.' The mother had an affair with the psychiatrist afterward. That is the story, as she reports it, of what launched her into the life of a tough having to make her way on her own. Ran away from home, from high school, went down south, worked there, came back up this way, got whatever work she could, and at twenty married this farmer, older than herself, a dairy farmer, a Vietnam vet, thinking that if they worked hard and raised kids and made the farm work she could have a stable, ordinary life, even if the guy was on the dumb side. Especially if he was on the dumb side. She thought she might be better off being the one with the brains. She thought that was her advantage. She was wrong. All they had together was trouble. The farm failed. 'Jerk-off,' she tells me, 'bought one tractor too many.' And regularly beat her up. Beat her black and blue. You know what she presents as the high point of the marriage? The event she calls 'the great warm shit fight.' One evening they are in the barn after the milking arguing about something, and a cow next to her takes a big shit, and Faunia picks up a handful and flings it in Lester's face. He flings a handful back, and that's how it started. She said to me, 'The warm shit fight may have been the best time we had together.' At the end, they were covered with cow shit and roaring with laughter, and, after washing off with the hose in the barn, they went up to the house to fuck. But that was carrying a good thing too far. That wasn't one-hundredth of the fun of the fight. Fucking Lester wasn't ever fun—according to Faunia, he didn't know how to do it. 'Too dumb even to fuck right.' When she tells me that I am the perfect man, I tell her that I see how that might seem so to her, coming to me after him."

"And fighting the Lesters of life with warm shit since she's fourteen has made her what at thirty-four," I asked, "aside from savagely wise? Tough? Shrewd? Enraged? Crazy?"

"The fighting life has made her tough, certainly sexually tough, but it hasn't made her crazy. At least I don't think so yet. Enraged? If it's there—and why wouldn't it be?—it's a furtive rage. Rage without the rage. And, for someone who seems to have lived entirely without luck, there's no lament in her—none she shows to me, anyway. But as for shrewd, no. She says things sometimes that sound shrewd. She says, 'Maybe you ought to think of me as a companion of equal age who happens to look younger. I think that's where

I'm at.' When I asked, 'What do you want from me?' she said, 'Some companionship. Maybe some knowledge. Sex. Pleasure. Don't worry. That's it.' When I told her once she was wise beyond her years, she told me, 'I'm dumb beyond my years.' She was sure smarter than Lester, but shrewd? No. Something in Faunia is permanently fourteen and as far as you can get from shrewd. She had an affair with her boss, the guy who hired her. Smoky Hollenbeck. *I* hired *him*—guy who runs the college's physical plant. Smoky used to be a football star here. Back in the seventies I knew him as a student. Now he's a civil engineer. He hires Faunia for the custodial staff, and even while he's hiring her, she understands what's on his mind. The guy is attracted to her. He's locked into an unexciting marriage, but he's not angry with her about it—he's not looking at her disdainfully, thinking, Why haven't you settled down, why are you still tramping and whoring around? No bourgeois superiority from Smoky. Smoky is doing all the right things and doing them beautifully—a wife, kids, *five* kids, married as a man can be, a sports hero still around the college, popular and admired in town—but he has a gift: he can also step outside of that. You wouldn't believe it to talk to him. Mr. Athena Square squared, performing in every single way he is supposed to perform. Appears to have bought into the story of himself one hundred percent. You would expect him to think, This stupid bitch with her fucked-up life? Get her the fuck out of my office. But he doesn't. Unlike everyone else in Athena, he is not so caught up in the legend of Smoky that he is incapable of thinking, Yeah, this is a real cunt I'd like to fuck. Or incapable of acting. He fucks her, Nathan. Gets Faunia in bed with him and another of the women from the custodial staff. Fucks 'em together. Goes on for six months. Then a real estate woman, newly divorced, fresh on the local scene, *she* joins the act. Smoky's circus. Smoky's secret three-ring circus. But then, after six months, he drops her—takes Faunia out of the rotation and drops her. I knew nothing about any of this till she told me. And she only told me because one night in bed, her eyes roll back into her head and she calls me by his name. Whispers to me, 'Smoky.' On top of old Smoky. Her being with him in that ménage gave me a better idea of the dame I was dealing with. Upped the ante. Gave me a jolt, actually—this is no amateur. When I ask her how Smoky manages to attract his hordes, she tells me, 'By the force of his prick.' 'Explain,' I say, and she tells me, 'You know how when a real cunt walks into a room, a man knows it? Well, the same thing happens the other way round. With certain people, no matter what the disguise, you understand what they're there to do.' In bed is the only place where Faunia is in any way shrewd, Nathan. A spontaneous physical shrewdness plays the leading role in bed—second lead played by transgressive audacity. In bed nothing escapes Faunia's attention. Her flesh has eyes. Her flesh sees everything. In bed she is a powerful, coherent, unified being whose pleasure is in overstepping the boundaries. In bed she is a deep phenomenon. Maybe that's a gift of the molestation. When we go downstairs to the kitchen, when I scramble some eggs and we sit there eating together, she's a kid. Maybe that's a gift of the molestation too. I am in the company of a blank-eyed, distracted, incoherent kid. This happens nowhere else. But whenever we eat, there it is: me and my kid. Seems to be all the daughter that's left in her. She can't sit up straight in her chair, she can't string two sentences together having anything to do with each other. All the seeming nonchalance about sex and tragedy, all of that disappears, and I'm sitting there wanting to say to her, 'Pull yourself up to the table, get the sleeve of my bathrobe out of your plate, try to listen to what I'm saying, and look at me, damn it, when you speak.'"

"*Do* you say it?"

"Doesn't seem advisable. No, I don't—not as long as I prefer to preserve the intensity of what *is* there. I think of that canister under her bed, where she keeps the ashes she doesn't know what to do with, and I want to say, 'It's two years. It's time to bury them. If you can't put them in the ground, then go down to the river and shake out the ashes from the bridge. Let them float off. Let them go. I'll go do it with you. We'll do it together.' But I am not the father to this daughter—that's not the role I play here. I'm not her professor. I'm not anyone's professor. From teaching people, correcting people, advising and examining and enlightening people, I am retired. I am a seventy-one-year-old man with a thirty-four-year-old mistress; this disqualifies me, in the commonwealth of Massachusetts, from enlightening anyone. I'm taking Viagra, Nathan. *There's* La Belle Dame sans Merci. I owe all of this turbulence and happiness to Viagra. Without Viagra none of this would be happening. Without Viagra I would have a picture of the world appropriate to my age and wholly different aims. Without Viagra I would have the dignity of an elderly gentleman free from desire who behaves correctly. I would not be doing something that makes no sense. I would not be doing something unseemly, rash, ill considered, and potentially disastrous for all involved. Without Viagra, I could continue, in my declining years, to develop the broad impersonal perspective of an experienced and educated honorably discharged man who has long ago given up the sensual enjoyment of life. I could continue to draw profound philosophical conclusions and have a steadying moral influence on the young, instead of having put myself back into the perpetual state of emergency that is sexual intoxication. Thanks to Viagra I've come to understand Zeus's amorous transformations. That's what they should have called Viagra. They should have called it Zeus."

Is he astonished to be telling me all this? I think he may be. But he's too enlivened by it all to stop. The impulse is the same one that drove him to dance with me. Yes, I thought, it's no longer writing *Spooks* that's the defiant rebound from humiliation; it's fucking Faunia. But there's more even than that driving him. There's the wish to let the brute out, let that force out—for half an hour, for two hours, for whatever, to be freed into the natural thing. He was married a long time. He had kids. He was the dean at a college. For forty years he was doing what was necessary to do. He was busy, and the natural thing that is the brute was moved into a box. And now that box is opened. Being a dean, being a father, being a husband, being a scholar, a teacher, reading the books, giving the lectures, marking the papers, giving the grades, it's over. At seventy-one you're not the high-spirited, horny brute you were at twenty-six, of course. But the remnants of the brute, the remnants of the natural thing—he is in touch now with the remnants. And he's happy as a result, he's grateful to be in touch with the remnants. He's more than happy—he's thrilled, and he's bound, deeply bound to her already, because of the thrill. It's not family that's doing it—biology has no use for him anymore. It's not family, it's not responsibility, it's not duty, it's not money, it's not a shared philosophy or the love of literature, it's not big discussions of great ideas. No, what binds him to her is the thrill. Tomorrow he develops cancer, and boom. But today he has this thrill.

Why is he telling me? Because to be able to abandon oneself to this freely, someone has to know it. He's free to be abandoned, I thought, because there's nothing at stake. Because there is no future. Because he's seventy-one and she's thirty-four. He's in it not for learning, not for planning, but for adventure; he's in it as she is: for the ride. He's been given a lot of license by those thirty-seven years. An old man and, one last time, the sexual charge. What is more moving for anybody?

"Of course I have to ask," Coleman said, "what she's doing with *me*. What is really going through her mind? An exciting new experience for her, to be with a man as old as her grandfather?"

"I suppose there is that type of woman," I said, "for whom it *is* an exciting experience. There's every other type, why shouldn't there be that type? Look, there is obviously a department somewhere, Coleman, a federal agency that deals with old men, and she comes from that agency."

"As a young guy," Coleman told me, "I was never involved with ugly women. But in the navy I had a friend, Farriello, and ugly women were his specialty. Down at Norfolk, if we went to a dance at a church, if we went at night to the USO, Farriello made a beeline for the ugliest girl. When I laughed at him, he told me I didn't know what I was missing. They're frustrated, he told me. They're not as beautiful, he told me, as the empresses you choose, so they'll do whatever you want. Most men are stupid, he said, because they don't know this. They don't understand that if only you approach the ugliest woman, she is the one who is the most extraordinary. If you can open her up, that is. But if you succeed? If you succeed in opening her up, you don't know what to do first, she is vibrating so. And all because she's ugly. Because she is never chosen. Because she is in the corner when all the other girls dance. And that's what it's like to be an old man. To be like that ugly girl. To be in the corner at the dance."

"So Faunia's your Farriello."

He smiled. "More or less."

"Well, whatever else may be going on," I told him, "thanks to Viagra you're no longer suffering the torture of writing that book."

"I think that's so," Coleman said. "I think that's true. That stupid book. And did I tell you that Faunia can't read? I found this out when we drove up to Vermont one night for dinner. Couldn't read the menu. Tossed it aside. She has a way, when she wants to look properly contemptuous, of lifting just a half of her upper lip, lifting it a hair, and then speaking what's on her mind. Properly contemptuous, she says to the waitress, 'Whatever he has, ditto.'"

"She went to school until she was fourteen. How come she can't read?"

"The ability to read seems to have perished right along with the childhood when she learned how. I asked her how this could happen, but all she did was laugh. 'Easy,' she says. The good liberals down at Athena are trying to encourage her to enter a literacy program, but Faunia's not having it. 'And don't *you* try to teach me. Do anything you want with me, anything,' she told me that night, 'but don't pull that shit. Bad enough having to hear people speak. Start teaching me to read, force me into that, push reading on me, and it'll be you who push me over the edge.' All the way back from Vermont, I was silent, and so was she. Not until we reached the house did we utter a word to each other. 'You're not up to fucking somebody who can't read,' she said. 'You're going to drop me because I'm not a worthy, legitimate person who *reads*. You're going to say to me, 'Learn to read or go.' 'No,' I told her, 'I'm going to fuck you all the harder because you can't read.' 'Good,' she said, 'we understand each other. I don't do it like those literate girls and I don't want to be done to like them.' 'I'm going to fuck you,' I said, 'for just what you are.' 'That's the ticket,' she says. We were both laughing by then. Faunia's got the laugh of a barmaid who keeps a baseball bat at her feet in case of trouble, and so she was laughing that laugh of hers, that scrappy, I've-seen-it-all laugh—you know, the coarse, easy laugh of the woman with a past—and by then she's unzipping my fly. But she was right on the money about my having decided to give her up. All the way back from Vermont I was thinking exactly what she said I was thinking. But I'm not going to do that. I'm not going to impose my wonderful virtue on her. Or on myself. That's over. I know these things don't come without a cost. I know that there's no insurance you can buy on this. I know how the thing that's restoring you can wind up killing you. I know that every mistake that a man can make usually has a sexual accelerator. But right now I happen not to care. I wake up in the morning, there's a towel on the floor, there's baby oil on the bedside table. How did all that get there? Then I remember. Got there because I'm alive again. Because I'm back in the tornado. Because this is what it is with a capital isness. I'm not going to give her up, Nathan. I've started to call her Voluptas."

As a result of surgery I had several years ago to remove my prostate—cancer surgery that, though successful, was not without the adverse aftereffects almost unavoidable in such operations because of nerve damage and internal scarring—I've been left incontinent, and so, the first thing I did when I got home from Coleman's was to dispose of the absorbent cotton pad that I wear night and day, slipped inside the crotch of my underwear the way a hot dog lies in a roll. Because of the heat that evening, and because I wasn't going out to a public place or a social gathering, I'd tried to get by with ordinary cotton briefs pulled on over the pad instead of the plastic ones, and the result was that the urine had seeped through to my khaki trousers. I discovered when I got home that the trousers were discolored at the front and that I smelled a little—the pads are treated, but there was, on this occasion, an odor. I'd been so engaged by Coleman and his story that I'd failed to monitor myself. All the while I was there, drinking a beer, dancing with him, attending to the clarity—the predictable rationality and descriptive clarity—with which he worked to make less unsettling to himself this turn that life had taken, I hadn't gone off to check myself, as ordinarily I do during my waking hours, and so, what from time to time now happens to me happened that night.

No, a mishap like this one doesn't throw me as much as it used to when, in the months after the surgery, I was first experimenting with the ways of handling the problem—and when, of course, I was habituated to being a free and easy, dry and odorless adult possessing an adult's mastery of the body's elementary functions, someone who for some sixty years had gone about his everyday business unworried about the status of his underclothes. Yet I do suffer at least a pang of distress when I have to deal with something messier than the ordinary inconvenience that is now a part of my life, and I still despair to think that the contingency that virtually defines the infant state will never be alleviated.

I was also left impotent by the surgery. The drug therapy that was practically brand-new in the summer of 1998 and that had already, in its short time on the market, proved to be something like a miraculous elixir, restoring functional potency to many otherwise healthy, elderly men like Coleman, was of no use to me because of the extensive nerve damage done by the operation. For conditions like mine Viagra could do nothing, though even had it proved helpful, I don't believe I would have taken it.

I want to make clear that it wasn't impotence that led me into a reclusive existence. To the contrary. I'd already been living and writing for some eighteen months in my two-room cabin up here in the Berkshires when, following a routine physical exam, I received a preliminary diagnosis of prostate cancer and, a month later, after the follow-up tests, went to Boston for the prostatectomy. My point is that by moving here I had altered deliberately my relationship to the sexual caterwaul, and not because the exhortations or, for that matter, my erections had been effectively weakened by time, but because I couldn't meet the costs of its clamoring anymore, could no longer marshal the wit, the strength, the patience, the illusion, the irony, the ardor, the egoism, the resilience— or the toughness, or the shrewdness, or the falseness, the dissembling, the dual being, the erotic *professionalism*—to deal with its array of misleading and contradictory meanings. As a result, I was able to lessen a little my postoperative shock at the prospect of permanent impotence by remembering that all the surgery had done was to make me hold to a renunciation to which I had already voluntarily submitted. The operation did no more than to enforce with finality a decision I'd come to on my own, under the pressure of a lifelong experience of entanglements but in a time of full, vigorous, and restless potency, when the venturesome masculine mania to repeat the act—repeat it and repeat it and repeat it—remained undeterred by physiological problems.

It wasn't until Coleman told me about himself and his Voluptas that all the comforting delusions about the serenity achieved through enlightened resignation vanished, and I completely lost my equilibrium. Well into the morning I lay awake, powerless as a lunatic to control my thinking, hypnotized by the other couple and comparing them to my own washed-out state. I lay awake not even trying to prevent myself from mentally reconstructing the "transgressive audacity" Coleman was refusing to relinquish. And my having danced around like a harmless eunuch with this still vital, potent participant in the frenzy struck me now as anything but charming self-satire.

How can one say, "No, this isn't a part of life," since it always is? The contaminant of sex, the redeeming corruption that de-idealizes the species and keeps us everlastingly mindful of the matter we are.

In the middle of the next week, Coleman got the anonymous letter, one sentence long, subject, predicate, and pointed modifiers boldly inscribed in a large hand across a single sheet of white typing paper, the twelve-word message, intended as an indictment, filling the sheet from top to bottom:

> Everyone knows you're
> sexually exploiting an
> abused, illiterate
> woman half your
> age.

The writing on both the envelope and the letter was in red ball-point ink. Despite the envelope's New York City postmark, Coleman recognized the handwriting immediately as that of the young French woman who'd been his department chair when he'd returned to teaching after stepping down from the deanship and who, later, had been among those most eager to have him exposed as a racist and reprimanded for the insult he had leveled at his absent black students.

In his *Spooks* files, on several of the documents generated by his case, he found samples of handwriting that confirmed his identification of Professor Delphine Roux, of Languages and Literature, as the anonymous letter writer. Aside from her having printed rather than written in script the first couple of words, she hadn't made any effort that Coleman could see to put him off the trail by falsifying her hand. She might have begun with that intention but appeared to have abandoned it or forgotten about it after getting no further than "Everyone knows." On the envelope, the French-born professor hadn't even bothered to eschew the telltale European sevens in Coleman's street address and zip code. This laxness, an odd disregard—in an anonymous letter—for concealing the signs of one's identity, might have been explained by some extreme emotional state she was in that hadn't allowed her to think through what she was doing before firing off the letter, except that it hadn't been posted locally—and hastily—but appeared from the postmark to have been transported some hundred and forty miles south before being mailed. Maybe she had figured that there was nothing distinctive or eccentric enough in her handwriting for him

to be able to recognize it from his days as dean; maybe she had
failed to remember the documents pertaining to his case, the notes
of her two interviews with Tracy Cummings that she had passed on
to the faculty investigating committee along with the final report
that bore her signature. Perhaps she didn't realize that, at Coleman's request, the committee had provided him with a photocopy
of her original notes and all the other data pertinent to the complaint against him. Or maybe she didn't care if he did determine
who out there had uncovered his secret: maybe she wanted both to
taunt him with the menacing aggressiveness of an anonymous indictment and, at the same time, to all but disclose that the indictment had been brought by someone now far from powerless.

The afternoon Coleman called and asked me to come over to see
the anonymous letter, all the samples of Delphine Roux's handwriting from the *Spooks* files were neatly laid out on the kitchen table,
both the originals and copies of the originals that he'd already run
off and on which he'd circled, in red, every stroke of the pen that he
saw as replicating the strokes in the anonymous letter. Marked off
mainly were letters in isolation—a *y*, an *s*, an *x*, here a word-ending
e with a wide loop, here an *e* looking something like an *i* when nestled up against an adjacent *d* but more like a conventionally written
e when preceding an *r*—and, though the similarities in writing
between the letter and the *Spooks* documents were noteworthy, it
wasn't until he showed me where his full name appeared on the envelope and where it appeared in her interview notes with Tracy
Cummings that it seemed to me indisputable that he had nailed the
culprit who'd set out to nail him.

Everyone knows you're
sexually exploiting an
abused, illiterate
woman half your
age.

While I held the letter in my hand and as carefully as I could—
and as Coleman would have me do—appraised the choice of words

and their linear deployment as if they'd been composed not by Delphine Roux but by Emily Dickinson, Coleman explained to me that it was Faunia, out of that savage wisdom of hers, and not he who had sworn them both to the secrecy that Delphine Roux had somehow penetrated and was more or less threatening to expose. "I don't want anybody butting in my life. All I want is a no-pressure bang once a week, on the sly, with a man who's been through it all and is nicely cooled out. Otherwise it's nobody's fucking business."

The nobody Faunia turned out mostly to be referring to was Lester Farley, her ex-husband. Not that she'd been knocked around in her life by this man alone—"How could I be, being out there on my own since I was fourteen?" When she was seventeen, for example, and down in Florida waitressing, the then-boyfriend not only beat her up and trashed her apartment, he stole her vibrator. "That hurt," Faunia said. And always, the provocation was jealousy. She'd looked at another man the wrong way, she'd invited another man to look at *her* the wrong way, she hadn't explained convincingly where she'd been for the previous half hour, she'd spoken the wrong word, used the wrong intonation, signaled, unsubstantially, *she* thought, that she was an untrustworthy two-timing slut—whatever the reason, whoever he might be would be over her swinging his fists and kicking his boots and Faunia would be screaming for her life.

Lester Farley had sent her to the hospital twice in the year before their divorce, and as he was still living somewhere in the hills and, since the bankruptcy, working for the town road crew, and as there was no doubting that he was still crazy, she was as frightened for Coleman, she said, as she was for herself, should he ever discover what was going on. She suspected that why Smoky had so precipitously dumped her was because of some sort of run-in or brush he'd had with Les Farley—because Les, a periodic stalker of his ex-wife, had somehow found out about her and her boss, even though Hollenbeck's trysting places were remarkably well hidden, tucked away in remote corners of old buildings that no one but the boss of the college physical plant could possibly know existed or have access to. Reckless as it might seem for Smoky to be recruiting girlfriends from his own custodial staff and then to be rendezvousing with them right on campus, he was otherwise as meticulous in the management of his sporting life as he was in his work for the college. With the same professional dispatch that could get the campus roads cleared of a blizzard in a matter of hours, he could, if need be, equally expeditiously rid himself of one of his girls.

"So what do I do?" Coleman asked me. "I wasn't against keeping this thing concealed even before I'd heard about the violent ex-husband. I knew that something like this was coming. Forget that I was once the dean where she now cleans the toilets. I'm seventy-one and she's thirty-four. I could count on that alone to do it, I was sure, and so, when she told me that it was nobody's business, I figured, She's taken it out of my hands. I don't even have to broach the subject. Play it like adultery? Fine with me. That's why we went for dinner up in Vermont. That's why if our paths cross at the post office, we don't even bother to say hello."

"Maybe somebody saw you in Vermont. Maybe somebody saw you driving together in your car."

"True—that's probably what happened. That's all that *could* have happened. It might have been Farley himself who saw us. Christ, Nathan, I hadn't been on a date in almost fifty years—I thought the restaurant . . . I'm an idiot."

"No, it wasn't idiocy. No, no—you just got claustrophobic. Look," I said, "Delphine Roux—I won't pretend I understand why she should care so passionately who you are screwing in your retirement, but since we know that other people don't do well with somebody who fails at being conventional, let's assume that she is one of these other people. But you're not. You're free. A free and independent man. A free and independent *old* man. You lost plenty quitting that place, but what about what you've gained? It's no longer your job to enlighten anyone—you said as much yourself. Nor is this a test of whether you can or cannot rid yourself of every last social inhibition. You may now be retired but you're a man who led virtually the whole of life within the bounds of the communal academic society—if I read you right, this is a most unusual thing for you. Perhaps you never wanted Faunia to have happened. You may even believe that you shouldn't want her to have happened. But the strongest defenses are riddled with weakness, and so in slips the last thing in the world you expected. At seventy-one, there is Faunia; in 1998, there is Viagra; there once again is the all-but-forgotten thing. The enormous comfort. The crude power. The disorienting intensity. Out of nowhere, Coleman Silk's last great fling. For all we know, the last great last-*minute* fling. So the particulars of Faunia Farley's biography form an unlikely contrast to your own. So they don't conform to decency's fantasy blueprint for who should be in bed with a man of your years and your position—if anyone should be. Did what resulted from your speaking the word 'spooks' conform to decency's blueprint? Did Iris's stroke conform to decency's blueprint? Ignore the inanely stupid letter. Why should you let it deter you?"

"*Anonymous* inanely stupid letter," he said. "Who has ever sent me an anonymous letter? Who capable of rational thought sends anyone an anonymous letter?"

"Maybe it's a French thing," I said. "Isn't there a lot of it in Balzac? In Stendhal? Aren't there anonymous letters in *The Red and the Black*?"

"I don't remember."

"Look, for some reason everything you do must have ruthlessness as its explanation, and everything Delphine Roux does must have virtue as its explanation. Isn't mythology full of giants and monsters and snakes? By defining you as a monster, she defines herself as a heroine. This is her slaying of the monster. This is her revenge for your preying on the powerless. She's giving the whole thing mythological status."

From the smile indulgently offered me, I saw that I wasn't making much headway by spinning off, even jokingly, a pre-Homeric interpretation of the anonymous indictment. "You can't find in mythmaking," he told me, "an explanation for her mental processes. She hasn't the imaginative resources for mythmaking. Her métier is the stories that the peasants tell to account for their misery. The evil eye. The casting of spells. I've cast a spell over Faunia. Her métier is folktales full of witches and wizards."

We were enjoying ourselves now, and I realized that in my effort to distract him from his rampaging pique by arguing for the primacy of his pleasure, I had given a boost to his feeling for me—and exposed mine for him. I was gushing and I knew it. I surprised myself with my eagerness to please, felt myself saying too much, explaining too much, overinvolved and overexcited in the way you are when you're a kid and you think you've found a soul mate in the new boy down the street and you feel yourself drawn by the force of the courtship and so act as you don't normally do and a lot more openly than you may even want to. But ever since he had banged on my door the day after Iris's death and proposed that I write *Spooks* for him, I had, without figuring or planning on it, fallen into a serious friendship with Coleman Silk. I wasn't paying attention to his predicament as merely a mental exercise. His difficulties mattered to me, and this despite my determination to concern myself, in whatever time *I* have left, with nothing but the daily demands of work, to be engrossed by nothing but solid work, in search of adventure nowhere else—to have not even a life of my own to care about, let alone somebody else's.

And I realized all this with some disappointment. Abnegation of society, abstention from distraction, a self-imposed separation from every last professional yearning and social delusion and cultural poison and alluring intimacy, a rigorous reclusion such as that practiced by religious devouts who immure themselves in caves or cells or isolated forest huts, is maintained on stuff more obdurate than I am made of. I had lasted alone just five years—five years of reading and writing a few miles up Madamaska Mountain in a pleasant two-room cabin situated between a small pond at the back of my place and, through the scrub across the dirt road, a ten-acre marsh where the migrating Canada geese take shelter each evening and a patient blue heron does its solitary angling all summer long.

The secret to living in the rush of the world with a minimum of pain is to get as many people as possible to string along with your delusions; the trick to living alone up here, away from all agitating entanglements, allurements, and expectations, apart especially from one's own intensity, is to organize the silence, to think of its mountaintop plenitude as capital, silence as wealth exponentially increasing. The encircling silence as your chosen source of advantage and your only intimate. The trick is to find sustenance in (Hawthorne again) "the communications of a solitary mind with itself." The secret is to find sustenance in *people* like Hawthorne, in the wisdom of the brilliant deceased.

It took time to face down the difficulties set by this choice, time and heronlike patience to subdue the longings for everything that had vanished, but after five years I'd become so skillful at surgically carving up my days that there was no longer an hour of the eventless existence I'd embraced that didn't have its importance to me. Its necessity. Its excitement even. I no longer indulged the pernicious wish for *something else,* and the last thing I thought I could endure again was the sustained company of *someone else.* The music I play after dinner is not a relief from the silence but something like its substantiation: listening to music for an hour or two every evening doesn't deprive me of the silence—the music is the silence coming true. I swim for thirty minutes in my pond first thing every summer morning, and, for the rest of the year, after my morning of writing—and so long as the snow doesn't make hiking impossible—I'm out on the mountain trails for a couple of hours nearly every afternoon. There has been no recurrence of the cancer that cost me my prostate. Sixty-five, fit, well, working hard—and I know the score. I *have* to know it.

So why, then, having turned the experiment of radical seclusion into a rich, full solitary existence—why, with no warning, should I be lonely? Lonely for what? What's gone is gone. There's no relaxing the rigor, no undoing the renunciations. Lonely for precisely what? Simple: for what I had developed an aversion to. For what I had turned my back on. For life. The entanglement with life.

This was how Coleman became my friend and how I came out from under the stalwartness of living alone in my secluded house and dealing with the cancer blows. Coleman Silk danced me right back into life. First Athena College, then me—here was a man who made things happen. Indeed, the dance that sealed our friendship was also what made his disaster my subject. And made his disguise my subject. And made the proper presentation of his secret my problem to solve. That was how I ceased being able to live apart from the turbulence and intensity that I had fled. I did no more than find a friend, and all the world's malice came rushing in.

Later that afternoon, Coleman took me to meet Faunia at a small dairy farm six miles from his house, where she lived rent-free in exchange for sometimes doing the milking. The dairy operation, a few years old now, had been initiated by two divorced women, college-educated environmentalists, who'd each come from a New England farming family and who had pooled their resources—pooled their young children as well, six children who, as the owners liked to tell their customers, weren't dependent on *Sesame Street* to learn where milk comes from—to take on the almost impossible task of making a living by selling raw milk. It was a unique operation, nothing like what was going on at the big dairy farms, nothing impersonal or factorylike about it, a place that wouldn't seem like a dairy farm to most people these days. It was called Organic Livestock, and it produced and bottled the raw milk that could be found in local general stores and in some of the region's supermarkets and was available, at the farm, for steady customers who purchased three or more gallons a week.

There were just eleven cows, purebred Jerseys, and each had an old-fashioned cow name rather than a numbered ear tag to identify it. Because their milk was not mixed with the milk of the huge herds that are injected with all sorts of chemicals, and because, uncompromised by pasteurization and unshattered by homogenization, the milk took on the tinge, even faintly the flavor, of whatever they were eating season by season—feed that had been grown

without the use of herbicides, pesticides, or chemical fertilizers—
and because their milk was richer in nutrients than blended milk, it
was prized by the people around who tried to keep the family diet
to whole rather than processed foods. The farm has a strong following particularly among the numerous people tucked away up here,
the retired as well as those raising families, in flight from the pol-
lutants, frustrations, and debasements of a big city. In the local
weekly, a letter to the editor will regularly appear from someone
who has recently found a better life out along these rural roads, and
in reverent tones mention will be made of Organic Livestock milk,
not simply as a tasty drink but as the embodiment of a freshen-
ing, sweetening country purity that their city-battered idealism requires. Words like "goodness" and "soul" crop up regularly in these
published letters, as if downing a glass of Organic Livestock milk
were no less a redemptive religious rite than a nutritional blessing.
"When we drink Organic Livestock milk, our body, soul, and spirit
are getting nourished as a whole. Various organs in our body receive this wholeness and appreciate it in a way we may not per-
ceive." Sentences like that, sentences with which otherwise sensible
adults, liberated from whatever vexation had driven them from
New York or Hartford or Boston, can spend a pleasant few minutes
at the desk pretending that they are seven years old.

Though Coleman probably used, all told, no more than the half
cup of milk a day he poured over his morning cereal, he'd signed on
with Organic Livestock as a three-gallon-a-week customer. Doing
this allowed him to pick up his milk, fresh from the cow, right at the
farm—to drive his car in from the road and down the long tractor
path to the barn and to walk into the barn and get the milk cold out
of the refrigerator. He'd arranged to do this not so as to be able to
procure the price break extended to three-gallon customers but because the refrigerator was set just inside the entryway to the barn
and only some fifteen feet from the stall where the cows were led in
to be milked one at a time, twice a day, and where at 5 P.M. (when he
showed up) Faunia, fresh from her duties at the college, would be
doing the milking a few times a week.

All he ever did there was watch her work. Even though there was rarely anyone else around at that time, Coleman remained outside the stall looking in and let her get on with the job without having to bother to talk to him. Often they said nothing, because saying nothing intensified their pleasure. She knew he was watching her; knowing she knew, he watched all the harder—and that they weren't able to couple down in the dirt didn't make a scrap of difference. It was enough that they should be alone together somewhere *other* than in his bed, it was enough to have to maintain the matter-of-factness of being separated by unsurpassable social obstacles, to play their roles as farm laborer and retired college professor, to perform consummately at her being a strong, lean working woman of thirty-four, a wordless illiterate, an elemental rustic of muscle and bone who'd just been in the yard with the pitchfork cleaning up from the morning milking, and at his being a thoughtful senior citizen of seventy-one, an accomplished classicist, an amplitudinous brain of a man replete with the vocabularies of two ancient tongues. It was enough to be able to conduct themselves like two people who had nothing whatsoever in common, all the while remembering how they could distill to an orgasmic essence everything about them that was irreconcilable, the human discrepancies that produced all the power. It was enough to feel the thrill of leading a double life.

There was, at first glance, little to raise unduly one's carnal expectations about the gaunt, lanky woman spattered with dirt, wearing shorts and a T-shirt and rubber boots, whom I saw in with the herd that afternoon and whom Coleman identified as his Voluptas. The carnally authoritative-looking creatures were those with the bodies that took up all the space, the creamy-colored cows with the free-swinging, girderlike hips and the barrel-wide paunches and the disproportionately cartoonish milk-swollen udders, the unagitated, slow-moving, strife-free cows, each a fifteen-hundred-pound industry of its own gratification, big-eyed beasts for whom chomping at one extremity from a fodder-filled trough while being sucked dry at the other by not one or two or three but by four pulsating, untiring mechanical mouths—for whom sensual stimulus simultaneously at both ends was their voluptuous due. Each of them deep into a bestial existence blissfully lacking in spiritual depth: to squirt and to chew, to crap and to piss, to graze and to sleep—that was their whole raison d'être. Occasionally (Coleman explained to me) a human arm in a long plastic glove is thrust into the rectum to haul out the manure and then, by feeling with the glove through the rectal wall, guides the other arm in inserting a syringelike breeding gun up the reproductive tract to deposit semen. They propagate, that means, without having to endure the disturbance of the bull, coddled even in breeding and then assisted in delivery— and in what Faunia said could prove to be an emotional process for everyone involved—even on below-zero nights when a blizzard is blowing. The best of carnal everything, including savoring at their leisure mushy, dripping mouthfuls of their own stringy cud. Few courtesans have lived as well, let alone workaday women.

Among those pleasured creatures and the aura they exuded of an opulent, earthy oneness with female abundance, it was Faunia who labored like the beast of burden for all that she seemed, with the cows framing her figure, one of evolution's more pathetic flyweights. Calling them to come out from the open shed where they were reposefully sprawled in a mix of hay and shit—"Let's go, Daisy, don't give me a hard time. C'mon now, Maggie, that's a good girl. Move your ass, Flossie, you old bitch"—grabbing them by the collar and driving and cajoling them through the sludge of the yard and up one step onto the concrete floor of the milking parlor, shoving these cumbersome Daisys and Maggies in toward the trough until they were secure in the stanchion, measuring out and pouring them each their portion of vitamins and feed, disinfecting the teats and wiping them clean and starting the milk flow with a few jerks of the hand, then attaching to the sterilized teats the suction cups at the end of the milk claw, she was in motion constantly, fixed unwaveringly on each stage of the milking but, in exaggerated contrast to their stubborn docility, moving all the time with a beelike adroitness until the milk was streaming through the clear milk tube into the shining stainless-steel pail, and she at last stood quietly by, watching to make certain that everything was working and that the cow too was standing quietly. Then she was again in motion, massaging the udder to be sure the cow was milked out, removing the teat cups, pouring out the feed portion for the cow she would be milking after undoing the milked cow from the stanchion, getting the grain for the next cow in front of the alternate stanchion, and then, within the confines of that smallish space, grabbing the milked cow by the collar again and maneuvering her great bulk around, backing her up with a push, shoving her with a shoulder, bossily telling her, "Get out, get on out of here, just get—" and leading her back through the mud to the shed.

Faunia Farley: thin-legged, thin-wristed, thin-armed, with clearly discernible ribs and shoulder blades that protruded, and yet when she tensed you saw that her limbs were hard; when she reached or stretched for something you saw that her breasts were surprisingly substantial; and when, because of the flies and the gnats buzzing the herd on this close summer day, she slapped at her neck or her backside, you saw something of how frisky she could be, despite the otherwise straight-up style. You saw that her body was something more than efficiently lean and severe, that she was a firmly made woman precipitously poised at the moment when she is no longer ripening but not yet deteriorating, a woman in the prime of her prime, whose fistful of white hairs is fundamentally beguiling just because the sharp Yankee contour of her cheeks and her jaw and the long unmistakably female neck haven't yet been subject to the transformations of aging.

"This is my neighbor," Coleman said to her when she took a moment to wipe the sweat from her face with the crook of her elbow and to look our way. "This is Nathan."

I hadn't expected composure. I was expecting someone openly angrier. She acknowledged me with no more than a jerk of her chin, but it was a gesture from which she got a lot of mileage. It was a *chin* from which she got a lot of mileage. Keeping it up as she normally did, it gave her—virility. That was in the response too: something virile and implacable, as well as a little disreputable, in that dead-on look. The look of someone for whom both sex and betrayal are as basic as bread. The look of the runaway and the look that results from the galling monotony of bad luck. Her hair, the golden blond hair in the poignant first stage of its unpreventable permutation, was twisted at the back through an elastic band, but a lock kept falling toward her eyebrow as she worked, and now, while silently looking our way, she pushed it back with her hand, and for the first time I noticed in her face a small feature that, perhaps wrongly, because I was searching for a sign, had the effect of something telling: the convex fullness of the narrow arch of flesh between the ridge of eyebrow and the upper eyelids. She was a thin-lipped woman with a straight nose and clear blue eyes and good teeth and a prominent jaw, and that puff of flesh just beneath her eyebrows was her only exotic marking, the only emblem of allure, something swollen with desire. It also accounted for a lot that was unsettlingly obscure about the hard flatness of her gaze.

In all, Faunia was not the enticing siren who takes your breath away but a clean-cut-looking woman about whom one thinks, As a child she must have been very beautiful. Which she was: according to Coleman, a golden, beautiful child with a rich stepfather who wouldn't leave her alone and a spoiled mother who wouldn't protect her.

We stood there watching while she milked each of the eleven cows—Daisy, Maggie, Flossie, Bessy, Dolly, Maiden, Sweetheart, Stupid, Emma, Friendly, and Jill—stood there while she went through the same unvarying routine with every one of them, and when that was finished and she moved into the whitewashed room with the big sinks and the hoses and the sterilizing units adjacent to the milking parlor, we watched her through that doorway mixing up the lye solution and the cleansing agents and, after separating the vacuum line from the pipeline and the teat cups from the claw and the two milker pails from their covers—after disassembling the whole of the milking unit that she'd taken in there with her—setting to work with a variety of brushes and with sinkful after sinkful of clear water to scrub every surface of every tube, valve, gasket, plug, plate, liner, cap, disc, and piston until each was spotlessly clean and sanitized. Before Coleman took his milk and we got back into his car to leave, he and I had stood together by the refrigerator for close to an hour and a half and, aside from the words he uttered to introduce me to her, nobody human said anything more. All you could hear was the whirring and the chirping of the barn swallows who nested there as they whished through the rafters where the barn opened out behind us, and the pellets dropping into the cement trough when she shook out the feed pail, and the shuffling clump of the barely lifted hooves on the milking parlor floor as Faunia, shoving and dragging and steering the cows, positioned them into the stanchion, and then the suction noise, the soft deep breathing of the milk pump.

After they were each buried four months later, I would remember that milking session as though it were a theatrical performance in which I had played the part of a walk-on, an extra, which indeed I now am. Night after night, I could not sleep because I couldn't stop being up there on the stage with the two leading actors and the chorus of cows, observing this scene, flawlessly performed by the entire ensemble, of an enamored old man watching at work the cleaning woman–farmhand who is secretly his paramour: a scene of pathos and hypnosis and sexual subjugation in which everything the woman does with those cows, the way she handles them, touches them, services them, talks to them, his greedy fascination appropriates; a scene in which a man taken over by a force so long suppressed in him that it had all but been extinguished revealed, before my eyes, the resurgence of its stupefying power. It was something, I suppose, like watching Aschenbach feverishly watching Tadzio—his sexual longing brought to a boil by the anguishing fact of mortality—except that we weren't in a luxury hotel on the Venice Lido nor were we characters in a novel written in German or even, back then, in one written in English: it was high summer and we were in a barn in the Northeast of our country, in America in the year of America's presidential impeachment, and, as yet, we were no more novelistic than the animals were mythological or stuffed. The light and heat of the day (*that* blessing), the unchanging quiet of each cow's life as it paralleled that of all the others, the enamored old man studying the suppleness of the efficient, energetic woman, the adulation rising in him, his looking as though nothing more stirring had ever before happened to him, and, too, my own willing waiting, my own fascination with their extensive disparity as human types, with the nonuniformity, the variability, the teeming irregularity of sexual arrangements—and with the injunction upon us, human and bovine, the highly differentiated and the all but undifferentiated, to live, not merely to endure but to *live*, to go on taking, giving, feeding, milking, acknowledging wholeheartedly, as the enigma that it is, the pointless meaningfulness of living—all was recorded as real by tens of thousands of minute impressions. The sensory fullness, the copiousness, the abundant—superabundant—detail of life, which is the rhapsody. And Coleman and Faunia, who are now dead, deep in the flow of the unexpected, day by day, minute by minute, themselves details in that superabundance.

Nothing lasts, and yet nothing passes, either. And nothing passes just because nothing lasts.

The trouble with Les Farley began later that night, when Coleman heard something stirring in the bushes outside his house, decided it wasn't a deer or a raccoon, got up from the kitchen table where he and Faunia had just finished their spaghetti dinner, and, from the kitchen door, in the summer evening half-light, caught sight of a man running across the field back of the house and toward the woods. "Hey! You! Stop!" Coleman shouted, but the man neither stopped nor looked back and disappeared quickly into the trees. This wasn't the first time in recent months that Coleman believed he was being watched by someone hiding within inches of the house, but previously it had been later in the evening and too dark for him to know for sure whether he had been alerted by the movements of a peeping Tom or of an animal. And previously he had always been alone. This was the first time Faunia was there, and it was she who, without having to see the man's silhouette cutting across the field, identified the trespasser as her ex-husband.

After the divorce, she told Coleman, Farley had spied on her all the time, but in the months following the death of the two children, when he was accusing her of having killed them by her negligence, he was frighteningly unrelenting. Twice he popped up out of no-where—once in the parking lot of a supermarket, once when she was at a gas station—and screamed out of the pickup window, "Murdering whore! Murdering bitch! You murdered my kids, you murdering bitch!" There were many mornings when, on her way to the college, she'd look in the rearview mirror and there would be his pickup truck and, back of the windshield, his face with the lips mouthing, "You murdered my kids." Sometimes he'd be on the road behind her when she was driving home from the college. She was then still living in the unburned half of the bungalow-garage where the children had been asphyxiated in the heater fire, and it was out of fear of him that she'd moved from there to a room in Seeley Falls and then, after a foiled suicide attempt, into the room at the dairy farm, where the two owners and their small children were almost always around and the danger was not so great of her being ac-costed by him. Farley's pickup appeared in her rearview mirror less frequently after the second move, and then, when there was no sign of him for months, she hoped he might be gone for good. But now, Faunia was sure of it, he'd somehow found out about Coleman and, enraged again with everything that had always enraged him about her, he was back at his crazy spying, hiding outside Coleman's house to see what she was doing there. What *they* were doing there.

That night, when Faunia got into her car—the old Chevy that Coleman preferred her to park, out of sight, inside his barn— Coleman decided to follow close behind her in his own car for the six miles until she was safely onto the dirt driveway that led past the cow barn to the farmhouse. And then all the way back to his own house he looked to see if anyone was behind *him*. At home, he walked from the car shed to the house swinging a tire iron in one hand, swinging it in all directions, hoping in that way to keep at bay anyone lurking in the dark.

By the next morning, after eight hours on his bed contending with his worries, Coleman had decided against lodging a complaint with the state police. Because Farley's identity couldn't be positively established, the police would be unable to do anything about him anyway, and should it leak out that Coleman had contacted them, his call would have served only to corroborate the gossip already circulating about the former dean and the Athena janitor. Not that, after his sleepless night, Coleman could resign himself to doing nothing about *everything:* following breakfast, he phoned his lawyer, Nelson Primus, and that afternoon went down to Athena to consult with him about the anonymous letter and there, overriding Primus's suggestion that he forget about it, prevailed on him to write, as follows, to Delphine Roux at the college: "Dear Ms. Roux: I represent Coleman Silk. Several days ago, you sent an anonymous letter to Mr. Silk that is offensive, harassing, and denigrating to Mr. Silk. The content of your letter reads: 'Everyone knows you're sexually exploiting an abused, illiterate woman half your age.' You have, unfortunately, interjected yourself and become a participant in something that is not your business. In doing that, you have violated Mr. Silk's legal rights and are subject to suit."

A few days later Primus received three curt sentences back from Delphine Roux's lawyer. The middle sentence, flatly denying the charge that Delphine Roux was the author of the anonymous letter, Coleman underlined in red. "None of the assertions in your letter are correct," her lawyer had written to Primus, "and, indeed, they are defamatory."

Immediately Coleman got from Primus the name of a certified documents examiner in Boston, a handwriting analyst who did forensic work for private corporations, U.S. government agencies, and the state, and the next day, he himself drove the three hours to Boston to deliver into the hands of the documents examiner his samples of Delphine Roux's handwriting along with the anonymous letter and its envelope. He received the findings in the mail the next week. "At your request," read the report, "I examined and compared copies of known handwriting of Delphine Roux with a questioned anonymous note and an envelope addressed to Coleman Silk. You asked for a determination of the authorship of the handwriting on the questioned documents. My examination covers handwriting characteristics such as slant, spacing, letter formation, line quality, pressure pattern, proportion, letter height relationship, connections and initials and terminal stroke formation. Based on the documents submitted, it is my professional opinion that the hand that penned all the known standards as Delphine Roux is one and the same hand that penned the questioned anonymous note and envelope. Sincerely, Douglas Gordon, CDE." When Coleman turned the examiner's report over to Nelson Primus, with instructions to forward a copy to Delphine Roux's lawyer, Primus no longer put up an argument, however distressing it was to him to see Coleman nearly as enraged as he'd been back during the crisis with the college.

In all, eight days had passed since the evening he'd seen Farley fleeing into the woods, eight days during which he had determined it would be best if Faunia stayed away and they communicated by phone. So as not to invite spying on either of them from any quarter, he didn't go out to the farm to fetch his raw milk but stayed at home as much as he could and kept a careful watch there, especially after dark, to determine if anyone was snooping around. Faunia, in turn, was told to keep a lookout of her own at the dairy farm and to check her rearview mirror when she drove anywhere. "It's as though we're a menace to public safety," she told him, laughing her laugh. "No, public health," he replied—"we're in noncompliance with the board of health."

By the end of the eight days, when he had been able at least to confirm Delphine Roux's identification as the letter writer if not yet Farley's as the trespasser, Coleman decided to decide that he'd done everything within his power to defend against all of this disagreeable and provocative meddling. When Faunia phoned him that afternoon during her lunch break and asked, "Is the quarantine over?" he at last felt free of enough of his anxiety—or decided to decide to be—to give the all-clear sign.

As he expected her to show up around seven that evening, he swallowed a Viagra tablet at six and, after pouring himself a glass of wine, walked outside with the phone to settle into a lawn chair and telephone his daughter. He and Iris had reared four children: two sons now into their forties, both college professors of science, married and with children and living on the West Coast, and the twins, Lisa and Mark, unmarried, in their late thirties, and both living in New York. All but one of the Silk offspring tried to get up to the Berkshires to see their father three or four times a year and stayed in touch every month by phone. The exception was Mark, who'd been at odds with Coleman all his life and sporadically cut himself off completely.

Coleman was calling Lisa because he realized that it was more than a month and maybe even two since he'd spoken to her. Perhaps he was merely surrendering to a transient feeling of loneliness that would have passed when Faunia arrived, but whatever his motive, he could have had no inkling, before the phone call, of what was in store. Surely the last thing he was looking for was yet more opposition, least of all from that child whose voice alone—soft, melodic, girlish still, despite twelve difficult years as a teacher on the Lower East Side—he could always depend on to soothe him, to calm him, sometimes to do even more: to infatuate him with this daughter all over again. He was doing probably what most any aging parent will do when, for any of a hundred reasons, he or she looks to a long-distance phone call for a momentary reminder of the old terms of reference. The unbroken, unequivocal history of tenderness between Coleman and Lisa made of her the least affrontable person still close to him.

Some three years earlier—back before the spooks incident—when Lisa was wondering if she hadn't made an enormous mistake by giving up classroom teaching to become a Reading Recovery teacher, Coleman had gone down to New York and stayed several days to see how bad off she was. Iris was alive then, very much alive, but it wasn't Iris's enormous energy Lisa had wanted—it wasn't to be put into motion the way Iris could put you in motion that she wanted—rather, it was the former dean of faculty with his orderly, determined way of untangling a mess. Iris was sure to tell her to forge ahead, leaving Lisa overwhelmed and feeling trapped; with him there was the possibility that, if Lisa made a compelling case against her own persevering, he would tell her that, if she wished, she could cut her losses and quit—which would, in turn, give her the gumption to go on.

He'd not only spent the first night sitting up late in her living room and listening to her woes, but the next day he'd gone to the school to see what it was that was burning her out. And he saw, all right: in the morning, first thing, four back-to-back half-hour sessions, each with a six- or seven-year-old who was among the lowest-achieving students in the first and second grades, and after that, for the rest of the day, forty-five-minute sessions with groups of eight kids whose reading skills were no better than those of the one-on-one kids but for whom there wasn't yet enough trained staff in the intensive program.

"The regular class sizes are too big," Lisa told him, "and so the teachers can't reach these kids. I was a classroom teacher. The kids who are struggling—it's three out of thirty. Three or four. It's not too bad. You have the progress of all the other kids helping you along. Instead of stopping and giving the hopeless kids what they need, teachers just sort of shuffle them through, thinking—or pretending—they are moving with the continuum. They're shuffled to the second grade, the third grade, the fourth grade, and then they seriously fail. But here it's *only* these kids, the ones who can't be reached and don't get reached, and because I'm very emotional about my kids and teaching, it affects my whole being—my whole *world*. And the school, the leadership—Dad, it's not good. You have a principal who doesn't have a vision of what she wants, and you have a mishmash of people doing what they think is best. Which is not necessarily what *is* best. When I came here twelve years ago it was great. The principal was really good. She turned the whole school around. But now we've gone through twenty-one teachers in four years. Which is a lot. We've lost a lot of good people. Two years ago I went into Reading Recovery because I just got burnt out in the classroom. Ten years of *that* day in and day out. I couldn't take any more."

He let her talk, said little, and, because she was but a few years from forty, suppressed easily enough the impulse to take in his arms this battered-by-reality daughter as he imagined she suppressed the same impulse with the six-year-old kid who couldn't read. Lisa had all of Iris's intensity without Iris's authority, and for someone whose life existed only for others—incurable altruism was Lisa's curse—she was, as a teacher, perpetually hovering at the edge of depletion. There was generally a demanding boyfriend as well from whom she could not withhold kindness, and for whom she turned herself inside out, and for whom, unfailingly, her uncontaminated ethical virginity became a great big bore. Lisa was always morally in over her head, but without either the callousness to disappoint the need of another or the strength to disillusion herself about her strength. This was why he knew she would never quit the Reading Recovery program, and also why such paternal pride as he had in her was not only weighted with fear but at times tinged with an impatience bordering on contempt.

"Thirty kids you have to take care of, the different levels that the kids come in at, the different experiences they've had, and you've got to make it all work," she was telling him. "Thirty diverse kids from thirty diverse backgrounds learning thirty diverse ways. That's a lot of management. That's a lot of paperwork. That's a lot of *everything*. But that is still *nothing* compared to *this*. Sure, even with this, even in Reading Recovery, I have days when I think, Today I was good, but most days I want to jump out the window. I struggle a lot as to whether this is the right program for me. Because I'm very intense, in case you didn't know. I want to do it the right way, and there is no right way—every kid is different and every kid is hopeless, and I'm supposed to go in there and make it all work. Of course everybody always struggles with the kids who can't learn.

What do you do with a kid who can't read? Think of it—a kid who can't read. It's difficult, Daddy. Your ego gets a little caught up in it, you know."

Lisa, who contains within her so much concern, whose conscientiousness knows no ambivalence, who wishes to exist only to assist. Lisa the Undisillusionable, Lisa the Unspeakably Idealistic. Phone Lisa, he told himself, little imagining that he could ever elicit from this foolishly saintly child of his the tone of steely displeasure with which she received his call.

"You don't sound like yourself."

"I'm fine," she told him.

"What's wrong, Lisa?"

"Nothing."

"How's summer school? How's teaching?"

"Fine."

"And Josh?" The latest boyfriend.

"Fine."

"How are your kids? What happened to the little one who couldn't recognize the letter *n*? Did he ever get to level ten? The kid with all the *n*'s in his name—Hernando."

"Everything's fine."

He then asked lightly, "Would you care to know how I am?"

"I know how you are."

"Do you?"

No answer.

"What's eating you, sweetheart?"

"Nothing." A "nothing," the second one, that meant all too clearly, *Don't you sweetheart me.*

Something incomprehensible was happening. Who had told her? *What* had they told her? As a high school kid and then in college after the war he had pursued the most demanding curriculum; as dean at Athena he had thrived on the difficulties of a taxing job; as the accused in the spooks incident he had never once weakened in fighting the false accusation against him; even his resignation from the college had been an act not of capitulation but of outraged protest, a deliberate manifestation of his unwavering contempt. But in all his years of holding his own against whatever the task or the setback or the shock, he had never—not even after Iris's death—felt as stripped of all defenses as when Lisa, the embodiment of an almost mockable kindness, gathered up into that one word "nothing" all the harshness of feeling for which she had never before, in the whole of her life, found a deserving object.

And then, even as Lisa's "nothing" was exuding its awful meaning, Coleman saw a pickup truck moving along the blacktop road down from the house—rolling at a crawl a couple of yards forward, braking, very slowly rolling again, then braking again . . . Coleman came to his feet, started uncertainly across the mown grass, craning his head to get a look, and then, on the run, began to shout, "You! What are you up to! Hey!" But the pickup quickly increased its speed and was out of sight before Coleman could get near enough to discern anything of use to him about either driver or truck. As he didn't know one make from another and, from where he'd wound up, couldn't even tell if the truck was new or old, all that he came away with was its color, an indeterminate gray.

And now the phone was dead. In running across the lawn, he'd inadvertently touched the off button. That, or Lisa had deliberately broken the connection. When he redialed, a man answered. "Is this Josh?" Coleman asked. "Yes," the man said. "This is Coleman Silk. Lisa's father." After a moment's silence, the man said, "Lisa doesn't want to talk," and hung up.

Mark's doing. It had to be. Could not be anyone else's. Couldn't be this fucking Josh's—who was he? Coleman had no more idea how Mark could have found out about Faunia than how Delphine Roux or anyone else had, but that didn't matter right now—it was Mark who had assailed his twin sister with their father's crime. For crime it would be to that boy. Almost from the time he could speak, Mark couldn't give up the idea that his father was against him: *for* the two older sons because they were older and starred at school and imbibed without complaint their father's intellectual pretensions; *for* Lisa because she was Lisa, the family's little girl, indisputably the child most indulged by her daddy; *against* Mark because everything his twin sister was—adorable, adoring, virtuous, touching, noble to the core—Mark was not and refused to be.

Mark's was probably the most difficult personality it was ever Coleman's lot to try, not to understand—the resentments were all too easy to understand—but to grapple with. The whining and sulking had begun before he was old enough to go off to kindergarten, and the protest against his family and their sense of things started soon after and, despite all attempts at propitiation, solidified over the years into *his* core. At the age of fourteen he vociferously supported Nixon during the impeachment hearings while the rest of them were rooting for the president to be imprisoned for life; at sixteen he became an Orthodox Jew while the rest of them, taking their cue from their anticlerical, atheistic parents, were Jews in little more than name; at twenty he enraged his father by dropping out of Brandeis with two semesters to go, and now, almost into his forties, having taken up and jettisoned a dozen different jobs to which he considered himself superior, he had discovered that he was a narrative poet.

Because of his unshakable enmity for his father, Mark had made himself into whatever his family wasn't—more sadly to the point, into whatever *he* wasn't. A clever boy, well read, with a quick mind and a sharp tongue, he nonetheless could never see his way around Coleman until, at thirty-eight, as a narrative poet on biblical themes, he had come to nurse his great life-organizing aversion with all the arrogance of someone who has succeeded at nothing. A devoted girlfriend, a humorless, high-strung, religiously observant young woman, earned their keep as a dental technician in Manhattan while Mark stayed home in their Brooklyn walk-up and wrote the biblically inspired poems that not even the Jewish magazines would publish, interminable poems about how David had wronged his son Absalom and how Isaac had wronged his son Esau and how Judah had wronged his brother Joseph and about the curse of the prophet Nathan after David sinned with Bathsheba—

poems that, in one grandiosely ill-disguised way or another, harked back to the idée fixe on which Markie had staked everything and lost everything.

How could Lisa listen to him? How could Lisa take seriously any charge brought by Markie when she knew what had been driving him all his life? But then Lisa's being generous toward her brother, however misbegotten she found the antagonisms that deformed him, went back almost to their birth as twins. Because it was her nature to be benevolent, and because even as a little schoolgirl she had suffered the troubled conscience of the preferred child, she had always gently indulged her twin brother's grievances and acted as his comforter in family disputes. But must her solicitousness toward the less favored of their twosome extend even to this crazy charge? And what *was* the charge? What harmful act had the father committed, what injury had he inflicted on his children that should put these twins in league with Delphine Roux and Lester Farley? And the other two, his scientist sons—were they and their scruples in on this too? When had he last heard from *them*?

He remembered now that awful hour at the house after Iris's funeral, remembered and was stung all over again by the charges that Mark had brought against his father before the older boys moved in and physically removed him to his old room for the rest of the afternoon. In the days that followed, while the kids were all still around, Coleman was willing to blame Markie's grief and not Mark for what the boy had dared to say, but that didn't mean that he'd forgotten or that he ever would. Markie had begun berating him only minutes after they'd driven back from the cemetery. "The college didn't do it. The blacks didn't do it. Your enemies didn't do it. *You* did it. You killed mother. The way you kill everything! Because you have to be right! Because you won't apologize, because every time you are a hundred percent right, now it's *Mother* who's dead! And it all could have been settled so easily—all of it settled in twenty-four hours if you knew how once in your life to *apologize*. 'I'm sorry that I said "spooks."' That's all you had to do, great man, just go to those students and say you were sorry, and Mother would not be dead!"

Out on his lawn, Coleman was seized suddenly with the sort of indignation he had not felt since the day following Markie's outburst, when he'd written and submitted his resignation from the college all in an hour's time. He knew that it was not correct to have such feelings toward his children. He knew, from the spooks incident, that indignation on such a scale was a form of madness, and one to which he could succumb. He knew that indignation like this could lead to no orderly and reasoned approach to the problem. He knew as an educator how to educate and as a father how to father and as a man of over seventy that one must regard nothing, particularly within a family, even one containing a grudge-laden son like Mark, as implacably unchangeable. And it wasn't from the spooks incident alone that he knew about what can corrode and warp a man who believes himself to have been grievously wronged. He knew from the wrath of Achilles, the rage of Philoctetes, the fulminations of Medea, the madness of Ajax, the despair of Electra, and the suffering of Prometheus the many horrors that can ensue when the highest degree of indignation is achieved and, in the name of justice, retribution is exacted and a cycle of retaliation begins.

And it was lucky that he knew all this, because it took no less than this, no less than the prophylaxis of the whole of Attic tragedy and Greek epic poetry, to restrain him from phoning on the spot to remind Markie what a little prick he was and always had been.

The head-on confrontation with Farley came some four hours later. As I reconstruct it, Coleman, so as to be certain that no one was spying on the house, was himself in and out the front door and the back door and the kitchen door some six or seven times in the hours after Faunia's arrival. It wasn't until somewhere around ten, when the two of them were standing together inside the kitchen screen door, holding each other before parting for the night, that he was able to rise above all the corroding indignation and to allow the really serious thing in his life—the intoxication with the last fling, what Mann, writing of Aschenbach, called the "late adventure of the feelings"—to reassert itself and take charge of him. As she was about to leave, he at last found himself craving for her as though nothing else mattered—and none of it did, not his daughter, not his sons, not Faunia's ex-husband or Delphine Roux. This is not merely life, he thought, this is the *end* of life. What was unendurable wasn't all this ridiculous antipathy he and Faunia had aroused; what was unendurable was that he was down to the last bucket of days, to the bottom of the bucket, the time if there ever was a time to quit the quarrel, to give up the rebuttal, to undo himself from the conscientiousness with which he had raised the four lively children, persisted in the combative marriage, influenced the recalcitrant colleagues, and guided Athena's mediocre students, as best he could, through a literature some twenty-five hundred years old. It was the time to yield, to let this simple craving be *his* guide. Beyond their accusation. Beyond their indictment. Beyond their judgment. Learn, he told himself, before you die, to live beyond the jurisdiction of their enraging, loathsome, stupid blame.

The encounter with Farley. The encounter that night with Farley, the confrontation with a dairy farmer who had not meant to fail but did, a road crew employee who gave his all to the town no matter how lowly and degrading the task assigned him, a loyal American who'd served his country with not one tour but two, who'd gone back a second time to finish the goddamn job. Re-upped and went back because when he comes home the first time everybody says that he isn't the same person and that they don't recognize him, and he sees that it's true: they're all afraid of him. He comes home to them from jungle warfare and not only is he not appreciated but he is feared, so he might as well go back. He wasn't expecting the hero treatment, but everybody looking at him like that? So he goes back for the second tour, and this time he is geared up. Pissed off. Pumped up. A very aggressive warrior. The first time he wasn't all that gung ho. The first time he was easygoing Les, who didn't know what it meant to feel hopeless. The first time he was the boy from the Berkshires who put a lot of trust in people and had no idea how cheap life could be, didn't know what medication was, didn't feel inferior to anyone, happy-go-lucky Les, no threat to society, tons of friends, fast cars, all that stuff. The first time he'd cut off ears because he was there and it was being done, but that was it. He wasn't one of those who once they were in all that lawlessness couldn't wait to get going, the ones who weren't too well put together or were pretty aggressive to start off with and only needed the slightest opportunity to go ape-shit. One guy in his unit, guy they called Big Man, he wasn't there one or two days when he'd slashed some pregnant woman's belly open. Farley was himself only beginning to get good at it at the end of his first tour. But the second time, in this unit where there are a lot of other guys who'd also come back and who hadn't come back just to kill time or to make a couple extra bucks, this second time, in with these guys who are always looking to be put out in front, ape-shit guys who recognize the horror but know it is the very best moment of their lives, he is ape-shit too. In a firefight, running from danger, blasting with guns, you can't not be frightened, but you can go berserk and get the rush, and so the second time he goes berserk. The second time he fucking wreaks havoc. Living right out there on the edge, full throttle, the excitement and the fear, and there's nothing in civilian life that can match it. Door gunning. They're losing helicopters and they need door gunners. They ask at some point for door gunners and he jumps at it, he volunteers. Up there above the action, and everything looks small from above, and he just guns down *huge*. Whatever moves. Death and destruction, that is what door gunning is all about. With the added attraction that you don't have to be down in the jungle the whole time. But then he comes home and it's not better than the first time, it's worse. Not like the guys in World War II: they had the ship, they got to relax, someone took care of them, asked them how they were. There's no transition. One day he's door gunning in Vietnam, seeing choppers explode, in midair seeing his buddies explode, down so low he smells skin cooking, hears the cries, sees whole villages going up in flames, and the next day he's back in the Berkshires. And now he *really* doesn't belong, and, besides, he's got fears now about things going over his head. He doesn't want to be around other people, he can't laugh or joke, he feels that he is no longer a part of their world, that he has seen and done things so outside what these people know about that he cannot connect to them and they cannot connect to him. They told him he could go home? How could he go home? He doesn't have a helicopter at home. He stays by himself and he drinks, and when he tries the VA they tell him he is just there to get the money while he knows he is there to get the help. Early on, he tried to get government help and all they gave him was some sleeping pills, so fuck the government. Treated him like garbage. You're young, they told him, you'll get over it. So he tries to get over it. Can't deal with the government, so he'll have to do it on his own. Only it isn't easy after two tours to come back and get settled all on his own. He's not calm. He's agitated. He's restless. He's drinking. It doesn't take much to put him into a rage. There are these things going over his head. Still he tries: eventually gets the wife, the home, the kids, the farm. He wants to be alone, but she wants to settle down and farm with him, so he tries to want to settle down too. Stuff he remembers easygoing Les wanting ten, fifteen years back, before Vietnam, he tries to want again. The trouble is, he can't really feel for these folks. He's sitting in the kitchen and he's eating with them and there's nothing. No way he can go from that to this. Yet *still* he tries. A couple times in the middle of the night he wakes up choking her, but it isn't his fault—it's the government's fault. The government did that to him. He thought she was the fucking enemy. What did she think he was going to do? She knew he was going to come out of it. He never hurt her and he never hurt the kids. That was all lies. She never cared about anything except herself. He should have known never to let her go off with those kids. She waited until he was in rehab—that was why she wanted to get him into rehab. She said she wanted him to be better so that they could be together again, and instead she used the whole thing against him to get the kids away from him. The bitch. The cunt. She tricked him. He should have known never to let her go off with those kids. It was partly his own fault because he was so drunk and they could get him to rehab by force, but it would have been better if he'd taken them all out when he said he would. Should have killed her, should have killed the kids, and would have if it hadn't been for rehab. And she knew it, knew he'd have killed them like *that* if she'd ever tried to take them away. He was the father—if anybody was going to raise his kids it was him. If he couldn't take care of them, the kids would be better off dead. She'd had no right to steal his kids. Steals them, then *she* kills them. The payback for what he did in Vietnam. They all said that at rehab—payback this and payback that, but because everyone said it, didn't make it not so. It *was* payback, *all* payback, the death of the kids was payback and the carpenter she was fucking was payback. He didn't know why he hadn't killed him. At first he just smelled the smoke. He was in the bushes down the road watching the two of them in the carpenter's pickup. They were parked in her driveway. She comes downstairs—the apartment she's renting is over a garage back of some bungalow—and she gets in the pickup and there's no light and there's no moon but he knows what's going on. Then he smelled the smoke. The only way he'd survived in Vietnam was that any change, a noise, the smell of an animal, any movement at all in the jungle, and he could detect it before anyone else—alert in the jungle like he was born there. Couldn't see the smoke, couldn't see the flames, couldn't see anything it was so dark, but all of a sudden he could smell the smoke and these things are flying over his head and he began running. They see him coming and they think he is going to steal the kids. They don't know the building is on fire. They think he's gone nuts. But he can smell the smoke and he knows it's coming from the second story and he knows the kids are in there. He knows his wife, stupid bitch cunt, isn't going to do anything because she's in the truck blowing the carpenter. He runs right by them. He doesn't know where he is now, forgets where he is, all he knows is that he's got to get in there and up the stairs, and so he bashes in the side door and he's running up to where the fire is, and that's when he sees the kids on the stairs, huddled there at the top of the stairs, and they're gasping, and that's when he picks them up. They're crumpled together on the stairs and he picks them up and tears out the door. They're alive, he's sure. He doesn't think there's a chance that they're not alive. He just thinks they're scared. Then he looks up and who does he see outside the door, standing there looking, but the carpenter. That's when he lost it. Didn't know what he was doing. That's when he went straight for his throat. Started choking him, and that bitch, instead of going to the kids, worries about him choking the fucking boyfriend. Fucking bitch worries about him killing her boyfriend instead of about her own goddamn kids. And they would have made it. That's why they died. Because she didn't give two shits about the kids. She never did. They weren't dead when he picked them up. They were *warm*. He knows what dead is. Two tours in Vietnam you're not going to tell him what dead is. He can *smell* death when he needs to. He can *taste* death. He knows what death *is*. They—were—not—dead. It was the boyfriend who was going to be fucking dead, until the police, in cahoots with the government, came with their guns, and that's when they put him away. The bitch kills the kids, it's her neglect, and they put *him* away. Jesus Christ, let me be right for a minute! The bitch wasn't paying attention! She never does. Like when he had the hunch they were headed for an ambush. Couldn't say why but he knew they were being set up, and nobody believed him, and he was *right*. Some new dumb officer comes into the company, won't listen to him, and that's how people get killed. That's how people get burned to hell! That's how assholes cause the death of your two best buddies! They don't listen to him! They don't give him credit! He came back alive, didn't he? He came back with all his limbs, he came back with his dick—you know what that took? But she won't listen! Never! She turned her back on him and she turned her back on his kids. He's just a crazy Vietnam vet. But he *knows* things, goddamnit. And she knows *nothing*. But do they put away the stupid bitch? They put *him* away. They shoot him up with stuff. Again they put him in restraints, and they won't let him out of the Northampton VA. And all he did was what they had trained him to do: you see the enemy, you kill the enemy. They train you for a year, then they try to kill you for a year, and when you're just doing what they trained you to do, that is when they fucking put the leather restraints on you and shoot you full of shit. He did what they were training him to do, and while he was doing that, his fucking wife is turning her back on his kids. He should have killed them all when he could. Him especially. The boyfriend. He should have cut their fucking heads off. He doesn't know why he didn't. Better not come fucking near him. If he knows where the fucking boyfriend is, he'll kill him so fast he won't know what hit him, and they won't know he did it because he knows how to do it so no one can hear it. Because that's what the government trained him to do. He is a trained killer thanks to the government of the United States. He did his job. He did what he was told to do. And this is how he fucking gets treated? They get him down in the lockup ward, they put him in the bubble, they send *him* to the fucking bubble! And they won't even cut him a check. For all this he gets fucking twenty percent. Twenty percent. He put his whole family through hell for twenty percent. And even for that he has to grovel. "So, tell me what happened," they say, the little social workers, the little psychologists with their college degrees. "Did you kill anyone when you were in Vietnam?" Was there anyone he *didn't* kill when he was in Vietnam? Wasn't that what he was *supposed* to do when they sent him to Vietnam? Fucking kill gooks. They said everything goes? So everything went. It all relates to the word "kill." Kill gooks! If "Did you kill anyone?" isn't bad enough, they give him a fucking gook psychiatrist, this like Chink shit. He serves his country and he can't even get a doctor who fucking speaks English. All round Northampton they've got Chinese restaurants, they've got Vietnamese restaurants, Korean markets—but him? If you're some Vietnamese, you're some Chink, you make out, you get a restaurant, you get a market, you get a grocery store, you get a family, you get a good education. But they got fuck-all for him. Because they want him dead. They wish he never came back. He is their worst nightmare. He was not *supposed* to come back. And now this college professor. Know where he was when the government sent us in there with one arm tied behind our backs? He was out there leading the fucking protesters. They pay them, when they go to college, to teach, to teach the kids, not to fucking protest the Vietnam War. They didn't give us a fucking chance. They say we lost the war. *We* didn't lose the war, the government lost the war. But when fancy-pants professors felt like it, instead of teaching class some day they go picketing out there against the war, and that is the thanks he gets for serving his country. That is the thanks for the shit he had to put up with day in and day out. He can't get a goddamn night's sleep. He hasn't had a good night's sleep in fucking twenty-six years. And for that, for *that* his wife goes down on some two-bit kike professor? There weren't too many kikes in Vietnam, not that he can remember. They were too busy getting their degrees. Jew bastard. There's something wrong with those Jew bastards. They don't look right. She goes down on *him?* Jesus Christ. Vomit, man. What was it all *for?* She doesn't know what it's like. Never had a hard day in her life. He never hurt her and he never hurt the kids. "Oh, my stepfather was mean to me." Stepfather used to finger her. Should have fucked her, that would have straightened her out a little. The kids would be alive today. His fucking kids would be alive today! He'd be like all the rest of those guys out there, with their families and their nice cars. Instead of locked up in a fucking VA facility. That was the thanks he got: Thorazine. His thanks was the Thorazine shuffle. Just because he thought he was back in the Nam.

This was the Lester Farley who came roaring out of the bushes. This was the man who came upon Coleman and Faunia as they stood just inside the kitchen doorway, who came roaring at them out of the darkness of the bushes at the side of the house. And all of that was just a little of what was inside his head, night after night, all through the spring and now into early summer, hiding for hours on end, cramped, still, living through so much emotion, and waiting there in hiding to see her doing it. Doing what she was doing when her own two kids were suffocating to death in the smoke. This time it wasn't even with a guy her age. Not even Farley's age. This time it wasn't with her boss, the great All-American Hollenbeck. Hollenbeck could give her something in return at least. You could almost respect her for Hollenbeck. But now the woman was so far gone she would do it for nothing with anybody. Now it was with a gray-haired skin-and-bones old man, with a high-and-mighty Jew professor, his yellow Jew face contorted with pleasure and his trembling old hands gripping her head. Who else has a wife sucks off an old Jew? Who else! This time the wanton, murdering, moaning bitch was pumping into her whoring mouth the watery come of a disgusting old Jew, and Rawley and Les Junior were still dead.

Payback. There was no end to it.

It felt like flying, it felt like Nam, it felt like the moment in which you go wild. Crazier, suddenly, because she is sucking off that Jew than because she killed the kids, Farley is flying upward, screaming, and the Jew professor is screaming back, the Jew professor is raising a tire iron, and it is only because Farley is unarmed—because that night he'd come there right from fire department drill and without a single one of the guns from his basement full of guns—that he doesn't blow them away. How it happened that he didn't reach for the tire iron and take it from him and end everything that way, he would never know. Beautiful what he could have achieved with that tire iron. "Put it down! I'll open your fuckin' head with it! Fuckin' put it *down!*" And the Jew put it down. Luckily for the Jew, he put it down.

After he made it home that night (never know how he did that either) and right through to the early hours of the morning—when it took five men from the fire department, five buddies of his, to hold him down and get him into restraints and drive him over to Northampton—Lester saw it all, everything, all at once, right there in his own house enduring the heat, enduring the rain, the mud, giant ants, killer bees on his own linoleum floor just beside the kitchen table, being sick with diarrhea, headaches, sick from no food and no water, short of ammo, certain this is his last night, waiting for it to happen, Foster stepping on the booby trap, Quillen drowning, himself almost drowning, freaking out, throwing grenades in every direction and shouting "I don't want to die," the warplanes all mixed up and shooting at them, Drago losing a leg, an arm, his nose, Conrity's burned body sticking to his hands, unable to get a chopper to land, the chopper saying they cannot land because we are under attack and him so fucking angry knowing that he is going to die that he is trying to shoot it down, shoot down our own chopper—the most inhuman night he ever witnessed and it is right there now in his own scumbag house, and the longest night too, his longest night on earth and petrified with every move he makes, guys hollering and shitting and crying, himself unprepared to hear so much crying, guys hit in the face and dying, taking their last breath and dying, Conrity's body all over his hands, Drago bleeding all over the place, Lester trying to shake somebody dead awake and hollering, screaming without stopping, "I don't want to die." No time out from death. No break time from death. No running from death. No letup from death. Battling death right through till morning and everything intense. The fear intense, the anger intense, no helicopter willing to land and the terrible smell of Drago's blood there in his own fucking house. He did not know how bad it could smell. EVERYTHING SO INTENSE AND EVERYBODY FAR FROM HOME AND ANGRY ANGRY ANGRY ANGRY RAGE!

Nearly all the way to Northampton—till they couldn't stand it anymore and gagged him—Farley is digging in late at night and waking up in the morning to find that he's slept in someone's grave with the maggots. "Please!" he cried. "No more of this! No more!" And so they had no choice but to shut him up.

At the VA hospital, a place to which he could be brought only by force and from which he'd been running for years—fleeing his whole life from the hospital of a government he could not deal with—they put him on the lockup ward, tied him to the bed, rehydrated him, stabilized him, detoxified him, got him off the alcohol, treated him for liver damage, and then, during the six weeks that followed, every morning in his group therapy session he recounted how Rawley and Les Junior had died. He told them all what happened, told them every day what had failed to happen when he saw the suffocated faces of his two little kids and knew for sure that they were dead.

"Numb," he said. "Fuckin' numb. No emotions. Numb to the death of my own kids. My son's eyes are rolled in back of his head and he has no pulse. He has no heartbeat. My son isn't fucking breathing. My son. Little Les. The only son I will ever have. But I did not feel anything. I was acting as if he was a stranger. Same with Rawley. She was a stranger. My little girl. That fucking Vietnam, you caused this! After all these years the war is over, and you caused this! All my feelings are all fucked up. I feel like I've been hit on the side of the head with a two-by-four when nothing is happening. Then something is happening, something fucking *huge*, I don't feel a fucking thing. Numbed out. My kids are dead, but my body is numb and my mind is blank. Vietnam. That's why! I never did cry for my kids. He was five and she was eight. I said to myself, 'Why can't I feel?' I said, 'Why didn't I save them? Why couldn't I save them?' Payback. Payback! I kept thinking about Vietnam. About all the times I think I died. That's how I began to know that I can't die. Because I died already. Because I died already in Vietnam. Because I am a man who fucking *died*."

The group consisted of Vietnam vets like Farley except for two from the Gulf War, crybabies who got a little sand in their eyes in a four-day ground war. A hundred-hour war. A bunch of waiting in the desert. The Vietnam vets were men who, in their postwar lives, had themselves been through the worst—divorce, booze, drugs, crime, the police, jail, the devastating lowness of depression, uncontrollable crying, wanting to scream, wanting to smash something, the hands trembling and the body twitching and the tightness in the face and the sweats from head to toe from reliving the metal flying and the brilliant explosions and the severed limbs, from reliving the killing of the prisoners and the families and the old ladies and the kids—and so, though they nodded their heads about Rawley and Little Les and understood how he couldn't feel for them when he saw them with their eyes rolled back because he himself was dead, they nonetheless agreed, these really ill guys (in that rare moment when any of them could manage to talk about anybody other than themselves wandering around the streets ready to snap and yelling "Why?" at the sky, about anybody else not getting the respect they should receive, about anybody else not being happy until they were dead and buried and forgotten), that Farley had better put it behind him and get on with his life.

Get on with his life. He knows it's shit, but it's all he has. Get on with it. Okay.

He was let out of the hospital late in August determined to do that. And with the help of a support group that he joined, and one guy in particular who walked with a cane and whose name was Jimmy Borrero, he succeeded at least halfway; it was tough, but with Jimmy's help he was doing it more or less, was on the wagon for nearly three whole months, right up until November. But then—and not because of something somebody said to him or because of something he saw on TV or because of the approach of another familyless Thanksgiving, but because there was no alternative for Farley, no way to prevent the past from building back up, building up and calling him to action and demanding from him an enormous response—instead of it all being behind him, it was in front of him.

Once again, it *was* his life.

2

Slipping the Punch

WHEN COLEMAN went down to Athena the next day to ask what could be done to ensure against Farley's ever again trespassing on his property, the lawyer, Nelson Primus, told him what he did not want to hear: that he should consider ending his love affair. He'd first consulted Primus at the outset of the spooks incident and, because of the sound advice Primus had given—and because of a strain of cocky bluntness in the young attorney's manner reminiscent of himself at Primus's age, because of a repugnance in Primus for sentimental nonessentials that he made no effort to disguise behind the regular-guy easygoingness prevailing among the other lawyers in town—it was Primus to whom he'd brought the Delphine Roux letter.

Primus was in his early thirties, the husband of a young Ph.D.—a philosophy professor whom Coleman had hired some four years earlier—and the father of two small children. In a New England college town like Athena, where most all the professionals were outfitted for work by L. L. Bean, this sleekly good-looking, raven-haired young man, tall, trim, athletically flexible, appeared at his office every morning in crisply tailored suits, gleaming black shoes, and starched white shirts discreetly monogrammed, attire that bespoke not only a sweeping self-confidence and sense of personal significance but a loathing for slovenliness of any kind—and that suggested as well that Nelson Primus was hungry for something more than an office above the Talbots shop across from the green. His wife was teaching here, so for now he was here. But not for long. A young panther in cufflinks and a pinstriped suit—a panther ready to pounce.

"I don't doubt that Farley's psychopathic," Primus told him, measuring each word with staccato exactitude and keeping a sharp watch on Coleman as he spoke. "I'd worry if he were stalking *me*. But did he stalk you before you took up with his ex-wife? He didn't know who you were. The Delphine Roux letter is something else entirely. You wanted me to write to her—against my better judgment I did that for you. You wanted an expert to analyze the handwriting—against my better judgment I got you somebody to analyze the handwriting. You wanted me to send the handwriting analysis to her lawyer—against my better judgment I sent him the results. Even though I wished you'd had it in you to treat a minor nuisance for what it was, I did whatever you instructed me to do. But Lester Farley is no minor nuisance. Delphine Roux can't hold a candle to Farley, not as a psychopath and not as an adversary. Farley's is the world that Faunia only barely managed to survive and that she can't help but bring with her when she comes through your door. Lester Farley works on the road crew, right? We get a restraining order on Farley and your secret is all over your quiet little backwoods town. Soon it's all over *this* town, it's all over the college, and what you started out with is going to bear no resemblance to the malevolent puritanism with which you will be tarred and feathered. I remember the precision with which the local comic weekly failed to understand the ridiculous charge against you and the meaning of your resignation. 'Ex-Dean Leaves College under Racist Cloud.' I remember the caption below your photograph. 'A denigrating epithet used in class forces Professor Silk into retirement.' I remember what it was like for you then, I think I know what it's like now, and I believe I know what it will be like in the future, when the whole county is privy to the sexcapades of the guy who left the college under the racist cloud. I don't mean to imply that what goes on behind your bedroom door is anybody's business but yours. I know it should not be like this. It's 1998. It's years now since Janis Joplin and Norman O. Brown changed everything for the better. But we've got people here in the Berkshires, hicks and college professors alike, who just won't bring their values into line and politely give way to the sexual revolution. Narrow-minded churchgoers, sticklers for propriety, all sorts of retrograde folks eager to expose and punish guys like you. They can heat things up for you, Coleman—and not the way your Viagra does."

Clever boy to come up with the Viagra all on his own. Showing off, but he's helped before, thought Coleman, so don't interrupt, don't put him down, however irritating his being so with-it is. There are no compassionate chinks in his armor? Fine with me. You asked his advice, so hear him out. You don't want to make a mistake for lack of being warned.

"Sure I can get you a restraining order," Primus told him. "But is that going to restrain him? A restraining order is going to inflame him. I got you a handwriting expert, I can get you your restraining order, I can get you a bulletproof vest. But what I can't provide is what you're never going to know as long as you're involved with this woman: a scandal-free, censure-free, Farley-free life. The peace of mind that comes of not being stalked. Or caricatured. Or snubbed. Or misjudged. Is she HIV negative, by the way? Did you have her tested, Coleman? Do you use a condom, Coleman?"

Hip as he imagines himself, he really can't get this old man and sex, can he? Seems utterly anomalous to him. But who can grasp at thirty-two that at seventy-one it's exactly the same? He thinks, How and why does he *do* this? My old-fart virility and the trouble it causes. At thirty-two, thought Coleman, I couldn't have understood it either. Otherwise, however, he speaks with the authority of someone ten or twenty years his senior about the way the world works. And how much experience can he have had, how much exposure to life's difficulties, to speak in such a patronizing manner to a man more than twice his age? Very, very little, if not none.

"Coleman, if you don't," Primus was saying, "does *she* use something? And if she says she does, can you be sure it's so? Even down-and-out cleaning women have been known to shade the truth from time to time, and sometimes even to seek remedy for all the shit they've taken. What happens when Faunia Farley gets pregnant? She may think the way a lot of women have been thinking ever since the act of begetting a bastard was destigmatized by Jim Morrison and The Doors. Faunia might very well want to go ahead and become the mother of a distinguished retired professor's child despite all your patient reasoning to the contrary. Becoming the mother of a distinguished professor's child might be an uplifting change after having been the mother of the children of a deranged total failure. And, once she's pregnant, if she decides that she doesn't want to be a menial anymore, that she wishes never again to work at *anything*, an enlightened court will not hesitate to direct you to support the child *and* the single mother. Now, I can represent you in the paternity suit, and if and when I have to, I will fight to keep your liability down to half your pension. I will do everything in my power to see that something is left in your bank account as you advance into your eighties. Coleman, listen to me: this is a bad deal. In every possible way, it is a bad deal. If you go to your hedonist counselor, he's going to tell you something else, but I am your counselor at law, and I'm going to tell you that it's a *terrible* deal. If I were you, I would not put myself in the path of Lester Farley's wild grievance. If I were you, I would rip up the Faunia contract and get out."

Everything he had to say having been said, Primus got up from behind his desk, a large, well-polished desk conscientiously kept cleared of all papers and files, pointedly bare of everything but the framed photographs of his young professor wife and their two children, a desk whose surface epitomized the unsullied *clean slate* and could only lead Coleman to conclude that there was nothing disorganized standing in the way of this voluble young man, neither weaknesses of character nor extreme views nor rash compulsions nor even the possibility of inadvertent error, nothing ill or well concealed that would ever crop up to prevent him from attaining every professional reward and bourgeois success. There'll be no spooks in Nelson Primus's life, no Faunia Farleys or Lester Farleys, no Markies to despise him or Lisas to desert him. Primus has drawn the line and no incriminating impurity will be permitted to breach it. But didn't I too draw the line and draw it no less rigorously? Was I less vigilant in the pursuit of legitimate goals and of an estimable, even-keeled life? Was I any less confident marching in step behind my own impregnable scruples? Was I any less arrogant? Isn't this the very way I took on the old guard in my first hundred days as Roberts's strongman? Isn't this how I drove them crazy and pushed them out? Was I any less ruthlessly sure of myself? Yet that one word did it. By no means the English language's most inflammatory, most heinous, most horrifying word, and yet word enough to lay bare, for all to see, to judge, to find wanting the truth of who and what I am.

The lawyer who'd not minced a single word—who'd laced virtually every one of them with a cautionary sarcasm that amounted to outright admonishment, whose purpose he would not disguise from his distinguished elderly client with a single circumlocution —came around from behind his desk to escort Coleman out of the office and then, at the doorway, went so far as to accompany him down the stairway and out onto the sunny street. It was largely on behalf of Beth, his wife, that Primus had wanted to be sure to say everything he could to Coleman as tellingly as he could, to say what had to be said no matter how seemingly unkind, in the hope of preventing this once considerable college personage from disgracing himself any further. That spooks incident—coinciding as it did with the sudden death of his wife—had so seriously unhinged Dean Silk that not only had he taken the rash step of resigning (and just when the case against him had all but run its spurious course), but now, two full years later, he remained unable to gauge what was and wasn't in his long-term interest. To Primus, it seemed almost as though Coleman Silk had not been unfairly diminished *enough*, as though, with a doomed man's cunning obtuseness, like someone who falls foul of a god, he was in crazy pursuit of a final, malicious, degrading assault, an ultimate injustice that would validate his aggrievement forever. A guy who'd once enjoyed a lot of power in his small world seemed not merely unable to defend himself against the encroachments of a Delphine Roux and a Lester Farley but, what was equally compromising to his embattled self-image, unable to shield himself against the pitiful sorts of temptations with which the aging male will try to compensate for the loss of a spirited, virile manhood. Primus could tell from Coleman's demeanor that he'd guessed right about the Viagra. Another chemical menace, the young man thought. The guy might as well be smoking crack, for all the good that Viagra is doing him.

Out on the street, the two shook hands. "Coleman," said Primus, whose wife, that very morning, when he'd said that he'd be seeing Dean Silk, had expressed her chagrin about his leavetaking from Athena, again speaking contemptuously of Delphine Roux, whom she despised for her role in the spooks affair—"Coleman," Primus said, "Faunia Farley is not from your world. You got a good look last night at the world that's shaped her, that's quashed her, and that, for reasons you know as well as I do, she'll never escape. Something worse than last night can come of all this, something much worse. You're no longer battling in a world where they are out to destroy you and drive you from your job so as to replace you with one of their own. You're no longer battling a well-mannered gang of elitist egalitarians who hide their ambition behind high-minded ideals. You're battling now in a world where nobody's ruthlessness bothers to cloak itself in humanitarian rhetoric. These are people whose fundamental feeling about life is that they have been fucked over unfairly right down the line. What you suffered because of how your case was handled by the college, awful as that was, is what these people feel every minute of every hour of . . ."

That's enough was by now so clearly written in Coleman's gaze that even Primus realized that it was time to shut up. Throughout the meeting, Coleman had silently listened, suppressing his feelings, trying to keep an open mind and to ignore the too apparent delight Primus took in floridly lecturing on the virtues of prudence a professional man nearly forty years his senior. In an attempt to humor himself, Coleman had been thinking, Being angry with me makes them all feel better—it liberates everyone to tell me I'm wrong. But by the time they were out on the street, it was no longer possible to isolate the argument from the utterance—or to separate himself from the man in charge he'd always been, the man in charge and the man deferred to. For Primus to speak directly to the point to his client had not required quite this much satiric ornamentation. If the purpose was to advise in a persuasive lawyerly fashion, a very *small* amount of mockery would have more effectively done the job. But Primus's sense of himself as brilliant and destined for great things seemed to have got the best of him, thought Coleman, and so the mockery of a ridiculous old fool made potent by a pharmaceutical compound selling for ten dollars a pill had known no bounds.

"You're a vocal master of extraordinary loquaciousness, Nelson. So perspicacious. So fluent. A vocal master of the endless, ostentatiously overelaborate sentence. And so rich with contempt for every last human problem you've never had to face." The impulse was overwhelming to grab the lawyer by the shirt front and slam the insolent son of a bitch through Talbots's window. Instead, drawing back, reining himself in, strategically speaking as softly as he could—yet not nearly so mindfully as he might have—Coleman said, "I never again want to hear that self-admiring voice of yours or see your smug fucking lily-white face."

"'Lily-white'?" Primus said to his wife that evening. "Why 'lily-white'? One can never hold people to what they lash out with when they think they've been made use of and deprived of their dignity. But did I *mean* to seem to be attacking him? Of course not. It's worse than that. Worse because this old guy has lost his bearings and I wanted to help him. Worse because the man is on the brink of carrying a mistake over into a catastrophe and I wanted to *stop* him. What he took to be an attack on him was actually a wrong-headed attempt to be taken seriously by him, to impress him. I failed, Beth, completely mismanaged it. Maybe because I *was* intimidated. In his slight, little-guy way, the man is a force. I never knew him as the big dean. I've known him only as someone in trouble. But you feel the presence. You see why people were intimidated by him. Somebody's *there* when he's sitting there. Look, I don't know what it is. It's not easy to know what to make of somebody you've seen half a dozen times in your life. Maybe it's primarily something stupid about me. But whatever caused it, I made every amateurish mistake in the book. Psychopathology, Viagra, The Doors, Norman O. Brown, contraception, AIDS. I knew everything about everything. Particularly if it happened before I was born, I knew everything that could possibly be known. I should have been concise, matter-of-fact, unsubjective; instead I was provocative. I wanted to help him and instead I insulted him and made things worse for him. No, I don't fault him for unloading on me like that. But, honey, the question remains: why *white?*"

Coleman hadn't been on the Athena campus for two years and by now no longer went to town at all if he could help it. He didn't any longer hate each and every member of the Athena faculty, he just wanted nothing to do with them, fearful that should he stop to chat, even idly, he'd be incapable of concealing his pain or concealing himself concealing his pain—unable to prevent himself from standing there seething or, worse, from coming apart and breaking unstoppably into an overly articulate version of the wronged man's blues. A few days after his resignation, he'd opened new accounts at the bank and the supermarket up in Blackwell, a depressed mill town on the river some eighteen miles from Athena, and even got a card for the local library there, determined to use it, however meager the collection, rather than to wander ever again through the stacks at Athena. He joined the YMCA in Blackwell, and instead of taking his swim at the Athena college pool at the end of the day or exercising on a mat in the Athena gym as he'd done after work for nearly thirty years, he did his laps a couple of times a week at the less agreeable pool of the Blackwell Y—he even went upstairs to the rundown gym and, for the first time since graduate school, began, at a far slower pace than back in the forties, to work out with the speed bag and to hit the heavy bag. To go north to Blackwell took twice as long as driving down the mountain to Athena, but in Blackwell he was unlikely to run into ex-colleagues, and when he did, it was less self-consciously fraught with feeling for him to nod unsmilingly and go on about his business than it would have been on the pretty old streets of Athena, where there was not a street sign, a bench, a tree, not a monument on the green, that didn't somehow remind him of himself before he was the college racist and everything was different. The string of shops across from the green hadn't even been there until his tenure as dean had brought all sorts of new people to Athena as staff and as students and as parents of students, and so, over time, he'd wound up changing the community no less than he had shaken up the college. The moribund antique shop, the bad restaurant, the subsistence-level grocery store, the provincial liquor store, the hick-town barbershop, the nineteenth-century haberdasher, the understocked bookshop, the genteel tearoom, the dark pharmacy, the depressing tavern, the newspaperless newsdealer, the empty, enigmatic magic shop—all of them had disappeared, to be replaced by establishments where you could eat a decent meal and get a good cup of coffee and have a prescription filled and buy a good bottle of wine and find a book about something other than the Berkshires and also find something other than long underwear to keep you warm in wintertime. The "revolution of quality" that he had once been credited with imposing on the Athena faculty and curriculum, he had, albeit inadvertently, bestowed on Town Street as well. Which only added to the pain and surprise of being the alien he was.

By now, two years down the line, he felt himself besieged not so much by *them*—apart from Delphine Roux, who at Athena cared any longer about Coleman Silk and the spooks incident?—as by weariness with his own barely submerged, easily galvanized bitterness; down in the streets of Athena, he now felt (to begin with) a greater aversion to himself than to those who, out of indifference or cowardice or ambition, had failed to mount the slightest protest in his behalf. Educated people with Ph.D.s, people he had himself hired because he believed that they were capable of thinking reasonably and independently, had turned out to have no inclination to weigh the preposterous evidence against him and reach an appropriate conclusion. Racist: at Athena College, suddenly the most emotionally charged epithet you could be stuck with, and to that emotionalism (and to fear for their personnel files and future promotions) his entire faculty had succumbed. "Racist" spoken with the official-sounding resonance, and every last potential ally had scurried for cover.

Walk up to the campus? It was summer. School was out. After nearly four decades at Athena, after all that had been destroyed and lost, after all that he had gone through to get there, why not? First "spooks," now "lily-white"—who knows what repellent deficiency will be revealed with the next faintly antiquated locution, the next idiom almost charmingly out of time that comes flying from his mouth? How one is revealed or undone by the perfect word. What burns away the camouflage and the covering and the concealment? This, the right word uttered spontaneously, without one's even having to think.

"For the thousandth time: I said spooks because I meant spooks. My father was a saloon keeper, but he insisted on precision in my language, and I have kept the faith with him. Words have meanings—with only a seventh-grade education, even my father knew that much. Back of the bar, he kept two things to help settle arguments among his patrons: a blackjack and a dictionary. My best friend, he told me, the dictionary—and so it is for me today. Because if we look in the dictionary, what do we find as the first meaning of 'spook'? The primary meaning. '1. *Informal.* a ghost; specter.'" "But Dean Silk, that is not the way it was taken. Let me read to you the *second* dictionary meaning. '2. *Disparaging.* A Negro.' That's the way it was taken—and you can see the logic of that as well: Does anybody know them, or are they blacks whom you don't know?" "Sir, if my intention was to say, 'Does anybody know

them, or do you not know them because they are black?' that is
what I would have said. 'Does anybody know them, or do none
of you know them because these happen to be two black students? Does anybody know them, or are they blacks whom nobody
knows?' If I had meant that, I would have said it *just like that.* But
how could I know they were black students if I had never laid eyes
on them and, other than their names, had no knowledge of them?
What I did know, indisputably, was that they were *invisible* students—and the word for invisible, for a ghost, for a specter, is the
word that I used in its primary meaning: spook. Look at the ad-
jective 'spooky,' which is the next dictionary entry after 'spook.'
Spooky. A word we all remember from childhood, and what does *it*
mean? According to the unabridged dictionary: '*Informal.* 1. like or
befitting a spook or ghost; suggestive of spooks. 2. eerie; scary. 3.
(esp. of horses) nervous; skittish.' Especially of horses. Now, would
anyone care to suggest that my two students were being characterized by me as horses as well? No? But why not? While you're at it,
why not that, too?"

One last look at Athena, and then let the disgrace be complete.

Silky. Silky Silk. The name by which he had not been known for
over fifty years, and yet he all but expected to hear someone shouting, "Hey, Silky!" as though he were back in East Orange, walking
up Central Avenue after school—instead of crossing Athena's Town
Street and, for the first time since his resignation, starting up the
hill to the campus—walking up Central Avenue with his sister,
Ernestine, listening to that crazy story she had to tell about what
she'd overheard the evening before when Dr. Fensterman, the Jewish doctor, the big surgeon from Mom's hospital down in Newark,
had come to call on their parents. While Coleman had been at the
gym working out with the track team, Ernestine was home in the
kitchen doing her homework and from there could hear Dr. Fensterman, seated in the living room with Mom and Dad, explaining
why it was of the utmost importance to him and Mrs. Fensterman
that their son Bertram graduate as class valedictorian. As the Silks

knew, it was now Coleman who was first in their class, with Bert second, though behind Coleman by a single grade. The one B that Bert had received on his report card the previous term, a B in physics that by all rights should have been an A—that B was all that was separating the top two students in the senior class. Dr. Fensterman explained to Mr. and Mrs. Silk that Bert wanted to follow his father into medicine, but that to do so it was essential for him to have a perfect record, and not merely perfect in college but extraordinary going back to kindergarten. Perhaps the Silks were not aware of the discriminatory quotas that were designed to keep Jews out of medical school, especially the medical schools at Harvard and Yale, where Dr. and Mrs. Fensterman were confident that, were Bert given the opportunity, he could emerge as the brightest of the brightest. Because of the tiny Jewish quotas in most medical schools, Dr. Fensterman had had himself to go down to Alabama for his schooling, and there he'd seen at first hand all that colored people have to strive against. Dr. Fensterman knew that prejudice in academic institutions against colored students was far worse than it was against Jews. He knew the kind of obstacles that the Silks themselves had had to overcome to achieve all that distinguished them as a model Negro family. He knew the tribulations that Mr. Silk had had to endure ever since the optical shop went bankrupt in the Depression. He knew that Mr. Silk was, like himself, a college graduate, and he knew that in working for the railroad as a steward—"That's what he called a waiter, Coleman, a 'steward'"—he was employed at a level in no way commensurate with his professional training. Mrs. Silk he of course knew from the hospital. In Dr. Fensterman's estimation, there was no finer nurse on the hospital staff, no nurse more intelligent, knowledgeable, reliable, or capable than Mrs. Silk—and that included the nursing supervisor herself. In his estimation, Gladys Silk should long ago have been appointed the head nurse on the medical-surgical floor; one of the promises that Dr. Fensterman wanted to make to the Silks was that he was prepared to do everything he could with the chief of staff to procure that very position for Mrs. Silk upon the retirement of Mrs. Noonan, the current medical-surgical head nurse. Moreover, he was prepared to assist the Silks with an interest-free, nonreturnable "loan" of three thousand dollars, payable in a lump sum when Coleman would be off to college and the family was sure to be incurring additional expenses. And in exchange he asked not so much as they might think. As salutatorian, Coleman would still be the highest-ranking colored student in the 1944 graduating class, not to mention the highest-ranking colored student ever to graduate E. O. With his grade average, Coleman would more than likely be the highest-ranking colored student in the county, even in the state, and his having finished high school as salutatorian rather than as valedictorian would make no difference whatsoever when he enrolled at Howard University. The chances were negligible of his suffering the slightest hardship with a ranking like that. Coleman would lose nothing, while the Silks would have three thousand dollars to put toward the children's college expenses; in addition, with Dr. Fensterman's support and backing, Gladys Silk could very well rise, in just a few years, to become the first colored head nurse on any floor of any hospital in the city of Newark. And from Coleman nothing more was required than his choosing his two weakest subjects and, instead of getting A's on the final exams, getting B's. It would then be up to Bert to get an A in all his subjects— doing that would constitute holding up *his* end of the bargain. And should Bert let everyone down by not working hard enough to get all those A's, then the two boys would finish in a flat-footed tie—or Coleman could even emerge as valedictorian, and Dr. Fensterman would still make good on his promises. Needless to say, the arrangement would be kept confidential by everyone involved.

So delighted was he by what he heard that Coleman broke loose from Ernestine's grasp and burst away up the street, in exuberant delight running up Central to Evergreen and then back, crying aloud, "My two weakest subjects—which are those?" It was as though in attributing to Coleman an academic weakness, Dr. Fensterman had told the most hilarious joke. "What'd they say, Ern? What did Dad say?" "I couldn't hear. He said it too low." "What did

Mom say?" "I don't know. I couldn't hear Mom either. But what they were saying after the doctor left, I heard that." "Tell me! What?" "Daddy said, 'I wanted to kill that man.'" "He did?" "Really. Yes." "And Mom?" "'I just bit my tongue.' That's what Mom said—'I just bit my tongue.'" "But you didn't hear what they said to *him?*" "No." "Well, I'll tell you one thing—I'm not going to do it." "Of course not," Ernestine said. "But suppose Dad told him I would?" "Are you crazy, Coleman?" "Ernie, three thousand dollars is more than Dad makes in a whole year. Ernie, three thousand dollars!" And the thought of Dr. Fensterman handing over to his father a big paper bag stuffed with all that money set him running again, goofily taking the imaginary low hurdles (for successive years now, he had been Essex County high school champ in low hurdles and run second in the hundred-yard dash) up to Evergreen and back. Another triumph—that's what he was thinking. Yet another rec-ord-breaking triumph for the great, the incomparable, the one and only Silky Silk! He was class valedictorian, all right, as well as a track star, but as he was also only seventeen, Dr. Fensterman's proposal meant no more to him than that he was of the greatest importance to just about everyone. The larger picture he didn't get yet.

In East Orange, where mostly everyone was white, either poor Italian—and living up at the Orange edge of town or down by Newark's First Ward—or Episcopalian and rich—and living in the big houses out by Upsala or around South Harrison—there were fewer Jews even than there were Negroes, and yet it was the Jews and their kids who these days loomed larger than anyone in Cole-man's extracurricular life. First there was Doc Chizner, who had as good as adopted him the year before, when Coleman joined his evening boxing class, and now there was Dr. Fensterman offering three thousand dollars for Coleman to place second academically so as to enable Bert to come in first. Doc Chizner was a dentist who loved boxing. Went to the fights whenever he had a chance—in Jer-sey at Laurel Garden and at the Meadowbrook Bowl, to New York to the Garden and out to St. Nick's. People would say, "You think you know fights until you sit next to Doc. Sit next to Doc Chizner, and you realize you're not watching the same fight." Doc officiated at amateur fights all over Essex County, including the Golden Gloves in Newark, and to his local classes in boxing Jewish parents from all over the Oranges, from Maplewood, from Irvington—from as far away as the Weequahic section over at Newark's southwest corner—sent their sons to learn how to defend themselves. Coleman had wound up in Doc Chizner's class not because he didn't know how but because his own father had found out that since his second year of high school, after track practice, all on his own—and as often sometimes as three times a week—Coleman had been sneaking down to the Newark Boys Club, below High Street in the Newark slums to Morton Street, and secretly training to be a fighter. Fourteen years old when he began, a hundred and eleven pounds, and he would work out there for two hours, loosen up, spar three rounds, hit the heavy bag, hit the speed bag, skip rope, do his exercises, and then head home to do his homework. A couple of times he even got to spar with Cooper Fulham, who the year before had won the National Championships up in Boston. Coleman's mother was working a shift and a half, even two shifts running at the hospital, his father was waiting tables on the train and hardly at home other than to sleep, his older brother, Walt, was away first at college, then in the army, and so Coleman came and went as he liked, swearing Ernestine to secrecy and making sure not to let his grades slip, in study hall, at night in bed, on the buses back and forth to Newark—two buses each way—plugging away even harder than usual at his schoolwork to be sure nobody found out about Morton Street.

If you wanted to box amateur, the Newark Boys Club was where you went, and if you were good and you were between thirteen and eighteen, you got matched up against guys from the Boys Club in Paterson, in Jersey City, in Butler, from the Ironbound PAL, and so on. There were loads of kids down at the Boys Club, some from Rahway, from Linden, from Elizabeth, a couple from as far away as Morristown, there was a deaf-mute they called Dummy who came from Belleville, but mostly they were from Newark and all of them were colored, though the two guys who ran the club were white. One was a cop in West Side Park, Mac Machrone, and he had a pistol, and he told Coleman that if he ever found out Coleman wasn't doing his roadwork, he'd shoot him. Mac believed in speed, and that's why he believed in Coleman. Speed and pacing and counterpunching. Once he'd taught Coleman how to stand and how to move and how to throw the punches, once Mac saw how quickly the boy learned and how smart he was and how quick his reflexes were, he began to teach him the finer things. How to move his head. How to slip punches. How to block punches. How to counter. To teach him the jab, Mac repeated, "It's like you flick a flea off your nose. Just flick it off him." He taught Coleman how to win a fight by using only his jab. Throw the jab, knock the punch down, counter. A jab comes, you slip it, come over with the right counter. Or you slip it inside, you come over with a hook. Or you just duck down, hit him a right to the heart, a left hook to the stomach. Slight as he was, Coleman would sometimes quickly grab the jab with both his hands, pull the guy and then hook him to the stomach, come up, hook him to the head. "Knock the punch down. Counterpunch. You're a counterpuncher, Silky. That's what you are, that's all you are." Then they went to Paterson. His first amateur tournament fight. This kid would throw a jab and Coleman would lean back, but his feet would be planted and he could come back and counter the kid with a right, and he kept catching him like that for the whole fight. The kid kept doing it, so Coleman kept doing it and won all three rounds. At the Boys Club, that became Silky Silk's style. When he threw punches, it was so nobody could say he was standing there doing nothing. Mostly he would wait for the other guy to throw, then he'd throw two, three back, and then he'd get out and wait again. Coleman could hit his opponent more by waiting for him to lead than by leading him. The result was that by the time Coleman was sixteen, in Essex and Hudson counties alone, at amateur shows at the armory, at the Knights of Pythias, at exhibitions for the veterans at the veterans hospital, he must have beaten three guys who were Golden Gloves champs. As he figured it, he could by then have won 112, 118, 126 . . . except there was no way he could fight in the Golden Gloves without its getting in the papers and his family finding out. And then they found out anyway. He didn't know how. He didn't have to. They found out because somebody told them. Simple as that.

They were all sitting down to dinner on a Sunday, after church, when his father said, "How did you do, Coleman?"

"How did I do at what?"

"Last night. At the Knights of Pythias. How did you do?"

"What's the Knights of Pythias?" Coleman asked.

"Do you think I was born yesterday, son? The Knights of Pythias is where they had the tournament last night. How many fights on the card?"

"Fifteen."

"And how did you do?"

"I won."

"How many fights have you won so far? In tournaments. In exhibitions. How many since you began?"

"Eleven."

"And how many have you lost?"

"So far, none."

"And how much did you get for the watch?"

"What watch?"

"The watch you won at the Lyons Veterans Hospital. The watch the vets gave you for winning the fight. The watch you hocked on Mulberry Street. Down in Newark, Coleman—the watch you hocked in Newark last week."

The man knew everything.

"What do you think I got?" Coleman dared to reply, though not looking up as he spoke—instead looking at the embroidered design on the good Sunday tablecloth.

"You got two dollars, Coleman. When are you planning on turning pro?"

"I don't do it for money," he said, still with his eyes averted. "I don't care about money. I do it for enjoyment. It's not a sport you take up if you don't enjoy it."

"You know, if I were your father, Coleman, you know what I'd tell you now?"

"You are my father," Coleman said.

"Oh, am I?" his father said.

"Well, sure . . ."

"Well—I'm not sure at all. I was thinking that maybe Mac Machrone, at the Newark Boys Club, was your father."

"Come on, Dad. Mac's my trainer."

"I see. So who then is your father, if I may ask?"

"You know. You are. You are, Dad."

"I am? Yes?"

"No!" Coleman shouted. "No, you're not!" And here, at the very start of Sunday dinner, he ran out of the house and for nearly an hour he did his roadwork, up Central Avenue and over the Orange line, and then through Orange all the way to the West Orange line, and then crossing over on Watchung Avenue to Rosedale Cemetery, and then turning south down Washington to Main, running and throwing punches, sprinting, then just running, then just sprinting, then shadowboxing all the way back to Brick Church Station, and finally sprinting the stretch, sprinting to the house, going back inside to where the family was eating their dessert and where he knew to sit back down at his place, far calmer than when he had bolted, and to wait for his father to resume where he had left off. The father who never lost his temper. The father who had another way of beating you down. With words. With speech. With what he called "the language of Chaucer, Shakespeare, and Dickens." With the English language that no one could ever take away from you and that Mr. Silk richly sounded, always with great fullness and clarity and bravado, as though even in ordinary conversation he were reciting Marc Antony's speech over the body of Caesar. Each of his three children had been given a middle name drawn from Mr. Silk's best-memorized play, in his view English literature's high point and the most educational study of treason ever written: the eldest Silk son was Walter Antony, the second son, Coleman Brutus; Ernestine Calpurnia, their younger sister, took her middle name from Caesar's loyal wife.

Mr. Silk's life in business for himself had come to a bitter end with the closing of the banks. It had taken him quite a time to get over losing the optician's store up in Orange, if he ever did. Poor Daddy, Mother would say, he always wanted to work for himself. He'd attended college in the South, in Georgia where he came from—Mother was from New Jersey—and took farming and animal husbandry. But then he quit and up north, in Trenton, he went to optician's school. Then he was drafted into the army for World War I, then he met Mother, moved with her to East Orange, opened the store, bought the house, then there was the crash, and now he was a waiter on a dining car. But if he couldn't in the dining car, at least at home he was able to speak with all his deliberateness and precision and directness and could wither you with words. He was very fussy about his children's speaking properly. Growing up, they never said, "See the bow-wow." They didn't even say, "See the doggie." They said, "See the Doberman. See the beagle. See the terrier." They learned things had classifications. They learned the power of naming precisely. He was teaching them English all the time. Even the kids who came into the house, his children's friends, had their English corrected by Mr. Silk.

When he was an optician and wore a white medical smock over a ministerial dark suit and was working more or less regular hours, he would sit after dessert and read the newspaper at the dinner table. They all would read from it. Each one of the children, even the baby, even Ernestine, would have to take a turn at the *Newark Evening News*, and not with the funnies. His mother, Coleman's grandmother, had been taught to read by her mistress and after Emancipation had gone to what was then called Georgia State Normal and Industrial School for Colored. His father, Coleman's paternal grandfather, had been a Methodist minister. In the Silk family they had read all the old classics. In the Silk family the children were not taken to prizefights, they were taken to the Metropolitan Museum of Art in New York to see the armor. They were taken to the Hayden Planetarium to learn about the solar system. Regularly they were taken to the Museum of Natural History. And then in 1937, on the Fourth of July, despite the cost, they were all taken by Mr. Silk to the Music Box Theatre on Broadway to see George M. Cohan in *I'd Rather Be Right*. Coleman still remembered what his father told his brother, Uncle Bobby, on the phone the next day. "When the curtain came down on George M. Cohan after all his curtain calls, do you know what the man did? He came out for an hour and sang all his songs. Every one of them. What better introduction could a child have to the theater?"

"If I were your father," Coleman's father resumed, while the boy sat solemnly before his empty plate, "you know what I would tell you now?"

"What?" said Coleman, speaking softly, and not because he was winded from all the roadwork but because he was chastened by having told his own father, who was no longer an optician but a dining car waiter and who would remain a dining car waiter till he died, that he was not his father.

"I would say, 'You won last night? Good. Now you can retire undefeated. You're retired.' That's what I'd say, Coleman."

It was much easier when Coleman spoke to him later, after he had spent the afternoon doing his homework and after his mother had a chance to talk and reason with his father. They were all able to sit more or less peaceably together then in the living room and listen to Coleman describe the glories of boxing and how, given all the resources you had to call on to excel, they exceeded even winning at track.

It was his mother who asked the questions now, and answering her was no problem. Her younger son was wrapped like a gift in every ameliorating dream Gladys Silk had ever had, and the handsomer he became and the smarter he became, the more difficult it was for her to distinguish the child from the dreams. As sensitive and gentle as she could be with the patients at the hospital, she could also be, with the other nurses, even with the doctors, with the white doctors, exacting and stern, imposing on them a code of conduct no less stringent than the one she imposed on herself. She could be that way with Ernestine as well. But never with Coleman. Coleman got what the patients got: her conscientious kindness and care. Coleman got just about anything he wanted. The father leading the way, the mother feeding the love. The old one-two.

"I don't see how you get mad at somebody you don't know. You especially," she said, "with your happy nature."

"You don't get mad. You just concentrate. It's a sport. You warm up before a fight. You shadowbox. You get yourself ready for whatever is going to come at you."

"If you've never seen the opponent before?" asked his father, with all the restraint on his sarcasm he could muster.

"All I mean," Coleman said, "is you don't *have* to get mad."

"But," his mother asked, "what if the other boy is mad?"

"It doesn't matter. It's brains that win, not getting mad. Let him get mad. Who cares? You have to think. It's like a chess game. Like a cat and a mouse. You can lead a guy. Last night, I had this guy, he was about eighteen or nineteen and he was sort of slow. He hit me with a jab on the top of my head. So the next time he did it, I was ready for it, and boom. I came over with the right counter and he didn't know where it came from. I knocked him down. I don't knock guys down, but I knocked this guy down. And I did it because I got him into thinking that he could catch me again with this punch."

"Coleman," his mother said, "I do not like the sound of what I'm hearing."

He stood up to demonstrate for her. "Look. It was a slow punch. You see? I saw his jab was slow and he wasn't catching me. It was nothing that hurt me, Mom. I just was thinking that if he does it again, I'll slip it and bang over with the right. So when he threw it again, I saw it coming because it was so slow, and I was able to counter and catch him. I knocked him down, Mom, but not because I was angry. Because I box better."

"But these Newark boys you fight. They're nothing like the

friends you have," and, with affection, she mentioned the names of the two other best-behaved, brightest Negro boys in his year at East Orange High, who were indeed the pals he had lunch with and hung around with at school. "I see these Newark boys on the street. These boys are so *tough*," she said. "Track is so much more civilized than boxing, so much more like you, Coleman. Dear, you run so beautifully."

"It doesn't *matter* how tough they are or how tough they think they are," he told her. "On the street it matters. But not in the ring. In the street this guy could probably have beat me silly. But in the ring? With rules? With gloves? No, no—he couldn't land a punch."

"But what happens when they *do* hit you? It has to hurt you. The impact. It must. And that's so dangerous. Your head. Your *brain*."

"You're rolling with the punch, Mom. That's where they teach you how to roll your head. Like this, see? That reduces the impact. Once, and only once, and only because I was a jerk, only because of my own stupid mistake and because I wasn't used to fighting a southpaw, did I get a little stunned. And it's only like if you bang your head against the wall, you feel a little dizzy or shaky. But then all of a sudden your body comes right back. All you have to do is just hold on to the guy or move away, and then your head clears up. Sometimes, you get hit in the nose, your eyes get a little watery for a second, but that's it. If you know what you're doing, it's not dangerous at all."

With that remark, his father had heard enough. "I've seen men get hit with a punch that they never saw coming. And when that happens," Mr. Silk said, "their eyes don't get watery—when that happens, it knocks them cold. Even Joe Louis, if you recall, was knocked cold—wasn't he? Am I mistaken? And if Joe Louis can be knocked cold, Coleman, so can you."

"Yeah, but Dad, Schmeling, when he fought Louis that first fight, he saw a weakness. And the weakness was that when Louis threw his jab, instead of coming back—" On his feet again, the boy demonstrated to his parents what he meant. "Instead of coming back, he dropped his left hand—see?—and Schmeling kept coming over

—see?—and that's how Schmeling knocked him out. It's all thinking. Really. It *is*, Dad. I swear to you."

"Don't say that. Don't say, 'I swear to you.'"

"I won't, I won't. But see, if he doesn't come back, where he's back in position, if he comes here instead, then the guy's going to come over with his right hand and eventually he's going to catch him. That's what happened that first time. That's exactly what happened."

But Mr. Silk had seen plenty of fights, in the army had seen fights among soldiers staged at night for the troops where fighters were not only knocked out like Joe Louis but so badly cut up nothing could be done to stop the bleeding. On his base he had seen colored fighters who used their heads as their main weapon, who should have had a glove on their heads, tough street fighters, stupid men who butted and butted with their heads until the face of the other fighter was unrecognizable as a face. No, Coleman was to retire undefeated, and if he wanted to box for the enjoyment of it, for the sport, he would do so not at the Newark Boys Club, which to Mr. Silk was for slum kids, for illiterates and hoodlums bound for either the gutter or jail, but right there in East Orange, under the auspices of Doc Chizner, who'd been the dentist for the United Electrical Workers when Mr. Silk was the optician providing the union's members with eyeglasses before he lost the business. Doc Chizner was still a dentist but after hours taught the sons of the Jewish doctors and lawyers and businessmen the basic skills of boxing, and nobody in his classes, you could be sure, ended up hurt or maimed for life. For Coleman's father, the Jews, even audaciously unsavory Jews like Dr. Fensterman, were like Indian scouts, shrewd people showing the outsider his way in, showing the social possibility, showing an intelligent colored family how it might be done.

That was how Coleman got to Doc Chizner and became the colored kid whom all the privileged Jewish kids got to know—probably the only one they would ever know. Quickly Coleman came to be Doc's assistant, teaching these Jewish kids not exactly the fine points of how to economize energy and motion that Mac

Machrone had taught his ace student but the basics, which was all they were up to anyway—"I say one, you jab. I say one-one, you double-jab. I say one-two, left jab, right cross. One-two-three, left jab, right cross, left hook." After the other pupils went home—with the occasional one who got a bloody nose packing it in, never to return—Doc Chizner worked alone with Coleman, some nights building up his endurance mainly by doing infighting with him, where you're tugging, you're pulling, you're hitting, and so afterward, by comparison, sparring is kid's play. Doc had Coleman up and out doing his roadwork and his shadowboxing even as the milkman's horse, drawing the wagon, would arrive in the neighborhood with the morning delivery. Coleman would be out there at 5 A.M. in his gray hooded sweatshirt, in the cold, the snow, it made no difference, out there three and a half hours before the first school bell. No one else around, nobody running, long before anybody knew what running was, doing three quick miles, and throwing punches the whole way, stopping only so as not to frighten that big, brown, lumbering old beast when, tucked sinisterly within his monklike cowl, Coleman drew abreast of the milkman and sprinted ahead. He hated the boredom of the running—and he never missed a day.

Some four months before Dr. Fensterman came to the house to make his offer to Coleman's parents, Coleman found himself one Saturday in Doc Chizner's car being driven up to West Point, where Doc was going to referee a match between Army and the University of Pittsburgh. Doc knew the Pitt coach and he wanted the coach to see Coleman fight. Doc was sure that, what with Coleman's grades, the coach could get him a four-year scholarship to Pitt, a bigger scholarship than he could ever get for track, and all he'd have to do was box for the Pitt team.

Now, it wasn't that on the way up Doc told him to tell the Pitt coach that he was white. He just told Coleman not to mention that he was colored.

"If nothing comes up," Doc said, "you don't bring it up. You're neither one thing or the other. You're Silky Silk. That's enough.

That's the deal." Doc's favorite expression: that's the deal. Something else Coleman's father would not allow him to repeat in the house.

"He won't know?" Coleman asked.

"How? How will he know? How the hell is he going to know? Here is the top kid from East Orange High, and he is with Doc Chizner. You know what he's going to think, if he thinks anything?"

"What?"

"You look like you look, you're with me, and so he's going to think that you're one of Doc's boys. He's going to think that you're Jewish."

Coleman never regarded Doc as much of a comedian—nothing like Mac Machrone and his stories about being a Newark cop—but he laughed loudly at that one and then reminded him, "I'm going to Howard. I can't go to Pitt. I've got to go to Howard." For as long as Coleman could remember, his father had been determined to send him, the brightest of the three kids, to a historically black college along with the privileged children of the black professional elite.

"Coleman, box for the guy. That's all. That's the whole deal. Let's see what happens."

Except for educational trips to New York City with his family, Coleman had never been out of Jersey before, and so first he spent a great day walking around West Point pretending he was at West Point because he was going to *go* to West Point, and then he boxed for the Pitt coach against a guy like the guy he'd boxed at the Knights of Pythias—slow, so slow that within seconds Coleman realized that there was no way this guy was going to beat him, even if he was twenty years old and a college boxer. Jesus, Coleman thought at the end of the first round, if I could fight this guy for the rest of my life, I'd be better than Ray Robinson. It wasn't just that Coleman weighed some seven pounds more than when he'd boxed on the amateur card at the Knights of Pythias. It was that something he could not even name made him want to be more damaging than he'd ever dared before, to do something more that day than merely win. Was it because the Pitt coach didn't know he was colored? Could it be because who he really was was entirely his secret? He did love secrets. The secret of nobody's knowing what was going on in your head, thinking whatever you wanted to think with no way of anybody's knowing. All the other kids were always blabbing about themselves. But that wasn't where the power was or the pleasure either. The power and pleasure were to be found in the opposite, in being counterconfessional in the same way you were a counterpuncher, and he knew that with nobody having to tell him and without his having to think about it. That's why he liked shadowboxing and hitting the heavy bag: for the secrecy in it. That's why he liked track, too, but this was even better. Some guys just banged away at the heavy bag. Not Coleman. Coleman *thought,* and the same way that he thought in school or in a race: rule everything else out, let nothing else in, and immerse yourself in the thing, the subject, the competition, the exam—whatever's to be mastered, become that thing. He could do that in biology and he could do it in the dash and he could do it in boxing. And not only did nothing external make any difference, neither did anything internal. If there were people in the fight crowd shouting at him, he could pay no attention to that, and if the guy he was fighting was his best friend, he could pay no attention to that. After the fight there was plenty of time for them to be friends again. He managed to force himself to ignore his feelings, whether of fear, uncertainty, even friendship— to have the feelings but have them separately from himself. When he was shadowboxing, for instance, he wasn't just loosening up. He was also imagining another guy, in his head fighting through a secret fight with another guy. And in the ring, where the other guy was real—stinky, snotty, wet, throwing punches as real as could be—the guy still could have no idea what you were thinking. There wasn't a teacher to ask for the answer to the question. All the answers that you came up with in the ring, you kept to yourself, and when you let the secret out, you let it out through everything *but* your mouth.

So at magic, mythical West Point, where it looked to him that day as though there were more of America in every square inch of the flag flapping on the West Point flagpole than in any flag he'd ever seen, and where the iron faces of the cadets had for him the most powerful heroic significance, even here, at the patriotic center, the marrow of his country's unbreakable spine, where his sixteen-year-old's fantasy of the place matched perfectly the official fantasy, where everything he saw made him feel a frenzy of love not only for himself but for all that was visible, as if everything in nature were a manifestation of his own life—the sun, the sky, the mountains, the river, the trees, just Coleman Brutus "Silky" Silk carried to the millionth degree—even here nobody knew his secret, and so he went out there in the first round and, unlike Mac Machrone's undefeated counterpuncher, started hitting this guy with everything he had. When the guy and he were of the same caliber, he would have to use his brains, but when the guy was easy and when Coleman saw that early, he could always be a more aggressive fighter and begin to pound away. And that's what happened at West Point. Before you turned around, he had cut the guy's eyes, the guy's nose was bleeding, and he was knocking him all over the place. And then something happened that had never happened before. He threw a hook, one that seemed to go three-quarters of the way into the guy's body. It went so deep he was astonished, though not half as astonished as the Pitt guy. Coleman weighed a hundred and twenty-eight pounds, hardly a young boxer who knocked people out. He never really planted his feet to throw that one good shot, that was not his style; and still this punch to the body went so deep that the guy just folded forward, a college boxer already twenty years old, and Coleman caught him in what Doc Chizner called "the labonz." Right in the labonz, and the guy folded forward, and for a moment Coleman thought the guy was even going to throw up, and so before he threw up and before he went down, Coleman set himself to whack him with the right one more time—all he saw as this white guy was going down was somebody he wanted to beat the living shit out of—but suddenly the Pitt coach, who was the referee, called, "Don't, Silky!" and as Coleman started to throw that last right, the coach grabbed him and stopped the fight.

"And that kid," said Doc on the drive home, "that kid was a goddamn good fighter, too. But when they dragged him back to his corner, they had to tell him the fight was over. This kid is already back in his corner, and *still* he didn't know what hit him."

Deep in the victory, in the magic, in the ecstasy of that last punch and of the sweet flood of fury that had broken out and into the open and overtaken him no less than its victim, Coleman said—almost as though he were speaking in his sleep rather than aloud in the car as he replayed the fight in his head—"I guess I was too quick for him, Doc."

"Sure, quick. Of course quick. I know you're quick. But also strong. That is the best hook you ever threw, Silky. My boy, you were too *strong* for him."

Was he? Truly strong?

He went to Howard anyway. Had he not, his father would—with words alone, with just the English language—have killed him. Mr. Silk had it all figured out: Coleman was going to Howard to become a doctor, to meet a light-skinned girl there from a good Negro family, to marry and settle down and have children who would in turn go to Howard. At all-Negro Howard, Coleman's tremendous advantages of intellect and of appearance would launch him into the topmost ranks of Negro society, make of him someone people would forever look up to. And yet within his first week at Howard, when he eagerly went off on Saturday with his roommate, a lawyer's son from New Brunswick, to see the Washington Monument, and they stopped in Woolworth's to get a hot dog, he was called a nigger. His first time. And they wouldn't give him the hot dog. Refused a hot dog at Woolworth's in downtown Washington, on the way out called a nigger, and, as a result, unable to divorce himself from his feelings as easily as he did in the ring. At East Orange High the class valedictorian, in the segregated South just another nigger.

In the segregated South there were no separate identities, not even for him and his roommate. No such subtleties allowed, and the impact was devastating. Nigger—and it meant *him*.

Of course, even in East Orange he had not escaped the minimally less malevolent forms of exclusion that socially separated his family and the small colored community from the rest of East Orange—everything that flowed from what his father called the country's "Negrophobia." And he knew, too, that working for the Pennsylvania Railroad, his father had to put up with insults in the dining car and, union or no union, prejudicial treatment from the company that were far more humbling than anything Coleman would have known as an East Orange kid who was not only as light-skinned as a Negro could get but a bubbling, enthusiastic, quick-witted boy who happened also to be a star athlete and a straight-A student. He would watch his father do everything he could so as not to explode when he came home from work after something had happened on the job about which, if he wanted to keep the job, he could do nothing but meekly say, "Yes, suh." That Negroes who were lighter were treated better didn't always hold true. "Any time a white deals with you," his father would tell the family, "no matter how well intentioned he may be, there is the presumption of intellectual inferiority. Somehow or other, if not directly by his words then by his facial expression, by his tone of voice, by his impatience, even by the opposite—by his forbearance, by his wonderful display of *humaneness*—he will always talk to you as though you are dumb, and then, if you're not, he will be astonished." "What happened, Dad?" Coleman would ask. But, as much out of pride as disgust, rarely would his father elucidate. To make the pedagogical point was enough. "What happened," Coleman's mother would explain, "is beneath your father even to repeat."

At East Orange High, there were teachers from whom Coleman sensed an unevenness of acceptance, an unevenness of endorsement compared to what they lavished on the smart white kids, but never to the degree that the unevenness was able to block his aims. No matter what the slight or the obstacle, he took it the way he took the low hurdles. If only to feign impregnability, he shrugged things off that Walter, say, could not and would not. Walt played varsity football, got good grades, as a Negro was no less anomalous in his skin color than Coleman, and yet he was always a little angrier about everything. When, for instance, he didn't get invited into a white kid's house but was made to wait outside, when he wasn't asked to the birthday party of a white teammate whom he'd been foolish enough to consider a buddy, Coleman, who shared a bedroom with him, would hear about it for months. When Walt didn't get his A in trigonometry, he went right to the teacher and stood there and, to the man's white face, said, "I think you made a mistake." When the teacher went over his grade book and looked again at Walt's test scores, he came back to Walt and, even while allowing his mistake, had the nerve to say, "I couldn't believe your grades were as high as they were," and only after a remark like that made the change from a B to an A. Coleman wouldn't have dreamed of asking a teacher to change a grade, but then he'd never had to. Maybe because he didn't have Walt's brand of bristling defiance, or maybe because he was lucky, or maybe because he was smarter and excelling academically wasn't the same effort for him that it was for Walt, he got the A in the first place. And when, in the seventh grade, *he* didn't get invited to some white friend's birthday party (and this was somebody who lived just down the block in the corner apartment house, the little white son of the building's super who'd been walking back and forth to school with Coleman since they'd started kindergarten), Coleman didn't take it as rejection by white people—after his initial mystification, he took it as rejection by Dicky Watkin's stupid mother and father. When he taught Doc Chizner's class, he knew there were kids who were repelled by him, who didn't like to be touched by him or to come in contact with his sweat, there was occasionally a kid who dropped out—again, probably because of parents who didn't want him taking boxing instruction, or any instruction, from a colored boy—and yet, unlike Walt, on whom no slight failed to register, Coleman, in the end, could forget it, dismiss it, or decide to appear to. There was the time one of the white runners on the track team was injured seriously in a car crash and guys from the team rushed to offer blood to the family for the transfusions, and Coleman was one of them, yet his was the blood the family didn't take. They thanked him and told him that they had enough, but he knew what the real reason was. No, it wasn't that he didn't know what was going on. He was too smart not to know. He competed against plenty of white Newark guys at track meets, Italians from Barringer, Poles from East Side, Irish from Central, Jews from Weequahic. He saw, he heard—he *overheard*. Coleman knew what was going on. But he also knew what wasn't going on, at the center of his life anyway. The protection of his parents, the protection provided by Walt as his older, six-foot-two-and-a-half-inch brother, his own innate confidence, his bright charm, his running prowess ("the fastest kid in the Oranges"), even his color, which made of him someone that people sometimes couldn't quite figure out—all this combined to mute for Coleman the insults that Walter found intolerable. Then there was the difference of personality: Walt was Walt, vigorously Walt, and Coleman was vigorously not. There was probably no better explanation than that for their different responses.

But "nigger"—directed at *him?* That infuriated him. And yet, unless he wanted to get in serious trouble, there was nothing he could do about it except to keep walking out of the store. This wasn't the amateur boxing card at the Knights of Pythias. This was Woolworth's in Washington, D.C. His fists were useless, his footwork was useless, so was his rage. Forget Walter. How could his *father* have taken this shit? In one form or another taken shit like this in that dining car every single day! Never before, for all his precocious cleverness, had Coleman realized how protected his life had been, nor had he gauged his father's fortitude or realized the powerful force that man was—powerful not merely by virtue of being his father. At last he saw all that his father had been condemned to accept. He saw all his father's defenselessness, too, where before he had been a naïve enough youngster to imagine, from the lordly, austere, sometimes insufferable way Mr. Silk conducted himself, that there was nothing vulnerable there. But because somebody, belatedly, had got around to calling Coleman a nigger to his face, he finally recognized the enormous barrier against the great American menace that his father had been for him.

But that didn't make life better at Howard. Especially when he began to think that there was something of the nigger about him even to the kids in his dorm who had all sorts of new clothes and money in their pockets and in the summertime didn't hang around the hot streets at home but went to "camp"—and not Boy Scout camp out in the Jersey sticks but fancy places where they rode horses and played tennis and acted in plays. What the hell was a "cotillion"? Where was Highland Beach? What were these kids talking about? He was among the very lightest of the light-skinned in the freshman class, lighter even than his tea-colored roommate, but he could have been the blackest, most benighted field hand for all they knew that he didn't. He hated Howard from the day he arrived, within the week hated Washington, and so in early October, when his father dropped dead serving dinner on the Pennsylvania Railroad dining car that was pulling out of 30th Street Station in Philadelphia for Wilmington, and Coleman went home for the funeral, he told his mother he was finished with that college. She pleaded with him to give it a second chance, assured him that there had to be boys from something like his own modest background, scholarship boys like him, to mix with and befriend, but nothing his mother said, however true, could change his mind. Only two people were able to get Coleman to change his mind once he'd made it up, his father and Walt, and even they had to all but break his will to do it. But Walt was in Italy with the U.S. Army, and the father whom Coleman had to placate by doing as he was told was no longer around to sonorously dictate anything.

Of course he wept at the funeral and knew how colossal this thing was that, without warning, had been taken away. When the minister read, along with the biblical stuff, a selection from *Julius Caesar* out of his father's cherished volume of Shakespeare's plays —the oversized book with the floppy leather binding that, when

Coleman was a small boy, always reminded him of a cocker span-
iel—the son felt his father's majesty as never before: the grandeur
of both his rise and his fall, the grandeur that, as a college freshman
away for barely a month from the tiny enclosure of his East Orange
home, Coleman had begun faintly to discern for what it was.

> Cowards die many times before their deaths;
> The valiant never taste of death but once.
> Of all the wonders that I yet have heard,
> It seems to me most strange that men should fear;
> Seeing that death, a necessary end,
> Will come when it will come.

The word "valiant," as the preacher intoned it, stripped away Coleman's manly effort at sober, stoical self-control and laid bare a
child's longing for that man closest to him that he'd never see again,
the mammoth, secretly suffering father who talked so easily, so
sweepingly, who with just his powers of speech had inadvertently
taught Coleman to want to be stupendous. Coleman wept with the
most fundamental and copious of all emotions, reduced helplessly
to everything he could not bear. As an adolescent complaining
about his father to his friends, he would characterize him with far
more scorn than he felt or had the capacity to feel—pretending to
an impersonal way of judging his own father was one more method
he'd devised to invent and claim impregnability. But to be no longer circumscribed and defined by his father was like finding that all
the clocks wherever he looked had stopped, and all the watches, and
that there was no way of knowing what time it was. Down to the
day he arrived in Washington and entered Howard, it was, like it or
not, his father who had been making up Coleman's story for him;
now he would have to make it up himself, and the prospect was terrifying. And then it wasn't. Three terrible, terrifying days passed, a
terrible week, two terrible weeks, until, out of nowhere, it was exhilarating.

"What can be avoided / Whose end is purposed by the mighty

gods?" Lines also from *Julius Caesar,* quoted to him by his father, and yet only with his father in the grave did Coleman at last bother to hear them—and when he did, instantaneously to aggrandize them. *This* had been purposed by the mighty gods! Silky's freedom. The raw I. All the subtlety of being Silky Silk.

At Howard he'd discovered that he wasn't just a nigger to Washington, D.C.—as if that shock weren't strong enough, he discovered at Howard that he was a Negro as well. A Howard Negro at that. Overnight the raw I was part of a we with all of the we's overbearing solidity, and he didn't want anything to do with it or with the next oppressive we that came along either. You finally leave home, the Ur of we, and you find *another* we? Another place that's just like that, the *substitute* for that? Growing up in East Orange, he was of course a Negro, very much of their small community of five thousand or so, but boxing, running, studying, at everything he did concentrating and succeeding, roaming around on his own all over the Oranges and, with or without Doc Chizner, down across the Newark line, he was, without thinking about it, everything else as well. He was Coleman, the greatest of the great *pioneers* of the I.

Then he went off to Washington and, in the first month, he was a nigger and nothing else and he was a *Negro* and nothing else. No. No. He saw the fate awaiting him, and he wasn't having it. Grasped it intuitively and recoiled spontaneously. You can't let the big they impose its bigotry on you any more than you can let the little they become a we and impose its ethics on you. Not the tyranny of the we and its we-talk and everything that the we wants to pile on your head. Never for him the tyranny of the we that is dying to suck you in, the coercive, inclusive, historical, inescapable moral *we* with its insidious *E pluribus unum.* Neither the they of Woolworth's nor the we of Howard. Instead the raw I with all its agility. *Self*-discovery— *that* was the punch to the labonz. Singularity. The passionate struggle for singularity. The singular animal. The sliding relationship with everything. Not static but sliding. Self-knowledge but *concealed.* What is as powerful as that?

"Beware the ides of March." Bullshit—beware *nothing.* Free.

With both bulwarks gone—the big brother overseas and the father dead—he is repowered and free to be whatever he wants, free to pursue the hugest aim, the confidence right in his bones to be his particular I. Free on a scale unimaginable to his father. As free as his father had been unfree. Free now not only of his father but of all that his father had ever had to endure. The impositions. The humiliations. The obstructions. The wound and the pain and the posturing and the shame—all the inward agonies of failure and defeat. Free instead on the big stage. Free to go ahead and be stupendous. Free to enact the boundless, self-defining drama of the pronouns we, they, and I.

The war was still on, and unless it ended overnight he was going to be drafted anyway. If Walt was in Italy fighting Hitler, why shouldn't he fight the bastard too? It was October of 1944, and he was still a month shy of being eighteen. But he could easily lie about his age—to move his birth date back by a month, from November 12 to October 12, was no problem at all. And dealing as he was with his mother's grief—and with her shock at his quitting college—it didn't immediately occur to him that, if he chose to, he could lie about his race as well. He could play his skin however he wanted, color himself just as he chose. No, that did not dawn on him until he was seated in the federal building in Newark and had all the navy enlistment forms spread out in front of him and, before filling them out, and carefully, with the same meticulous scrutiny that he'd studied for his high school exams—as though whatever he was doing, large or small, was, for however long he concentrated on it, the most important thing in the world—began to read them through. And even then it didn't occur to *him*. It occurred first to his heart, which began banging away like the heart of someone on the brink of committing his first great crime.

In '46, when Coleman came out of the service, Ernestine was already enrolled in the elementary education program at Montclair State Teachers College, Walt was at Montclair State finishing up, and both of them were living at home with their widowed mother. But Coleman, determined to live by himself, on his own, was across the river in New York, enrolled at NYU. He wanted to live in Greenwich Village far more than to go to NYU, wanted to be a poet or a playwright far more than to study for a degree, but the best way he could think to pursue his goals without having to get a job to support himself was by cashing in on the GI Bill. The problem was that as soon as he started taking classes, he wound up getting A's, getting interested, and by the end of his first two years he was on the track for Phi Beta Kappa and a summa cum laude degree in classics. His quick mind and prodigious memory and classroom fluency made his performance at school as outstanding as it had always been, with the result that what he had come to New York wanting most was displaced by his success at what everybody else thought he should do and encouraged him to do and admired him for doing brilliantly. This was beginning to look like a pattern: he kept getting co-opted because of his academic prowess. Sure, he could take it all in and even enjoy it, the pleasure of being conventional unconventionally, but that wasn't really the idea. He had been a whiz at Latin and Greek in high school and gotten the Howard scholarship when what he wanted was to box in the Golden Gloves; now he was no less a whiz in college, while his poetry, when he showed it to his professors, didn't kindle any enthusiasm. At first he kept up his roadwork and his boxing for the fun of it, until one day at the gym he was approached to fight a four-rounder at St. Nick's Arena, offered thirty-five dollars to take the place of a fighter who'd pulled out, and mostly to make up for all he'd missed at the Golden Gloves, he accepted and, to his delight, secretly turned pro.

So there was school, poetry, professional boxing, and there were girls, girls who knew how to walk and how to wear a dress, how to *move* in a dress, girls who conformed to everything he'd been imagining when he'd set out from the separation center in San Francisco for New York—girls who put the streets of Greenwich Village and the crisscrossing walkways of Washington Square to their proper use. There were warm spring afternoons when nothing in triumphant postwar America, let alone in the world of antiquity, could be of more interest to Coleman than the legs of the girl walking in front of him. Nor was he the only one back from the war beset by this fixation. In those days in Greenwich Village there seemed to be no more engrossing off-hours entertainment for NYU's ex-GIs than appraising the legs of the women who passed by the coffeehouses and cafés where they congregated to read the papers and play chess. Who knows why sociologically, but whatever the reason, it was the great American era of aphrodisiacal legs, and once or twice a day at least, Coleman followed a pair of them for block after block so as not to lose sight of the way they moved and how they were shaped and what they looked like at rest while the corner light was changing from red to green. And when he gauged the moment was right—having followed behind long enough to become both verbally poised and insanely ravenous—and quickened his pace so as to catch up, when he spoke and ingratiated himself enough so as to be allowed to fall in step beside her and to ask her name and to make her laugh and to get her to accept a date, he was, whether she knew it or not, proposing the date to her legs.

And the girls, in turn, liked Coleman's legs. Steena Palsson, the eighteen-year-old exile from Minnesota, even wrote a poem about Coleman that mentioned his legs. It was handwritten on a sheet of lined notebook paper, signed "S," then folded in quarters and stuck into his mail slot in the tiled hallway above his basement room. It had been two weeks since they'd first flirted at the subway station, and this was the Monday after the Sunday of their first twenty-four-hour marathon. Coleman had rushed off to his morning class while Steena was still making up in the bathroom; a few minutes later, she herself set out for work, but not before leaving him the poem that, in spite of all the stamina they'd so conscientiously demonstrated over the previous day, she'd been too shy to hand him directly. Since Coleman's schedule took him from his classes to the library to his late evening workout in the ring of a rundown

Chinatown gym, he didn't find the poem jutting from the mail slot
until he got back to Sullivan Street at eleven-thirty that night.

> He has a body.
> He has a beautiful body—
> the muscles on the backs of his legs and the back of his neck.
>
> Also he is bright and brash.
> He's four years older,
> but sometimes I feel he is younger.
>
> He is sweet, still, and romantic,
> though he says he is not romantic.
>
> I am almost dangerous for this man.
>
> How much can I tell
> of what I see in him?
> I wonder what he does
> after he swallows me whole.

Rapidly reading Steena's handwriting by the dim hall light, he at
first mistook "neck" for "negro"—*and the back of his negro* . . . His
negro *what?* Till then he'd been surprised by how easy it was. What
was supposed to be hard and somehow shaming or destructive was
not only easy but without consequences, no price paid at all. But
now the sweat was pouring off him. He kept reading, faster even
than before, but the words formed themselves into no combination
that made sense. His negro WHAT? They had been naked together
a whole day and night, for most of that time never more than
inches apart. Not since he was an infant had anyone other than
himself had so much time to study how he was made. Since there
was nothing about her long pale body that he had not observed and
nothing that she had concealed and nothing now that he could not
picture with a painterlike awareness, a lover's excited, meticulous
connoisseurship, and since he had spent all day stimulated no less
by her presence in his nostrils than by her legs spread-eagled in
his mind's eye, it had to follow that there was nothing about *his*

body that *she* had not microscopically absorbed, nothing about that extensive surface imprinted with his self-cherishing evolutionary uniqueness, nothing about his singular configuration as a man, his skin, his pores, his whiskers, his teeth, his hands, his nose, his ears, his lips, his tongue, his feet, his balls, his veins, his prick, his armpits, his ass, his tangle of pubic hair, the hair on his head, the fuzz on his frame, nothing about the way he laughed, slept, breathed, moved, smelled, nothing about the way he shuddered convulsively when he came that she had not registered. And remembered. And pondered.

Was it the act itself that did it, the absolute intimacy of it, when you are not just inside the body of the other person but she is tightly enveloping you? Or was it the physical nakedness? You take off your clothes and you're in bed with somebody, and that is indeed where whatever you've concealed, your particularity, whatever it may be, however encrypted, is going to be found out, and that's what the shyness is all about and what *everybody* fears. In that anarchic crazy place, how much of me is being seen, how much of me is being discovered? *Now I know who you are. I see clear through to the back of your negro.*

But how, by seeing *what?* What could it have been? Was it seeable to her, whatever it was, because she was a blond Icelandic Dane from a long line of blond Icelanders and Danes, Scandinavian-raised, at home, in school, at church, in the company all her life of nothing but . . . and then Coleman recognized the word in the poem as a four- and not a five-letter word. What she'd written wasn't "negro." It was "neck." Oh, my *neck!* It's only my neck! . . . *the muscles on the backs of his legs and the back of his neck.*

But what then did this mean: "How much can I tell / of what I see in him?" What was so ambiguous about what she saw in him? If she'd written "tell from" instead of "tell of," would that have made her meaning clearer? Or would that have made it less clear? The more he reread that simple stanza, the more opaque the meaning became—and the more opaque the meaning, the more certain he was that she distinctly sensed the problem that Coleman brought to her life. Unless she meant by "what I see in him" no more than what is colloquially meant by skeptical people when they ask someone in love, "What can you possibly see in him?"

And what about "tell"? How much can she tell to *whom?* By tell does she mean make—"how much can I make," et cetera—or does she mean reveal, expose? And what about "I am almost dangerous for this man." Is "dangerous for" different from "dangerous to"? Either way, what's the danger?

Each time he tried to penetrate her meaning, it slipped away. After two frantic minutes on his feet in the hallway, all he could be sure of was his fear. And this astonished him—and, as always with Coleman, his susceptibility, by catching him unprepared, shamed him as well, triggering an SOS, a ringing signal to self-vigilance to take up the slack.

Bright and game and beautiful as Steena was, she was only eighteen years old and fresh to New York from Fergus Falls, Minnesota, and yet he was now more intimidated by her—and her almost preposterous, unequivocal goldenness—than by anybody he had ever faced in the ring. Even on that night in the Norfolk whorehouse, when the woman who was watching from the bed as he began to peel off his uniform—a big-titted, fleshy, mistrustful whore not entirely ugly but certainly no looker (and maybe herself two thirty-fifths something other than white)—smiled sourly and said, "You're a black nigger, ain't you, boy?" and the two goons were summoned to throw him out, only then had he been as undone as he was by Steena's poem.

> I wonder what he does
> after he swallows me whole.

Even *that* he could not understand. At the desk in his room, he battled into the morning with the paradoxical implications of this final stanza, ferreting out and then renouncing one complicated formulation after another until, at daybreak, all he knew for sure was that for Steena, ravishing Steena, not everything he had eradicated from himself had vanished into thin air.

Dead wrong. Her poem didn't mean anything. It wasn't even a poem. Under the pressure of her own confusion, fragments of ideas, raw bits of thought, had all chaotically come tumbling into her head while she was under the shower, and so she'd torn a page from one of his notebooks, scribbled out at his desk whatever words jelled, then jammed the page into the mail slot before rushing off for work. Those lines were just something she'd done—that she'd *had* to do—with the exquisite newness of her bewilderment. A poet? Hardly, she laughed: just somebody leaping through a ring of fire.

They were together in the bed in his room every weekend for over a year, feeding on each other like prisoners in solitary madly downing their daily ration of bread and water. She astonished him—astonished *herself*—with the dance she did one Saturday night, standing at the foot of his foldout sofa bed in her half slip and nothing else. She was getting undressed, and the radio was on—Symphony Sid—and first, to get her moving and in the mood, there was Count Basie and a bunch of jazz musicians jamming on "Lady Be Good," a wild live recording, and following that, more Gershwin, the Artie Shaw rendition of "The Man I Love" that featured Roy Eldridge steaming everything up. Coleman was lying semi-upright on the bed, doing what he most loved to do on a Saturday night after they'd returned from their five bucks' worth of Chianti and spaghetti and cannoli in their favorite Fourteenth Street basement restaurant: watch her take her clothes off. All at once, with no prompting from him—seemingly prompted only by Eldridge's trumpet—she began what Coleman liked to describe as the single most slithery dance ever performed by a Fergus Falls girl after little more than a year in New York City. She could have raised Gershwin himself from the grave with that dance, and with the way she sang the song. Prompted by a colored trumpet player playing it like a black torch song, there to see, plain as day, was all the power of her whiteness. That big white thing. "Some day he'll come along . . . the man I love . . . and he'll be big and strong . . . the man I love." The language was ordinary enough to have been lifted from the most innocent first-grade primer, but when the record was over, Steena put her hands up to hide her face, half meaning, half pretending to cover her shame. But the gesture protected her against nothing, least of all from his enravishment. The gesture merely transported him further. "Where did I find you, Voluptas?" he asked. "*How* did I find you? Who are you?"

It was during this, the headiest of times that Coleman gave up his evening workout at the Chinatown gym and cut back his early morning five-mile run and, in the end, relinquished in any way taking seriously his having turned pro. He had fought and won a total of four professional bouts, three four-rounders and then, his finale, a six-rounder, all of them Monday night fights at the old St. Nicholas Arena. He never told Steena about the fights, never told anyone at NYU, and certainly never let on to his family. For those first few years of college, that was one more secret, even though at the arena he boxed under the name of Silky Silk and the results from St. Nick's were printed in small type in a box on the sports page of the tabloids the next day. From the first second of the first round of the first thirty-five-dollar four-round fight, he went into the ring as a pro with an attitude different from that of his amateur days. Not that he had ever wanted to lose as an amateur. But as a pro he put out twice as hard, if only to prove to himself that he could stay there if he wanted to. None of the fights went the distance, and in the last fight, the six-rounder—with Beau Jack at the top of the card—and for which he got one hundred dollars, he stopped the guy in two minutes and some-odd seconds and was not even tired when it was over. Walking down the aisle for the six-rounder, Coleman had had to pass the ringside seat of Solly Tabak, the promoter, who was already dangling a contract in front of Coleman to sign away a third of his earnings for the next ten years. Solly slapped him on the behind and, in his meaty whisper, told him, "Feel the nigger out in the first round, see what he's got, Silky, and give the people their money's worth." Coleman nodded at Tabak and smiled but, while climbing into the ring, thought, Fuck you. I'm getting a hundred dollars, and I'm going to let some guy hit me to give the people their money's worth? I'm supposed to give a shit about some jerk-off sitting in the fifteenth row? I'm a hundred and thirty-nine pounds and five foot eight and a half, he's a hundred and forty-five and five foot ten, and I'm supposed to let the guy hit me in the head four, five, ten extra times in order to put on a show? Fuck the show.

After the fight Solly was not happy with Coleman's behavior. It struck him as juvenile. "You could have stopped the nigger in the fourth round instead of the first and gave the people their money's worth. But you didn't. I ask you nicely, and you don't do what I ask you. Why's that, wise guy?"

"Because I don't carry no nigger." That's what he said, the classics major from NYU and valedictorian son of the late optician, dining car waiter, amateur linguist, grammarian, disciplinarian, and student of Shakespeare Clarence Silk. That's how obstinate he was, that's how secretive he was—no matter what he undertook, that's how much he meant business, this colored kid from East Orange High.

He stopped fighting because of Steena. However mistaken he was about the ominous meaning hidden in her poem, he remained convinced that the mysterious forces that made their sexual ardor inexhaustible—that transformed them into lovers so unbridled that Steena, in a neophyte's distillation of self-marveling self-mockery, midwesternly labeled them "two mental cases"—would one day work to dissolve his story of himself right before her eyes. How this would happen he did not know, and how he could forestall it he did not know. But the boxing wasn't going to help. Once she found out about Silky Silk, questions would be raised that would inevitably lead her to stumble on the truth. She knew that he had a mother in East Orange who was a registered nurse and a regular churchgoer, that he had an older brother who'd begun teaching seventh and eighth grades in Asbury Park and a sister finishing up for her teaching certificate from Montclair State, and that once each month the Sunday in his Sullivan Street bed had to be cut short because Coleman was expected in East Orange for dinner. She knew that his father had been an optician—just that, an optician—and even that he'd come originally from Georgia. Coleman was scrupulous in seeing that she had no reason to doubt the truth of whatever she was told by him, and once he'd given up the boxing for good, he didn't even have to lie about that. He didn't lie to Steena about anything. All he did was to follow the instructions that Doc Chizner had given him the day they were driving up to West Point (and that already had gotten him through the navy): if nothing comes up, you don't bring it up.

His decision to invite her to East Orange for Sunday dinner, like all his other decisions now—even the decision at St. Nick's to silently say fuck you to Solly Tabak by taking out the other guy in the first round—was based on nobody's thinking but his own. It was close to two years since they'd met, Steena was twenty and he was twenty-four, and he could no longer envision himself walking down Eighth Street, let alone proceeding through life, without her. Her undriven, conventional daily demeanor in combination with the intensity of her weekend abandon—all of it subsumed by a physical incandescence, a girlish American flashbulb radiance that was practically voodooish in its power—had achieved a startling supremacy over a will as ruthlessly independent as Coleman's: she had not only severed him from boxing and the combative filial defiance encapsulated in being Silky Silk the undefeated welterweight pro, but had freed him from the desire for anyone else.

Yet he couldn't tell her he was colored. The words he heard himself having to speak were going to make everything sound worse than it was—make *him* sound worse than *he* was. And if he then left it to her to imagine his family, she was going to picture people wholly unlike what they were. Because she knew no Negroes, she would imagine the kind of Negroes she saw in the movies or knew from the radio or heard about in jokes. He realized by now that she was not prejudiced and that if only she were to meet Ernestine and Walt and his mother, she would recognize right off how conventional they were and how much they happened to have in common with the tiresome respectability she had herself been all too glad to leave behind in Fergus Falls. "Don't get me wrong—it's a lovely city," she hastened to tell him, "it's a beautiful city. It's unusual, Fergus Falls, because it has the Otter Tail Lake just to the east, and not far from our house it has the Otter Tail River. And it's, I suppose, a little more sophisticated than other towns out there that size, because it's just south and to the east of Fargo-Moorhead, which is the college town in that section of the country." Her father owned a hardware supply store and a small lumberyard. "An irrepressible, gigantic, amazing person, my father. Huge. Like a slab of ham. He drinks in one night an entire container of whatever alcohol you have around. I could never believe it. I still can't. He just keeps going. He gets a big gash in his calf muscle wrestling with a piece of machinery—he just leaves it there, he doesn't wash it. They tend to be like this, the Icelanders. Bulldozer types. What's interesting is his personality. Most astonishing person. My father in a conversation takes over the whole room. And he's not the only one. My Palsson grandparents, too. His father is that way. His *mother* is that way." "Icelanders. I didn't even know you call them Icelanders. I didn't even know they were here. I don't know anything about Icelanders at all. When," Coleman asked, "did they come to Minnesota?" She shrugged and laughed. "Good question. I'm going to say after the dinosaurs. That's what it seems like." "And it's him you're escaping?" "I guess. Hard to be the daughter of that sort of feistiness. He kind of submerges you." "And your mother? He submerges her?" "That's the Danish side of the family. That's the Rasmussens. No, she's unsubmergeable. My mother's too practical to be submerged. The characteristics of her family—and I don't think it's peculiar to that family, I think Danes are this way, and they're not too different from Norwegians in this way either—they're interested in objects. *Objects.* Tablecloths. Dishes. Vases. They talk endlessly about how much each object costs. My mother's father is like this too, my grandfather Rasmussen. Her whole family. They don't have any dreams in them. They don't have any unreality. Everything is made up of objects and what they cost and how much you can get them for. She goes into people's houses and examines all the objects and knows where they got half of them and tells them where they could have got them for less. And clothing. Each object of clothing. Same thing. Practicality. A bare-boned practicality about the whole bunch of them. Thrifty. Extremely thrifty. Clean. Extremely clean. She'll notice, when I come home from school, if I have one bit of ink under one fingernail from filling a fountain pen. When she's having guests on a Saturday evening, she sets the table Friday night at about five o'clock. It's there, every glass, every piece of silver. And then she throws a light gossamer thing over it so it won't get dust specks on it. Everything organized perfectly. And a fantastically good cook if you don't like any spices or salt or pepper. Or taste of any kind. So that's my parents. I can't get to the bottom with her particularly. On anything. It's all surface. She's organizing everything and my father's disorganizing everything, and so I got to be eighteen and graduated high school and came here. Since if I'd gone up to Moorhead or North Dakota State, I'd still have to be living at home, I said the heck with college and came to New York. And so here I am. Steena."

That's how she explained who she was and where she came from and why she'd left. For him it was not going to be so simple. *Afterward,* he told himself. Afterward—that's when he could make his explanations and ask her to understand how he could not allow his prospects to be unjustly limited by so arbitrary a designation as race. If she was calm enough to hear him out, he was sure he could make her see why he had chosen to take the future into his own hands rather than to leave it to an unenlightened society to determine his fate—a society in which, more than eighty years after the Emancipation Proclamation, bigots happened to play too large a role to suit him. He would get her to see that far from there being anything wrong with his decision to identify himself as white, it was the most natural thing for someone with his outlook and temperament and skin color to have done. All he'd ever wanted, from earliest childhood on, was to be free: not black, not even white— just on his own and free. He meant to insult no one by his choice, nor was he trying to imitate anyone whom he took to be his superior, nor was he staging some sort of protest against his race or hers.

He recognized that to conventional people for whom everything was ready-made and rigidly unalterable what he was doing would never look correct. But to dare to be nothing more than correct had never been his aim. The objective was for his fate to be determined not by the ignorant, hate-filled intentions of a hostile world but, to whatever degree humanly possible, by his own resolve. Why accept a life on any other terms?

This is what he would tell her. And wouldn't it all strike her as nonsense, like one big sales pitch of a pretentious lie? Unless she had first met his family—confronted head-on the fact that he was as much a Negro as they were, and that they were as unlike what she might imagine Negroes to be as he was—these words or any others would seem to her only another form of concealment. Until she sat down to dinner with Ernestine, Walt, and his mother, and they all took a turn over the course of a day at swapping reassuring banalities, whatever explanation he presented to her would sound like so much preening, self-glorifying, self-justifying baloney, high-flown, highfalutin talk whose falseness would shame him in her eyes no less than in his own. No, he couldn't speak this shit either. It was beneath him. If he wanted this girl for good, then it was boldness that was required now and not an elocutionary snow job, à la Clarence Silk.

In the week before the visit, though he didn't prepare anyone else, he readied himself in the same concentrated way he used to prepare mentally for a fight, and when they stepped off the train at the Brick Church Station that Sunday, he even summoned up the phrases that he always chanted semi-mystically in the seconds before the bell sounded: "The task, nothing but the task. At one with the task. Nothing else allowed in." Only then, at the bell, breaking from his corner—or here, starting up the porch stairs to the front door—did he add the ordinary Joe's call to arms: "Go to work."

The Silks had been in their one-family house since 1925, the year before Coleman was born. When they got there, the rest of the street was white, and the small frame house was sold to them by a couple who were mad at the people next door and so were determined to sell it to colored to spite them. But no one in the private houses ran because they'd moved in, and even if the Silks never socialized with their neighbors, everyone was agreeable on that stretch of street leading up toward the Episcopal rectory and church. Agreeable even though the rector, when he arrived some years earlier, had looked around, seen a fair number of Bajians and Barbadians, who were Church of England—many of them domestics working for East Orange's white rich, many of them island people who knew their place and sat at the back and thought they were accepted—leaned on his pulpit, and, before beginning the sermon on his first Sunday, said, "I see we have some colored families here. We'll have to do something about that." After consulting with the seminary in New York, he had seen to it that various services and Sunday schools for the colored were conducted, outside basic church law, in the colored families' houses. Later, the swimming pool at the high school was shut down by the school superintendent so that the white kids wouldn't have to swim with the colored kids. A big swimming pool, used for swimming classes and a swimming team, a part of the physical education program for years, but since there were objections from some of the white kids' parents who were employers of the black kids' parents—the ones working as maids and housemen and chauffeurs and gardeners and yardmen—the pool was drained and covered over.

Within the four square miles of this residential flyspeck of a Jersey town of not quite seventy thousand people, as throughout the country during Coleman's youth, there existed these rigid distinctions between classes and races sanctified by the church and legitimized by the schools. Yet on the Silks' own modest tree-lined side street ordinary people needed not to be quite so responsible to God and the state as those whose vocation it was to maintain a human community, swimming pool and all, untainted by the impurities, and so the neighbors were on the whole friendly with the ultrarespectable, light-skinned Silks—Negroes, to be sure, but, in the words of one tolerant mother of a kindergarten playmate of Coleman's, "people of a very pleasing shade, rather like eggnog"—even to the point of borrowing a tool or a ladder or helping to figure out what was wrong with the car when it wouldn't start. The big apartment house at the corner remained all white until after the war. Then, in late 1945, when colored people began coming in at the Orange end of the street—the families of professional men mainly, of teachers, doctors, and dentists—there was a moving van outside the apartment building every day, and half the white tenants disappeared within months. But things soon settled down, and, though the landlord of the apartment building began renting to colored just in order to keep the place going, the whites who remained in the immediate neighborhood stayed around until they had a reason other than Negrophobia to leave.

Go to work. And he rang the doorbell and pushed open the front door and called, "We're here."

Walt had been unable to make it up that day from Asbury Park but there, coming out of the kitchen and into the hallway, were his mother and Ernestine. And here, in their house, was his girl. She may or may not have been what they were expecting. Coleman's mother hadn't asked. Since he'd unilaterally made his decision to join the navy as a white man, she hardly dared ask him anything, for fear of what she might hear. She was prone now, outside the hospital—where she had at last become the first colored head floor nurse of a Newark hospital, and without help from Dr. Fensterman—to let Walt take charge of her life and of the family altogether. No, she hadn't asked anything about the girl, politely declined to know, and encouraged Ernestine not to inquire. Coleman, in turn, hadn't told anyone anything, and so, fair-complexioned as fair could be, and—with her matching blue handbag and pumps, in her cotton floral shirtwaist dress and her little white gloves and pillbox hat—as immaculately trim and correct as any girl alive and young in 1950, here was Steena Palsson, Iceland and Denmark's American progeny, of the bloodline going back to King Canute and beyond.

He had done it, got it his own way, and no one so much as flinched. Talk about the ability of the species to adapt. Nobody

groped for words, nobody went silent, nor did anyone begin jab-
bering a mile a minute. Commonplaces, yes, cornballisms, you
bet—generalities, truisms, clichés aplenty. Steena hadn't been
raised along the banks of the Otter Tail River for nothing: if it was
hackneyed, she knew how to say it. Chances were that if Coleman
had gotten to blindfold the three women before introducing them
and to keep them blindfolded throughout the day, their conversation would have had no weightier a meaning than it had while they
smilingly looked one another right in the eye. Nor would it have
embodied an intention other than the standard one: namely, I
won't say anything you can possibly take offense with if you won't
say anything I can take offense with. Respectability at any cost—
that's where the Palssons and the Silks were one.

The point at which all three got addled was, strangely enough,
while discussing Steena's height. True, she was five eleven, nearly
three full inches taller than Coleman and six inches taller than either his sister or his mother. But Coleman's father had been six one
and Walt was an inch and a half taller than that, so tallness in and
of itself was nothing new to the family, even if, with Steena and
Coleman, it was the woman who happened to be taller than the
man. Yet those three inches of Steena's—the distance, say, from her
hairline to her eyebrows—caused a careening conversation about
physical anomalies to veer precipitously close to disaster for some
fifteen minutes before Coleman smelled something acrid and the
women—the three of them—rushed for the kitchen to save the biscuits from going up in flames.

After that, throughout dinner and until it was time for the young
couple to return to New York, it was all unflagging rectitude, exter-
nally a Sunday like every nice family's dream of total Sunday happiness and, consequently, strikingly in contrast with life, which, as experience had already taught even the youngest of these four, could
not for half a minute running be purged of its inherent instability,
let alone be beaten down into a predictable essence.

Not until the train carrying Coleman and Steena back to New

York pulled into Pennsylvania Station early that evening did Steena break down in tears.

As far as he knew, until then she had been fast asleep with her head on his shoulder all the way from Jersey—virtually from the moment they had boarded at Brick Church Station sleeping off the exhaustion of the afternoon's effort at which she had so excelled.

"Steena—what is wrong?"

"I can't do it!" she cried, and, without another word of explanation, gasping, violently weeping, clutching her bag to her chest—and forgetting her hat, which was in his lap, where he'd been holding it while she slept—she raced alone from the train as though from an attacker and did not phone him or try ever to see him again.

It was four years later, in 1954, that they nearly collided outside Grand Central Station and stopped to take each other's hand and to talk just long enough to stir up the original wonder they'd awakened in each other at twenty-two and eighteen and then to walk on, crushed by the certainty that nothing as statistically spectacular as this chance meeting could possibly happen again. He was married by then, an expectant father, in the city for the day from his job as a classics instructor at Adelphi, and she was working in an ad agency down the street on Lexington Avenue, still single, still pretty, but womanly now, very much a smartly dressed New Yorker and clearly someone with whom the trip to East Orange might have ended on a different note if only it had taken place further down the line.

The way it might have ended—the conclusion against which reality had decisively voted—was all he could think about. Stunned by how little he'd gotten over her and she'd gotten over him, he walked away understanding, as outside his reading in classical Greek drama he'd never had to understand before, how easily life can be one thing rather than another and how accidentally a destiny is made . . . on the other hand, how accidental fate may seem when things can never turn out other than they do. That is, he walked away understanding nothing, knowing he could understand nothing, though with the illusion that he *would* have metaphysically understood something of enormous importance about this stubborn determination of his to become his own man if . . . if only such things were understandable.

The charming two-page letter she sent the next week, care of the college, about how incredibly good he'd been at "swooping" their first time together in his Sullivan Street room—"swooping, almost like birds do when they fly over land or sea and spy something moving, something bursting with life, and dive down . . . and seize upon it"—began, "Dear Coleman, I was very happy to see you in New York. Brief as our meeting was, after I saw you I felt an autumnal sadness, perhaps because the six years since we first met make it wrenchingly obvious how many days of my life are 'over.' You look very good, and I'm glad you're happy . . ." and ended in a languid, floating finale of seven little sentences and a wistful closing that, after numerous rereadings, he took as the measure of her regret for *her* loss, a veiled admission of remorse as well, poignantly signaling to him a subaudible apology: "Well, that's it. That's enough. I shouldn't even bother you. I promise I won't ever again. Take care. Take care. Take care. Very fondly, Steena."

He never threw the letter away, and when he happened upon it in his files and, in the midst of whatever else he was doing, paused to look it over—having otherwise forgotten it for some five or six years—he thought what he thought out on the street that day after lightly kissing her cheek and saying goodbye to Steena forever: that had she married him—as he'd wanted her to—she would have known everything—as he had wanted her to—and what followed with his family, with hers, with their own children, would have been different from what it was with Iris. What happened with his mother and Walt could as easily never have occurred. Had Steena said fine, he would have lived another life.

I can't do it. There was wisdom in that, an awful lot of wisdom for a young girl, not the kind one ordinarily has at only twenty. But that's why he'd fallen for her—because she had the wisdom that is solid, thinking-for-yourself common sense. If she hadn't . . . but if she hadn't, she wouldn't have been Steena, and he wouldn't have wanted her as a wife.

He thought the same useless thoughts—useless to a man of no great talent like himself, if not to Sophocles: how accidentally a fate is made . . . or how accidental it all may seem when it is inescapable.

As she first portrayed herself and her origins to Coleman, Iris Gittelman had grown up willful, clever, furtively rebellious—secretly plotting, from the second grade on, how to escape her oppressive surroundings—in a Passaic household rumbling with hatred for every form of social oppression, particularly the authority of the rabbis and their impinging lies. Her Yiddish-speaking father, as she characterized him, was such a thoroughgoing heretical anarchist that he hadn't even had Iris's two older brothers circumcised, nor had her parents bothered to acquire a marriage license or to submit to a civil ceremony. They considered themselves husband and wife, claimed to be American, even called themselves Jews, these two uneducated immigrant atheists who spat on the ground when a rabbi walked by. But they called themselves what they called themselves freely, without asking permission or seeking approval from what her father contemptuously described as the hypocritical enemies of everything that was natural and good—namely, officialdom, those illegitimately holding the power. On the cracking, filth-caked wall over the soda fountain of the family candy store on Myrtle Avenue—a cluttered shop so small, she said, "you couldn't bury the five of us there side by side"—hung two framed pictures, one of Sacco, the other of Vanzetti, photographs torn from the rotogravure section of the newspaper. Every August 22—the anniversary of the day in 1927 when Massachusetts executed the two anarchists for murders Iris and her brothers were taught to believe neither man had committed—business was suspended and the family retreated upstairs to the tiny, dim apartment whose lunatic disorder exceeded even the store's, so as to observe a day of fasting. This was a ritual Iris's father had, like a cult leader, dreamed up all on his own, modeling it wackily on the Jewish Day of Atonement.

Her father had no real ideas about what he thought of as ideas—all
that ran deep was desperate ignorance and the bitter hopelessness
of dispossession, the impotent revolutionary hatred. Everything
was said with a clenched fist, and everything was a harangue. He
knew the names Kropotkin and Bakunin, but nothing of their writ-
ings, and the anarchist Yiddish weekly *Freie Arbeiter Stimme,* which
he was always carrying around their apartment, he rarely read more
than a few words of each night before dropping off to sleep. Her
parents, she explained to Coleman—and all this dramatically, scan-
dalously dramatically, in a Bleecker Street café minutes after he had
picked her up in Washington Square—her parents were simple
people in the grips of a pipe dream that they could not begin to articulate or rationally defend but for which they were zealously willing to sacrifice friends, relatives, business, the good will of neighbors, even their own sanity, even their *children's* sanity. They knew
only what they had nothing in common with, which to Iris, the
older she got, appeared to be everything. Society as it was consti-
tuted—its forces all in constant motion, the intricate underweb-
bing of interests stretched to its limit, the battle for advantage that
is ongoing, the subjugation that is ongoing, the factional collisions
and collusions, the shrewd jargon of morality, the benign despot
that is convention, the unstable illusion of stability—society as it
was made, always has been and *must* be made, was as foreign to
them as was King Arthur's court to the Connecticut Yankee. And
yet, this wasn't because they'd been bound by the strongest ties to
some other time and place and then forcefully set down in a wholly
alien world: they were more like people who'd stepped directly into
adulthood from the cradle, having had no intervening education in
how human beastliness is run and ruled. Iris could not decide, from
the time she was a tot, whether she was being raised by crackpots or
visionaries, or whether the passionate loathing she was meant to
share was a revelation of the awful truth or utterly ridiculous and
possibly insane.

All that afternoon she told Coleman folklorishly enchanting stories that made having survived growing up above the Passaic candy

store as the daughter of such vividly benighted individualists as Morris and Ethel Gittelman appear to have been a grim adventure not so much out of Russian literature as out of the Russian funny papers, as though the Gittelmans had been the deranged next-door neighbors in a Sunday comic strip called "The Karamazov Kids." It was a strong, brilliant performance for a girl barely nineteen years old who had fled from Jersey across the Hudson—as who among his Village acquaintances wasn't fleeing, and from places as far away as Amarillo?—without any idea of being anything other than free, a new impoverished exotic on the Eighth Street stage, a theatrically big-featured, vivacious dark girl, emotionally a dynamic force and, in the parlance of the moment, "stacked," a student uptown at the Art Students League who partly earned her scholarship there modeling for the life drawing classes, someone whose style was to hide nothing and who appeared to have no more fear of creating a stir in a public place than a belly dancer. Her head of hair was something, a labyrinthine, billowing wreath of spirals and ringlets, fuzzy as twine and large enough for use as Christmas ornamentation. All the disquiet of her childhood seemed to have passed into the convolutions of her sinuous thicket of hair. Her irreversible hair. You could polish pots with it and no more alter its construction than if it were harvested from the inky depths of the sea, some kind of wiry reef-building organism, a dense living onyx hybrid of coral and shrub, perhaps possessing medicinal properties.

For three hours she held Coleman entranced by her comedy, her outrage, her hair, and by her flair for manufacturing excitement, by a frenzied, untrained adolescent intellect and an actressy ability to enkindle herself and believe her every exaggeration that made Coleman—a cunning self-concoction if ever there was one, a product on which no one but he held a patent—feel by comparison like somebody with no conception of himself at all.

But when he got her back to Sullivan Street that evening, everything changed. It turned out that she had no idea in the world who she was. Once you'd made your way past the hair, all she was was molten. The antithesis of the arrow aimed at life who was twenty-five-year-old Coleman Silk—a self-freedom fighter too, but the agitated version, the *anarchist* version, of someone wanting to find her way.

It wouldn't have fazed her for five minutes to learn that he had been born and raised in a colored family and identified himself as a Negro nearly all his life, nor would she have been burdened in the slightest by keeping that secret for him if it was what he'd asked her to do. A tolerance for the unusual was not one of Iris Gittelman's deficiencies—unusual to her was what most conformed to the standards of legitimacy. To be two men instead of one? To be two colors instead of one? To walk the streets incognito or in disguise, to be neither this nor that but something in between? To be possessed of a double or a triple or a quadruple personality? To her there was nothing frightening about such seeming deformities. Iris's open-mindedness wasn't even a moral quality of the sort liberals and libertarians pride themselves on; it was more on the order of a mania, the cracked antithesis of bigotry. The expectations indispensable to most people, the assumption of meaning, the confidence in authority, the sanctification of coherence and order, struck her as nothing else in life did—as nonsensical, as totally nuts. Why would things happen as they do and history read as it does if inherent to existence was something called normalcy?

And yet, what he told Iris was that he was Jewish, Silk being an Ellis Island attenuation of Silberzweig, imposed on his father by a charitable customs official. He even bore the biblical mark of circumcision, as not many of his East Orange Negro friends did in that era. His mother, working as a nurse at a hospital staffed predominantly by Jewish doctors, was convinced by burgeoning medical opinion of the significant hygienic benefits of circumcision, and so the Silks had arranged for the rite that was traditional among Jews—and that was beginning, back then, to be elected as a postnatal surgical procedure by an increasing number of Gentile parents—to be performed by a doctor on each of their infant boys in the second week of life.

Coleman had been allowing that he was Jewish for several years now—or letting people think so if they chose to—since coming to realize that at NYU as in his café hangouts, many people he knew seemed to have been assuming he was a Jew all along. What he'd learned in the navy is that all you have to do is give a pretty good and consistent line about yourself and nobody ever inquires, because no one's that interested. His NYU and Village acquaintances could as easily have surmised—as buddies of his had in the service—that he was of Middle Eastern descent, but as this was a moment when Jewish self-infatuation was at a postwar pinnacle among the Washington Square intellectual avant-garde, when the aggrandizing appetite driving their Jewish mental audacity was beginning to look to be uncontrollable and an aura of cultural significance emanated as much from their jokes and their family anecdotes, from their laughter and their clowning and their wisecracks and their arguments—even from their insults—as from *Commentary, Midstream,* and the *Partisan Review,* who was he not to go along for the ride, especially as his high school years assisting Doc Chizner as a boxing instructor of Essex County Jewish kids made claiming a New Jersey Jewish boyhood not so laden with pitfalls as pretending to being a U.S. sailor with Syrian or Lebanese roots. Taking on the ersatz prestige of an aggressively thinking, self-analytic, irreverent American Jew reveling in the ironies of the marginal Manhattan existence turned out to be nothing like so reckless as it might have seemed had he spent years dreaming up and elaborating the disguise on his own, and yet, pleasurably enough, it felt spectacularly reckless—and when he remembered Dr. Fensterman, who'd offered his family three thousand dollars for Coleman to take a dive on his final exams so as to make brilliant Bert the class valedictorian, it struck him as spectacularly comical too, a colossal sui generis score-settling joke. What a great all-encompassing idea the world had had to turn him into this—what sublimely earthly mischief! If ever there was a perfect one-of-a-kind creation—and hadn't singularity been his inmost ego-driven ambition all along? —it was this magical convergence into his father's Fensterman son.

No longer was he playing at something. With Iris—the churned-up, untamed, wholly un-Steena-like, non-Jewish Jewish Iris—as the medium through which to make himself anew, he'd finally got it right. He was no longer trying on and casting off, endlessly practicing and preparing to be. This was it, the solution, the secret to his secret, flavored with just a drop of the ridiculous—the redeeming, reassuring ridiculous, life's little contribution to every human decision.

As a heretofore unknown amalgam of the most unalike of America's historic undesirables, he now made sense.

There was an interlude, however. After Steena and before Iris there was a five-month interlude named Ellie Magee, a petite, shapely colored girl, tawny-skinned, lightly freckled across the nose and cheeks, in appearance not quite over the dividing line between adolescence and womanhood, who worked at the Village Door Shop on Sixth Avenue, excitedly selling shelving units for books and selling doors—doors on legs for desks and doors on legs for beds. The tired old Jewish guy who owned the place said that hiring Ellie had increased his business by fifty percent. "I had nothing going here," he told Coleman. "Eking out a living. But now every guy in the Village wants a door for a desk. People come in, they don't ask for me—they ask for Ellie. They call on the phone, they want to talk to Ellie. This little gal has changed everything." It was true, nobody could resist her, including Coleman, who was struck, first, by her legs up on high heels and then with all her naturalness. Goes out with white NYU guys who are drawn to her, goes out with colored NYU guys who are drawn to her—a sparkling twenty-three-year-old kid, as yet wounded by nothing, who has moved to the Village from Yonkers, where she grew up, and is living the unconventional life with a small *u*, the Village life as advertised. She is a find, and so Coleman goes in to buy a desk he doesn't need and that night takes her for a drink. After Steena and the shock of losing someone he'd so much wanted, he is having a good time again, he's alive again, and all this from the moment they start flirting in the store. Does she think he's a white guy in the store? He doesn't know. Interesting. Then that evening she laughs and, comically squinting at him, says, "What are you anyway?" Right out she spots something and goes ahead and says it. But now the sweat is not pouring off him as it did when he misread Steena's poem. "What am I? Play it any way you like," Coleman says. "Is that the way *you* play it?" she asks. "Of course that's the way I play it," he says. "So white girls think you're white?" "Whatever they think," he says, "I let them think." "And whatever I think?" Ellie asks. "Same deal," Coleman says. That's the little game they play, and that becomes the excitement for them, playing the ambiguity of it. He's not that close to anybody particularly, but the guys he knows from school think he's taking out a colored girl, and her friends all think she's going around with a white guy. There's some real fun in having other people find them important, and most everywhere they go, people do. It's 1951. Guys ask Coleman, "What's she like?" "Hot," he says, drawing the word out while floppily wiggling one hand the way the Italians did back in East Orange. There's a day-to-day, second-to-second kick in all this, a little movie-star magnitude to his life now: he's always in a scene when he's out with Ellie. Nobody on Eighth Street knows what the hell is going on, and he enjoys that. She's got the legs. She laughs all the time. She's a woman in a natural way—full of ease and a lively innocence that's enchanting to him. Something like Steena, except she's not white, with the result that they don't go rushing off to visit his family and they don't go visiting hers. Why should they? They live in the Village. Taking her to East Orange doesn't even occur to him. Maybe it's because he doesn't want to hear the sigh of relief, to be told, even wordlessly, that he's doing the right thing. He thinks about his motivation for bringing Steena home. To be honest with everyone? And what did that achieve? No, no families—not for now anyway.

Meanwhile, he so enjoys being with her that one night the truth just comes bubbling out. Even about his being a boxer, which he could never tell Steena. It's so easy to tell Ellie. That she's not disapproving gives her another boost up in his estimation. She's not conventional—and yet so sound. He is dealing with someone utterly unnarrow-minded. The splendid girl wants to hear it all. And so he talks, and without restraints he is an extraordinary talker, and Ellie is enthralled. He tells her about the navy. He tells her about his family, which turns out to be a family not much different from hers, except that her father, a pharmacist with a drugstore in Harlem, is living, and though he isn't happy about her having moved to the Village, fortunately for Ellie he can't stop himself from adoring her. Coleman tells her about Howard and how he couldn't stand the place. They talk a lot about Howard because that was where her parents had wanted her to go too. And always, whatever they're talking about, he finds he is effortlessly making her laugh. "I'd never seen so many colored people before, not even in south Jersey at the family reunion. Howard University looked to me like just too many Negroes in one place. Of all persuasions, of every stripe, but I just did not want to be around them like that. Did not at all see what it had to do with me. Everything there was just so concentrated that any sort of pride I ever had was diminished. Completely diminished by a concentrated, false environment." "Like a soda that's too sweet," Ellie said. "Well," he told her, "it's not so much that too much has been put in, it's that everything else has been taken out." Talking openly with Ellie, Coleman finds all his relief. True, he's not a hero anymore, but then he's not in any way a villain either. Yes, she's a contender, this one. Her transcendence into independence, her transformation into a Village girl, the way she handles her folks—she seems to have grown up the way you're supposed to be able to.

One evening she takes him around to a tiny Bleecker Street jewelry shop where the white guy who owns it makes beautiful things out of enamel. Just shopping the street, out looking, but when they leave she tells Coleman that the guy is black. "You're wrong," Coleman tells her, "he can't be." "Don't tell me that I'm wrong"—she laughs—"*you're* blind." Another night, near midnight, she takes him to a bar on Hudson Street where painters congregate to drink. "See that one? The smoothie?" she says in a soft voice, inclining her head toward a good-looking white guy in his mid-twenties charming all the girls at the bar. "Him," she says. "*No,*" says Coleman, who's the one laughing now. "You're in Greenwich Village, Coleman Silk, the four freest square miles in America. There's one on every other block. You're so vain, you thought you'd dreamed it up yourself." And if *she* knows of three—which she does, positively—there are ten, if not more. "From all over everywhere," she says, "they make straight for Eighth Street. Just like you did from little East Orange." "And," he says, "I don't see it at all." And that too makes them laugh, laugh and laugh and laugh because he is hopeless and cannot see it in others and because Ellie is his guide, pointing them out.

In the beginning, he luxuriates in the solution to his problem. Losing the secret, he feels like a boy again. The boy he'd been before he had the secret. A kind of imp again. He gets from all her naturalness the pleasure and ease of being natural himself. If you're going to be a knight and a hero, you're armored, and what he gets now is the pleasure of being unarmored. "You're a lucky man," Ellie's boss tells him. "A lucky man," he repeats, and means it. With Ellie the secret is no longer operative. It's not only that he can tell her everything and that he does, it's that if and when he wants to, he can now go home. He can deal with his brother, and the other way, he knows, he could never have. His mother and he can go on back and resume being as close and easygoing as they always were. And then he meets Iris, and that's it. It's been fun with Ellie, and it continues to be fun, but some dimension is missing. The whole thing lacks the ambition—it fails to feed that conception of himself that's been driving him all his life. Along comes Iris and he's back in the ring. His father had said to him, "Now you can retire undefeated. You're retired." But here he comes roaring out of his corner—he has the secret again. And the *gift* to be secretive again, which is hard to come by. Maybe there *are* a dozen more guys like him hanging around the Village. But not just everybody has that gift. That is, they have it, but in petty ways: they simply lie all the time. They're not secretive in the grand and elaborate way that Coleman is. He's back on the trajectory outward. He's got the elixir of the secret, and

it's like being fluent in another language—it's being somewhere
that is constantly fresh to you. He's lived without it, it was fine,
nothing horrible happened, it wasn't objectionable. It was fun. Innocent fun. But insufficiently everything else. Sure, he'd regained
his innocence. Ellie gave him that all right. But what use is innocence? Iris gives more. She raises everything to another pitch. Iris
gives him back his life on the scale he wants to live it.

Two years after they met, they decided to get married, and that was
when, for this license he'd taken, this freedom he'd sounded, the
choices he had dared to make—and could he really have been any
more artful or clever in arriving at an actable self big enough to
house his ambition and formidable enough to take on the world?—
the first large payment was exacted.

Coleman went over to East Orange to see his mother. Mrs. Silk
did not know of Iris Gittelman's existence, though she wasn't at all
surprised when he told her that he was going to get married and
that the girl was white. She wasn't even surprised when he told her
that the girl didn't know he was colored. If anyone was surprised,
it was Coleman, who, having openly declared his intention, all at
once wondered if this entire decision, the most monumental of
his life, wasn't based on the least serious thing imaginable: Iris's
hair, that sinuous thicket of hair that was far more Negroid than
Coleman's—more like Ernestine's hair than his. As a little girl,
Ernestine was famous for asking, "Why don't I have blow hair like
Mommy?"—meaning, why didn't her hair blow in the breeze, not
only like her mother's but like the hair of all the women on the ma-
ternal side of the family.

In the face of his mother's anguish, there floated through Coleman the eerie, crazy fear that all that he had ever wanted from Iris
Gittelman was the explanation her appearance could provide for
the texture of their children's hair.

But how could a motive as bluntly, as dazzlingly utilitarian as
that have escaped his attention till now? Because it wasn't in any

way true? Seeing his mother suffering like this—inwardly shaken by his own behavior and yet resolved, as Coleman always was, to carry through to the finish—how could this startling idea seem to him anything *other* than true? Even as he remained seated across from his mother in what appeared to be a state of perfect self-control, he had the definite impression that he had just chosen a wife for the stupidest reason in the world and that he was the emptiest of men.

"And she believes your parents are dead, Coleman. That's what you told her."

"That's right."

"You have no brother, you have no sister. There is no Ernestine. There is no Walt."

He nodded.

"And? What else did you tell her?"

"What else do you think I told her?"

"Whatever it suited you to tell her." That was as harsh as she got all afternoon. Her capacity for anger never had been and never would be able to extend to him. The mere sight of him, from the moment of his birth, stimulated feelings against which she had no defenses and that had nothing to do with what he was worthy of. "I'm never going to know my grandchildren," she said.

He had prepared himself. The important thing was to forget about Iris's hair and let her speak, let her find her fluency and, from the soft streaming of her own words, create for him his apologia.

"You're never going to let them see me," she said. "You're never going to let them know who I am. 'Mom,' you'll tell me, 'Ma, you come to the railroad station in New York, and you sit on the bench in the waiting room, and at eleven twenty-five A.M., I'll walk by with my kids in their Sunday best.' That'll be my birthday present five years from now. 'Sit there, Mom, say nothing, and I'll just walk them slowly by.' And you know very well that I will be there. The railroad station. The zoo. Central Park. Wherever you say, of course I'll do it. You tell me the only way I can ever touch my grandchildren is for you to hire me to come over as Mrs. Brown to baby-sit and put them to bed, I'll do it. Tell me to come over as Mrs. Brown to clean your house, I'll do *that*. Sure I'll do what you tell me. I have no choice."

"Don't you?"

"A choice? Yes? What is my choice, Coleman?"

"To disown me."

Almost mockingly, she pretended to give that idea some thought. "I suppose I could be that ruthless with you. Yes, that's possible, I suppose. But where do you think I'm going to find the strength to be that ruthless with myself?"

It was not a moment for him to be recalling his childhood. It was not a moment for him to be admiring her lucidity or her sarcasm or her courage. It was not a moment to allow himself to be subjugated by the all-but-pathological phenomenon of mother love. It was not a moment for him to be hearing all the words that she was not saying but that were sounded more tellingly even than what she did say. It was not a moment to think thoughts other than the thoughts he'd come armed with. It was certainly not a moment to resort to explanations, to start brilliantly toting up the advantages and the disadvantages and pretend that this was no more than a logical decision. There was no explanation that could begin to address the outrage of what he was doing to her. It was a moment to deepen his focus on what he was there to achieve. If disowning him was a choice foreclosed to her, then taking the blow was all she could do. Speak quietly, say little, forget Iris's hair, and, for however long is required, let her continue to employ her words to absorb into her being the brutality of the most brutal thing he had ever done.

He was murdering her. You don't have to murder your father. The world will do that for you. There are plenty of forces out to get your father. The world will take care of him, as it had indeed taken care of Mr. Silk. Who there is to murder is the mother, and that's what he saw he was doing to her, the boy who'd been loved as he'd been loved by this woman. Murdering her on behalf of his exhilarating notion of freedom! It would have been much easier without her. But only through this test can he be the man he has chosen to be, unalterably separated from what he was handed at birth, free to struggle at being free like any human being would wish to be free. To get that from life, the alternate destiny, on one's own terms, he must do what must be done. Don't most people want to walk out of the fucking lives they've been handed? But they don't, and that's what makes them them, and this was what was making him him. Throw the punch, do the damage, and forever lock the door. You can't do this to a wonderful mother who loves you unconditionally and has made you happy, you can't inflict this pain and then think you can go back on it. It's so awful that all you can do is live with it. Once you've done a thing like this, you have done so much violence it can *never* be undone—which is what Coleman wants. It's like that moment at West Point when the guy was going down. Only the referee could save him from what Coleman had it in him to do. Then as now, he was experiencing the power of it as a fighter. Because that is the test too, to give the brutality of the repudiation its real, unpardonable human meaning, to confront with all the realism and clarity possible the moment when your fate intersects with something enormous. This is his. This man and his mother. This woman and her beloved son. If, in the service of honing himself, he is out to do the hardest thing imaginable, this is it, short of stabbing her. This takes him right to the heart of the matter. This is the major act of his life, and vividly, consciously, he feels its immensity.

"I don't know why I'm not better prepared for this, Coleman. I should be," she said. "You've been giving fair warning almost from the day you got here. You were seriously disinclined even to take the breast. Yes, you were. Now I see why. Even that might delay your escape. There was always something about our family, and I don't mean color—there was something about us that impeded you. You think like a prisoner. You do, Coleman Brutus. You're white as snow and you think like a slave."

It was not a moment to give credence to her intelligence, to take even the most appealing turn of phrase as the embodiment of some special wisdom. It often happened that his mother could say something that made it sound as though she knew more than she did. The rational other side. That was what came of leaving the orating to his father and so seeming by comparison to say what counted.

"Now, I could tell you that there is no escape, that all your attempts to escape will only lead you back to where you began. That's what your father would tell you. And there'd be something in *Julius Caesar* to back him up. But for a young man like you, whom everybody falls for? A good-looking, charming, clever young fellow with your physique, your determination, your shrewdness, with all your wonderful gifts? You with your green eyes and your long dark lashes? Why, this should cause you no trouble at all. I expect coming to see me is about as hard as it's going to get, and look how calmly you're sitting here. And that is because you know what you're doing makes great sense. *I* know it makes sense, because you would not pursue a goal that didn't. Of course you will have disappointments. Of course little is going to turn out as you imagine it, sitting so calmly across from me. Your special destiny will be special all right—but how? Twenty-six years old—you can't begin to know. But wouldn't the same be true if you did nothing? I suppose any profound change in life involves saying 'I don't know you' to someone."

She went on for nearly two hours, a long speech about his autonomy dating back to infancy, expertly taking in the pain by delineating all she was up against and couldn't hope to oppose and would have to endure, during which Coleman did all he could not to notice—in the simplest things, like the thinning of her hair (his mother's hair, not Iris's hair) and the jutting of her head, the swelling of her ankles, the bloating of her belly, the exaggerated splay of her large teeth—how much further along toward her death she'd been drawn since the Sunday three years back when she'd done everything gracious she could to put Steena at her ease. At some point midway through the afternoon, she seemed to Coleman to step up to the very edge of the big change: the point of turning, as the elderly do, into a tiny, misshapen being. The longer she talked, the more he believed he was seeing this happen. He tried not to think about the disease that would kill her, about the funeral they would give her, about the tributes that would be read and the prayers offered up at the side of her grave. But then he tried not to think about her going on living either, of his leaving and her being here and alive, the years passing and her thinking about him and his children and his wife, more years passing and the connection between the two of them only growing stronger for her because of its denial.

Neither his mother's longevity nor her mortality could be allowed to have any bearing on what he was doing, nor could the struggles her family had been through in Lawnside, where she'd been born in a dilapidated shack and lived with her parents and four brothers until her father died when she was seven. Her father's people had been in Lawnside, New Jersey, since 1855. They were runaway slaves, brought north on the Underground Railroad from Maryland and into southwest Jersey by the Quakers. The Negroes first called the place Free Haven. No whites lived there then, and only a handful did now, out on the fringes of a town of a couple of thousand where just about everybody was descended from runaway slaves whom the Haddonfield Quakers had protected—the mayor was descended from them, the fire chief, the police chief, the tax collector, the teachers in the grade school, the kids in the grade school. But the uniqueness of Lawnside as a Negro town had no bearing on anything either. Nor did the uniqueness of Gouldtown, farther south in Jersey, down by Cape May. That's where her mother's people were from, and that's where the family went to live after the death of her father. Another settlement of colored people, many nearly white, including her own grandmother, everyone somehow related to everyone else. "Way, way back," as she used to explain to Coleman when he was a boy—simplifying and condensing as best she could all the lore she'd ever heard—a slave was owned by a Continental Army soldier who'd been killed in the French and Indian War. The slave looked after the soldier's widow. He did everything, from dawn to dark didn't stop doing what needed to be done. He chopped and hauled the wood, gathered the crops, excavated and built a cabbage house and stowed the cabbages there, stored the pumpkins, buried the apples, turnips, and potatoes in the ground for winter, stacked the rye and wheat in the barn, slaughtered the pig, salted the pork, slaughtered the cow and corned the beef, until one day the widow married him and they had three sons. And those sons married Gouldtown girls whose families reached back to the settlement's origins in the 1600s, families that by the Revolution were all intermarried and thickly intermingled. One or another or all of them, she said, were descendants of the Indian from the large Lenape settlement at Indian Fields who married a Swede—locally Swedes and Finns had superseded the original Dutch settlers—and who had five children with her; one or another or all were descendants of the two mulatto brothers brought from the West Indies on a trading ship that sailed up the river from Greenwich to Bridgeton, where they were indentured to the landowners who had paid their passage and who themselves later paid the passage of two Dutch sisters to come from Holland to become their wives; one or another or all were descendants of the granddaughter of John Fenwick, an English baronet's son, a cavalry officer in Cromwell's Commonwealth army and a member of the Society of Friends who died in New Jersey not that many years after New Cesarea (the province lying between the Hudson and the Delaware that was deeded by the brother of the king of England to two English proprietors) *became* New Jersey. Fenwick died in 1683 and was buried somewhere in the personal colony he purchased, founded, and governed, and which stretched north of Bridgeton to Salem and south and east to the Delaware.

Fenwick's nineteen-year-old granddaughter, Elizabeth Adams, married a colored man, Gould. "That black that hath been the ruin of her" was her grandfather's description of Gould in the will from which he excluded Elizabeth from any share of his estate until such time as "the Lord open her eyes to see her abominable transgression against Him." As the story had it, only one son of the five sons of Gould and Elizabeth survived to maturity, and he was Benjamin Gould, who married a Finn, Ann. Benjamin died in 1777, the year after the signing of the Declaration of Independence across the Delaware in Philadelphia, leaving a daughter, Sarah, and four sons, Anthony, Samuel, Abijah, and Elisha, from whom Gouldtown took its name.

Through his mother, Coleman learned the maze of family history going back to the days of aristocratic John Fenwick, who was to that southwestern region of New Jersey what William Penn was to the part of Pennsylvania that encompassed Philadelphia—and from whom it sometimes seemed all of Gouldtown had descended—and then he heard it again, though never the same in all its details, from great-aunts and great-uncles, from great-*great*-aunts and -uncles, some of them people close to a hundred, when, as children, he, Walt, and Ernestine went with their parents down to Gouldtown for the annual reunion—almost two hundred relatives from southwest Jersey, from Philadelphia, from Atlantic City, from as far off as Boston, eating fried bluefish, stewed chicken, fried chicken, homemade ice cream, sugared peaches, pies, and cakes—eating favorite family dishes and playing baseball and singing songs and reminiscing all day long, telling stories about the women way back spinning and knitting, boiling fat pork and baking huge breads for the men to take to the fields, making the clothes, drawing the water from the well, administering medicines obtained mainly from the woods, herb infusions to treat measles, the syrups of molasses and onions to counter whooping cough. Stories about family women who kept a dairy making fine cheeses, about women who went to the city of Philadelphia to become housekeepers, dressmakers, and schoolteachers, and about women at home of remarkable hospitality. Stories about the men in the woods, trapping and shooting the winter game for meat, about the farmers plowing the fields, cutting the cordwood and the rails for fences, buying, selling, slaughtering the cattle, and the prosperous ones, the dealers, selling tons of salt hay for packing to the Trenton pottery works, hay cut from the salt marsh they owned along the bay and river shores. Stories about the men who left the woods, the farm, the marsh, and the cedar swamp to serve—some as white soldiers, some as black—

in the Civil War. Stories about men who went to sea to become blockade runners and who went to Philadelphia to become undertakers, printers, barbers, electricians, cigar makers, and ministers in the African Methodist Episcopal Church—one who went to Cuba to ride with Teddy Roosevelt and his Rough Riders, and a few men who got in trouble, ran away, and never came back. Stories about family children like themselves, often dressed poorly, without shoes sometimes or coats, asleep on winter nights in the freezing rooms of simple houses, in the heat of summer pitching, loading, and hauling hay with the men, but taught manners by their parents, and catechized in the schoolhouse by the Presbyterians—where they also learned to spell and read—and always eating all they wanted, even in those days, of pork and potatoes and bread and molasses and game, and growing up strong and healthy and honest.

But one no more decides not to become a boxer because of the history of Lawnside's runaway slaves, the abundance of everything at the Gouldtown reunions, and the intricacy of the family's American genealogy—or not to become a teacher of classics because of the history of Lawnside's runaway slaves, the abundance of the Gouldtown reunions, and the intricacy of the family's American genealogy—than one decides not to become anything else for such reasons. Many things vanish out of a family's life. Lawnside is one, Gouldtown another, genealogy a third, and Coleman Silk was a fourth.

Over these last fifty years or more, he was not the first child, either, who'd heard about the harvesting of the salt hay for the Trenton pottery works or eaten fried bluefish and sugared peaches at the Gouldtown reunions and grown up to vanish like this—to vanish, as they used to say in the family, "till all trace of him was lost." "Lost himself to all his people" was another way they put it.

Ancestor worship—that's how Coleman put it. Honoring the past was one thing—the idolatry that is ancestor worship was something else. The hell with that imprisonment.

That night after coming back to the Village from East Orange, Coleman got a call from his brother in Asbury Park that took things further faster than he had planned. "Don't you ever come around her," Walt warned him, and his voice was resonant with something barely suppressed—all the more frightening for *being* suppressed— that Coleman hadn't heard since his father's time. There's another force in that family, pushing him now *all* the way over on the other side. The act was committed in 1953 by an audacious young man in Greenwich Village, by a specific person in a specific place at a specific time, but now he will be over on the other side forever. Yet that, as he discovers, is exactly the point: freedom is dangerous. Freedom is very dangerous. And nothing is on your own terms for long. "Don't you even *try* to see her. No contact. No calls. Nothing. Never. Hear me?" Walt said. "*Never.* Don't you dare ever show your lily-white face around that house again!"

3

What Do You Do with the Kid Who Can't Read?

"I F CLINTON had fucked her in the ass, she might have shut her mouth. Bill Clinton is not the man they say he is. Had he turned her over in the Oval Office and fucked her in the ass, none of this would have happened."

"Well, he never dominated her. He played it safe."

"You see, once he got to the White House, he didn't dominate anymore. Couldn't. He didn't dominate Willey either. That's why she got angry with him. Once he became president, he lost his Arkansas ability to dominate women. So long as he was attorney general and governor of an obscure little state, that was perfect for him."

"Sure. Gennifer Flowers."

"What happens in Arkansas? If you fall when you're still back in Arkansas, you don't fall from a very great height."

"Right. And you're expected to be an ass man. There's a tradition."

"But when you get to the White House, you can't dominate. And when you can't dominate, then Miss Willey turns against you, and Miss Monica turns against you. Her loyalty would have been earned by fucking her in the ass. That should be the pact. That should seal you together. But there was no pact."

"Well, she was frightened. She was close to not saying anything, you know. Starr overwhelmed her. Eleven guys in the room with her at that hotel? Hitting on her? It was a gang bang. It was a gang rape that Starr staged there at that hotel."

"Yeah. True. But she was talking to Linda Tripp."

"Oh, right."

"She was talking to everybody. She's part of that dopey culture. Yap, yap, yap. Part of this generation that is proud of its shallowness. The sincere performance is everything. Sincere and empty, totally empty. The sincerity that goes in all directions. The sincerity that is worse than falseness, and the innocence that is worse than corruption. All the rapacity hidden under the sincerity. And under the lingo. This wonderful language they all have—that they appear to *believe*—about their 'lack of self-worth,' all the while what they actually believe is that they're entitled to everything. Their shamelessness they call lovingness, and the ruthlessness is camouflaged as lost 'self-esteem.' Hitler lacked self-esteem too. That was his problem. It's a con these kids have going. The hyperdramatization of the pettiest emotions. Relationship. My relationship. Clarify my relationship. They open their mouths and they send me up the wall. Their whole language is a summation of the stupidity of the last forty years. Closure. *There's* one. My students cannot stay in that place where thinking must occur. Closure! They fix on the conventionalized narrative, with its beginning, middle, and end—every experience, no matter how ambiguous, no matter how knotty or mysterious, must lend itself to this normalizing, conventionalizing, anchorman cliché. Any kid who says 'closure' I flunk. They want closure, there's their closure."

"Well, whatever she is—a total narcissist, a conniving little bitch, the most exhibitionistic Jewish girl in the history of Beverly Hills, utterly corrupted by privilege—he knew it all beforehand. He could read her. If he can't read Monica Lewinsky, how can he read Saddam Hussein? If he can't read and outfox Monica Lewinsky, the

guy *shouldn't* be president. There's *genuine* grounds for impeachment. No, he saw it. He saw it all. I don't think he was hypnotized by
her cover story for long. That she was totally corrupt and totally innocent, of course he saw it. The extreme innocence *was* the corruption—it was her corruption and her madness and her cunning.
That was her force, that combination. That she had no depth, that
was her charm at the end of his day of being commander in chief.
The intensity of the shallowness was its appeal. Not to mention the
shallowness of the intensity. The stories about her childhood. The
boasting about her adorable willfulness: 'See, I was three but I was
already a personality.' I'm sure he understood that everything he
did that didn't conform to her delusions was going to be yet another brutal blow to her self-esteem. But what he didn't see was that
he had to fuck her in the ass. Why? To shut her up. Strange behavior
in our president. It was the first thing she showed him. She stuck it
in his face. She offered it to him. And he did nothing about it. I
don't get this guy. Had he fucked her in the ass, I doubt she would
have talked to Linda Tripp. Because she wouldn't have wanted to
talk about that."

"She wanted to talk about the cigar."

"That's different. That's kid stuff. No, he didn't give her regularly
something she didn't want to talk about. Something he wanted that
she didn't. That's the mistake."

"In the ass is how you create loyalty."

"I don't know if that would have shut her up. I don't know that
shutting her up is humanly possible. This isn't Deep Throat. This is
Big Mouth."

"Still, you have to admit that this girl has revealed more about
America than anybody since Dos Passos. *She* stuck a thermometer
up the *country's* ass. Monica's *U.S.A.*"

"The trouble was she was getting from Clinton what she got
from all these guys. She wanted something else from him. He's the
president, she's a love terrorist. She wanted him to be different from
this teacher she had an affair with."

"Yeah, the niceness did him in. Interesting. Not his brutality but his niceness. Playing it not by his rules but by hers. She controls him because he wants it. Has to have it. It's all wrong. You know what Kennedy would have told her when she came around asking for a job? You know what Nixon would have told her? Harry Truman, even Eisenhower would have told it to her. The general who ran World War II, he knew how not to be nice. They would have told her that not only would they not give her a job, but nobody would ever give her a job again as long as she lived. That she wouldn't be able to get a job driving a cab in Horse Springs, New Mexico. *Nothing*. That her father's practice would be sabotaged, and *he'd* be out of work. That her mother would never work again, that her brother would never work again, that nobody in her family would earn another dime, if she so much as dared to open her mouth about the eleven blow jobs. Eleven. Not even a round dozen. I don't think under a dozen in over two years qualifies for the Heisman in debauchery, do you?"

"His caution, his caution did him in. Absolutely. He played it like a lawyer."

"He didn't want to give her any evidence. That's why he wouldn't come."

"There he was right. The moment he came, he was finished. She had the goods. Collected a sample. The smoking come. Had he fucked her in the ass, the nation could have been spared this terrible trauma."

They laughed. There were three of them.

"He never really abandoned himself to it. He had an eye on the door. He had his own system there. She was trying to up the ante."

"Isn't this what the Mafia does? You give somebody something they can't talk about. Then you've got them."

"You involve them in a mutual transgression, and you have a mutual corruption. Sure."

"So his problem is that he's *insufficiently* corrupt."

"Oh, yes. Absolutely. And unsophisticated."

"It's just the opposite of the charge that he's reprehensible. He's insufficiently reprehensible."

"Of course. If you're engaged in that behavior, why draw the line there? Wasn't that fairly artificial?"

"Once you draw the line, you make it clear that you're frightened. And when you're frightened, you're finished. Your destruction is no further than Monica's cell phone."

"He didn't want to lose control, you see. Remember he said, I don't want to be hooked on you, I don't want to be addicted to you? That struck me as true."

"I thought that was a line."

"I don't think so. I think probably the way she remembered it, it sounds like a line, but I think the motivation—no, he didn't want the sexual hook. She was good but she was replaceable."

"Everybody's replaceable."

"But you don't know what his experience was. He wasn't into hookers and that kind of stuff."

"Kennedy was into hookers."

"Oh yeah. The real stuff. This guy Clinton, this is schoolboy stuff."

"I don't think he was a schoolboy when he was down in Arkansas."

"No, the scale was right in Arkansas. Here it was all out of whack. And it must have driven him crazy. President of the United States, he has access to everything, and he can't touch it. This was hell. Especially with that goody two-shoes wife."

"She's goody two-shoes, you think?"

"Oh, sure."

"Her and Vince Foster?"

"Well, she would fall in love with somebody, but she never would have done anything crazy because he was *married*. She could make even adultery boring. She's a real de-transgressor."

"You think she was fucking Foster?"

"Yes. Oh yeah."

"Now the whole world has fallen in love with goody two-shoes. That's exactly what they've fallen in love with."

"Clinton's genius was to give Vince Foster a job in Washington.

Put him right there. Make him do his personal bit for the administration. That's genius. There Clinton acted like a good Mafia don
and had that on her."

"Yeah. That's okay. But that isn't what he did with Monica. You
see, he had only Vernon Jordan to talk to about Monica. Who was
probably the best person to talk to. But they couldn't figure that
out. Because they thought she was blabbing just to her stupid little
California Valley Girls. Okay. So what. But that this Linda Tripp,
this Iago, this undercover Iago that Starr had working in the White
House—"

At this point, Coleman got up from where he was seated and
headed toward the campus. That was all of the chorus Coleman
overheard while sitting on a bench on the green, contemplating
what move he'd make next. He didn't recognize their voices, and
since their backs were to him and their bench was around the other
side of the tree from his, he couldn't see their faces. His guess was
that they were three young guys, new to the faculty since his time,
on the town green drinking bottled water or decaf out of contain-
ers, just back from a workout on the town tennis courts, and relaxing together, talking over the day's Clinton news before heading
home to their wives and children. To him they sounded sexually
savvy and sexually confident in ways he didn't associate with young
assistant professors, particularly at Athena. Pretty rough talk, pretty
raw for academic banter. Too bad these tough guys hadn't been
around in his time. They might have served as a cadre of resistance
against ... No, no. Up on the campus, where not everyone's a tennis
buddy, this sort of force tends to get dissipated in jokes when it's
not entirely self-suppressed—they would probably have been no
more forthcoming than the rest of the faculty when it came to ral-
lying behind him. Anyway, he didn't know them and didn't want to.
He knew no one any longer. For two years now, all the while he was
writing *Spooks*, he had cut himself off completely from the friends
and colleagues and associates of a lifetime, and so not until today—
just before noon, following the meeting with Nelson Primus that
had ended not merely badly but stunningly badly, with Coleman

astounding *himself* by his vituperative words—had he come any-where near leaving Town Street, as he was doing now, and heading down South Ward and then, at the Civil War monument, climbing the hill to the campus. Chances were there'd be no one he knew for him to bump into, except perhaps whoever might be teaching the retired who came in July to spend a couple of weeks in the college's Elderhostel program, which included visits to the Tanglewood con-certs, the Stockbridge galleries, and the Norman Rockwell Mu-seum.

It was these very summer students he saw first when he reached the crest of the hill and emerged from behind the old astronomy building onto the sun-speckled main quadrangle, more kitschily collegiate-looking at that moment than even on the cover of the Athena catalog. They were heading to the cafeteria for lunch, me-andering in pairs along one of the tree-lined quadrangle's criss-crossing paths. A procession of twos: husbands and wives together, pairs of husbands and pairs of wives, pairs of widows, pairs of wid-owers, pairs of rearranged widows and widowers—or so Coleman took them to be—who had teamed up as couples after meeting here in their Elderhostel classes. All were neatly dressed in light summer clothes, a lot of shirts and blouses of bright pastel shades, trousers of white or light khaki, some Brooks Brothers summer-time plaid. Most of the men were wearing visored caps, caps of ev-ery color, many of them stitched with the logos of professional sports teams. No wheelchairs, no walkers, no crutches, no canes that he could see. Spry people his age, seemingly no less fit than he was, some a bit younger, some obviously older but enjoying what retirement freedom was meant to provide for those fortunate enough to breathe more or less easily, to ambulate more or less painlessly, and to think more or less clearly. This was where he was supposed to be. Paired off properly. Appropriately.

Appropriate. The current code word for reining in most any de-viation from the wholesome guidelines and thereby making every-body "comfortable." Doing not what he was being judged to be doing but doing instead, he thought, what was deemed suitable by God only knows which of our moral philosophers. Barbara Walters? Joyce Brothers? William Bennett? *Dateline NBC*? If he were around this place as a professor, he could teach "Appropriate Behavior in Classical Greek Drama," a course that would be over before it began.

They were on their way to lunch, passing within sight of North Hall, the ivied, beautifully weathered colonial brick building where, for over a decade, Coleman Silk, as faculty dean, had occupied the office across from the president's suite. The college's architectural marker, the six-sided clock tower of North Hall, topped by the spire that was topped by the flag—and that, from down in Athena proper, could be seen the way the massive European cathedrals are discerned from the approaching roadways by those repairing for the cathedral town—was tolling noon as he sat on a bench shadowed by the quadrangle's most famously age-gnarled oak, sat and calmly tried to consider the coercions of propriety. The *tyranny* of propriety. It was hard, halfway through 1998, for even him to believe in American propriety's enduring power, and he was the one who considered himself tyrannized: the bridle it still is on public rhetoric, the inspiration it provides for personal posturing, the persistence just about everywhere of this de-virilizing pulpit virtue-mongering that H. L. Mencken identified with boobism, that Philip Wylie thought of as Momism, that the Europeans unhistorically call American puritanism, that the likes of a Ronald Reagan call America's core values, and that maintains widespread jurisdiction by masquerading itself as something else—as *everything* else. As a force, propriety is protean, a dominatrix in a thousand disguises, infiltrating, if need be, as civic responsibility, WASP dignity, women's rights, black pride, ethnic allegiance, or emotion-laden Jewish ethical sensitivity. It's not as though Marx or Freud or Darwin or Stalin or Hitler or Mao had never happened—it's as though Sinclair Lewis had not happened. It's, he thought, as though *Babbitt* had never been written. It's as though not even that most basic level of imaginative thought had been admitted into consciousness to cause the slightest disturbance. A century of destruction unlike any other in its extremity befalls and blights the human race—scores of millions of ordinary people condemned to suffer deprivation upon deprivation, atrocity upon atrocity, evil upon evil, half the world or more subjected to pathological sadism as social policy, whole societies organized and fettered by the fear of violent persecution, the degradation of individual life engineered on a scale unknown throughout history, nations broken and enslaved by ideological criminals who rob them of everything, entire populations so demoralized as to be unable to get out of bed in the morning with the minutest desire to face the day . . . all the terrible touchstones presented by this century, and here they are up in arms about Faunia Farley. Here in America either it's Faunia Farley or it's Monica Lewinsky! The luxury of these lives disquieted so by the inappropriate comportment of Clinton and Silk! *This,* in 1998, is the wickedness they have to put up with. *This,* in 1998, is their torture, their torment, and their spiritual death. Their source of greatest moral despair, Faunia blowing me and me fucking Faunia. I'm depraved not simply for having once said the word "spooks" to a class of white students—and said it, mind you, not while standing there reviewing the legacy of slavery, the fulminations of the Black Panthers, the metamorphoses of Malcolm X, the rhetoric of James Baldwin, or the radio popularity of *Amos 'n' Andy,* but while routinely calling the roll. I am depraved not merely because of . . .

All this after less than five minutes sitting on a bench and looking at the pretty building where he had once been dean.

But the mistake had been made. He was back. He was there. He was back on the hill from which they had driven him, and so was his contempt for the friends who hadn't rallied round him and the colleagues who hadn't cared to support him and the enemies who'd disposed so easily of the whole meaning of his professional career. The urge to expose the capricious cruelty of their righteous idiocy flooded him with rage. He was back on the hill in the bondage of his rage and he could feel its intensity driving out all sense and demanding that he take immediate action.

Delphine Roux.

He got up and started for her office. At a certain age, he thought, it is better for one's health not to do what I am about to do. At a certain age, a man's outlook is best tempered by moderation, if not resignation, if not outright capitulation. At a certain age, one should live without either harking too much back to grievances of the past or inviting resistance in the present by embodying a challenge to the pieties that be. Yet to give up playing any but the role socially assigned, in this instance assigned to the respectably retired—at seventy-one, that is surely what is appropriate, and so, for Coleman Silk, as he long ago demonstrated with requisite ruthlessness to his very own mother, that is what is unacceptable.

He was not an embittered anarchist like Iris's crazy father, Gittelman. He was not a firebrand or an agitator in any way. Nor was he a madman. Nor was he a radical or a revolutionary, not even intellectually or philosophically speaking, unless it is revolutionary to believe that disregarding prescriptive society's most restrictive demarcations and asserting independently a free personal choice that is well within the law was something other than a basic human right—unless it is revolutionary, when you've come of age, to refuse to accept automatically the contract drawn up for your signature at birth.

By now he had passed behind North Hall and was headed for the long bowling green of a lawn leading to Barton and the office of Delphine Roux. He had no idea what he was going to say should he even catch her at her desk on a midsummer day as glorious as this one, with the fall semester not scheduled to begin for another six or seven weeks—nor did he find out, because, before he got anywhere near the wide brick path encircling Barton, he noticed around at the back of North Hall, gathered on a shady patch of grass adjacent to a basement stairwell, a group of five college janitors, in custodial staff shirts and trousers of UPS brown, sharing a pizza out of a delivery box and heartily laughing at somebody's joke. The only woman of the five and the focus of her coworkers' lunchtime attention—she who had told the joke or made the wisecrack or done the teasing and who happened also to be laughing loudest—was Faunia Farley.

The men appeared to be in their early thirties or thereabouts. Two were bearded, and one of the bearded ones, sporting a long ponytail, was particularly broad and oxlike. He was the only one up on his feet, the better, it seemed, to hover directly over Faunia as she sat on the ground, her long legs stretched out before her and her head thrown back in the gaiety of the moment. Her hair was a surprise to Coleman. It was down. In his experience, it was unfailingly drawn tightly back through an elastic band—down only in bed when she removed the band so as to allow it to fall to her unclothed shoulders.

With the boys. These must be "the boys" she referred to. One of them was recently divorced, a successless one-time garage mechanic who kept her Chevy running for her and drove her back and forth from work on the days when the damn thing wouldn't start no matter what he did, and one of them wanted to take her to a porn film on the nights his wife was working the late shift at the Blackwell paper box plant, and one of the boys was so innocent he didn't know what a hermaphrodite was. When the boys came up in conversation, Coleman listened without comment, expressing no chagrin over what she had to say about them, however much he wondered about their interest in her, given the meat of their talk as Faunia reported it. But as she didn't go endlessly on about them, and as he didn't encourage her with questions about them, the boys didn't make the impression on Coleman that they would have had, say, on Lester Farley. Of course she might herself choose to be a little less carefree and feed herself less cooperatively into their fantasies, but even when Coleman was impelled to suggest that, he easily managed to restrain himself. She could speak as pointlessly or pointedly as she liked to anyone, and whatever the consequences, she would have to bear them. She was not his daughter. She was not even his "girl." She was—what she was.

But watching unseen from where he had ducked back into the shadowed wall of North Hall, it was not nearly so easy to take so detached and tolerant a view. Because now he saw not only what he invariably saw—what attaining so little in life had done to her—but perhaps why so little had been attained; from his vantage point no more than fifty feet away, he could observe almost microscopically how, without him to take her cues from, she took cues instead from the gruffest example around, the coarsest, the one whose human expectations were the lowest and whose self-conception the shallowest. Since, no matter how intelligent you may be, Voluptas makes virtually anything you want to think come true, certain possibilities are never even framed, let alone vigorously conjectured, and assessing correctly the qualities of your Voluptas is the last thing you are equipped to do . . . until, that is, you slip into the shadows and observe her rolling onto her back on the grass, her knees bent and falling slightly open, the cheese of the pizza running down one hand, a Diet Coke brandished in the other, and laughing her head off—at what? at hermaphroditism?—while over her looms, in the person of a failed grease monkey, everything that is the antithesis of your own way of life. Another Farley? Another Les Farley? Maybe nothing so ominous as that, but more of a substitute for Farley than for him.

A campus scene that would have seemed without significance had Coleman encountered it on a summer day back when he was dean—as he undoubtedly had numerous times—a campus scene that would have seemed back then not merely harmless but appealingly expressive of the pleasure to be derived from eating out of doors on a beautiful day was freighted now with nothing *but* significance. Where neither Nelson Primus nor his beloved Lisa nor even the cryptic denunciation anonymously dispatched by Delphine Roux had convinced him of anything, this scene of no great moment on the lawn back of North Hall exposed to him at last the underside of his own disgrace.

Lisa. Lisa and those kids of hers. Tiny little Carmen. That's who came flashing into his thoughts, tiny Carmen, six years old but, in Lisa's words, like a much younger kid. "She's cute," Lisa said, "but she's like a baby." And adorably cute Carmen was when he saw her:

pale, pale brown skin, pitch-black hair in two stiff braids, eyes un-like any he'd ever seen on another human being, eyes like coals blue with heat and lit from within, a child's quick and flexible body, attired neatly in miniaturized jeans and sneakers, wearing colorful socks and a white tube of a T-shirt nearly as narrow as a pipe cleaner—a frisky little girl seemingly attentive to everything, and particularly to him. "This is my friend Coleman," Lisa said when Carmen came strolling into the room, on her small, scrubbed first-thing-in-the-morning face a slightly amused, self-important mock smile. "Hello, Carmen," Coleman said. "He just wanted to see what we do," Lisa explained. "Okay," said Carmen, agreeably enough, but she studied him no less carefully than he was studying her, seem-ingly *with* the smile. "We're just gonna do what we always do," said Lisa. "Okay," Carmen said, but now she was trying out on him a rather more serious version of the smile. And when she turned and got to handling the movable plastic letters magnetized to the low little blackboard and Lisa asked her to begin sliding them around to make the words "want," "wet," "wash," and "wipe"—"I always tell you," Lisa was saying, "that you have to look at the first letters. Let's see you read the first letters. Read it with your finger"— Carmen kept periodically swiveling her head, then her whole body, to look at Coleman and stay in touch with him. "Anything is a dis-traction," Lisa said softly to her father. "Come on, Miss Carmen. Come on, honey. He's invisible." "What's that?" "Invisible," Lisa re-peated, "you can't see him." Carmen laughed—"I *can* see him." "Come on. Come on back to me. The first letters. That's it. Good work. But you also have to read the rest of the word too. Right? The first letter—and now the rest of the word. Good—'wash.' What's this one? You know it. You know that one. 'Wipe.' Good." Twenty-five weeks in the program on the day Coleman came to sit in on Reading Recovery, and though Carmen had made progress, it wasn't much. He remembered how she had struggled with the word "your" in the illustrated storybook from which she was reading aloud—scratching with her fingers around her eyes, squeezing and balling up the midriff of her shirt, twisting her legs onto the rung of her kiddie-sized chair, slowly but surely working her behind farther and farther off the seat of the chair—and was still unable to recognize "your" or to sound it out. "This is March, Dad. Twenty-five weeks. It's a long time to be having trouble with 'your.' It's a long time to be confusing 'couldn't' with 'climbed,' but at this point I'll settle for 'your.' It's supposed to be twenty weeks in the program, and out. She's been to kindergarten—she should have learned some basic sight words. But when I showed her a list of words back in September—and by then she was entering first grade—she said, 'What are these?' She didn't even know what words were. And the letters: *h* she didn't know, *j* she didn't know, she confused *u* for *c*. You see how she did that, it's visually similar, but she still has something of the problem twenty-five weeks later. The *m* and the *w*. The *i* and the *l*. The *g* and the *d*. Still problems for her. It's all a problem for her." "You're pretty dejected about Carmen," he said. "Well, every day for half an hour? That's a lot of instruction. That's a lot of work. She's supposed to read at home, but at home there's a sixteen-year-old sister who just had a baby, and the parents forget or don't care. The parents are immigrants, they're second-language learners, they don't find it easy reading to their children in English, though Carmen never got read to even in Spanish. And this is what I deal with day in and day out. Just seeing if a child can manipulate a book—I give it to them, a book like this one, with a big colorful illustration beneath the title, and I say, 'Show me the front of the book.' Some kids know, but most don't. Print doesn't mean anything to them. And," she said, smiling with exhaustion and nowhere near as enticingly as Carmen, "my kids supposedly aren't learning-disabled. Carmen doesn't look at the words while *I'm* reading. She doesn't care. And that's why you're wiped out at the end of the day. Other teachers have difficult tasks, I know, but at the end of a day of Carmen after Carmen after Carmen, you come home emotionally drained. By then *I* can't read. I can't even get on the phone. I eat something and go to bed. I do like these kids. I love these kids. But it's worse than draining—it's killing."

Faunia was sitting up on the grass now, downing the last of her drink while one of the boys—the youngest, thinnest, most boyish-looking of them, incongruously bearded at just the chin and wearing, with his brown uniform, a red-checkered bandanna and what looked like high-heeled cowboy boots—was collecting all the debris from lunch and stuffing it into a trash sack, and the other three were standing apart, out in the sunshine, each smoking a last cigarette before returning to work.

Faunia was alone. And quiet now. Sitting there gravely with the empty soda can and thinking what? About the two years of waitressing down in Florida when she was sixteen and seventeen, about the retired businessmen who used to come in for lunch without their wives and ask her if she wouldn't like to live in a nice apartment and have nice clothes and a nice new Pinto and charge accounts at all the Bal Harbour clothing shops and at the jewelry store and at the beauty parlor and in exchange do nothing more than be a girlfriend a few nights a week and every once in a while on weekends? Not one, two, three, but four such proposals in just the first year. And then the proposition from the Cuban. She clears a hundred bucks a john and no taxes. For a skinny blonde with big tits, a tall, good-looking kid like her with hustle and ambition and guts, got up in a miniskirt, a halter, and boots, a thousand bucks a night would be nothing. A year, two, and, if by then she wants to, she retires—she can afford to. "And you didn't do it?" Coleman asked. "No. Uh-uh. But don't think I didn't think about it," she said. "All the restaurant shit, those creepy people, the crazy cooks, a menu I can't read, orders I can't write, keeping everything straight in my head—it was no picnic. But if I can't read, I can count. I can add. I can subtract. I can't read words but I know who Shakespeare is. I know who Einstein is. I know who won the Civil War. I'm not stupid. I'm just an illiterate. A fine distinction but there it is. Numbers are something else. Numbers, believe me, I know. Don't think I didn't think it might not be a bad idea at all." But Coleman needed no such instruction. Not only did he think that at seventeen she thought being a hooker might be a good idea, he thought that it was an idea that she had more than simply entertained.

"What do you do with the kid who can't read?" Lisa had asked him in her despair. "It's the key to everything, so you have to do *something*, but doing it is burning me out. Your second year is supposed to be better. Your third year better than that. And this is my fourth." "And it isn't better?" he asked. "It's hard. It's so hard. Each year is *harder*. But if one-on-one tutoring doesn't work, what *do* you do?" Well, what *he* did with the kid who couldn't read was to make her his mistress. What Farley did was to make her his punching bag. What the Cuban did was to make her his whore, or one among them—so Coleman believed more often than not. And for how long his whore? Is that what Faunia was thinking about before getting herself up to head back to North Hall to finish cleaning the corridors? Was she thinking about how long it had all gone on? The mother, the stepfather, the escape from the stepfather, the places in the South, the places in the North, the men, the beatings, the jobs, the marriage, the farm, the herd, the bankruptcy, the children, the two dead children. No wonder half an hour in the sun sharing a pizza with the boys is paradise to her.

"This is my friend Coleman, Faunia. He's just going to watch."

"Okay," Faunia says. She is wearing a green corduroy jumper, fresh white stockings, and shiny black shoes, and is not nearly as jaunty as Carmen—composed, well mannered, permanently a little deflated, a pretty middle-class Caucasian child with long blond hair in butterfly barrettes at either side and, unlike Carmen, showing no interest in him, no curiosity about him, once he has been introduced. "Hello," she mumbles meekly, and goes obediently back to moving the magnetic letters around, pushing together the *w*'s, the *t*'s, the *n*'s, the *s*'s, and, on another part of the blackboard, grouping together all the vowels.

"Use two hands," Lisa tells her, and she does what she is told.

"Which are these?" Lisa asks.

And Faunia reads them. Gets all the letters right.

"Let's take something she knows," Lisa says to her father. "Make 'not,' Faunia."

Faunia does it. Faunia makes "not."

"Good work. Now something she doesn't know. Make 'got.'"

Looks long and hard at the letters, but nothing happens. Faunia makes nothing. Does nothing. Waits. Waits for the next thing to happen. Been waiting for the next thing to happen all her life. It always does.

"I want you to change the first part, Miss Faunia. Come on. You know this. What's the first part of 'got'?"

"*G*." She moves away the *n* and, at the start of the word, substitutes *g*.

"Good work. Now make it say 'pot.'"

She does it. Pot.

"Good. Now read it with your finger."

Faunia moves her finger beneath each letter while distinctly pronouncing its sound. "Puh—ah—tuh."

"She's quick," Coleman says.

"Yes, but that's supposed to be quick."

There are three other children with three other Reading Recovery teachers in other parts of the large room, and so all around him Coleman can hear little voices reading aloud, rising and falling in the same childish pattern regardless of the content, and he hears the other teachers saying, "You know that—*u*, like '*u*mbrella'—*u*, *u*—" and "You know that—*ing*, you know *ing*—" and "You know *I*—good, good work," and when he looks around, he sees that all the other children being taught are Faunia as well. There are alphabet charts everywhere, with pictures of objects to illustrate each of the letters, and there are plastic letters everywhere to pick up in your hand, differently colored so as to help you phonetically form the words a letter at a time, and piled everywhere are simple books that tell the simplest stories: ". . . on Friday we went to the beach. Saturday we went to the airport." "'Father Bear, is Baby Bear with you?' 'No,' said Father Bear." "In the morning a dog barked at Sara. She was frightened. 'Try to be a brave girl, Sara,' said Mom." In addition to all these books and all these stories and all these Saras and all these dogs and all these bears and all these beaches, there are four teachers, four teachers all for Faunia, and they *still* can't teach her to read at her level.

"She's in first grade," Lisa is telling her father. "We're hoping that if we all four work together with her all day long every day, by the end of the year we can get her up to speed. But it's hard to get her motivated on her own."

"Pretty little girl," Coleman says.

"Yes, you find her pretty? You like that type? Is that your type, Dad, the pretty, slow-at-reading type with the long blond hair and the broken will and the butterfly barrettes?"

"I didn't say that."

"You didn't have to. I've been watching you with her," and she points around the room to where all four Faunias sit quietly before the board, forming and reforming out of the colorful plastic letters the words "pot" and "got" and "not." "The first time she spelled out 'pot' with her finger, you couldn't take your eyes off the kid. Well, if that turns you on, you should have been here back in September. Back in September she misspelled her first name *and* her second name. Fresh from kindergarten and the only word on the word list she could recognize was 'not.' She didn't understand that print contains a message. She didn't know left page before right page. She didn't know 'Goldilocks and the Three Bears.' 'Do you know "Goldilocks and the Three Bears," Faunia?' 'No.' Which means that her kindergarten experience—because that's what they get there, fairy tales, nursery rhymes—wasn't very good. Today she knows 'Little Red Riding Hood,' but then? Forget it. Oh, if you'd met Faunia last September, fresh from failing at kindergarten, I guarantee you, Dad, she would have driven you wild."

What do you do with the kid who can't read? The kid who is sucking somebody off in a pickup in her driveway while, upstairs, in a tiny apartment over a garage, her small children are supposedly asleep with a space heater burning—two untended children, a kerosene fire, and she's with this guy in his truck. The kid who has been a runaway since age fourteen, on the lam from her inexplicable life for her entire life. The kid who marries, for the stability and the safeguard he'll provide, a combat-crazed veteran who goes for your throat if you so much as turn in your sleep. The kid who is false, the kid who hides herself and lies, the kid who can't read who *can* read, who *pretends* she can't read, takes willingly upon herself this crippling shortcoming all the better to impersonate a member of a subspecies to which she does not belong and need not belong but to which, for every wrong reason, she wants him to believe she belongs. Wants herself to believe she belongs. The kid whose existence became a hallucination at seven and a catastrophe at fourteen and a disaster after that, whose vocation is to be neither a waitress nor a hooker nor a farmer nor a janitor but forever the stepdaughter to a lascivious stepfather and the undefended offspring of a self-obsessed mother, the kid who mistrusts everyone, sees the con in everyone, and yet is protected against nothing, whose capacity to hold on, unintimidated, is enormous and yet whose purchase on life is minute, misfortune's favorite embattled child, the kid to whom everything loathsome that can happen has happened and whose luck shows no sign of changing and yet who excites and arouses him like nobody since Steena, not the most but, morally speaking, the *least* repellent person he knows, the one to whom he feels drawn because of having been aimed for so long in the opposite direction—because of all he has *missed* by going in the opposite direction—and because the underlying feeling of rightness that controlled him formerly is exactly what is propelling him now, the unlikely intimate with whom he shares no less a spiritual than a physical union, who is anything *but* a plaything upon whom he flings his body twice a week in order to sustain his animal nature, who is more to him like a comrade-in-arms than anyone else on earth.

And what do you do with such a kid? You find a pay phone as fast as you can and rectify your idiotic mistake.

He thinks she is thinking about how long it has all gone on, the mother, the stepfather, the escape from the stepfather, the places in the South, the places in the North, the men, the beatings, the jobs, the marriage, the farm, the herd, the bankruptcy, the children, the dead children . . . and maybe she is. Maybe she is even if, alone now on the grass while the boys are smoking and cleaning up from lunch, she thinks she is thinking about crows. She thinks about crows a lot of the time. They're everywhere. They roost in the woods not far from the bed where she sleeps, they're in the pasture when she's out there moving the fence for the cows, and today they are cawing all over the campus, and so instead of thinking of what she is thinking the way Coleman thinks she is thinking it, she is thinking about the crow that used to hang around the store in Seeley Falls when, after the fire and before moving to the farm, she took the furnished room up there to try to hide from Farley, the crow that hung around the parking lot between the post office and the store, the crow that somebody had made into a pet because it was abandoned or because its mother was killed—she never knew what orphaned it. And now it had been abandoned for a second time and had taken to hanging out in that parking lot, where most everybody came and went during the course of the day. This crow created many problems in Seeley Falls because it started dive-bombing people coming into the post office, going after the bar-rettes in the little girls' hair and so on—as crows will because it is their nature to collect shiny things, bits of glass and stuff like that—and so the postmistress, in consultation with a few interested townsfolk, decided to take it to the Audubon Society, where it was caged and only sometimes let out to fly; it couldn't be set free be-cause in the wild a bird that likes to hang around a parking lot sim-ply will not fit in. That crow's voice. She remembers it at all hours, day or night, awake, sleeping, or insomniac. Had a strange voice. Not like the voice of other crows probably because it hadn't been raised with other crows. Right after the fire, I used to go and visit that crow at the Audubon Society, and whenever the visit was over and I would turn to leave, it would call me back with this voice. Yes, in a cage, but being what it was, it was better off that way. There were other birds in cages that people had brought in because they couldn't live in the wild anymore. There were a couple of little owls. Speckled things that looked like toys. I used to visit the owls too. And a pigeon hawk with a piercing cry. Nice birds. And then I moved down here and, alone as I was, am, I have gotten to know crows like never before. And them me. Their sense of humor. Is that what it is? Maybe it's not a sense of humor. But to me it looks like it is. The way they walk around. The way they tuck their heads. The way they scream at me if I don't have bread for them. Faunia, go get the bread. They strut. They boss the other birds around. On Saturday, after having the conversation with the redtail hawk down by Cumberland, I came home and I heard these two crows back in the orchards. I knew something was up. This alarming crow-calling. Sure enough, saw three birds—two crows crowing and cawing off this hawk. Maybe the very one I'd been talking to a few minutes before. Chasing it. Obviously the redtail was up to no good. But taking on a hawk? Is that a good idea? It wins them points with the other crows, but I don't know if I would do that. Can even *two* of them take on a hawk? Aggressive bastards. Mostly hostile. Good for them. Saw a photo once—a crow going right up to an eagle and barking at it. The eagle doesn't give a shit. Doesn't even see him. But the crow is something. The way it flies. They're not as pretty as ravens when ravens fly and do those wonderful, beautiful acrobatics. They've got a big fuselage to get off the ground and yet they don't need a running start necessarily. A few steps will do it. I've watched that. It's more just a huge effort. They make this huge effort and they're up. When I used to take the kids to eat at Friendly's. Four years ago. There were millions of them. The Friendly's on East Main Street in Blackwell. In the late afternoon. Before dark. Millions of them in the parking lot. The crow convention at Friendly's. What is it with crows and parking lots? What is that all about? We'll never know what that's about or anything else. Other birds are kind of dull next to crows. Yes, bluejays have that terrific bounce. The trampoline walk. That's good. But crows can do the bounce *and* the chesty thrust. Most impressive. Turning their heads from left to right, casing the joint. Oh, they're hot shit. They're the coolest. The caw. The noisy caw. Listen. Just listen. Oh, I love it. Staying in touch like that. The frantic call that means danger. I love that. Rush outside then. It can be 5 A.M., I don't care. The frantic call, rush outside, and you can expect the show to begin any minute. The other calls, I can't say I know what they mean. Maybe nothing. Sometimes it's a quick call. Sometimes it's throaty. Don't want to confuse it with the raven's call. Crows mate with crows and ravens with ravens. It's wonderful that they never get confused. Not to my knowledge anyway. Everybody who says they're ugly scavenger birds—and most everybody does—is nuts. I think they're beautiful. Oh, yes. Very beautiful. Their sleekness. Their shades. It's so so black in there you can see purple in there. Their heads. At the start of the beak that sprout of hairs, that mustache thing, those hairs coming forward from the feathers. Probably has a name. But the name doesn't matter. Never does. All that matters is that it's there. And nobody knows why. It's like everything else—just *there*. All their eyes are black. Everybody gets black eyes. Black claws. What is it like flying? Ravens will do the soaring, crows just seem to go where they're going. They don't just fly around as far as I can tell. Let the ravens soar. Let the ravens do the soaring. Let the ravens pile up the miles and break the records and get the prizes. The crows have to get from one place to another. They hear that I have bread, so they're here. They hear somebody down the road two miles has bread, so they're there. When I throw their bread out to them, there'll always be one who is the guard and another you can hear off in the distance, and they're signaling back and forth just to let everybody know what's going on. It's hard to believe in everybody's looking out for everybody else, but that's what it looks like. There's a wonderful story I never forgot that a friend of mine told me when I was a kid that her mother told her. There were these crows who were so smart that they had figured out how to take these nuts they had that they couldn't break open out to the highway, and they would watch the lights, the traffic lights, and they would know when the cars would take off—they were that intelligent that they knew what was going on with the lights—and they would place the nuts right in front of the tires so they'd be cracked open and as soon as the light would change they'd move down. I believed that back then. Believed everything back then. And now that I know them and nobody else, I believe it again. Me and the crows. That's the ticket. Stick to the crows and you've got it made. I hear they preen each other's feathers. Never seen that. Seen them close together and wonder what they're doing. But never seen them actually doing it. Don't even see them preen their own. But then, I'm next door to the roost, not in it. Wish I were. Would have preferred to be one. Oh, yes, absolutely. No two ways about that. Much prefer to be a crow. They don't have to worry about moving to get away from anybody or anything. They just move. They don't have to pack anything. They just go. When they get smashed by something, that's it, it's over. Tear a wing, it's over. Break a foot, it's over. A much better way than this. Maybe I'll come back as one. What was I before that I came back as *this?* I was a crow! Yes! I was one! And I said, "God, I wish I was that big-titted girl down there," and I got my wish, and now, Christ, do I want to go back to my crow status. My status crow. Good name for a crow. Status. Good name for anything black and big. Goes with the strut. Status. I noticed everything as a kid. I loved birds. Always stuck on crows and hawks and owls. Still see the owls at night, driving home from Coleman's place. I can't help it if I get out of the car to talk to them. Shouldn't. Should drive straight on home before that bastard kills me. What do crows think when they hear the other birds singing? They think it's stupid. It is. Cawing. That's the only thing. It doesn't look good for a bird that struts to sing a sweet little song. No, caw your head off. That's the fucking ticket—cawing your head off and frightened of nothing and in there eating everything that's dead. Gotta get a lot of road kill in a day if you want to fly like that. Don't bother to drag it off but eat it right on the road. Wait until the last minute when a car is coming, and then they get up and go but not so far that they can't hop right back and dig back in soon as it's passed. Eating in the middle of the road. Wonder what happens when the meat goes bad. Maybe it doesn't for them. Maybe that's what it means to be a scavenger. Them and the turkey vultures—that's their job. They take care of all of those things out in the woods and out in the road that we don't want anything to do with. No crow goes hungry in all this world. Never without a meal. If it rots, you don't see the crow run away. If there's death, they're there. Something's dead, they come by and get it. I like that. I like that a lot. Eat that raccoon no matter what. Wait for the truck to come crack open the spine and then go back in there and suck up all the good stuff it takes to lift that beautiful black carcass off the ground. Sure, they have their strange behavior. Like anything else. I've seen them up in those trees, gathered all together, talking all together, and *something's* going on. But what it is I'll never know. There's some powerful arrangement there. But I haven't the faintest idea whether they know what it is themselves. It could be as meaningless as everything else. I'll bet it isn't, though, and that it makes a million fucking times more sense than any fucking thing down here. Or doesn't it? Is it just a lot of stuff that looks like something else but isn't? Maybe it's all just a genetic tic. Or tock. Imagine if the crows were in charge. Would it be the same shit all over again? The thing about them is that they're all practicality. In their flight. In their talk. Even in their color. All that blackness. Nothing but blackness. Maybe I was one and maybe I wasn't. I think I sometimes believe that I already am one. Yes, been believing that on and off for months now. Why not? There are men who are locked up in women's bodies and women who are locked up in men's bodies, so why can't I be a crow locked up in this body? Yeah, and where is the doctor who is going to do what they do to let me out? Where do I go to get the surgery that will let me be what I am? Who do I talk to? Where do I go and what do I do and how the fuck do I get out?

I am a crow. I know it. I know it!

At the student union building, midway down the hill from North Hall, Coleman found a pay phone in the corridor across from the cafeteria where the Elderhostel students were having their lunch. He could see inside, through the double doorway, to the long dining tables where the couples were all mingling happily at lunch.

Jeff wasn't at home—it was about 10 A.M. in L.A., and Coleman got the answering machine, and so he searched his address book for the office number at the university, praying that Jeff wasn't off in class yet. What the father had to say to his eldest son had to be said immediately. The last time he'd called Jeff in a state anything like this was to tell him that Iris had died. "They killed her. They set out to kill me and they killed her." It was what he said to everyone, and not just in those first twenty-four hours. That was the beginning of the disintegration: everything requisitioned by rage. But this is the end of it. The end—there was the news he had for his son. And for himself. The end of the expulsion from the previous life. To be content with something less grandiose than self-banishment and the overwhelming challenge that is to one's strength. To live with one's failure in a modest fashion, organized once again as a rational being and blotting out the blight and the indignation. If unyielding, unyielding quietly. Peacefully. Dignified contemplation—that's the ticket, as Faunia liked to say. To live in a way that does not bring Philoctetes to mind. He does not have to live like a tragic character in his course. That the primal seems a solution is not news— it always does. Everything changes with desire. The answer to all that has been destroyed. But choosing to prolong the scandal by perpetuating the protest? My stupidity everywhere. My derangement everywhere. And the grossest sentimentality. Wistfully remembering back to Steena. Jokingly dancing with Nathan Zuckerman. Confiding in him. Reminiscing with him. Letting him listen. Sharpening the writer's sense of reality. Feeding that great opportunistic maw, a novelist's mind. Whatever catastrophe turns up, he transforms into writing. Catastrophe is cannon fodder for him. But what can *I* transform this into? I am stuck with it. As is. Sans language, shape, structure, meaning—sans the unities, the catharsis, sans everything. More of the untransformed unforeseen. And why would anyone want more? Yet the woman who is Faunia *is* the unforeseen. Intertwined orgasmically with the unforeseen, and convention unendurable. Upright principles unendurable. Contact with her body the only principle. Nothing more important than that. And the stamina of her sneer. Alien to the core. Contact with *that.* The obligation to subject my life to hers and its vagaries. Its vagrancy. Its truancy. Its strangeness. The delectation of this elemental eros. Take the hammer of Faunia to everything outlived, all the exalted justifications, and smash your way to freedom. Freedom from? From the stupid glory of being right. From the ridiculous quest for significance. From the never-ending campaign for legitimacy. The onslaught of freedom at seventy-one, the freedom to leave a lifetime behind—known also as Aschenbachian madness. "And before nightfall"—the final words of *Death in Venice*—"a shocked and respectful world received the news of his decease." No, he does not have to live like a tragic character in *any* course.

"Jeff! It's Dad. It's your father."

"Hi. How's it going?"

"Jeff, I know why I haven't heard from you, why I haven't heard from Michael. Mark I wouldn't expect to hear from—and Lisa hung up on me last time I called."

"She phoned me. She told me."

"Listen, Jeff—my affair with this woman is over."

"Is it? How come?"

He thinks, Because there's no hope for her. Because men have beaten the shit out of her. Because her kids have been killed in a fire. Because she works as a janitor. Because she has no education and says she can't read. Because she's been on the run since she's fourteen. Because she doesn't even ask me, "What are you doing with me?" Because she knows what *everybody* is doing with her. Because she's seen it all and there's no hope.

But all he says to his son is, "Because I don't want to lose my children."

With the gentlest laugh, Jeff said, "Try as you might, you couldn't do it. You certainly aren't able to lose me. I don't believe you were going to lose Mike or Lisa, either. Markie is something else. Markie yearns for something *none* of us can give him. Not just you—none of us. It's all very sad with Markie. But that we were losing *you*? That we've been losing you since Mother died and you resigned from the college? That is something we've all been living with. Dad, nobody has known what to do. Since you went on the warpath with the college, it hasn't been easy to get to you."

"I realize that," said Coleman, "I understand that," but two minutes into the conversation and it was already insufferable to him. His reasonable, supercompetent, easygoing son, the eldest, the coolest head of the lot, speaking calmly about the family problem with the father who *was* the problem was as awful to endure as his irrational youngest son being enraged with him and going nuts. The excessive demand he had made on their sympathy—on the sympathy of his own children! "I understand," Coleman said again, and that he understood made it all the worse.

"I hope nothing too awful happened with her," Jeff said.

"With her? No. I just decided that enough was enough." He was afraid to say more for fear that he might start to say something very different.

"That's good," Jeff said. "I'm terrifically relieved. That there've been no repercussions, if that's what you're saying. That's just great."

Repercussions?

"I don't follow you," Coleman said. "Why repercussions?"

"You're free and clear? You're yourself again? You sound more like yourself than you have for years. That you've called—this is all that matters. I was waiting and I was hoping and now you've called. There's nothing more to be said. You're back. That's all we were worried about."

"I'm lost, Jeff. Fill me in. I'm lost as to what we're going on about here. Repercussions from what?"

Jeff paused before he spoke again, and when he did speak, it was reluctantly. "The abortion. The suicide attempt."

"Faunia?"

"Right."

"Had an abortion? Tried to commit suicide? When?"

"Dad, everyone in Athena knew. That's how it got to us."

"Everyone? Who is everyone?"

"Look, Dad, there are no repercussions—"

"It never happened, my boy, that's why there are no 'repercussions.' *It never happened.* There was no abortion, there was no suicide attempt—not that I know of. And not that she knows of. But just who is this *everyone?* Goddamnit, you hear a story like that, a senseless story like that, why don't you pick up the phone, why don't you come to *me?*"

"Because it isn't my business to come to you. I don't come to a man your age—"

"No, you don't, do you? Instead, whatever you're told about a man my age, however ludicrous, however malicious and absurd, you believe."

"If I made a mistake, I am truly sorry. You're right. Of course you're right. But it's been a long haul for all of us. You've not been that easy to reach now for—"

"Who told this to you?"

"Lisa. Lisa heard it first."

"Who did Lisa hear it from?"

"Several sources. People. Friends."

"I want names. I want to know who this everyone *is.* Which friends?"

"Old friends. Athena friends."

"Her darling childhood friends. The offspring of my colleagues. Who told them, I wonder."

"There was no suicide attempt," Jeff said.

"No, Jeffrey, there wasn't. No abortion that I know of, either."

"Well, fine."

"And if there were? If I *had* impregnated this woman and she'd gone for an abortion and after the abortion had attempted suicide? Suppose, Jeff, she had even succeeded at suicide. Then what? *Then what, Jeff?* Your father's mistress kills herself. Then what? Turn on your father? Your criminal father? No, no, no—let's go back, back

up a step, back up to the suicide *attempt*. Oh, I like that. I do wonder who came up with the suicide *attempt*. Is it because of the abortion that she attempts this suicide? Let's get straight this melo-
drama that Lisa got from her Athena friends. Because she doesn't
want the abortion? Because the abortion is *imposed* on her? I see. I
see the cruelty. A mother who has lost two little children in a fire
turns up pregnant by her lover. Ecstasy. A new life. Another chance.
A new child to replace the dead ones. But the lover—*no,* says he,
and drags her by her hair to the abortionist, and then—of course—
having worked his will on her, takes the naked, bleeding body—"

By this time Jeff had hung up.

But by this time Coleman didn't need Jeff to keep on going. He
had only to see the Elderhostel couples inside the cafeteria finishing
their coffee before returning to class, he had only to hear them in
there at their ease and enjoying themselves, the appropriate elderly
looking as they should look and sounding as they should sound, for
him to think that even the conventional things that he'd done afforded him no relief. Not just having been a professor, not just having been a dean, not just having remained married, through everything, to the same formidable woman, but having a family, having
intelligent children—and it all afforded him nothing. If anybody's
children should be able to understand this, shouldn't his? All the
preschool. All the reading to them. The sets of encyclopedias. The
preparation before quizzes. The dialogues at dinner. The endless
instruction, from Iris, from him, in the multiform nature of life.
The scrutinization of language. All this stuff we did, and then to
come back at me with this mentality? After all the schooling and all
the books and all the words and all the superior SAT scores, it is in-
supportable. After all the taking them seriously. When they said
something foolish, engaging it seriously. All the attention paid to
the development of reason and of mind and of imaginative sympathy. And of skepticism, of well-informed skepticism. Of thinking
for oneself. And then to absorb the first rumor? All the education
and nothing helps. Nothing can insulate against the lowest level of

thought. Not even to ask themselves, "But does that sound like our father? Does that sound like him to me?" Instead, your father is an open-and-shut case. Never allowed to watch TV and you manifest the mentality of a soap opera. Allowed to read nothing but the Greeks or their equivalent and you make life into a Victorian soap opera. Answering your questions. Your every question. Never turning one aside. You ask about your grandparents, you ask who they were and I told you. They died, your grandparents, when I was young. Grandpa when I was in high school, Grandma when I was away in the navy. By the time I got back from the war, the landlord had long ago put everything out on the street. There was nothing left. The landlord told me he couldn't afford to blah blah, there was no rent coming in, and I could have killed the son of a bitch. Photo albums. Letters. Stuff from my childhood, from *their* childhood, all of it, everything, the whole thing, gone. "Where were they born? Where did they live?" They were born in Jersey. The first of their families born here. He was a saloon keeper. I believe that in Russia his father, your great-grandfather, worked in the tavern business. Sold booze to the Russkies. "Do we have aunts and uncles?" My father had a brother who went to California when I was a little kid, and my mother was an only child, like me. After me she couldn't have children—I never knew why that was. The brother, my father's older brother, remained a Silberzweig—he never took the changed name as far as I know. Jack Silberzweig. Born in the old country and so kept the name. When I was shipping out from San Francisco, I looked in all the California phone books to try to locate him. He was on the outs with my father. My father considered him a lazy bum, wanted nothing to do with him, and so nobody was sure what city Uncle Jack lived in. I looked in all the phone books. I was going to tell him that his brother had died. I wanted to meet him. My one living relative on that side. So what if he's a bum? I wanted to meet his children, my cousins, if there were any. I looked under Silberzweig. I looked under Silk. I looked under Silber. Maybe in California he'd become a Silber. I didn't know. And

I don't know. I have no idea. And then I stopped looking. When you don't have a family of your own, you concern yourself with these things. Then I had you and I stopped worrying about having an uncle and having cousins . . . Each kid heard the same thing. And the only one it didn't satisfy was Mark. The older boys didn't ask that much, but the twins were insistent. "Were there any twins in the past?" My understanding—I believe I was told this—was that there was either a great- or a great-great-grandfather who was a twin. This was the story he told Iris as well. All of it was invented for Iris. This was the story he told her on Sullivan Street when they first met and the story he stuck to, the original boilerplate. And the only one never satisfied was Mark. "Where did our great-grandparents come from?" Russia. "But what city?" I asked my father and mother, but they never seemed to know for sure. One time it was one place, one time another. There was a whole generation of Jews like that. They never really knew. The old people didn't talk about it much, and the American children weren't that curious, they were het up on being Americans, and so, in my family as in many families, there was a general Jewish geographical amnesia. All I got when I asked, Coleman told them, was the answer "Russia." But Markie said, "Russia is gigantic, Dad. *Where* in Russia?" Markie would not be still. And why? *Why?* There was no answer. Markie wanted the knowledge of who they were and where they came from—all that his father could never give him. And that's why he becomes the Orthodox Jew? That's why he writes the biblical protest poems? That's why Markie hates him so? Impossible. There were the Gittelmans. Gittelman grandparents. Gittelman aunts and uncles. Little Gittelman cousins all over Jersey. Wasn't that enough? How many relatives did he need? There had to be Silks and Silberzweigs too? That made no sense at all as a grievance—it could not be! Yet Coleman wondered anyway, irrational as it might be to associate Markie's brooding anger with his own secret. So long as Markie was at odds with him, he was never able to stop himself from wondering, and never more agonizingly than after Jeff had hung up the phone on

him. If the children who carried his origins in their genes and who
would pass those origins on to their own children could find it so
easy to suspect him of the worst kind of cruelty to Faunia, what explanation could there be? Because he could never tell them about
their family? Because he'd owed it to them to tell them? Because to
deny them such knowledge was wrong? That made no sense! Retribution was not unconsciously or unknowingly enacted. There was
no such quid pro quo. *It could not be.* And yet, after the phone
call—leaving the student union, leaving the campus, all the while
he was driving in tears back up the mountain—that was exactly
what it felt like.

And all the while he was driving home he was remembering the
time he'd almost told Iris. It was after the twins were born. The
family was now complete. They'd done it—he'd made it. With not
a sign of his secret on any of his kids, it was as though he had
been *delivered* from his secret. The exuberance that came of having
pulled it off brought him to the very brink of giving the whole
thing away. Yes, he would present his wife with the greatest gift he
possessed: he would tell the mother of his four children who their
father really was. He would tell Iris the truth. That was how excited
and relieved he was, how solid the earth felt beneath his feet after
she had their beautiful twins, and he took Jeff and Mikey to the
hospital to see their new brother and sister, and the most frightening apprehension of them all had been eradicated from his life.

But he never did give Iris that gift. He was saved from doing it—
or damned to leave it undone—because of the cataclysm that be-
fell a dear friend of hers, her closest associate on the art association board, a pretty, refined amateur watercolorist named Claudia
McChesney, whose husband, owner of the county's biggest building firm, turned out to have quite a stunning secret of his own: a
second family. For some eight years, Harvey McChesney had been
keeping a woman years younger than Claudia, a bookkeeper at a
chair factory over near the Taconic by whom he'd had two children,
little kids aged four and six, living in a small town just across the

Massachusetts line in New York State, whom he visited each week, whom he supported, whom he seemed to love, and whom nobody in the McChesneys' Athena household knew anything about until an anonymous phone call—probably from one of Harvey's building-trade rivals—revealed to Claudia and the three adolescent children just what McChesney was up to when he wasn't out on the job. Claudia collapsed that night, came completely apart and tried to slash her wrists, and it was Iris who, beginning at 3 A.M., with the help of a psychiatrist friend, organized the rescue operation that got Claudia installed before dawn in Austin Riggs, the Stockbridge psychiatric hospital. And it was Iris who, all the while she was nursing two newborns and mothering two preschool boys, visited the hospital every day, talking to Claudia, steadying her, reassuring her, bringing her potted plants to tend and art books to look at, even combing and braiding Claudia's hair, until, after five weeks—and as much a result of Iris's devotion as of the psychiatric program—Claudia returned home to begin to take the steps necessary to rid herself of the man who had caused all her misery.

In just days, Iris had got Claudia the name of a divorce lawyer up in Pittsfield and, with all the Silk kids, including the infants, strapped down in the back of the station wagon, she drove her friend to the lawyer's office to be absolutely certain that the separation arrangements were initiated and Claudia's deliverance from McChesney was under way. On the ride home that day, there'd been a lot of bucking up to do, but bucking people up was Iris's specialty, and she saw to it that Claudia's determination to right her life was not washed away by her residual fears.

"What a wretched thing to do to another person," Iris said. "Not the girlfriend. Bad enough, but that happens. And not the little children, not even that—not even the other woman's little boy and girl, painful and brutal as that would be for any wife to discover. No, it's the secret—that's what did it, Coleman. That's why Claudia doesn't want to go on living. 'Where's the intimacy?' That's what gets her crying every time. 'Where is the intimacy,' she says, 'when there is such a secret?' That he could hide this from her, that he *would* have gone on hiding it from her—that's what Claudia's defenseless against, and that's why she still wants to do herself in. She says to me, 'It's like discovering a corpse. Three corpses. Three human bodies hidden under our floor.'" "Yes," Coleman said, "it's like something out of the Greeks. Out of *The Bacchae*." "Worse," Iris said, "because it's not out of *The Bacchae*. It's out of Claudia's life."

When, after almost a year of outpatient therapy, Claudia had a rapprochement with her husband and he moved back into the Athena house and the McChesneys resumed life together as a family—when Harvey agreed to give up the other woman, if not his other children, to whom he swore to remain a responsible father— Claudia seemed no more eager than Iris to keep their friendship alive, and after Claudia resigned from the art association, the women no longer saw each other socially or at any of the organization meetings where Iris was generally kingpin.

Nor did Coleman go ahead—as his triumph dictated when the twins were born—to tell his wife *his* stunning secret. Saved, he thought, from the most childishly sentimental stunt he could ever have perpetrated. Suddenly to have begun to think the way a fool thinks: suddenly to think the best of everything and everyone, to shed entirely one's mistrust, one's caution, one's *self*-mistrust, to think that all one's difficulties have come to an end, that all complications have ceased to be, to forget not only where one is but how one has got there, to surrender the diligence, the discipline, the taking the measure of every last situation . . . As though the battle that is each person's singular battle could somehow be abjured, as though voluntarily one could pick up and leave off being one's self, the characteristic, the immutable self in whose behalf the battle is undertaken in the first place. The last of his children having been born perfectly white had all but driven him to taking what was strongest in him and wisest in him and tearing it to bits. Saved he was by the wisdom that says, "Don't do anything."

But even earlier, after the birth of their first child, he had done something almost equally stupid and sentimental. He was a young classics professor from Adelphi down at the University of Pennsylvania for a three-day conference on *The Iliad;* he had given a paper, he had made some contacts, he'd even been quietly invited by a renowned classicist to apply for a position opening at Princeton, and, on the way home, thinking himself at the pinnacle of existence, instead of heading north on the Jersey Turnpike, to get to Long Island, he had very nearly turned south and made his way down along the back roads of Salem and Cumberland counties to Gouldtown, to his mother's ancestral home where they used to hold the annual family picnic when he was a boy. Yes, then as well, having become a father, he was going to try to give himself the easy pleasure of one of those meaningful feelings that people will go in search of whenever they cease to think. But because he had a son didn't require him to turn south to Gouldtown any more than on that same journey, when he reached north Jersey, his having had this son required him to take the Newark exit and head toward East Orange. There was yet another impulse to be suppressed: the impulse he felt to see his mother, to tell her what had happened and to bring her the boy. The impulse, two years after jettisoning her, and despite Walter's warning, to show *himself* to his mother. No. Absolutely not. And instead he continued straight on home to his white wife and his white child.

And, some four decades later, all the while he was driving home from the college, besieged by recrimination, remembering some of the best moments of his life—the birth of his children, the exhilaration, the all-too-innocent excitement, the wild wavering of his resolve, the relief so great that it nearly *undid* his resolve—he was remembering also the worst night of his life, remembering back to his navy stint and the night he was thrown out of that Norfolk whorehouse, the famous white whorehouse called Oris's. "You're a black nigger, ain't you, boy?" and seconds later the bouncers had hurled him from the open front door, over the stairs to the sidewalk and into the street. The place he was looking for was Lulu's, over on Warwick Avenue—Lulu's, they shouted after him, was where his black ass belonged. His forehead struck the pavement, and yet he got himself up, ran until he saw an alleyway, and there cut away from the street and the Shore Patrol, who were all over the place on a Saturday, swinging their billy clubs. He wound up in the toilet of the only bar he dared to enter looking as battered as he did—a colored bar just a few hundred feet from Hampton Roads and the Newport News ferry (the ferry conveying the sailors to Lulu's) and some ten blocks from Oris's. It was his first colored bar since he was an East Orange schoolkid, back when he and a friend used to run the football pools out of Billy's Twilight Club down on the Newark line. During his first two years of high school, on top of the surreptitious boxing, he would be in and out of Billy's Twilight all through the fall, and it was there that he'd garnered the barroom lore he claimed to have learned—as an East Orange white kid—in a tavern owned by his Jewish old man.

He was remembering how he'd struggled to stanch his cut face and how he'd swabbed vainly away at his white jumper but how the blood dripped steadily down to spatter everything. The seatless bowl was coated with shit, the soggy plank floor awash with piss, the sink, if that thing was a sink, a swillish trough of sputum and puke—so that when the retching began because of the pain in his wrist, he threw up onto the wall he was facing rather than lower his face into all that filth.

It was a hideous, raucous dive, the worst, like no place he had ever seen, the most abominable he could have imagined, but he had to hide somewhere, and so, on a bench as far as he could get from the human wreckage swarming the bar, and in the clutches of all his fears, he tried to sip at a beer, to steady himself and dim the pain and to avoid drawing attention. Not that anyone at the bar had bothered looking his way after he'd bought the beer and disappeared against the wall back of the empty tables: just as at the white cathouse, nobody took him here for anything other than what he was.

He still knew, with the second beer, that he was where he should not be, yet if the Shore Patrol picked him up, if they discovered why he'd been thrown out of Oris's, he was ruined: a court-martial, a conviction, a long stretch at hard labor followed by a dishonorable discharge—and all for having lied to the navy about his race, all for having been stupid enough to step through a door where the only out-and-out Negroes on the premises were either laundering the linens or mopping up the slops.

This was it. He'd serve out his stint, do his time as a white man, and this would be it. Because I can't pull it off, he thought—I don't even want to. He'd never before known real disgrace. He'd never before known what it was to hide from the police. Never before had he bled from taking a blow—in all those rounds of amateur boxing he had not lost a drop of blood or been hurt or damaged in any way. But now the jumper of his whites was as red as a surgical dressing, his pants were soggy with caking blood and, from where he'd landed on his knees in the gutter, they were torn and dark with grime. And his wrist had been injured, maybe even shattered, from when he'd broken the fall with his hand—he couldn't move it or bear to touch it. He drank off the beer and then got another in order to try to deaden the pain.

This was what came of failing to fulfill his father's ideals, of flouting his father's commands, of deserting his dead father altogether. If only he'd done as his father had, as Walter had, everything would be happening another way. But first he had broken the law by lying to get into the navy, and now, out looking for a white woman to fuck, he had plunged into the worst possible disaster. "Let me get through to my discharge. Let me get out. Then I'll never lie again. Just let me finish my time, and that's it!" It was the first he'd spoken to his father since he'd dropped dead in the dining car.

If he kept this up, his life would amount to nothing. How did Coleman know that? Because his father was speaking back to him

—the old admonishing authority rumbling up once again from his father's chest, resonant as always with the unequivocal legitimacy of an upright man. If Coleman kept on like this, he'd end up in a ditch with his throat slit. Look at where he was now. Look where he had come to hide. And how? Why? Because of his credo, because of his insolent, arrogant "I am not one of you, I can't bear you, I am not part of your Negro we" credo. The great heroic struggle against their we—and look at what he now looked like! The passionate struggle for precious singularity, his revolt of one against the Negro fate—and just look where the defiant great one had ended up! Is this where you've come, Coleman, to seek the deeper meaning of existence? A world of love, that's what you had, and instead you forsake it for this! The tragic, reckless thing that you've done! And not just to yourself—to us all. To Ernestine. To Walt. To Mother. To me. To me in my grave. To my father in his. What else grandiose are you planning, Coleman Brutus? Whom next are you going to mislead and betray?

Still, he couldn't leave for the street because of his fear of the Shore Patrol, and of the court-martial, and of the brig, and of the dishonorable discharge that would hound him forever. Everything in him was too stirred up for him to do anything but keep on drinking until, of course, he was joined on the bench by a prostitute who was openly of his own race.

When the Shore Patrol found him in the morning, they attributed the bloody wounds and the broken wrist and the befouled, disheveled uniform to his having spent a night in niggertown, another swingin' white dick hot for black poon who—having got himself reamed, steamed, and dry-cleaned (as well as properly tattooed in the bargain)—had been deposited for the scavengers to pick over in that glass-strewn lot back of the ferry slip.

"U.S. Navy" is all the tattoo said, the words, no more than a quarter inch high, inscribed in blue pigment between the blue arms of a blue anchor, itself a couple inches long. A most unostentatious design as military tattoos go and, discreetly positioned just below the joining of the right arm to the shoulder, a tattoo certainly easy enough to hide. But when he remembered how he'd got it, it was the mark evocative not only of the turbulence of the worst night of his life but of all that underlay the turbulence—it was the sign of the whole of his history, of the indivisibility of the heroism and the disgrace. Embedded in that blue tattoo was a true and total image of himself. The ineradicable biography was there, as was the proto-type of the ineradicable, a tattoo being the very emblem of what cannot ever be removed. The enormous enterprise was also there. The outside forces were there. The whole chain of the unforeseen, all the dangers of exposure and all the dangers of concealment—even the senselessness of life was there in that stupid little blue tattoo.

His difficulties with Delphine Roux had begun the first semester he was back in the classroom, when one of his students who happened to be a favorite of Professor Roux's went to her, as department chair, to complain about the Euripides plays in Coleman's Greek tragedy course. One play was *Hippolytus,* the other *Alcestis;* the stu-dent, Elena Mitnick, found them "degrading to women."

"So what shall I do to accommodate Miss Mitnick? Strike Euripi-des from my reading list?"

"Not at all. Clearly everything depends on how you teach Euri-pides."

"And what," he asked, "is the prescribed method these days?" thinking even as he spoke that this was not a debate for which he had the patience or the civility. Besides, confounding Delphine Roux was easier *without* engaging in the debate. Brimming though she was with intellectual self-importance, she was twenty-nine years old and virtually without experience outside schools, new to her job and relatively new both to the college and to the country. He understood from their previous encounters that her attempt to appear to be not merely his superior but a supercilious superior— "Clearly everything depends" and so on—was best repulsed by displaying complete indifference to her judgment. For all that she could not bear him, she also couldn't bear that the academic credentials that so impressed other of her Athena colleagues hadn't yet overwhelmed the ex-dean. Despite herself, she could not escape from being intimidated by the man who, five years earlier, had reluctantly hired her fresh from the Yale graduate school and who, afterward, never denied regretting it, especially when the psychological numbskulls in his department settled on so deeply confused a young woman as their chair.

To this day, she continued to be disquieted by Coleman Silk's presence just to the degree that she wished for him now to be unsettled by her. Something about him always led her back to her childhood and the precocious child's fear that she is being seen through; also to the precocious child's fear that she is not being seen enough. Afraid of being exposed, dying to be seen—there's a dilemma for you. Something about him made her even second-guess her English, with which otherwise she felt wholly at ease. Whenever they were face to face, something made her think that he wanted nothing more than to tie her hands behind her back.

This something was what? The way he had sexually sized her up when she first came to be interviewed in his office, or the way he had failed to sexually size her up? It had been impossible to read his reading of her, and that on a morning when she knew she had maximally deployed all her powers. She had wanted to look terrific and she did, she had wanted to be fluent and she was, she had wanted to sound scholarly and she'd succeeded, she was sure. And yet he looked at her as if she were a schoolgirl, Mr. and Mrs. Inconsequential's little nobody child.

Now, perhaps that was because of the plaid kilt—the miniskirt-like kilt might have made him think of a schoolgirl's uniform, especially as the person wearing it was a trim, tiny, dark-haired young woman with a small face that was almost entirely eyes and who weighed, clothes and all, barely a hundred pounds. All she'd intended, with the kilt as with the black cashmere turtleneck, black

tights, and high black boots, was neither to desexualize herself by
what she chose to wear (the university women she'd met so far in
America seemed all too strenuously to be doing just that) nor to
appear to be trying to tantalize him. Though he was said to be in his
mid-sixties, he didn't look to be any older than her fifty-year-old
father; he in fact resembled a junior partner in her father's firm,
one of several of her father's engineering associates who'd been eye-
ing her since she was twelve. When, seated across from the dean, she
had crossed her legs and the flap of the kilt had fallen open, she had
waited a minute or two before pulling it closed—and pulling it
closed as perfunctorily as you close a wallet—only because, however young she looked, she *wasn't* a schoolgirl with a schoolgirl's
fears and a schoolgirl's primness, caged in by a schoolgirl's rules.
She did not wish to leave that impression any more than to give
the opposite impression by allowing the flap to remain open and
thereby inviting him to imagine that she meant him to gaze
throughout the interview at her slim thighs in the black tights.
She had tried as best she could, with the choice of clothing as
with her manner, to impress upon him the intricate interplay of *all*
the forces that came together to make her so interesting at twenty-
four.

Even her one piece of jewelry, the large ring she'd placed that
morning on the middle finger of her left hand, her sole decorative
ornament, had been selected for the sidelight it provided on the intellectual she was, one for whom enjoying the aesthetic surface of
life openly, nondefensively, with her appetite and connoisseurship
undisguised, was nonetheless subsumed by a lifelong devotion to
scholarly endeavor. The ring, an eighteenth-century copy of a Roman signet ring, was a man-sized ring formerly worn by a man. On
the oval agate, set horizontally—which was what made the ring so
masculinely chunky—was a carving of Danaë receiving Zeus as a
shower of gold. In Paris, four years earlier, when Delphine was
twenty, she had been given the ring as a love token from the professor to whom it belonged—the one professor whom she'd been unable to resist and with whom she'd had an impassioned affair. Co-

incidentally, he had been a classicist. The first time they met, in his office, he had seemed so remote, so judging, that she found herself paralyzed with fear until she realized that he was playing the seduction against the grain. Was that what this Dean Silk was up to?

However conspicuous the ring's size, the dean never did ask to see the shower of gold carved in agate, and that, she decided, was just as well. Though the story of how she'd come by the ring testified, if anything, to an audacious adultness, he would have thought the ring a frivolous indulgence, a sign that she *lacked* maturity. Except for the stray hope, she was sure that he was thinking about her along those lines from the moment they'd shaken hands—and she was right. Coleman's take on her was of someone too young for the job, incorporating too many as yet unresolved contradictions, at once a little too grand about herself and, simultaneously, playing at self-importance like a child, an imperfectly self-governed child, quick to respond to the scent of disapproval, with a considerable talent for being wounded, and drawn on, as both child *and* woman, to achievement upon achievement, admirer upon admirer, conquest upon conquest, as much by uncertainty as by confidence. Someone smart for her age, even too smart, but off the mark emotionally and seriously underdeveloped in most other ways.

From her c.v. and from a supplementary autobiographical essay of fifteen pages that accompanied it—which detailed the progress of an intellectual journey begun at age six—he got the picture clearly enough. Her credentials were indeed excellent, but everything about her (including the credentials) struck him as particularly wrong for a little place like Athena. Privileged 16th *arrondissement* childhood on the rue de Longchamp. Monsieur Roux an engineer, owner of a firm employing forty; Madame Roux (née de Walincourt) born with an ancient noble name, provincial aristocracy, wife, mother of three, scholar of medieval French literature, master harpsichordist, scholar of harpsichord literature, papal historian, "etc." And what a telling "etc." that was! Middle child and only daughter Delphine graduated from the Lycée Janson de Sailly, where she studied philosophy and literature, English and German, Latin, French literature: ". . . read the entire body of French literature in a very canonical way." After the Lycée Janson, Lycée Henri IV: ". . . grueling in-depth study of French literature and philosophy, English language and literary history." At twenty, after the Lycée Henri IV, the École Normale Supérieure de Fontenay: ". . . with the élite of French intellectual society . . . only thirty a year selected." Thesis: "Self-Denial in Georges Bataille." Bataille? Not another one. Every ultra-cool Yale graduate student is working on either Mallarmé or Bataille. It isn't difficult to understand what she intends for him to understand, especially as Coleman knows something of Paris from being a young professor with family on a Fulbright one year, and knows something about these ambitious French kids trained in the elite lycées. Extremely well prepared, intellectually well connected, very smart immature young people endowed with the most snobbish French education and vigorously preparing to be envied all their lives, they hang out every Saturday night at the cheap Vietnamese restaurant on rue St. Jacques talking about great things, never any mention of trivialities or small talk—ideas, politics, philosophy only. Even in their spare time, when they are all alone, they think only about the reception of Hegel in twentieth-century French intellectual life. The intellectual must not be frivolous. Life only about thought. Whether brainwashed to be aggressively Marxist or to be aggressively anti-Marxist, they are congenitally appalled by everything American. From this stuff and more she comes to Yale: applies to teach French language to undergraduates and to be incorporated into the Ph.D. program, and, as she notes in her autobiographical essay, she is but one of two from all of France who are accepted. "I arrived at Yale very Cartesian, and there everything was much more pluralistic and polyphonic." Amused by the undergraduates. Where's their intellectual side? Completely shocked by their having fun. Their chaotic, nonideological way of thinking—of living! They've never even seen a Kurosawa film—they don't know *that* much. By the time she was their age, she'd seen all the Kurosawas, all the Tarkovskys, all the Fellinis, all the Antonionis, all the Fassbinders, all the Wertmüllers, all the Satyajit Rays, all the René Clairs, all the Wim Wenderses, all the Truffauts, the Godards, the Chabrols, the Resnaises, the Rohmers, the Renoirs, and all these kids have seen is *Star Wars*. In earnest at Yale she resumes her intellectual mission, taking classes with the most hip professors. A bit lost, however. Confused. Especially by the other graduate students. She is used to being with people who speak the same intellectual language, and these Americans . . . And not everybody finds her that interesting. Expected to come to America and have everyone say, "Oh, my God, she's a *normalienne*." But in America no one appreciates the very special path she was on in France and its enormous prestige. She's not getting the type of recognition she was trained to get as a budding member of the French intellectual elite. She's not even getting the kind of resentment she was trained to get. Finds an adviser and writes her dissertation. Defends it. Is awarded the degree. Gets it extraordinarily rapidly because she had already worked so hard in France. So much schooling and hard work, ready now for the big job at the big school—Princeton, Columbia, Cornell, Chicago—and when she gets nothing, she is crushed. A visiting position at Athena College? Where and what is Athena College? She turns up her nose. Until her adviser says, "Delphine, in this market, you get your big job from another job. Visiting assistant professor at Athena College? *You* may not have heard of it, but we have. Perfectly decent institution. Perfectly decent job for a first job." Her fellow foreign graduate students tell her that she's too good for Athena College, it would be too déclassé, but her fellow American graduate students, who would kill for a job teaching in the Stop & Shop boiler room, think that her uppityness is characteristically Delphine. Begrudgingly, she applies—and winds up in her minikilt and boots across the desk from Dean Silk. To get the second job, the fancy job, she first needs this Athena job, but for nearly an hour Dean Silk listens to her all but talk her way out of the Athena job. Narrative structure and temporality. The internal contradictions of the work of art. Rousseau hides himself and then his rhetoric gives him away. (A little like her, thinks the dean, in that autobiographical essay.) The critic's voice is as legitimate as the voice of Herodotus. Narratology. The diegetic. The difference between diegesis and mimesis. The bracketed experience. The proleptic quality of the text. Coleman doesn't have to ask what all this means. He knows, in the original Greek meaning, what all the Yale words mean and what all the École Normale Supérieure words mean. Does she? As he's been at it for over three decades, he hasn't time for any of this stuff. He thinks: Why does someone so beautiful want to hide from the human dimension of her experience behind these words? Perhaps just because she is so beautiful. He thinks: So carefully self-appraising and so utterly deluded.

Of course she had the credentials. But to Coleman she embodied the sort of prestigious academic crap that the Athena students needed like a hole in the head but whose appeal to the faculty second-raters would prove irresistible.

At the time he thought that he was being open-minded by hiring her. But more likely it was because she was so goddamn enticing. So lovely. So alluring. And all the more so for looking so daughterly.

Delphine Roux had misread his gaze by thinking, a bit melodramatically—one of the impediments to her adroitness, this impulse not merely to leap to the melodramatic conclusion but to succumb erotically to the melodramatic spell—that what he wanted was to tie her hands behind her back: what he wanted, for every possible reason, was not to have her around. And so he'd hired her. And thus they seriously began not to get on.

And now it was she calling him to her office to be the interviewee. By 1995, the year that Coleman had stepped down from the deanship to return to teaching, the lure of petitely pretty Delphine's all-encompassing chic, with its gaminish intimations of a subterranean sensuality, along with the blandishments of her École Normale sophistication (what Coleman described as "her permanent act of self-inflation"), had appeared to him to have won over just about every wooable fool professor and, not yet out of her twenties—but with an eye perhaps on the deanship that had once been Coleman's—she succeeded to the chair of the smallish department that some dozen years earlier had absorbed, along with the other language departments, the old Classics Department in which Coleman had begun as an instructor. In the new Department of Languages and Literature there was a staff of eleven, one professor in Russian, one in Italian, one in Spanish, one in German, there was Delphine in French and Coleman Silk in classics, and there were five overworked adjuncts, fledgling instructors as well as a few local foreigners, teaching the elementary courses.

"Miss Mitnick's misreading of those two plays," he was telling her, "is so grounded in narrow, parochial ideological concerns that it does not lend itself to correction."

"Then you don't deny what she says—that you didn't try to help her."

"A student who tells me that I speak to her in 'engendered language' is beyond being assisted by me."

"Then," Delphine said lightly, "there's the problem, isn't it?"

He laughed—both spontaneously and for a purpose. "Yes? The English I speak is insufficiently nuanced for a mind as refined as Miss Mitnick's?"

"Coleman, you've been out of the classroom for a very long time."

"And you haven't been out of it ever. My dear," he said, deliberately, and with a deliberately irritating smile, "I've been reading and thinking about these plays all my life."

"But never from Elena's feminist perspective."

"Never even from Moses's Jewish perspective. Never even from the fashionable Nietzschean perspective about perspective."

"Coleman Silk, alone on the planet, has no perspective other than the purely disinterested literary perspective."

"Almost without exception, my dear"—again? why not?—"our students are abysmally ignorant. They've been incredibly badly educated. Their lives are intellectually barren. They arrive knowing nothing and most of them leave knowing nothing. Least of all do they know, when they show up in my class, how to read classical drama. Teaching at Athena, particularly in the 1990s, teaching what is far and away the dumbest generation in American history, is the same as walking up Broadway in Manhattan talking to yourself, except instead of the eighteen people who hear you in the street talking to yourself, they're all in the room. They know, like, *nothing*. After nearly forty years of dealing with such students—and Miss Mitnick is merely typical—I can tell you that a feminist perspective on Euripides is what they *least* need. Providing the most naive of readers with a feminist perspective on Euripides is one of the best ways you could devise to close down their thinking before it's even had a chance to begin to demolish a single one of their brainless 'likes.' I have trouble believing that an educated woman coming from a French academic background like your own believes there *is* a feminist perspective on Euripides that isn't simply foolishness. Have you really been edified in so short a time, or is this just old-fashioned careerism grounded right now in the fear of one's feminist colleagues? Because if it *is* just careerism, it's fine with me. It's human and I understand. But if it's an intellectual commitment to this idiocy, then I am mystified, because you are not an idiot. Because you know better. Because in France surely nobody from the École Normale would dream of taking this stuff seriously. Or would they? To read two plays like *Hippolytus* and *Alcestis,* then to listen to a week of classroom discussion on each, then to have nothing to say about either of them other than that they are 'degrading to women,' isn't a 'perspective,' for Christ's sake—it's mouthwash. It's just the latest mouthwash."

"Elena's a student. She's twenty years old. She's learning."

"Sentimentalizing one's students ill becomes you, my dear. Take them seriously. Elena's not learning. She's parroting. Why she ran directly to you is because it's more than likely you she's parroting."

"That is not true, though if it pleases you to culturally frame me like that, that is okay too, and entirely predictable. If you feel safely superior putting me in that silly frame, so be it, my dear," she delighted now in saying with a smile of her own. "Your treatment of

Elena was offensive to her. That was why she ran to me. You frightened her. She was upset."

"Well, I develop irritating personal mannerisms when I am confronting the consequences of my ever having hired someone like you."

"And," she replied, "some of our students develop irritating personal mannerisms when they are confronting fossilized pedagogy. If you persist in teaching literature in the tedious way you are used to, if you insist on the so-called humanist approach to Greek tragedy you've been taking since the 1950s, conflicts like this are going to arise continually."

"Good," he said. "Let them come." And walked out. And then that very next semester when Tracy Cummings ran to Professor Roux, close to tears, barely able to speak, baffled at having learned that, behind her back, Professor Silk had employed a malicious racial epithet to characterize her to her classmates, Delphine decided that asking Coleman to her office to discuss the charge could only be a waste of time. Since she was sure that he would behave no more graciously than he had the last time a female student had complained—and sure from past experience that should she call him in, he would once again condescend to her in his patronizing way, yet another upstart female daring to inquire into his conduct, yet another woman whose concerns he must trivialize should he deign even to address them—she had turned the matter over to the accessible dean of faculty who had succeeded him. From then on she was able to spend her time more usefully with Tracy, steadying, comforting, as good as taking charge of the girl, a parentless black youngster so badly demoralized that, in the first few weeks after the episode, to prevent her from picking up and running away— and running away to nothing—Delphine had gained permission to move her out of the dormitory into a spare room in her own apartment and to take her on, temporarily, as a kind of ward. Though by the end of the academic year, Coleman Silk, by removing himself from the faculty voluntarily, had essentially confessed to his malice in the spooks affair, the damage done Tracy proved too debilitating for someone so uncertain to begin with: unable to concentrate on her work because of the investigation and frightened of Professor Silk's prejudicing other teachers against her, she had failed all her courses. Tracy packed up not only to leave the college but to pull out of town altogether—out of Athena, where Delphine had been hoping to find her a job and get her tutored and keep an eye on her till she could get back into school. One day Tracy took a bus to Oklahoma, to stay with a half-sister in Tulsa, yet using the Tulsa address, Delphine had been unable to locate the girl ever again.

And then Delphine heard about Coleman Silk's relationship with Faunia Farley, which he was doing everything possible to hide. She couldn't believe it—two years into retirement, seventy-one years old, and the man was still at it. With no more female students who dared question his bias for him to intimidate, with no more young black girls needing nurturing for him to ridicule, with no more young women professors like herself threatening his hegemony for him to browbeat and insult, he had managed to dredge up, from the college's nethermost reaches, a candidate for subjugation who was the prototype of female helplessness: a full-fledged battered wife. When Delphine stopped by the personnel office to learn what she could about Faunia's background, when she read about the ex-husband and the horrifying death of the two small children—in a mysterious fire set, some suspected, *by* the ex-husband—when she read of the illiteracy that limited Faunia to performing only the most menial of janitorial tasks, she understood that Coleman Silk had managed to unearth no less than a misogynist's heart's desire: in Faunia Farley he had found someone more defenseless even than Elena or Tracy, the perfect woman to crush. For whoever at Athena had ever dared to affront his preposterous sense of prerogative, Faunia Farley would now be made to answer.

And no one to stop him, Delphine thought. No one to stand in his way.

With the realization that he was beyond the jurisdiction of the college and therefore restrained by nothing from taking his revenge on her—on *her,* yes, on her for everything she had done to prevent him from psychologically terrorizing his female students, on her for the role she had willingly played in having him stripped of authority and removed from the classroom—she was unable to contain her outrage. Faunia Farley was his substitute for her. Through Faunia Farley he was striking back at her. Who else's face and name and form does she suggest to you but mine—the mirror image of me, she could suggest to you no one else's. By luring a woman who is, as I am, employed by Athena College, who is, as I am, less than half your age—yet a woman otherwise my opposite in every way—you at once cleverly masquerade and flagrantly disclose just who it is you wish to destroy. You are not so unshrewd as not to know it, and, from your own august station, you are ruthless enough to enjoy it. But neither am I so stupid as not to recognize that it's me, in effigy, you are out to get.

Understanding had come so swiftly, in sentences so spontaneously explosive, that even as she signed her name at the bottom of the letter's second page and addressed an envelope to him in care of general delivery, she was still seething at the thought of the viciousness that could make of this dreadfully disadvantaged woman who had already lost everything a *toy,* that could capriciously turn a suffering human being like Faunia Farley into a plaything only so as to revenge himself on *her.* How could even *he* do this? No, she would not alter by one syllable what she'd written nor would she bother to type it up so as to make it easier for him to read. She refused to vitiate her message where it was graphically demonstrated by the propulsive, driven slant of her script. Let him not underestimate her resolve: nothing was now more important to her than exposing Coleman Silk for what he was.

But twenty minutes later she tore up the letter. And luckily. Luckily. When the unbridled idealism swept over her, she could not always see it as fantasy. Right she was to reprimand so reprehensible a predator. But to imagine saving a woman as far gone as Faunia Farley when she hadn't been able to rescue Tracy? To imagine prevailing against a man who, in his embittered old age, was free now not only of every institutional restraint but—humanist that he was!—of every humane consideration? For her there could be no greater delusion than believing herself a match for Coleman Silk's guile. Even a letter so clearly composed in the white heat of moral repulsion, a letter unmistakably informing him that his secret was out, that he was unmasked, exposed, tracked down, would some-how, in his hands, be twisted into an indictment with which to compromise *her* and, if the opportunity presented itself, to outright ruin her.

He was ruthless and he was paranoid, and whether she liked it or not, there were practical matters to take into account, concerns that might not have impeded her back when she was a Marxist-oriented lycée student whose inability to sanction injustice sometimes, ad-mittedly, overtook common sense. But now she was a college pro-fessor, awarded early tenure, already chairperson of her own de-partment, and all but certain of moving on someday to Princeton, to Columbia, to Cornell, to Chicago, perhaps even triumphantly back to Yale. A letter like this, signed by her and passed from hand to hand by Coleman Silk until, inevitably, it found its way to who-ever, out of envy, out of resentment, because she was just too damn successful too young, might wish to undermine her . . . Yes, bold as it was, with none of her fury censored out, this letter would be used by him to trivialize her, to contend that she lacked maturity and had no business being *anyone's* superior. He had connections, he knew people still—he could do it. He *would* do it, so falsify her meaning . . .

Quickly she tore the letter into tiny pieces and, at the center of a clean sheet of paper, with a red ballpoint pen of the kind she ordi-narily never used for correspondence and in big block letters that no one would recognize as hers, she wrote:

Everyone knows

But that was all. She stopped herself there. Three nights later, minutes after turning out the lights, she got up out of bed and, hav-ing come to her senses, went to her desk to crumple up and discard and forget forever the piece of paper beginning "Everyone knows" and instead, leaning over the desk, without even seating herself—fearing that in the time it took to sit down she would again lose her nerve—she wrote in a rush ten more words that would suffice to let him know that exposure was imminent. The envelope was addressed, stamped, the unsigned note sealed up inside it, the desk lamp flicked off, and Delphine, relieved at having decisively settled on the most telling thing to do within the practical limitations of her situation, was back in bed and morally primed to sleep untroubled.

But she had first to subdue everything driving her to get back up and tear open the envelope so as to reread what she'd written, to see if she had said too little or said it too feebly—or said it too stridently. Of course that wasn't her rhetoric. It couldn't be. That's why she'd used it—it was too blatant, too vulgar, far too sloganlike to be traced to her. But for that very reason, it was perhaps misjudged by her and unconvincing. She had to get up to see if she had remembered to disguise her handwriting—to see if, inadvertently, under the spell of the moment, in an angry flourish, she had forgotten herself and signed her name. She had to see if there was any way in which she had unthinkingly revealed who she was. And if she had? She *should* sign her name. Her whole life had been a battle not to be cowed by the Coleman Silks, who use their privilege to overpower everyone else and do exactly as they please. Speaking to men. Speaking *up* to men. Even to much older men. Learning not to be fearful of their presumed authority or their sage pretensions. Figuring out that her intelligence *did* matter. Daring to consider herself their equal. Learning, when she put forward an argument and it didn't work, to overcome the urge to capitulate, learning to summon up the logic and the confidence and the cool to *keep* arguing, no matter what they did or said to shut her up. Learning to take the second step, to sustain the effort instead of collapsing. Learning to argue her point *without backing down*. She didn't have to defer to him, she didn't have to defer to *anyone*. He was no longer the dean who had hired her. Nor was he department chair. She was. Dean

Silk was now nothing. She should indeed open that envelope to sign her name. He was nothing. It had all the comfort of a mantra: nothing.

She walked around with the sealed envelope in her purse for weeks, going over her reasons, not only to send it but to go ahead and sign it. He settles on this broken woman who cannot possibly fight back. Who cannot begin to compete with him. Who intellectually does not even exist. He settles on a woman who has never defended herself, who *cannot* defend herself, the weakest woman on this earth to take advantage of, drastically inferior to him in every possible way—and settles on her for the most transparent of antithetical motives: because he considers all women inferior and because he's frightened of any woman with a brain. Because I speak up for myself, because I will not be bullied, because I'm successful, because I'm attractive, because I'm independent-minded, because I have a first-rate education, a first-rate degree . . .

And then, down in New York, where she'd gone one Saturday to see the Jackson Pollock show, she pulled the envelope out of the purse and all but dropped the twelve-word letter, unsigned, into a mailbox in the Port Authority building, the first mailbox she saw after stepping from the Bonanza bus. It was still in her hand when she got on the subway, but once the train started moving she forgot about the letter, stuck it back in her bag, and let the meaningfulness of the subway take hold. She remained amazed and excited by the New York subway. When she was in the Métro in Paris she never thought about it, but the melancholic anguish of the people in the New York subway never failed to restore her belief in the rightness of her having come to America. The New York subway was the symbol of why she'd come—her refusal to shrink from reality.

The Pollock show emotionally so took possession of her that she felt, as she advanced from one stupendous painting to the next, something of that swelling, clamorous feeling that is the mania of lust. When a woman's cell phone suddenly went off while the whole

of the chaos of the painting entitled *Number 1A, 1948* was entering wildly into the space that previously that day—previously that
year—had been nothing more than her body, she was so furious
that she turned and exclaimed, "Madam, I'd like to strangle you!"

Then she went to the New York Public Library on Forty-second
Street. She always did this in New York. She went to the museums,
to the galleries, to concerts, she went to the movies that would
never make their way to the one dreadful theater in backwoods
Athena, and, in the end, no matter what specific things she'd come
to New York to do, she wound up for an hour or so reading whatever book she'd brought with her while sitting in the main reading
room of the library.

She reads. She looks around. She observes. She has little crushes
on the men there. In Paris she had seen the movie *Marathon Man* at
one of the festivals. (No one knows that at the movies she is a terrible sentimentalist and is often in tears.) In *Marathon Man*, the
character, the fake student, hangs out at the New York Public
Library and is picked up by Dustin Hoffman, and so it's in that romantic light that she has always thought of the New York Public
Library. So far no one has picked her up there, except for a medical
student who was too young, too raw, and immediately said the
wrong thing. Right off he had said something about her accent, and
she could not bear him. A boy who had not lived at all. He made
her feel like a grandmother. She had, by his age, been through so
many love affairs and so much thinking and rethinking, so many
levels of suffering—at twenty, years younger than him, she had already lived her big love story not once but twice. In part she had
come to America in *flight* from her love story (and, also, to make
her exit as a bit player in the long-running drama—entitled *Etc.*—
that was the almost criminally successful life of her mother). But
now she is extremely lonely in her plight to find a man to connect
with.

Others who try to pick her up sometimes say something acceptable enough, sometimes ironic enough or mischievous enough to

be charming, but then—because up close she is more beautiful than they had realized and, for one so petite, a little more arrogant than they may have expected—they get shy and back off. The ones who make eye contact with her are automatically the ones she doesn't like. And the ones who are lost in their books, who are charmingly oblivious and charmingly desirable, are . . . lost in their books. Whom is she looking for? She is looking for the man who is going to recognize *her*. She is looking for the Great Recognizer.

Today she is reading, in French, a book by Julia Kristeva, a treatise as wonderful as any ever written on melancholy, and across at the next table she sees a man reading, of all things, a book in French by Kristeva's husband, Philippe Sollers. Sollers is someone whose playfulness she refuses any longer to take seriously for all that she did at an earlier point in her intellectual development; the playful French writers, unlike the playful Eastern European writers like Kundera, no longer satisfy her . . . but that is not the issue at the New York Public Library. The issue is the coincidence, a coincidence that is almost sinister. In her craving, restless state, she launches into a thousand speculations about the man who is reading Sollers while she is reading Kristeva and feels the imminence not only of a pickup but of an affair. She knows that this dark-haired man of forty or forty-two has just the kind of gravitas that she cannot find in anyone at Athena. What she is able to surmise from the way he quietly sits and reads makes her increasingly hopeful that something is about to happen.

And something does: a girl comes by to meet him, decidedly a girl, someone younger even than she is, and the two of them go off together, and she gathers up her things and leaves the library and at the first mailbox she sees, she takes the letter from her purse—the letter she's been carrying there for over a month—and she thrusts it into the mailbox with something like the fury with which she told the woman at the Pollock show that she wanted to strangle her. There! It's gone! I did it! Good!

A full five seconds must pass before the magnitude of the blunder overwhelms her and she feels her knees weaken. "Oh, my God!" Even after her having left it unsigned, even after her having employed a vulgar rhetoric not her own, the letter's origins are going to be no mystery to someone as fixated on her as Coleman Silk.

Now he will *never* leave her alone.

4

What Maniac Conceived It?

I SAW COLEMAN ALIVE only one more time after that July. He himself never told me about the visit to the college or the phone call from the student union to his son Jeff. I learned of his having been on the campus that day because he'd been observed there—inadvertently, from an office window—by his former colleague Herb Keble, who, near the end of his speech at the funeral, alluded to seeing Coleman standing hidden back against the shadowed wall of North Hall, seemingly secreting himself for reasons that Keble only could guess at. I knew about the phone call because Jeff Silk, whom I spoke with after the funeral, mentioned something about it, enough for me to know that the call had gone wildly out of Coleman's control. It was directly from Nelson Primus that I learned of the visit that Coleman had made to the attorney's office earlier on the same day he'd phoned Jeff and that had ended, like the other call, with Coleman lashing out in vituperative disgust. After that, neither Primus nor Jeff Silk ever spoke to Coleman again. Coleman didn't return their calls or mine—turned out he didn't return anyone's—and then it seems he disconnected his answering machine, because soon enough the phone just rang on endlessly when I tried to reach him.

He was there alone in the house, however—he hadn't gone away. I knew he was there because, after a couple of weeks of phoning unsuccessfully, one Saturday evening early in August I drove by after dark to check. Only a few lamps were burning but, sure enough, when I pulled over beside Coleman's hugely branched ancient maples, cut my engine, and sat motionless in the car on the blacktop road down at the bottom of the undulating lawn, there was the dance music coming from the open windows of the black-shuttered, white clapboard house, the evening-long Saturday FM program that took him back to Steena Palsson and the basement room on Sullivan Street right after the war. He is in there now just with Faunia, each of them protecting the other against everyone else—each of them, to the other, *comprising* everyone else. There they dance, as likely as not unclothed, beyond the ordeal of the world, in an unearthly paradise of earthbound lust where their coupling is the drama into which they decant all the angry disappointment of their lives. I remembered something he'd told me Faunia had said in the afterglow of one of their evenings, when so much seemed to be passing between them. He'd said to her, "This is more than sex," and flatly she replied, "No, it's not. You just forgot what sex is. This is sex. All by itself. Don't fuck it up by pretending it's something else."

Who are they now? They are the simplest version possible of themselves. The essence of singularity. Everything painful congealed into passion. They may no longer even regret that things are not otherwise. They are too well entrenched in disgust for that. They are out from under everything ever piled on top of them. Nothing in life tempts them, nothing in life excites them, nothing in life subdues their hatred of life anything like this intimacy. Who are these drastically unalike people, so incongruously allied at seventy-one and thirty-four? They are the disaster to which they are enjoined. To the beat of Tommy Dorsey's band and the gentle crooning of young Sinatra, dancing their way stark naked right into a violent death. Everyone on earth does the end differently: this is

how the two of them work it out. There is now no way they will
stop themselves in time. It's done.

I am not alone in listening to the music from the road.

When my calls were not returned, I assumed that Coleman wished
to have nothing more to do with me. Something had gone wrong,
and I assumed, as one does when a friendship ends abruptly—a
new friendship particularly—that I was responsible, if not for some
indiscreet word or deed that had deeply irritated or offended him,
then by being who and what I am. Coleman had first come to me,
remember, because, unrealistically, he hoped to persuade me to
write the book explaining how the college had killed his wife; per-
mitting this same writer to nose around in his private life was probably the last thing he now wanted. I didn't know what to conclude
other than that his concealing from me the details of his life with
Faunia had, for whatever reason, come to seem to him far wiser
than his continuing to confide in me.

Of course I knew nothing then of the truth of his origins—that,
too, I'd learn about conclusively at the funeral—and so I couldn't
begin to surmise that the reason we'd never met in the years before
Iris's death, the reason that he'd wanted *not* to meet, was because I
had myself grown up only a few miles from East Orange and because, having more than a run-of-the-mill familiarity with the region, I might be too knowledgeable or too curious to leave his roots
in Jersey unscrutinized. Suppose I turned out to have been one
of the Newark Jewish boys in Doc Chizner's after-school boxing
classes? The fact is that I *was* one, but not until '46 and '47, by
which time Silky was no longer helping Doc teach kids like me the
right way to stand and move and throw a punch but was at NYU on
the GI Bill.

The fact is that, having befriended me during the time he was
writing his draft of *Spooks,* he had indeed taken the risk, and a foolish one at that, of being exposed, nearly six decades on, as East
Orange High's Negro valedictorian, the colored kid who'd boxed
around Jersey in amateur bouts out of the Morton Street Boys Club

before entering the navy as a white man; dropping me in the middle of that summer made sense for every possible reason, even if I had no way of imagining why.

Well, to the last time I saw him. One August Saturday, out of loneliness, I drove over to Tanglewood to hear the open rehearsal of the next day's concert program. A week after having parked down from his house, I was still both missing Coleman and missing the experience of having an intimate friend, and so I thought to make myself a part of that smallish Saturday-morning audience that fills about a quarter of the Music Shed for these rehearsals, an audience of summer folks who are music lovers and of visiting music students, but mainly of elderly tourists, people with hearing aids and people carrying binoculars and people paging through the *New York Times* who'd been bused to the Berkshires for the day.

Maybe it was the oddness born of my being out and about that did it, the momentary experience of being a sociable creature (or a creature feigning sociability), or maybe it was because of a fleeting notion I had of the elderly congregated together in the audience as embarkees, as deportees, waiting to be floated away on the music's buoyancy from the all-too-tangible enclosure of old age, but on this breezy, sunny Saturday in the last summer of Coleman Silk's life, the Music Shed kept reminding me of the open-sided piers that once extended cavernously out over the Hudson, as though one of those spacious, steel-raftered piers dating from when ocean liners docked in Manhattan had been raised from the water in all its hugeness and rocketed north a hundred and twenty miles, set down intact on the spacious Tanglewood lawn, a perfect landing amid the tall trees and sweeping views of mountainous New England.

As I made my way to a single empty seat that I spotted, one of the few empty seats close to the stage that nobody had as yet designated as reserved by slinging a sweater or a jacket across it, I kept thinking that we were all going somewhere together, had in fact gone and gotten there, leaving everything behind . . . when all we were doing was readying ourselves to hear the Boston Symphony rehearse

Rachmaninoff, Prokofiev, and Rimsky-Korsakov. Underfoot at the Music Shed there's a packed brown earth floor that couldn't make it clearer that your chair's aground on terra firma; roosting at the peak of the structure are the birds whose tweeting you hear in the weighty silence between orchestral movements, the swallows and wrens that wing busily in from the woods down the hill and then go zipping off again in a way no bird would have dared cut loose from Noah's floating Ark. We were about a three-hour drive west of the Atlantic, but I couldn't shake this dual sense of both being where I was and of having pushed off, along with the rest of the senior citizens, for a mysterious watery unknown.

Was it merely death that was on my mind in thinking of this debarkation? Death and myself? Death and Coleman? Or was it death and an assemblage of people able still to find pleasure in being bused about like a bunch of campers on a summer outing, and yet, as a palpable human multitude, an entity of sensate flesh and warm red blood, separated from oblivion by the thinnest, most fragile layer of life?

The program that preceded the rehearsal was just ending when I arrived. A lively lecturer dressed in a sport shirt and khaki trousers stood before the empty orchestra chairs introducing the audience to the last of the pieces they'd be hearing—on a tape machine playing for them bits of Rachmaninoff and speaking brightly of "the dark, rhythmic quality" of the *Symphonic Dances*. Only when he'd finished and the audience broke into applause did somebody emerge from the wings to uncover the timpani and begin to set out the sheet music on the music stands. At the far side of the stage, a couple of stagehands appeared carrying the harps, and then the musicians entered, chatting with one another as they drifted on, all of them, like the lecturer, casually dressed for the rehearsal—an oboist in a gray hooded sweatshirt, a couple of bass players wearing faded Levi's, and then the fiddle players, men and women alike outfitted, from the look of it, by Banana Republic. As the conductor was slipping on his glasses—a guest conductor, Sergiu Commissiona, an aged Romanian in a turtleneck shirt, white bush of hair up top, blue espadrilles below—and the childishly courteous audience once again began to applaud, I noticed Coleman and Faunia walking down the aisle, looking for a place close-up to sit.

The musicians, about to undergo their transformation from a bunch of seemingly untroubled vacationers into a powerful, fluid music machine, had already settled in and were tuning up as the couple—the tall, gaunt-faced blond woman and the slender, handsome, gray-haired man not so tall as she and much older, though still walking his light-footed athletic walk—made their way to two empty seats three rows down from me and off to my right some twenty feet.

The piece by Rimsky-Korsakov was a tuneful fairy tale of oboes and flutes whose sweetness the audience found irresistible, and when the orchestra came to the end of their first go-round enthusiastic applause again poured forth like an upsurge of innocence from the elderly crowd. The musicians had indeed laid bare the youngest, most innocent of our ideas of life, the indestructible yearning for the way things aren't and can never be. Or so I thought as I turned my gaze toward my former friend and his mistress and found them looking nothing like so unusual or humanly isolated as I'd been coming to envision the pair of them since Coleman had dropped out of sight. They looked nothing like immoderate people, least of all Faunia, whose sculpted Yankee features made me think of a narrow room with windows in it but no door. Nothing about these two seemed at odds with life or on the attack—or on the defensive, either. Perhaps by herself, in this unfamiliar environment, Faunia mightn't have been so at ease as she seemed, but with Coleman at her side, her affinity for the setting appeared no less natural than the affinity for him. They didn't look like a pair of desperadoes sitting there together but rather like a couple who had achieved their own supremely concentrated serenity, who took no notice whatsoever of the feelings and fantasies that their presence might foment anywhere in the world, let alone in Berkshire County.

I wondered if Coleman had coached her beforehand on how he

wanted her to behave. I wondered if she'd listen if he had. I wondered if coaching was necessary. I wondered why he'd chosen to bring her to Tanglewood. Simply because he wanted to hear the music? Because he wanted her to hear it and to see the live musicians? Under the auspices of Aphrodite, in the guise of Pygmalion, and in the environs of Tanglewood, was the retired classics professor now bringing recalcitrant, transgressive Faunia to life as a tastefully civilized Galatea? Was Coleman embarked on educating her, on influencing her—embarked on saving her from the tragedy of her strangeness? Was Tanglewood a first big step toward making of their waywardness something less unorthodox? Why so soon? Why at all? Why, when everything they had and were together had evolved out of the subterranean and the clandestinely crude? Why bother to normalize or regularize this alliance, why even attempt to, by going around as a "couple"? Since the publicness will tend only to erode the intensity, is this, in fact, what they truly want? What *he* wants? Was *taming* essential now to their lives, or did their being here have no such meaning? Was this some joke they were playing, an act designed to agitate, a deliberate provocation? Were they smiling to themselves, these carnal beasts, or merely there listening to the music?

Since they didn't get up to stretch or stroll around while the orchestra took a break and a piano was rolled onto the stage—for Prokofiev's Second Piano Concerto—I remained in place as well. There was a bit of a chill inside the shed, more of an autumnal than a summery coolness, though the sunlight, spread brilliantly across the great lawn, was warming those who preferred to listen and enjoy themselves from outside, a mostly younger audience of twenty-ish couples and mothers holding small children and picnicking families already breaking out the lunch from their hampers. Three rows down from me, Coleman, his head tipped slightly toward hers, was talking to Faunia quietly, seriously, but about what, of course, I did not know.

Because we don't know, do we? *Everyone knows* . . . How what happens the way it does? What underlies the anarchy of the train of events, the uncertainties, the mishaps, the disunity, the shocking ir-regularities that define human affairs? *Nobody* knows, Professor Roux. "Everyone knows" is the invocation of the cliché and the be-ginning of the banalization of experience, and it's the solemnity and the sense of authority that people have in voicing the cliché that's so insufferable. What we know is that, in an unclichéd way, nobody knows anything. You *can't* know anything. The things you *know* you don't know. Intention? Motive? Consequence? Meaning? All that we don't know is astonishing. Even more astonishing is what passes for knowing.

As the audience filed back in, I began, cartoonishly, to envisage the fatal malady that, without anyone's recognizing it, was working away inside us, within each and every one of us: to visualize the blood vessels occluding under the baseball caps, the malignancies growing beneath the permed white hair, the organs misfiring, atro-phying, shutting down, the hundreds of billions of murderous cells surreptitiously marching this entire audience toward the improba-ble disaster ahead. I couldn't stop myself. The stupendous decima-tion that is death sweeping us all away. Orchestra, audience, con-ductor, technicians, swallows, wrens—think of the numbers for Tanglewood alone just between now and the year 4000. Then mul-tiply that times everything. The ceaseless perishing. What an idea! What maniac conceived it? And yet what a lovely day it is today, a gift of a day, a perfect day lacking nothing in a Massachusetts vaca-tion spot that is itself as harmless and pretty as any on earth.

Then Bronfman appears. Bronfman the brontosaur! Mr. Fortis-simo! Enter Bronfman to play Prokofiev at such a pace and with such bravado as to knock my morbidity clear out of the ring. He is conspicuously massive through the upper torso, a force of nature camouflaged in a sweatshirt, somebody who has strolled into the Music Shed out of a circus where he is the strongman and who takes on the piano as a ridiculous challenge to the gargantuan strength he revels in. Yefim Bronfman looks less like the person who is going to play the piano than like the guy who should be moving it. I had never before seen anybody go at a piano like this sturdy little barrel of an unshaven Russian Jew. When he's finished, I thought, they'll have to throw the thing out. He crushes it. He doesn't let that piano conceal a thing. Whatever's in there is going to come out, and come out with its hands in the air. And when it does, everything there out in the open, the last of the last pulsation, he himself gets up and goes, leaving behind him our redemption. With a jaunty wave, he is suddenly gone, and though he takes all his fire off with him like no less a force than Prometheus, our own lives now seem inextinguishable. Nobody is dying, *nobody*—not if Bronfman has anything to say about it!

There was another break in the rehearsal, and when Faunia and Coleman got up this time, to leave the shed, so did I. I waited for them to precede me, not sure how to approach Coleman or—since it seemed that he no longer had any more use for me than for anyone else hereabouts—whether to approach him at all. Yet I did miss him. And what had I done? That yearning for a friend came to the surface just as it had when we'd first met, and once again, because of a magnetism in Coleman, an allure that I could never quite specify, I found no efficient way of putting it down.

I watched from some ten feet behind as they moved in a shuffling cluster of people slowly up the incline of the aisle toward the sunlit lawn, Coleman talking quietly to Faunia again, his hand between her shoulder blades, the palm of his hand against her spine guiding her along as he explained whatever he was now explaining about whatever it was she did not know. Once outside, they set off across the lawn, presumably toward the main gate and the dirt field beyond that was the parking lot, and I made no attempt to follow. When I happened to look back toward the shed, I could see inside, under the lights on the stage, that the eight beautiful bass fiddles were in a neat row where the musicians, before going off to take a break, had left them resting on their sides. Why this too should remind me of the death of all of us I could not fathom. A graveyard of horizontal instruments? Couldn't they more cheerily have put me in mind of a pod of whales?

I was standing on the lawn stretching myself, taking the warmth of the sun on my back for another few seconds before returning to my seat to hear the Rachmaninoff, when I saw them returning— apparently they'd left the vicinity of the shed only to walk the grounds, perhaps for Coleman to show her the views off to the south—and now they were headed back to hear the orchestra conclude its open rehearsal with the *Symphonic Dances*. To learn what I could learn, I decided then to head directly toward them for all that they still looked like people whose business was entirely their own. Waving at Coleman, waving and saying "Hello, there. Coleman, hello," I blocked their way.

"I thought I saw you," Coleman said, and though I didn't believe him, I thought, What better to say to put her at her ease? To put me at my ease. To put himself at his. Without a trace of anything but the easygoing, hard-nosed dean-of-faculty charm, seemingly irritated not at all by my sudden appearance, Coleman said, "Mr. Bronfman's something. I was telling Faunia that he took ten years at least out of that piano."

"I was thinking along those lines myself."

"This is Faunia Farley," he said to me, and to her, "This is Nathan Zuckerman. You two met out at the farm."

Closer to my height than to his. Lean and austere. Little, if anything, to be learned from the eyes. Decidedly uneloquent face. Sensuality? Nil. Nowhere to be seen. Outside the milking parlor, everything alluring shut down. She had managed to make herself so that *she* wasn't even here to be seen. The skill of an animal, whether predator or prey.

She wore faded jeans and a pair of moccasins—as did Coleman—and, with the sleeves rolled up, an old button-down tattersall shirt that I recognized as one of his.

"I've missed you," I said to him. "Maybe I can take you two to dinner some night."

"Good idea. Yes. Let's do that."

Faunia was no longer paying attention. She was looking off into the tops of the trees. They were swaying in the wind, but she was watching them as though they were speaking. I realized then that she was quite lacking in something, and I didn't mean the capacity to attend to small talk. What I meant I would have named if I could. It wasn't intelligence. It wasn't poise. It wasn't decorum or decency—she could pull off that ploy easily enough. It wasn't depth —shallowness wasn't the problem. It wasn't inwardness—one saw that inwardly she was dealing with plenty. It wasn't sanity—she was sane and, in a slightly sheepish way, haughty-seeming as well, superior through the authority of her suffering. Yet a piece of her was decidedly not there.

I noticed a ring on the middle finger of her right hand. The stone was milky white. An opal. I was sure that he had given it to her.

By contrast to Faunia, Coleman was very much of a piece, or appeared so. Glibly so. I knew he had no intention of taking Faunia out to dinner with me or anyone else.

"The Madamaska Inn," I said. "Eat outside. How about it?"

Never had I seen Coleman any more courtly than when he said to me, lying, "The inn—right. We must. We will. But let us take you. Nathan, let's speak," he said, suddenly in a rush and grabbing at Faunia's hand. Motioning with his head toward the Music Shed, he said, "I want Faunia to hear the Rachmaninoff." And they were gone, the lovers, "fled away," as Keats wrote, "into the storm."

In barely a couple of minutes so much had happened, or seemed to have happened—for nothing of any importance had actually occurred—that instead of returning to my seat, I began to wander about, like a sleepwalker at first, aimlessly heading across the lawn dotted with picnickers and halfway around the Music Shed, then doubling back to where the view of the Berkshires at the height of summer is about as good as views get east of the Rockies. I could hear in the distance the Rachmaninoff dances coming from the shed, but otherwise I might have been off on my own, deep in the fold of those green hills. I sat on the grass, astonished, unable to account for what I was thinking: he has a secret. This man constructed along the most convincing, believable emotional lines, this force with a history as a force, this benignly wily, smoothly charm-

ing, seeming totality of a manly man nonetheless has a gigantic secret. How do I reach this conclusion? Why a secret? Because it is
there when he's with her. And when he's not with her it's there
too—it's the secret that's his magnetism. It's something *not* there
that beguiles, and it's what's been drawing me all along, the enigmatic *it* that he holds apart as his and no one else's. He's set himself
up like the moon to be only half visible. And I cannot make him
fully visible. There is a blank. That's all I can say. They are, together,
a *pair* of blanks. There's a blank in her and, despite his air of being
someone firmly established, if need be an obstinate and purposeful
opponent—the angry faculty giant who quit rather than take their
humiliating crap—somewhere there's a blank in him too, a blotting
out, an excision, though of what I can't begin to guess . . . can't even
know, really, if I am making sense with this hunch or fancifully reg-
istering my ignorance of another human being.

Only some three months later, when I learned the secret and began this book—the book he had asked me to write in the first place,
but written not necessarily as he wanted it—did I understand the
underpinning of the pact between them: he had told her his whole
story. Faunia alone knew how Coleman Silk had come about being
himself. How do I know she knew? I don't. I couldn't know that either. I can't know. Now that they're dead, nobody can know. For
better or worse, I can only do what everyone does who thinks that
they know. I imagine. I am forced to imagine. It happens to be what
I do for a living. It is my job. It's now all I do.

After Les got out of the VA hospital and hooked up with his support group so as to stay off the booze and not go haywire, the long-
range goal set for him by Louie Borrero was for Les to make a pil-
grimage to the Wall—if not to the real Wall, the Vietnam Veterans
Memorial in Washington, then to the Moving Wall when it arrived
in Pittsfield in November. Washington, D.C., was a city Les had
sworn he would never set foot in because of his hatred of the government and, since '92, because of his contempt for that draft

dodger sleeping in the White House. To get him to travel all the way down to Washington from Massachusetts was probably asking too much anyway: for someone still fresh from the hospital, there would be too much emotion stretched over too many hours of coming and going on the bus.

The way to prepare Les for the Moving Wall was the same way Louie prepared everybody: start him off in a Chinese restaurant, get Les to go along with another four or five guys for a Chinese dinner, arrange as many trips as it took—two, three, seven, twelve, fifteen if need be—until he was able to last out one complete dinner, to eat all the courses, from soup to dessert, without sweating through his shirt, without trembling so bad he couldn't hold still enough to spoon his soup, without running outside every five minutes to breathe, without ending up vomiting in the bathroom and hiding inside the locked stall, without, of course, losing it completely and going ballistic with the Chinese waiter.

Louie Borrero had his hundred percent service connection, he'd been off drugs and on his meds now for twelve years, and helping veterans, he said, was how he got his therapy. Thirty-odd years on, there were a lot of Vietnam veterans still out there hurting, and so he spent just about all day every day driving around the state in his van, heading up support groups for veterans and their families, finding them doctors, getting them to AA meetings, listening to all sorts of troubles, domestic, psychiatric, financial, advising on VA problems, and trying to get the guys down to Washington to the Wall.

The Wall was Louie's baby. He organized everything: chartered the buses, arranged for the food, with his gift for gentle camaraderie took personal care of the guys terrified they were going to cry too hard or feel too sick or have a heart attack and die. Beforehand they all backed off by saying more or less the same thing: "No way. I can't go to the Wall. I can't go down there and see so-and-so's name. No way. No how. Can't do it." Les, for one, had told Louie, "I heard about your trip that last time. I heard all about how bad it went.

Twenty-five dollars a head for this charter bus. Supposed to include lunch, and the guys all say the lunch was shit—wasn't worth *two* bucks. And that New York guy didn't want to wait around, the driver. Right, Lou? Wanted to get back early to do a run to Atlantic City? Atlantic City! Fuck that shit, man. Rushin' everything and everybody and then lookin' for a big tip at the end? Not me, Lou. No fuckin' way. If I had to see a couple of guys in tiger suits falling into each other's arms and sobbin', I'd puke."

But Louie knew what a visit could mean. "Les, it's nineteen hundred and ninety-eight. It's the end of the twentieth century, Lester. It's time you started to face this thing. You can't do it all at once, I know that, and nobody is going to ask you to. But it's time to work your program, buddy. The time has *come*. We're not gonna start with the Wall. We're gonna start slow. We're gonna start off with a Chinese restaurant."

But for Les that wasn't starting slow; for Les, just going for the take-out down in Athena, he'd had to wait in the truck while Faunia picked up the food. If he went inside, he'd want to kill the gooks as soon as he saw them. "But they're Chinese," Faunia told him, "not Vietnamese." "Asshole! I don't care *what* the fuck they are! They count as gooks! A gook is a gook!"

As if he hadn't slept badly enough for the last twenty-six years, the week before the visit to the Chinese restaurant he didn't sleep at all. He must have telephoned Louie fifty times telling him he couldn't go, and easily half the calls were placed after 3 A.M. But Louie listened no matter what the hour, let him say everything on his mind, even agreed with him, patiently muttered "Uh-huh . . . uh-huh . . . uh-huh" right on through, but in the end he always shut him down the same way: "You're going to sit there, Les, as best you can. That's all you have to do. Whatever gets going in you, if it's sadness, if it's anger, whatever it is—the hatred, the rage—we're all going to be there with you, and you're going to try to sit there without running or doing anything." "But the *waiter*," Les would say, "how am I going to deal with the fucking waiter? I can't, Lou—I'll fuckin' lose it!" "I'll deal with the waiter. All you have to do is sit." To whatever objection Les raised, including the danger that he might kill the waiter, Louie replied that all he'd have to do was sit. As if that was all it took—sitting—to stop a man from killing his worst enemy.

They were five in Louie's van when they went up to Blackwell one evening barely two weeks after Les's release from the hospital. There was the mother-father-brother-leader, Louie, a bald guy, clean-shaven, neatly dressed, wearing freshly pressed clothes and his black Vietnam Vet cap and carrying his cane, and, what with his short stature, sloping shoulders, and high paunch, looking a little like a penguin because of the stiff way he walked on his bad legs. Then there were the big guys who never said much: Chet, the thrice-divorced housepainter who'd been a marine—three different wives scared out of their wits by this brute-sized, opaque, pony-tailed lug without any desire ever to speak—and Bobcat, an ex-rifleman who'd lost a foot to a land mine and worked for Midas Muffler. Last, there was an undernourished oddball, a skinny, twitchy asthmatic missing most of his molars, who called himself Swift, having legally changed his name after his discharge, as though his no longer being Joe Brown or Bill Green or whoever he was when he was drafted would cause him, back home, to leap out of bed every morning with joy. Since Vietnam, Swift's health had been close to destroyed by every variety of skin and respiratory and neurological ailment, and now he was being eaten away by an antagonism toward the Gulf War vets that exceeded even Les's disdain. All the way up to Blackwell, with Les already beginning to shake and feel queasy, Swift more than made up for the silence of the big guys. That wheezing voice of his would not stop. "Their biggest problem is they can't go to the beach? They get upset at the beach when they see the sand? Shit. Weekend warriors and all of a sudden they have to see some real action. That's why they're pissed off—all in the reserves, never thought they were going to be called up, and then they get called up. And they didn't do *dick*. They don't know what war *is*. Call that a war? Four-day ground war? How many gooks did *they* kill? They're all upset they didn't take out

Saddam Hussein. They got one enemy—Saddam Hussein. Gimme a break. There's nothin' wrong with these guys. They just want money without puttin' in the hard time. A rash. You know how many rashes I got from Agent Orange? I'm not goin' to live to see sixty, and these guys are worryin' about a rash!"

The Chinese restaurant sat up at the north edge of Blackwell, on the highway just beyond the boarded-up paper mill and backing onto the river. The concrete-block building was low and long and pink, with a plate-glass window at the front, and half of it was painted to look like brickwork—pink brickwork. Years ago it had been a bowling alley. In the big window, the erratically flickering letters of a neon sign meant to look Chinese spelled out "The Harmony Palace."

For Les, the sight of that sign was enough to erase the slightest glimmer of hope. He couldn't do it. He'd never make it. He'd lose it completely.

The monotonousness of repeating those words—and yet the force it took for him to surmount the terror. The river of blood he had to wade through to make it by the smiling gook at the door and take his seat at the table. And the horror—a deranging horror against which there was no protection—of the smiling gook handing him a menu. The outright grotesquerie of the gook pouring him a glass of water. Offering *him* water! The very source of all his suffering could have been that water. That's how crazy it made him feel.

"Okay, Les, you're doin' good. Doin' real good," said Louie. "Just have to take this one course at a time. Real good so far. Now I want you to deal with your menu. That's all. Just the menu. Just open the menu, open it up, and I want you to focus on the soups. The only thing you have to do now is order your soup. That's all you gotta do. If you can't make up your mind, we'll decide for you. They got mighty good wonton soup here."

"Fuckin' waiter," Les said.

"He's not the waiter, Les. His name is Henry. He's the owner. Les, we gotta focus on the soup. Henry, he's here to run his place. To be sure everything is running okay. No more, no less. He doesn't know about all that other stuff. Doesn't know about it, doesn't want to. What about your soup?"

"What are you guys having?" *He* had said that. Les. In the midst of this desperate drama, he, Les, had managed to stand apart from all the turmoil and ask what they were having to eat.

"Wonton," they all said.

"All right. Wonton."

"Okay," Louie said. "Now we're going to order the other stuff. Do we want to share? Would that be too much, Les, or do you want your own thing? Les, what do you want? You want chicken, vegetables, pork? You want lo mein? With the noodles?"

He tried to see if he could do it again. "What are you guys going to have?"

"Well, Les, some of us are having pork, some of us are having beef—"

"I don't care!" And why he didn't care was because this all was happening on some other planet, this pretending that they were ordering Chinese food. This was not what was really happening.

"Double-sautéed pork? Double-sautéed pork for Les. Okay. All you have to do now, Les, is concentrate and Chet'll pour you some tea. Okay? Okay."

"Just keep the fucking waiter away." Because from the corner of his eye he'd spotted some movement.

"Sir, sir—" Louie called to the waiter. "Sir, if you just stay there, we'll come to you with our order. If you wouldn't mind. We'll bring the order to you—you just keep a distance." But the waiter seemed not to understand, and when he again started toward them, clumsily but quickly Louie rose up on his bad legs. "*Sir!* We'll bring the order to *you*. To. You. Right? Right," Louie said, sitting back down again. "Good," he said, "good," nodding at the waiter, who stood stock-still some ten feet away. "That's it, sir. That's perfect."

The Harmony Palace was a dark place with fake plants scattered along the walls and maybe as many as fifty tables spaced in rows down the length of the long dining room. Only a few of them were occupied, and all of those far enough away so that none of the other customers seemed to have noticed the brief disturbance up at the end where the five men were eating. As a precaution, Louie always made certain, coming in, to get Henry to place his party at a table apart from everyone else. He and Henry had been through this before.

"Okay, Les, we got it under control. You can let go of the menu now. Les, let go of the menu. First with your right hand. Now your left hand. There. Chet'll fold it up for you."

The big guys, Chet and Bobcat, had been seated to either side of Les. They were assigned by Louie to be the evening's MPs and knew what to do if Les made a wrong move. Swift sat at the other side of the round table, next to Louie, who directly faced Les, and now, in the helpful tones a father might use with a son he was teaching to ride a bike, Swift said to Les, "I remember the first time I came here. I thought I'd never make it through. You're doin' real good. My first time, I couldn't even read the menu. The letters, they all were swimmin' at me. I thought I was goin' to bust through the window. Two guys, they had to take me out 'cause I couldn't sit still. You're doin' a good job, Les." If Les had been able to notice anything other than how much his hands were now trembling, he would have realized that he'd never before seen Swift not twitching. Swift neither twitching nor bitching. That was why Louie had brought him along —because helping somebody through the Chinese meal seemed to be the thing that Swift did best in this world. Here at The Harmony Palace, as nowhere else, Swift seemed for a while to remember what was what. Here one had only the faintest sense of him as someone crawling through life on his hands and knees. Here, made manifest in this embittered, ailing remnant of a man was a tiny, tattered piece of what had once been courage. "You're doin' a good job, Les. You're doin' all right. You just have to have a little tea," Swift suggested. "Let Chet pour some tea."

"Breathe," Louie said. "That's it. Breathe, Les. If you can't make it after the soup, we'll go. But you have to make it through the first course. If you can't make it through the double-sautéed pork, that's okay. But you have to make it through the soup. Let's make a code word if you have to get out. A code word that you can give me when there's just no two ways about it. How about 'tea leaf' for the code word? That's all you have to say and we're out of here. Tea leaf. If you need it, there it is. But *only* if you need it."

The waiter was poised at a little distance holding the tray with their five bowls of soup. Chet and Bobcat hopped right up and got the soup and brought it to the table.

Now Les just wants to say "tea leaf" and get the fuck out. Why doesn't he? I gotta get out of here. I gotta get out of here.

By repeating to himself "I gotta get out of here," he is able to put himself into a trance and, even without any appetite, to begin to eat his soup. To take down a little of the broth. "I gotta get out of here," and this blocks out the waiter and it blocks out the owner but it does not block out the two women at a wall-side table who are opening pea pods and dropping the shelled peas into a cooking pot. Thirty feet away, and Les can pick up the scent of whatever's the brand of cheap toilet water that they've sprayed behind their four gook ears—it's as pungent to him as the smell of raw earth. With the same phenomenal lifesaving powers that enabled him to detect the unwashed odor of a soundless sniper in the black thickness of a Vietnam jungle, he smells the women and begins to lose it. No one told him there were going to be women here doing that. How long are they going to be doing that? Two young women. Gooks. Why are they sitting there doing that? "I gotta get out of here." But he cannot move because he cannot divert his attention from the women.

"Why are those women doing that?" Les asks Louie. "Why don't they stop doing that? Do they have to keep doing that? Are they gonna keep doing that all night long? Are they gonna keep doing that over and over? Is there a reason? Can somebody tell me the reason? Make them stop doing that."

"Cool it," Louie says.

"I am cool. I just wanna know—are they gonna keep doing that? Can anyone stop them? Is there nobody who can think of a *way?*"

His voice rising now, and no easier to stop that happening than to stop those women.

"Les, we're in a restaurant. In a restaurant they prepare beans."

"Peas," Les says. "*Those are peas!*"

"Les, you got your soup and you got your next course coming. The next course: that's the whole world right now. That's everything. That's it. All you got to do next is eat some double-sautéed pork, and that's it."

"I had enough soup."

"Yeah?" Bobcat says. "You're not going to eat that? You done with that?"

Besieged on all sides by the disaster to come—how long can the agony be transformed into *eating?*—Les manages, beneath his breath, to say "Take it."

And that's when the waiter makes his move—purportedly going for the empty plates.

"No!" roars Les, and Louie is on his feet again, and now, looking like the lion tamer in the circus—and with Les taut and ready for the waiter to attack—Louie points the waiter back with his cane.

"You stay there," Louie says to the waiter. "Stay *there*. We bring the empty plates to you. You don't come to us."

The women shelling the peas have stopped, and without Les's even getting up and going over and showing them how to stop.

And Henry is in on it now, that's clear. This rangy, thin, smiling Henry, a young guy in jeans and a loud shirt and running shoes who poured the water and is the owner, is staring at Les from the door. Smiling but staring. That man is a menace. He is blocking the exit. Henry has got to go.

"Everything's okay," Louie calls to Henry. "Very good food. Wonderful food. That's why we come back." To the waiter he then says, "Just follow my lead," and then he lowers his cane and sits back down. Chet and Bobcat gather up the empty plates and go over and pile them on the waiter's tray.

"Anybody else?" Louie asks. "Anybody else got a story about his first time?"

"Uh-uh," says Chet while Bobcat sets himself the pleasant task of polishing off Les's soup.

This time, as soon as the waiter comes out of the kitchen carrying the rest of their order, Chet and Bobcat get right up and go over to the dumb fucking gook before he can even begin to forget and start approaching the table again.

And now it's out there. The food. The agony that is the food. Shrimp beef lo mein. Moo goo gai pan. Beef with peppers. Double-sautéed pork. Ribs. Rice. The agony of the rice. The agony of the steam. The agony of the smells. Everything out there is supposed to save him from death. Link him backward to Les the boy. That is the recurring dream: the unbroken boy on the farm.

"Looks good!"

"Tastes better!"

"You want Chet to put some on your plate, or you want to take for yourself, Les?"

"Not hungry."

"That's all right," Louie says, as Chet begins piling things on Les's plate for him. "You don't have to be hungry. That's not the deal."

"This almost over?" Les says. "I gotta get out of here. I'm not kiddin', guys. I really gotta get out of here. Had enough. Can't take it. I feel like I'm gonna lose control. I've had enough. You said I could leave. I gotta get out."

"I don't hear the code word, Les," Louie says, "so we're going to keep going."

Now the shakes have set in big-time. He cannot deal with the rice. It falls off the fork, he's shaking so bad.

And, Christ almighty, here comes a waiter with the water. Circling around and coming at Lester from the back, from out of fucking nowhere, another waiter. They are all at once but a split second away from Les yelling "Yahhh!" and going for the waiter's throat, and the water pitcher exploding at his feet.

"Stop!" cries Louie. "Back off!"

The women shelling the peas start screaming.

"He does not need any water!" Shouting, standing on his feet and shouting, with his cane raised over his head, Louie looks to the women like the one who is nuts. But they don't know what nuts is if they think that Louie's nuts. They have no idea.

At other tables some people are standing, and Henry rushes over and talks to them quietly until they are all sitting down. He has explained that those are Vietnam veterans, and whenever they come around, he takes it as a patriotic duty to be hospitable to them and to put up for an hour or two with their problems.

There is absolute quiet in the restaurant from then on. Les picks at a little food and the others eat up everything until the only food left on the table is the stuff still on Les's plate.

"You done with that?" Bobcat asks him. "You not gonna eat that?"

This time he can't even manage "take it." Say just those two words, and everybody buried beneath that restaurant floor will come rising up to seek revenge. Say *one* word, and if you weren't there the first time to see what it looked like, you sure as shit will see it now.

Here come the fortune cookies. Usually they love that. Read the fortunes, laugh, drink the tea—who doesn't love that? But Les shouts "Tea leaf!" and takes off, and Louie says to Swift, "Go out with him. Get him, Swiftie. Keep an eye on him. Don't let him out of your sight. We're gonna pay up."

On the way home there is silence: from Bobcat silence because he is laden with food; from Chet silence because he long ago learned through the repetitive punishment of too many brawls that for a man as fucked up as himself, silence is the only way to seem friendly; and from Swift silence too, a bitter and disgruntled silence, because once the flickering neon lights are behind them, so is the memory of himself that he seems to have had at The Harmony Palace. Swift is now busy stoking the pain.

Les is silent because he is sleeping. After the ten days of solid insomnia that led up to this trip, he is finally out.

It's when everybody else has been dropped off and Les and Louie are alone in the van that Louie hears him coming round and says,

"Les? Les? You did good, Lester. I saw you sweatin', I thought, Umm-umm-umm, no way he's gonna make it. You should have seen the color you were. I couldn't believe it. I thought the waiter was finished." Louie, who spent his first nights home handcuffed to a radiator in his sister's garage to assure himself he would not kill the brother-in-law who'd kindly taken him in when he was back from the jungle only forty-eight hours, whose waking hours are so organized around all the others' needs that no demonic urge can possibly squeeze back in, who, over a dozen years of being sober and clean, of working the Twelve Steps and religiously taking his meds—for the anxiety his Klonopin, for the depression his Zoloft, for the sizzling ankles and the gnawing knees and the relentlessly aching hips his Salsalate, an anti-inflammatory that half the time does little other than to give him a burning stomach, gas, and the shits—has managed to clear away enough debris to be able to talk civilly again to others and to feel, if not at home, then less crazily aggrieved at having to move inefficiently about for the rest of his life on those pain-ridden legs, at having to try to stand tall on a foundation of sand—happy-go-lucky Louie laughs. "I thought he didn't have a *chance*. But, man," says Louie, "you didn't just make it past the soup, you made it to the fucking fortune cookie. You know how many times it took me to make it to the fortune cookie? Four. Four times, Les. The first time I headed straight for the bathroom and it took them fifteen minutes to get me out. You know what I'm gonna tell my wife? I'm goin' to tell her, 'Les, did *okay*. Les did *all right*.'"

But when it came time to return, Les refused. "Isn't it enough that I sat there?" "I want you to eat," Louie said. "I want you to eat the meal. Walk the walk, talk the talk, eat the meal. We got a new goal, Les." "I don't want any more of your goals. I made it through. I didn't kill anyone. Isn't that enough?" But a week later back they drove to The Harmony Palace, same cast of characters, same glass of water, same menus, even the same cheap toilet water scent emitted by the sprayed Asian flesh of the restaurant women and wafting its sweet galvanic way to Les, the telltale scent by which he can track

his prey. The second time he eats, the third time he eats *and* orders—though they still won't let the waiter near the table—and the
fourth time they let the waiter serve them, and Les eats like a crazy
man, eats till he nearly bursts, eats as if he hasn't seen food in a year.

Outside The Harmony Palace, high fives all around. Even Chet is
joyous. Chet speaks, Chet *shouts*, "Semper fi!"

"Next time," says Les, while they're driving home and the feeling
is heady of being raised from the grave, "next time, Louie, you're
gonna go too far. Next time you're gonna want me to *like* it!"

But what is next is facing the Wall. He has to go look at Kenny's
name. And this he can't do. It was enough once to look up Kenny's
name in the book they've got at the VA. After, he was sick for a
week. That was all he could think about. That's all he can think
about anyway. Kenny there beside him without his head. Day and
night he thinks, Why Kenny, why Chip, why Buddy, why them and
not me? Sometimes he thinks that they're the lucky ones. It's over
for them. No, no way, no how, is he going to the Wall. That Wall.
Absolutely not. Can't do it. Won't do it. That's it.

Dance for me.

They've been together for about six months, and so one night he
says, "Come on, dance for me," and in the bedroom he puts on a
CD, the Artie Shaw arrangement of "The Man I Love," with Roy
Eldridge playing trumpet. Dance for me, he says, loosening the
arms that are tight around her and pointing toward the floor at
the foot of the bed. And so, undismayed, she gets up from where
she's been smelling that smell, the smell that is Coleman unclothed,
that smell of sun-baked skin—gets up from where she's been lying
deeply nestled, her face cushioned in his bare side, her teeth, her
tongue glazed with his come, her hand, below his belly, splayed
across the crinkled, buttery tangle of that coiled hair, and, with him
keeping an eagle eye on her—his green gaze unwavering through
the dark fringe of his long lashes, not at all like a depleted old man
ready to faint but like somebody pressed up against a window-
pane—she does it, not coquettishly, not like Steena did in 1948, not

because she's a sweet girl, a sweet young girl dancing for the plea-sure of giving him the pleasure, a sweet young girl who doesn't know much about what she's doing saying to herself, "I can give him that—he wants that, and I can do it, and so here it is." No, not quite the naive and innocent scene of the bud becoming the flower or the filly becoming the mare. Faunia can do it, all right, but with-out the budding maturity is how she does it, without the youthful, misty idealization of herself and him and everyone living and dead. He says, "Come on, dance for me," and, with her easy laugh, she says, "Why not? I'm generous that way," and she starts moving, smoothing her skin as though it's a rumpled dress, seeing to it that everything is where it should be, taut, bony, or rounded as it should be, a whiff of herself, the evocative vegetal smell coming familiarly off her fingers as she slides them up from her neck and across her warm ears and slowly from there over her cheeks to her lips, and her hair, her graying yellow hair that is damp and straggly from ex-ertion, she plays with like seaweed, pretends to herself that it's sea-weed, that it's always been seaweed, a great trickling sweep of sea-weed saturated with brine, and what's it cost her, anyway? What's the big deal? Plunge in. Pour forth. If this is what he wants, abduct the man, ensnare him. Wouldn't be the first one.

She's aware when it starts happening: that thing, that connection. She moves, from the floor that is now her stage at the foot of the bed she moves, alluringly tousled and a little greasy from the hours before, smeared and anointed from the preceding performance, fair-haired, white-skinned where she isn't tanned from the farm, scarred in half a dozen places, one kneecap abraded like a child's from when she slipped in the barn, very fine threadlike cuts half healed on both her arms and legs from the pasture fencing, her hands roughened, reddened, sore from the fiberglass splinters picked up while rotating the fence, from pulling out and putting in those stakes every week, a petal-shaped, rouge-colored bruise either from the milking parlor or from him precisely at the joining of her throat and torso, another bruise, blue-black at the turn of her unmuscled thigh, spots where she's been bitten and stung, a hair of his, an ampersand of his hair like a dainty grayish mole adhering to her cheek, her mouth open just wide enough to reveal the curve of her teeth, and in no hurry at all to go anywhere because it's the getting there that's the fun. She moves, and now he's seeing her, seeing this elongated body rhythmically moving, this slender body that is so much stronger than it looks and surprisingly so heavy-breasted dipping, dipping, dipping, on the long, straight handles of her legs stooping toward him like a dipper filled to the limit with his liquid. Unresisting, he's stretched across the wavelets of bedsheets, a sinuous swirl of pillows balled together to support his head, his head resting level with the span of her hips, with her belly, with her moving belly, and he's seeing her, every particle, he's seeing her and she knows that he's seeing her. They're connected. She knows he wants her to claim something. He wants me to stand here and move, she thinks, and to claim what is mine. Which is? Him. Him. He's offering me him. Okey-dokey, this is high-voltage stuff but here we go. And so, giving him her downturned look with the subtlety in it, she moves, she moves, and the formal transfer of power begins. And it's very nice for her, moving like this to that music and the power passing over, knowing that at her slightest command, with the flick of the finger that summons a waiter, he would crawl out of that bed to lick her feet. So soon in the dance, and already she could peel him and eat him like a piece of fruit. It's not all about being beat up and being the janitor and I'm at the college cleaning up other people's shit and I'm at the post office cleaning up other people's shit, and there's a terrible toughness that comes with that, with cleaning up everybody else's waste; if you want to know the truth, it sucks, and don't tell me there aren't better jobs, but I've got it, it's what I do, three jobs, because this car's got about six days left, I've got to buy a cheap car that runs, so three jobs is what I'm doing, and not for the first time, and by the way, the dairy farm is a lot of fucking work, to you it sounds great and to you it looks great, Faunia and the cows, but coming on top of everything else it breaks my fucking hump . . . But now I'm naked in a room with a man, seeing him lying there with his dick and that navy tattoo, and it's calm and he's calm, even getting a charge out of seeing me dance he's so very calm, and he's just had the shit kicked out of him, too. He's lost his wife, he's lost his job, publicly humiliated as a racist professor, and what's a racist professor? It's not that you've just become one. The story is you've been discovered, so it's been your whole life. It's not just that you did one thing wrong once. If you're a racist, then you've always been a racist. Suddenly it's your entire life you've been a racist. That's the stigma and it's not even true, and yet now he's calm. I can do that for him. I can make him calm like this, he can make me calm like this. All I have to do is just keep moving. He says dance for me and I think, Why not? Why not, except that it's going to make him think that I'm going to go along and pretend with him that this is something else. He's going to pretend that the world is ours, and I'm going to let him, and then I'm going to do it too. Still, why not? I can dance . . . but he has to remember. This is only what it is, even if I'm wearing nothing but the opal ring, nothing on me but the ring he gave me. This is standing in front of your lover naked with the lights on and moving. Okay, you're a man, and you're not in your prime, and you've got a life and I'm not part of it, but I know what's here. You come to me as a man. So I come to you. That's a lot. But that's all it is. I'm dancing in front of you naked with the lights on, and you're naked too, and all the other stuff doesn't matter. It's the simplest thing we've ever done—it's *it*. Don't fuck it up by thinking it's more than this. You don't, and I won't. It doesn't *have* to be more than this. You know what? I see you, Coleman.

Then she says it aloud. "You know what? I see you."

"Do you?" he says. "Then now the hell begins."

"You think—if you ever want to know—is there a God? You want to know why am I in this world? What is it about? It's about this. It's about, You're here, and I'll do it for you. It's about not thinking you're someone else somewhere else. You're a woman and you're in bed with your husband, and you're not fucking for fucking, you're not fucking to come, you're fucking because you're in bed with your husband and it's the right thing to do. You're a man and you're with your wife and you're fucking her, but you're thinking you want to be fucking the post office janitor. Okay—you know what? You're with the janitor."

He says softly, with a laugh, "And that proves the existence of God."

"If that doesn't, nothing does."

"Keep dancing," he says.

"When you're dead," she asks, "what does it matter if you didn't marry the right person?"

"It doesn't matter. It doesn't even matter when you're alive. Keep dancing."

"What is it, Coleman? What does matter?"

"This," he said.

"That's my boy," she replies. "Now you're learning."

"Is that what this is—you teaching me?"

"It's about time somebody did. Yes, I'm teaching you. But don't look at me now like I'm good for something other than this. Something more than this. Don't do that. Stay here with me. Don't go. Hold on to this. Don't think about anything else. Stay here with me. I'll do whatever you want. How many times have you had a woman really tell you that and mean it? I will do anything you want. Don't lose it. Don't take it somewhere else, Coleman. This is all we're here to do. Don't think it's about tomorrow. Close all the doors, before and after. All the social ways of thinking, shut 'em down. Everything the wonderful society is asking? The way we're set up socially? 'I should, I should, I should'? Fuck all that. What you're supposed to be, what you're supposed to do, all that, it just kills everything. I can keep dancing, if that's the deal. The secret little moment—if that's the whole deal. That slice you get. That slice out of time. It's no more than that, and I hope you know it."

"Keep dancing."

"This stuff is the important stuff," she says. "If I abandoned thinking that . . ."

"What? Thinking what?"

"I was a whoring little cunt from early on."

"Were you?"

"He always told himself it wasn't him, it was me."

"The stepfather."

"Yes. That's what he told himself. Maybe he was even right. But I had no choice at eight and nine and ten. It was the brutality that was wrong."

"What was it like when you were ten?"

"It was like asking me to pick up the whole house and carry it on my back."

"What was it like when the door opened at night and he came into your room?"

"It's like when you're a child in a war. You ever see those pictures in the paper of kids after they bomb their cities? It's like that. It's as big as a bomb. But no matter how many times I got blown over, I was still standing. That was my downfall: my still standing up. Then I was twelve and thirteen and starting to get tits. I was starting to bleed. Suddenly I was just a body that surrounded my pussy . . . But stick to the dancing. All doors closed, before and after, Coleman. I see you, Coleman. You're not closing the doors. You still have the fantasies of love. You know something? I really need a guy older than you. Who's had all the love-shit kicked out of him totally. You're too young for me, Coleman. Look at you. You're just a little boy falling in love with your piano teacher. You're falling for me, Coleman, and you're much too young for the likes of me. I need a much older man. I think I need a man at least a hundred. Do you have a friend in a wheelchair you can introduce me to? Wheelchairs are okay—I can dance and push. Maybe you have an older brother. Look at you, Coleman. Looking at me with those schoolboy eyes. Please, please, call your older friend. I'll keep dancing, just get him on the phone. I want to talk to him."

And she knows, while she is saying this, that it's this and the dancing that are making him fall in love with her. And it's so easy. I've attracted a lot of men, a lot of pricks, the pricks find me and they come to me, not just any man with a prick, not the ones who don't understand, which is about ninety percent of them, but men, young boys, the ones with the real male thing, the ones like Smoky who really understand it. You can beat yourself up over the things you don't have, but that I've got, even fully dressed, and some guys know it—they know what it is, and that's why they find me, and that's why they come, but this, this, this is taking candy from a baby. Sure—he remembers. How could he not? Once you've tasted it, you remember. My, my. After two hundred and sixty blow jobs and four hundred regular fucks and a hundred and six asshole fucks, the flirtation begins. But that's the way it goes. How many times has anyone in the world ever loved before they fucked? How many times have I loved *after* I fucked? Or is this it, the groundbreaker?

"Do you want to know what I feel like?" she asks him.

"Yes."

"I feel *so* good."

"So," he asks, "who can get out of this alive?"

"I'm with you there, mister. You're right, Coleman. This is going to lead to disaster. Into this at seventy-one? Turned around by this at seventy-one? Uh-uh. We'd better go back to the raw thing."

"Keep dancing," he says, and he hits a button on the bedside Sony and "The Man I Love" track starts up again.

"No. No. I beg you. There's my career as a janitor to think about."

"Don't stop."

"'Don't stop.'" she repeats. "I've heard those words somewhere before." In fact, rarely has she ever heard the word "stop" *without* "don't." Not from a man. Not much from herself either. "I've always thought 'don't stop' was one word," she says.

"It is. Keep dancing."

"Then don't lose it," she says. "A man and a woman in a room. Naked. We've got all we need. We don't need love. Don't diminish yourself—don't reveal yourself as a sentimental sap. You're dying to do it, but don't. Let's not lose this. Imagine, Coleman, imagine sustaining this."

He's never seen me dance like this, he's never heard me talk like this. Been so long since I talked like this, I'd have thought I'd forgotten how. So very long in hiding. *Nobody's* heard me talk like this. The hawks and the crows sometimes in the woods, but otherwise no one. This is not the usual way I entertain men. This is the most reckless I have ever been. Imagine.

"Imagine," she says, "showing up every day—and this. The woman who doesn't want to own everything. The woman who doesn't want to own *anything*."

But never had she wanted to own anything more.

"Most women want to own everything," she says. "They want to own your mail. They want to own your future. They want to own your fantasies. 'How dare you want to fuck anybody other than me. *I* should be your fantasy. Why are you watching porn when you have *me* at home?' They want to own who you are, Coleman. But the pleasure isn't owning the person. The pleasure is this. Having another contender in the room with you. Oh, I see you, Coleman. I could give you away my whole life and still have you. Just by dancing. Isn't that true? Am I mistaken? Do you like this, Coleman?"

"What luck," he says, watching, watching. "What incredible luck. Life owed me this."

"Did it now?"

"There's no one like you. Helen of Troy."

"Helen of Nowhere. Helen of Nothing."

"Keep dancing."

"I see you, Coleman. I do see you. Do you want to know what I see?"

"Sure."

"You want to know if I see an old man, don't you? You're afraid I'll see an old man and I'll run. You're afraid that if I see all the differences from a young man, if I see the things that are slack and the things that are gone, you'll lose me. Because you're too old. But you know what I see?"

"What?"

"I see a kid. I see you falling in love the way a kid does. And you mustn't. You mustn't. Know what else I see?"

"Yes."

"Yes, I see it now—I do see an old man. I see an old man dying."

"Tell me."

"You've lost everything."

"You see that?"

"Yes. Everything except me dancing. You want to know what I see?"

"What?"

"You didn't deserve that hand, Coleman. That's what I see. I see that you're furious. And that's the way it's going to end. As a furious old man. And it shouldn't have been. That's what I see: your fury. I see the anger and the shame. I see that you understand as an old man what time is. You don't understand that till near the end. But now you do. And it's frightening. Because you can't do it again. You can't be twenty again. It's not going to come back. And this is how it ended. And what's worse even than the dying, what's worse even than the being dead, are the fucking bastards who did this to you. Took it all away from you. I see that in you, Coleman. I see it because it's something I know about. The fucking bastards who changed everything within the blink of an eye. Took your life and threw it away. Took *your* life, and *they* decided they were going to throw it away. You've come to the right dancing girl. They decide what is garbage, and they decided *you're* garbage. Humiliated and humbled and destroyed a man over an issue everyone knew was bullshit. A pissy little word that meant nothing to them, absolutely nothing at all. And that's infuriating."

"I didn't realize you were paying attention."

She laughs the easy laugh. And dances. Without the idealism, without the idealization, without all the utopianism of the sweet young thing, despite everything she knows reality to be, despite the irreversible futility that is her life, despite all the chaos and callousness, she dances! And speaks as she's never spoken to a man before. Women who fuck like she does aren't supposed to talk like this— at least that's what the men who don't fuck women like her like to think. That's what the *women* who don't fuck like her like to think. That's what everyone likes to think—stupid Faunia. Well, let 'em. My pleasure. "Yes, stupid Faunia has been paying attention," she says. "How else does stupid Faunia get through? Being stupid

Faunia—that's my achievement, Coleman, that's me at my most sensible best. Turns out, Coleman, I've been watching *you* dance. How do I know this? Because you're with *me*. Why else would you be with me, if you weren't so fucking enraged? And why would I be with you, if *I* wasn't so fucking enraged? That's what makes for the great fucking, Coleman. The rage that levels everything. So don't lose it."

"Keep dancing."

"Till I drop?" she asks.

"Till you drop," he tells her. "Till the last gasp."

"Whatever you want."

"Where did I find you, Voluptas?" he says. "*How* did I find you? Who are you?" he asks, tapping the button that again starts up "The Man I Love."

"I am whatever you want."

All Coleman was doing was reading her something from the Sunday paper about the president and Monica Lewinsky, when Faunia got up and shouted, "Can't you avoid the fucking seminar? Enough of the seminar! I can't learn! I don't learn! I don't *want* to learn! Stop fucking teaching me—it won't work!" And, in the midst of their breakfast, she ran.

The mistake was to stay there. She didn't go home, and now she hates him. What does she hate most? That he really thinks his suffering is a big deal. He really thinks that what everybody thinks, what everybody says about him at Athena College, is so life-shattering. It's a lot of assholes not liking him—it's not a big deal. And for him this is the most horrible thing that ever happened? Well, it's not a big deal. Two kids suffocating and dying, that's a big deal. Having your stepfather put his fingers up your cunt, that's a big deal. Losing your job as you're about to retire isn't a big deal. That's what she hates about him—the privilegedness of his suffering. He thinks he never had a chance? There's real pain on this earth, and he thinks *he* didn't have a chance? You know when you don't have a chance? When, after the morning milking, he takes that iron pipe and hits you in the head with it. I don't even see it coming—and *he* didn't have a chance! Life owes *him* something!

What it amounts to is that at breakfast she doesn't want to be taught. Poor Monica might not get a good job in New York City? You know what? I don't care. Do you think Monica cares if my back hurts from milking those fucking cows after my day at the college? Sweeping up people's shit at the post office because they can't bother to use the fucking garbage can? Do you think Monica cares about that? She keeps calling the White House, and it must have been just terrible not to have her phone calls returned. And it's over for you? That's terrible too? It never *began* for me. Over before it *began*. Try having an iron pipe knock you down. Last night? It happened. It was nice. It was wonderful. I needed it too. But I still have three jobs. It didn't change anything. That's why you take it when it's happening, because it doesn't change a thing. Tell Mommy her husband puts his fingers in you when he comes in at night—it doesn't change a thing. Maybe now Mommy knows and she's going to help you. But nothing changes anything. We had this night of dancing. But it doesn't change anything. He reads to me about these things in Washington—what, what, what does it change? He reads to me about these escapades in Washington, Bill Clinton getting his dick sucked. How's that going to help me when my car craps out? You really think that this is the important stuff in the world? It's not that important. It's not important *at all*. I had two kids. They're dead. If I don't have the energy this morning to feel bad about Monica and Bill, chalk it up to my two kids, all right? If that's my shortcoming, so be it. I don't have any more left in me for all the great troubles of the world.

The mistake was to stay there. The mistake was to fall under the spell so completely. Even in the wildest thunderstorm, she'd driven home. Even when she was terrified of Farley following behind and forcing her off the road and into the river, she'd driven home. But she stayed. Because of the dancing she stayed, and in the morning she's angry. She's angry at him. It's a great new day, let's see what the paper has to say. After last night he wants to see what the paper has to say? Maybe if they hadn't talked, if they'd just had breakfast and she'd left, staying would have been okay. But to start the seminar. That was just about the worst thing he could have done. What *should* he have done? Given her something to eat and let her go home. But the dancing did its damage. I stayed. I stupidly stayed. Leaving at night—there is nothing more important for a girl like me. I'm not clear about a lot of things, but this I know: staying the next morning, it *means* something. The fantasy of Coleman-and-Faunia. It's the beginning of the indulgence of the fantasy of forever, the tritest fantasy in the world. I have a place to go to, don't I? It isn't the nicest place, but it's a place. Go to it! Fuck until all hours, but then *go.* There was the thunderstorm on Memorial Day, a thunderstorm ripping, pounding, volleying through the hills as though a war had broken out. The surprise attack on the Berkshires. But I got up at three in the morning, got my clothes on, and left. The lightning crackling, the trees splitting, the limbs crashing, the hail raining down like shot on my head, and I left. Whipped by all that wind, I left. The mountain is exploding, and still I left. Just between the house and the car I could have been killed, by a bolt of lightning ignited and killed, but I did not stay—*I left.* But to lie in bed with him all night? The moon big, the whole earth silent, the moon and moonlight everywhere, and I stayed. Even a blind man could have found his way home on a night like that, but I did not go. And I did not sleep. Couldn't. Awake all night. Didn't want to roll anywhere near the guy. Didn't want to touch this man. Didn't know *how,* this man whose asshole I've been licking for months. A leper till daybreak at the edge of the bed watching the shadows of his trees creep across his lawn. He said, "You should stay," but he didn't want me to, and I said, "I think I'll take you up on that," and I did. You could figure on at least one of us staying tough. But no. The two of us yielding to the worst idea ever. What the hookers told her, the whores' great wisdom: "Men don't pay you to sleep with them. They pay you to go home."

But even as she knows all she hates, she knows what she likes. His generosity. So rare for her to be anywhere near anyone's generosity.

And the strength that comes from being a man who doesn't swing a pipe at my head. If he pressed me, I'd even have to admit to him that I'm smart. Didn't I do as much last night? He listened to me and so I was smart. He listens to me. He's loyal to me. He doesn't reproach me for anything. He doesn't plot against me in any way. And is that a reason to be so fucking mad? He takes me seriously. That is sincere. That's what he meant by giving me the ring. They stripped him and so he's come to me naked. In his most mortal moment. My days have not been carpeted with men like this. He'd help me buy the car if I let him. He'd help me buy everything if I let him. It's painless with this man. Just the rise and fall of his voice, just *hearing* him, reassures me.

Are these the things you run away from? Is this why you pick a fight like a kid? A total accident that you even met him, your first lucky accident—your *last* lucky accident—and you flare up and run away like a kid? You really want to invite the end? To go back to what it was before him?

But she ran, ran from the house and pulled her car out of the barn and drove across the mountain to visit the crow at the Audubon Society. Five miles on, she swung off the road onto the narrow dirt entryway that twisted and turned for a quarter of a mile until the gray shingled two-story house cozily appeared between the trees, long ago a human habitat but now the society's local headquarters, sitting at the edge of the woods and the nature trails. She pulled onto the gravel drive, bumping right up to the edge of the log barrier, and parked in front of the birch with the sign nailed to it pointing to the herb garden, hers the only car to be seen. She'd made it. She could as easily have driven off the mountainside.

Wind chimes hanging adjacent to the entrance were tinkling in the breeze, glassily, mysteriously, as though, without words, a religious order were welcoming visitors to stay to meditate as well as to look around—as though something small but touching were being venerated here—but the flag hadn't been hoisted up the flagpole yet, and a sign on the door said the place wasn't open on Sundays until 1 P.M. Nonetheless, when she pushed, the door gave way and she stepped beyond the thin morning shadow of the leafless dog-woods and into the hallway, where large sacks heavy with different mixes of bird feed were stacked on the floor, ready for the winter buyers, and across from the sacks, piled up to the window along the opposite wall, were the boxes containing the various bird feeders. In the gift shop, where they sold the feeders along with nature books and survey maps and audiotapes of bird calls and an assortment of animal-inspired trinkets, there were no lights on, but when she turned in the other direction, into the larger exhibit room, home to the scanty collection of stuffed animals and a small assortment of live specimens—turtles, snakes, a few birds in cages—there was one of the staff, a chubby girl of about eighteen or nineteen, who said, "Hi," and didn't make a fuss about the place not yet being open. This far out on the mountain, once the autumn leaves were over, visitors were rare enough on the first of November, and she wasn't about to turn away someone who happened to show up at nine-fifteen in the morning, even this woman who wasn't quite dressed for the outdoors in the middle of fall in the Berkshire Hills but seemed to be wearing, above her gray sweatpants, the top of a man's striped pajamas, and on her feet nothing but backless house slippers, those things called mules. Nor had her long blond hair been brushed or combed as yet. But, all in all, she was more disheveled-looking than dissipated, and so the girl, who was feeding mice to a snake in a box at her feet—holding each mouse out to the snake at the end of a pair of tongs until the snake struck and took it and the infinitely slow process of ingestion began—just said, "Hi," and went back to her Sunday morning duties.

The crow was in the middle cage, an enclosure about the size of a clothes closet, between the cage holding the two saw-whet owls and the cage for the pigeon hawk. There he was. She felt better already.

"Prince. Hey, big guy." And she clicked at him, her tongue against her palate—click, click, click.

She turned to the girl feeding the snake. She hadn't been around in the past when Faunia came to see the crow, and more than likely she was new. Or relatively new. Faunia herself hadn't been to visit the crow for months now, and not at all since she'd begun seeing Coleman. It was a while now since she'd gone looking for ways to leave the human race. She hadn't been a regular visitor here since after the children died, though back then she sometimes stopped by four or five times a week. "He can come out, can't he? He can come just for a minute."

"Sure," the girl said.

"I'd like to have him on my shoulder," Faunia said, and stooped to undo the hook that held shut the glass door of the cage. "Oh, hello, Prince. Oh, Prince. Look at you."

When the door was open, the crow jumped from its perch to the top of the door and sat there with its head craning from side to side. She laughed softly. "What a great expression. He's checking me out," she called back to the girl. "Look," she said to the crow, and showed the bird her opal ring, Coleman's gift. The ring he'd given her in the car on that August Saturday morning that they'd driven to Tanglewood. "Look. Come over. Come on over," she whispered to the bird, presenting her shoulder.

But the crow rejected the invitation and jumped back into the cage and resumed life on the perch.

"Prince is not in the mood," the girl said.

"Honey?" cooed Faunia. "Come. Come on. It's Faunia. It's your friend. That's a boy. Come on." But the bird wouldn't move.

"If he knows that you want to get him, he won't come down," the girl said, and, using the tongs, picked up another mouse from a tray holding a cluster of dead mice and offered it to the snake that had, at long last, drawn into its mouth, millimeter by millimeter, the whole of the last one. "If he knows you're trying to get him, he usually stays out of reach, but if he thinks you're ignoring him, he'll come down."

They laughed together at the humanish behavior.

"Okay," said Faunia, "I'll leave him alone for a moment." She walked over to where the girl sat feeding the snake. "I love crows. They're my favorite bird. And ravens. I used to live in Seeley Falls, so I know all about Prince. I knew him when he was up there hang-

ing around Higginson's store. He used to steal the little girls' bar-
rettes. Goes right for anything shiny, anything colorful. He was famous for that. There used to be clippings about him from the
paper. All about him and the people who raised him after the nest
was destroyed and how he hung out like a big shot at the store.
Pinned up right there," she said, pointing back to a bulletin board
by the entryway to the room. "Where are the clippings?"

"He ripped 'em down."

Faunia burst out laughing, much louder this time than before.
"*He* ripped them down?"

"With his beak. Tore 'em up."

"He didn't want anybody to know his background! Ashamed of
his own background! Prince!" she called, turning back to face the
cage whose door was still wide open. "You're ashamed of your no-
torious past? Oh, you good boy. You're a good crow."

Now she took notice of one of the several stuffed animals scattered on mounts around the room. "Is that a bobcat there?"

"Yeah," the girl said, waiting patiently for the snake to finish
flicking its tongue out at the new dead mouse and grab hold of it.

"Is he from around here?"

"I don't know."

"I've seen them around, up in the hills. Looked just like that one,
the one I saw. Probably *is* him." And she laughed again. She wasn't
drunk—hadn't even got half her coffee down when she'd run from
the house, let alone had a drink—but the laugh sounded like the
laugh of someone who'd already had a few. She was just feeling
good being here with the snake and the crow and the stuffed bobcat, none of them intent on teaching her a thing. None of them going to read to her from the *New York Times*. None of them going to
try to catch her up on the history of the human race over the last
three thousand years. She knew all she needed to know about the
history of the human race: the ruthless and the defenseless. She
didn't need the dates and the names. The ruthless and the defenseless, there's the whole fucking deal. Nobody here was going to try to
encourage her to read, because nobody here knew how, with the ex-

ception of the girl. That snake certainly didn't know how. It just knew how to eat mice. Slow and easy. Plenty of time.

"What kind of snake is that?"

"A black rat snake."

"Takes the whole thing down."

"Yeah."

"Gets digested in the gut."

"Yeah."

"How many will it eat?"

"That's his seventh mouse. He took that one kind of slow even for him. That might be his last."

"Every day seven?"

"No. Every one or two weeks."

"And is it let out anywhere or is that life?" she said, pointing to the glass case from which the snake had been lifted into the plastic carton where it was fed.

"That's it. In there."

"Good deal," said Faunia, and she turned back to look across the room at the crow, still on its perch inside its cage. "Well, Prince, I'm over here. And you're over there. And I have no interest in you whatsoever. If you don't want to land on my shoulder, I couldn't care less." She pointed to another of the stuffed animals. "What's the guy over there?"

"That's an osprey."

She sized it up—a hard look at the sharp claws—and, again with a biggish laugh, said, "Don't mess with the osprey."

The snake was considering an eighth mouse. "If I could only get my kids to eat seven mice," Faunia said, "I'd be the happiest mother on earth."

The girl smiled and said, "Last Sunday, Prince got out and was flying around. All of the birds we have can't fly. Prince is the only one that can fly. He's pretty fast."

"Oh, I know that," Faunia said.

"I was dumping some water and he made a beeline for the door and went out into the trees. Within minutes there were three or four crows that came. Surrounded him in the tree. And they were going nuts. Harassing him. Hitting him on the back. Screaming. Smacking into him and stuff. They were there within minutes. He doesn't have the right voice. He doesn't know the crow language. They don't like him out there. Eventually he came down to me, because I was out there. They would have killed him."

"That's what comes of being hand-raised," said Faunia. "That's what comes of hanging around all his life with people like us. The human stain," she said, and without revulsion or contempt or condemnation. Not even with sadness. *That's how it is*—in her own dry way, that is all Faunia was telling the girl feeding the snake: we leave a stain, we leave a trail, we leave our imprint. Impurity, cruelty, abuse, error, excrement, semen—there's no other way to be here. Nothing to do with disobedience. Nothing to do with grace or salvation or redemption. It's in everyone. Indwelling. Inherent. Defining. The stain that is there before its mark. Without the sign it is there. The stain so intrinsic it doesn't require a mark. The stain that *precedes* disobedience, that *encompasses* disobedience and perplexes all explanation and understanding. It's why all the cleansing is a joke. A barbaric joke at that. The fantasy of purity is appalling. It's insane. What is the quest to purify, if not *more* impurity? All she was saying about the stain was that it's inescapable. That, naturally, would be Faunia's take on it: the inevitably stained creatures that we are. Reconciled to the horrible, elemental imperfection. She's like the Greeks, like Coleman's Greeks. Like their gods. They're petty. They quarrel. They fight. They hate. They murder. They fuck. All their Zeus ever wants to do is to fuck—goddesses, mortals, heifers, she-bears—and not merely in his own form but, even more excitingly, as himself made manifest as beast. To hugely mount a woman as a bull. To enter her bizarrely as a flailing white swan. There is never enough flesh for the king of the gods or enough perversity. All the craziness desire brings. The dissoluteness. The depravity. The crudest pleasures. And the fury from the all-seeing wife. Not the Hebrew God, infinitely alone, infinitely obscure, monomaniacally the only god there is, was, and always will be, with nothing better to do than worry about Jews. And not the perfectly desexualized Christian man-god and his uncontaminated mother and all the guilt and shame that an exquisite unearthliness inspires. Instead the Greek Zeus, entangled in adventure, vividly expressive, capricious, sensual, exuberantly wedded to his own rich existence, anything but alone and anything but hidden. Instead the *divine* stain. A great reality-reflecting religion for Faunia Farley if, through Coleman, she'd known anything about it. As the hubristic fantasy has it, made in the image of God, all right, but not ours—*theirs*. God debauched. God corrupted. A god of life if ever there was one. God in the image of *man*.

"Yeah. I suppose that's the tragedy of human beings raising crows," the girl replied, not exactly getting Faunia's drift though not entirely missing it either. "They don't recognize their own species. *He* doesn't. And he should. It's called imprinting," the girl told her. "Prince is really a crow that doesn't know how to be a crow."

Suddenly Prince started cawing, not in a true crow caw but in that caw that he had stumbled on himself and that drove the other crows nuts. The bird was out on top of the door now, practically shrieking.

Smiling temptingly, Faunia turned and said, "I take that as a compliment, Prince."

"He imitates the schoolkids that come here and imitate him," the girl explained. "When the kids on the school trips imitate a crow? That's his impression of the kids. The kids do that. He's invented his own language. From kids."

In a strange voice of her own, Faunia said, "I love that strange voice he invented." And in the meantime she had crossed back to the cage and stood only inches from the door. She raised her hand, the hand with the ring, and said to the bird, "Here. Here. Look what I brought you to play with." She took the ring off and held it up for him to examine at close range. "He likes my opal ring."

"Usually we give him keys to play with."

"Well, he's moved up in the world. Haven't we all. Here. Three hundred bucks," Faunia said. "Come on, play with it. Don't you know an expensive ring when somebody offers it to you?"

"He'll take it," the girl said. "He'll take it inside with him. He's like a pack rat. He'll take his food and shove it into the cracks in the wall of his cage and pound it in there with his beak."

The crow had now grasped the ring tightly in its beak and was jerkily moving its head from side to side. Then the ring fell to the floor. The bird had dropped it.

Faunia bent down and picked it up and offered it to the crow again. "If you drop it, I'm not going to give it to you. You know that. Three hundred bucks. I'm giving you a ring for three hundred bucks—what are you, a fancy man? If you want it, you have to take it. Right? Okay?"

With his beak he again plucked it from her fingers and firmly took hold of it.

"Thank you," said Faunia. "Take it inside," she whispered so that the girl couldn't hear. "Take it in your cage. Go ahead. It's for you."

But he dropped it again.

"He's very smart," the girl called over to Faunia. "When we play with him, we put a mouse inside a container and close it. And he figures out how to open the container. It's amazing."

Once again Faunia retrieved the ring and offered it, and again the crow took it and dropped it.

"Oh, Prince—that was *deliberate*. It's now a game, is it?"

Caw. Caw. Caw. Caw. Right into her face, the bird exploded with its special noise.

Here Faunia reached up with her hand and began to stroke the head and then, very slowly, to stroke the body downward from the head, and the crow allowed her to do this. "Oh, Prince. Oh, so beautifully shiny. He's *humming* to me," she said, and her voice was rapturous, as though she had at last uncovered the meaning of everything. "He's *humming*." And she began to hum back, "Ewwww . . . ewwww . . . ummmmm," imitating the bird, which was indeed making some sort of lowing sound as it felt the pressure of the hand smoothing its back feathers. Then suddenly, click click, it was clicking its beak. "Oh, that's *good*," whispered Faunia, and then she turned her head to the girl and, with her heartiest of laughs, said, "Is he for sale? That clicking did it. I'll take him." Meanwhile, closer and closer she came to his clicking beak with her own lips, whispering to the bird, "Yes, I'll take you, I'll buy you—"

"He does bite, so watch your eyes," the girl said.

"Oh, I know he bites. I've already had him bite me a couple of times. When we first met he bit me. But he clicks, too. Oh, listen to him click, children."

And she was remembering how hard she had tried to die. Twice. Up in the room in Seeley Falls. The month after the children died, twice tried to kill myself in that room. For all intents and purposes, the first time I did. I know from stories the nurse told me. The stuff on the monitor that defines a heartbeat wasn't even there. Usually lethal, she said. But some girls have all the luck. And I tried so hard. I remember taking the shower, shaving my legs, putting on my best skirt, the long denim skirt. The wraparound. And the blouse from Brattleboro that time, that summer, the embroidered blouse. I remember the gin and the Valium, and dimly remember this powder. I forget the name. Some kind of rat powder, bitter, and I folded it into the butterscotch pudding. Did I turn on the oven? Did I forget to? Did I turn blue? How long did I sleep? When did they decide to break down the door? I still don't know who did that. To me it was ecstatic, getting myself ready. There are times in life worth celebrating. Triumphant times. The occasions for which dressing up was intended. Oh, how I turned myself out. I braided my hair. I did my eyes. Would have made my own mother proud, and that's saying something. Called her just the week before to tell her the kids were dead. First phone call in twenty years. "It's Faunia, Mother." "I don't know anybody by that name. Sorry," and hung up. The bitch. After I ran away, she told everyone, "My husband is strict and Faunia couldn't live by the rules. She could never live by the rules." The classic cover-up. What privileged girl-child ever ran away because a stepfather was strict? She runs away, you bitch, because the stepfather isn't strict—because the stepfather is wayward and won't leave her alone. Anyway, I dressed myself in the best I owned. No less would do. The second time I didn't dress up. And that I didn't dress up tells the whole story. My heart wasn't in it anymore, not after the first time didn't work. The second time it was sudden and impulsive and joyless. That first time had been so long in coming, days and nights, all that anticipation. The concoctions. Buying the powder. Getting prescriptions. But the second time was hurried. Uninspired. I think I stopped because I couldn't stand the suffocating. My throat choking, really suffocating, not getting any air, and hurrying to unknot the extension cord. There wasn't any of that hurried business the first time. It was calm and peaceful. The kids are gone and there's no one to worry about and I have all the time in the world. If only I'd done it right. The pleasure there was in it. Finally where there is none, there is that last joyous moment, when death should come on your own angry terms, but you don't feel angry—just elated. I can't stop thinking about it. All this week. He's reading to me about Clinton from the *New York Times* and all I'm thinking about is Dr. Kevorkian and his carbon monoxide machine. Just inhale deeply. Just suck until there is no more to inhale.

"'They were such beautiful children,' he said. 'You never expect anything like this to happen to you or your friends. At least Faunia has the faith that her children are with God now.'"

That's what some jerk-off told the paper. 2 CHILDREN SUFFO-CATE IN LOCAL HOUSE FIRE. "'Based on the initial investigation,' Sergeant Donaldson said, 'evidence indicates that a space heater . . .' Residents of the rural road said they became aware of the fire when the children's mother . . .'"

When the children's mother tore herself free from the cock she was sucking.

"The father of the children, Lester Farley, emerged from the hallway moments later, neighbors said."

Ready to kill me once and for all. He didn't. And then I didn't. Amazing. Amazing how nobody's done it yet to the dead children's mother.

"No, I didn't, Prince. Couldn't make that work either. And so," she whispered to the bird, whose lustrous blackness beneath her hand was warm and sleek like nothing she had ever fondled, "here we are instead. A crow who really doesn't know how to be a crow, a woman who doesn't really know how to be a woman. We're meant for each other. Marry me. You're my destiny, you ridiculous bird." Then she stepped back and bowed. "Farewell, my Prince."

And the bird responded. With a high-pitched noise that so sounded like "Cool. Cool. Cool," that once again she broke into laughter. When she turned to wave goodbye to the girl, she told her, "Well, that's better than I get from the guys on the street."

And she'd left the ring. Coleman's gift. When the girl wasn't looking, she'd hid it away in the cage. Engaged to a crow. That's the ticket.

"Thank you," called Faunia.

"You're welcome. Have a good one," the girl called after her, and with that, Faunia drove back to Coleman's to finish her breakfast and see what developed with him next. The ring's in the cage. He's got the ring. He's got a three-hundred-dollar ring.

The trip to the Moving Wall up in Pittsfield took place on Veterans Day, when the flag is flown at half-mast and many towns hold parades—and the department stores hold their sales—and vets who feel as Les did are more disgusted with their compatriots, their country, and their government than on any other day of the year. *Now* he was supposed to be in some two-bit parade and march around while a band played and everyone waved the flag? *Now* it was going to make everybody feel good for a minute to be recognizing their Vietnam veterans? How come they spit on him when he came home if they were so eager to see him out there now? How come there were veterans sleeping in the street while that draft dodger was sleeping in the White House? Slick Willie, commander in chief. Son of a bitch. Squeezing that Jew girl's fat tits while the VA budget goes down the drain. Lying about sex? Shit. The goddamn government lies about *everything*. No, the U.S. government had already played enough bad jokes on Lester Farley without adding on the joke of Veterans Day.

And yet there he was, on that day of all days, driving up to Pittsfield in Louie's van. They were headed for the half-scale replica of the real Wall that for some fifteen years now had been touring the country; from the tenth through the sixteenth of November, it was to be on view in the parking lot of the Ramada Inn under the sponsorship of the Pittsfield VFW. With him was the same crew that had seen him through the trial of the Chinese meal. They weren't going to let him go alone, and they'd been reassuring him of that all along: we'll be there with you, we'll stand by you, we'll be with you 24/7 if we need to be. Louie had gone so far as to say that afterward Les could stay with him and his wife at their house, and, for however long it took, they would look after him. "You won't have to go home alone, Les, not if you don't want to. I don't think you should try. You come stay with me and Tess. Tessie's seen it all. Tessie understands. You don't have to worry about Tessie. When I got back, Tessie became my motivation. My outlook was, How can anyone tell me what to do. I'm going into a rage without any provocation. You know. You know it all, Les. But thank God Tessie steadfastly stood by me. If you want, she'll stand by you."

Louie was a brother to him, the best brother a man could ever hope to have, but because he would not leave him be about going to the Wall, because he was so fucking fanatical about him seeing that wall, Les had all he could do not to take him by the throat and throttle the bastard. Gimpy spic bastard, leave me alone! Stop telling me how it took you ten years to get to the Wall. Stop telling me how it fucking changed your life. Stop telling me how you made peace with Mikey. Stop telling me what Mikey said to you at the Wall. I don't want to know!

And yet they're off, they're on their way, and again Louie is repeating to him, "'It's all right, Louie'—that's what Mikey told me, and that's what Kenny is going to tell you. What he was telling me, Les, is that it was okay, I could get on with my life."

"I can't take it, Lou—turn around."

"Buddy, relax. We're halfway there."

"Turn the fucking thing around!"

"Les, you don't know unless you go. You got to go," said Louie kindly, "and you got to find out."

"I don't *want* to find out!"

"How about you take a little more of your meds? A little Ativan. A little Valium. A little extra won't hurt. Give him some water, Chet."

Once they reached Pittsfield and Louie had parked across the way from the Ramada Inn, it wasn't easy getting Les out of the van. "I'm not doin' it," he said, and so the others stood around outside smoking, letting Les have a little more time for the extra Ativan and Valium to kick in. From the street, Louie kept an eye on him. There were a lot of police cars around and a lot of buses. There was a ceremony going on at the Wall, you could hear somebody speaking over a microphone, some local politician, probably the fifteenth one to sound off that morning. "The people whose names are inscribed on this wall behind me are your relatives, friends, and neighbors. They are Christian, Jew, Muslim, black, white, native people—Americans all. They gave a pledge to defend and protect, and gave their lives to keep that pledge. There is no honor, no ceremony, that can fully express our gratitude and admiration. The following poem was left at this wall a few weeks ago in Ohio, and I'd like to share it with you. 'We remember you, smiling, proud, strong / You told us not to worry / We remember those last hugs and kisses . . .'"

And when that speech was over, there was another to come. ". . . but with this wall of names behind me, and as I look out into the crowd and see the faces of middle-aged men like me, some of them wearing medals and other remnants of a military uniform, and I see a slight sadness in their eyes—maybe that's what's left of the thousand-yard stare which we all picked up when we were just brother grunts, infantrymen, ten thousand miles away from home—when I see all this, I am somehow transported back thirty years. This traveling monument's permanent namesake opened on the Mall in Washington on November 13, 1982. It took me roughly about two and a half years to get there. Looking back over that time, I know, like many Vietnam veterans, I stayed away on purpose, because of painful memories that I knew it would conjure up. And so on a Washington evening, when dusk was settling, I went over to the Wall by myself. I left my wife and children at the hotel— we were on our way back from Disney World—and visited, stood alone at its apex, close to where I'm standing right now. And the memories came—a whirlwind of emotions came. I remembered people I grew up with, played ball with, who are on this wall, right here from Pittsfield. I remembered my radio operator, Sal. We met in Vietnam. We played the where-you-from game. Massachusetts. Massachusetts. Whereabouts in Massachusetts? West Springfield he was from. I said I was from Pittsfield. And Sal died a month after I left. I came home in April, and I picked up a local newspaper, and I saw that Sal was not going to meet me in Pittsfield or Springfield for drinks. I remembered other men I served with . . ."

And then there was a band—an army infantry band most likely —playing the "Battle Hymn of the Green Berets," which led Louie to conclude that it was best to wait till the ceremony was completely over before getting Les out of the van. Louie had timed their arrival so they wouldn't have to deal with the speeches or the emotional music, but the program had more than likely started late, and so they were still at it. Looking at his watch, though, seeing it was close to noon, he figured it must be near the end. And, yep—suddenly they were finishing up. The lone bugle playing taps. Just as well. Hard enough to hear taps standing out on the street amid all the empty buses and the cop cars, let alone to be right there, with all the weeping people, dealing with taps *and* the Wall. There was taps, agonizing taps, the last awful note of taps, and then the band was playing "God Bless America," and Louie could hear the people at the Wall singing along—"From the mountains, to the prairies, to the oceans, white with *foam*"—and a moment later it was over.

Inside the van, Les was still shaking, but he didn't appear to be looking behind him all the time and only occasionally was he looking over his head for "the things," and so Louie climbed awkwardly back up inside and sat down next to him, knowing that the whole of Les's life was now the dread of what he was about to find out, and so the thing to do was to get him there and get it done with.

"We're going to send Swift in advance, Les, to find Kenny for you. It's a pretty long wall. Better than you having to go through all those names, Swift and the guys'll go over and locate it in advance. The names are up there on panels in the order of time. They're up there by time, from first guy to last guy. We got Kenny's date, you gave us the date, so it won't take too long now to find him."

"I ain't doin' it."

When Swift came back to the van, he opened the door a crack and said to Louie, "We got Kenny. We found him."

"Okay, this is it, Lester. Suck it up. You're going to walk over there. It's around back of the inn. There are going to be other folks there doing the same thing we're doing. They had an official little ceremony, but that's finished and you don't have to worry about it. No speeches. No bullshit. It's just going to be kids and parents and grandparents and they are all going to be doing the same thing. They're going to be laying wreaths of flowers. They're going to be saying prayers. Mostly they're going to be looking for names. They're going to be talking among themselves like people do, Les. Some of them are going to be crying. That's all that's there. So you know just what's there. You're going to take your time but you're coming with us."

It was unusually warm for November, and approaching the Wall they saw that a lot of the guys were in shirtsleeves and some of the women were wearing shorts. People wearing sunglasses in mid-November but otherwise the flowers, the people, the kids, the grandparents—it was exactly as Louie had described. And the Moving Wall was no surprise: he'd seen it in magazines, on T-shirts, got a glimpse on TV once of the real full-sized D.C. Wall before he quickly switched off the set. Stretched the entire length of the macadam parking lot were all those familiar joined panels, a perpendicular cemetery of dark upright slabs sloping off gradually at either end and stamped in white lettering with all the tightly packed names. The name of each of the dead was about a quarter of the length of a man's little finger. That's what it took to get them all in there, 58,209 people who no longer take walks or go to the movies but who manage to exist, for whatever it is worth, as inscriptions on a portable black aluminum wall supported behind by a frame of two-by-fours in a Massachusetts parking lot back of a Ramada Inn.

The first time Swift had been to the Wall he couldn't get out of the bus, and the others had to drag him off and keep dragging until they got him face to face with it, and afterward he had said, "You can hear the Wall crying." The first time Chet had been to the Wall he'd begun to beat on it with his fists and to scream, "That shouldn't be Billy's name—no, Billy, no!—that there should be my name!" The first time Bobcat had been to the Wall he'd just put out his hand to touch it and then, as though the hand were frozen, could not pull it away—had what the VA doctor called some type of fit. The first time Louie had been to the Wall it didn't take him long to figure out what the deal was and get to the point. "Okay, Mikey," he'd said aloud, "here I am. I'm here," and Mikey, speaking in his own voice, had said right back to him, "It's all right, Lou. It's okay."

Les knew all these stories of what could happen the first time, and now he is there for the first time, and he doesn't feel a thing. Nothing happens. Everyone telling him it's going to be better, you're going to come to terms with it, each time you come back it's going to get better and better until we get you to Washington and you make a tracing at the big wall of Kenny's name, and that, that is going to be the real spiritual healing—this enormous buildup, and nothing happens. Nothing. Swift had heard the Wall crying—Les doesn't hear anything. Doesn't feel anything, doesn't hear anything, doesn't even remember anything. It's like when he saw his two kids dead. This huge lead-in, and nothing. Here he was so afraid he was going to feel too much and he feels nothing, and that is worse. It shows that despite everything, despite Louie and the trips to the Chinese restaurant and the meds and no drinking, he was right all along to believe he was dead. At the Chinese restaurant he felt something, and that temporarily tricked him. But now he knows for sure he's dead because he can't even call up Kenny's memory. He used to be tortured by it, now he can't be connected to it in any way.

Because he's a first-timer, the others are kind of hovering around. They wander off briefly, one at a time, to pay their respects to particular buddies, but there is always someone who stays with him to check him out, and when each guy comes back from being away, he puts an arm around Les and hugs him. They all believe they are right now more attuned to one another than they have ever been before, and they all believe, because Les has the requisite stunned look, that he is having the experience they all wanted him to have. They have no idea that when he turns his gaze up to one of the three American flags flying, along with the black POW/MIA flag, over the parking lot at half-mast, he is not thinking about Kenny or even about Veterans Day but thinking that they are flying all the flags at half-mast in Pittsfield because it has finally been established that Les Farley is dead. It's official: altogether dead and not merely inside. He doesn't tell this to the others. What's the point? The truth is the truth. "Proud of you," Louie whispers to him. "Knew you could do it. I knew this would happen." Swift is saying to him, "If you ever want to talk about it . . ."

A serenity has overcome him now that they all mistake for some therapeutic achievement. The Wall That Heals—that's what the sign says that's out front of the inn, and that is what it does. Finished with standing in front of Kenny's name, they're walking up and down with Les, the whole length of the Wall and back, all of them watching the folks searching for the names, letting Lester take it all in, letting him know that he is where he is doing what he is doing. "This is not a wall to climb, honey," a woman says quietly to a small boy she's gathered back from where he was peering over the low end. "What's the name? What's Steve's last name?" an elderly man is asking his wife as he is combing through one of the panels, counting carefully down with a finger, row by row, from the top. "Right there," they hear a woman say to a tiny tot who can barely walk; with one finger she is touching a name on the Wall. "Right there, sweetie. That's Uncle Johnny." And she crosses herself. "You sure that's line twenty-eight?" a woman says to her husband. "I'm sure." "Well, he's got to be there. Panel four, line twenty-eight. I found him in Washington." "Well, I don't see him. Let me count again." "That's my cousin," a woman is saying. "He opened a bottle of Coke over there, and it exploded. Booby-trapped. Nineteen years old. Behind the lines. He's at peace, please God." There is a veteran in an American Legion cap kneeling before one of the panels, helping out two black ladies dressed in their best church clothes. "What's his name?" he asks the younger of the two. "Bates. James." "Here he is," the vet says. "There he is, Ma," the younger woman says.

Because the Wall is half the size of the Washington Wall, a lot of people are having to kneel down to search for the names and, for the older ones, that makes locating them especially hard. There are flowers wrapped in cellophane lying up against the Wall. There is a handwritten poem on a piece of paper that somebody has taped to the bottom of the Wall. Louie stoops to read the words: "Star light, star bright / First star I see tonight . . ." There are people with red eyes from crying. There are vets with a black Vietnam Vet cap like Louie's, some of them with campaign ribbons pinned to the cap. There's a chubby boy of about ten, his back turned stubbornly to the Wall, saying to a woman, "I don't *wanna* read it." There's a heavily tattooed guy in a First Infantry Division T-shirt—"Big Red One," the T-shirt says—who is clutching himself and wandering around in a daze, having terrible thoughts. Louie stops, takes hold of him, and gives him a hug. They all hug him. They even get Les to hug him. "Two of my high school friends are on there, killed within forty-eight hours of each other," a fellow nearby is saying. "And both of them waked from the same funeral home. That was a sad day at Kingston High." "He was the first one to go to Nam," somebody else is saying, "and the only one of us to not come back. And you know what he'd want there under his name, at the Wall there? Just what he wanted in Nam. I'll tell you exactly: a bottle of Jack Daniel's, a pair of good boots, and pussy hairs baked into a brownie."

There is a group of four guys standing around talking, and when Louie hears them going at it, reminiscing, he stops to listen, and the others wait there with him. The four strangers are all gray-haired men—all of them now with stray gray hair or gray curls or, in one case, a gray ponytail poking out from back of the Vietnam Vet cap.

"You were mechanized when you were there, huh?"

"Yeah. We did a lot of humpin', but sooner or later you knew you'd get back to that fifty."

"We did a lot of walkin'. We walked all over the freakin' Central Highlands. All over them damn mountains."

"Another thing with the mech unit, we were never in the rear. I think out of the whole time I was there, almost eleven months, I went to base camp when I got there and I went on R&R—that was it."

"When the tracks were movin', they knew you were comin', and they knew when you were going to get there, so that B-40 rocket was sittin' there waitin'. He had a lot of time to polish it up and put your name on it."

Suddenly Louie butts in, speaks up. "We're here," he says straight out to the four strangers. "We're *here*, right? We're all here. Let me do names. Let me do names and addresses." And he takes his note-pad out of his back pocket and, while leaning on his cane, writes down all their information so he can mail them the newsletter he and Tessie publish and send out, on their own, a couple of times a year.

Then they are passing the empty chairs. They hadn't seen them on the way in, so intent were they on getting Les to the Wall without his falling down or breaking away. At the end of the parking lot, there are forty-one brownish-gray old metal bridge chairs, proba-bly out of some church basement and set up in slightly arced rows, as at a graduation or an award ceremony—three rows of ten, one row of eleven. Great care has been taken to arrange them just so. Taped to the backrest of each chair is somebody's name—above the empty seat, a name, a man's name, printed on a white card. A whole section of chairs off by itself, and, so as to be sure that nobody sits down there, it is roped off on each of the four sides with a sagging loop of intertwined black and purple bunting.

And a wreath is hanging there, a big wreath of carnations, and when Louie, who doesn't miss a thing, stops to count them, he finds, as he suspected, that the carnations number forty-one.

"What's this?" asks Swift.

"It's the guys from Pittsfield that died. It's their empty chairs," Louie says.

"Son of a bitch," Swift says. "What a fuckin' slaughter. Either fight to win or don't fight at all. Son of a fuckin' bitch."

But the afternoon isn't over for them yet. Out on the pavement in front of the Ramada Inn, there is a skinny guy in glasses, wearing a coat much too heavy for the day, who is having a serious problem—shouting at passing strangers, pointing at them, spitting because he's shouting so hard, and there are cops rushing in from the squad cars to try to talk him into calming down before he strikes out at someone or, if he has a gun hidden on him, pulls it out to take a shot. In one hand he holds a bottle of whiskey—that's all he *appears* to have on him. "Look at me!" he shouts. "I'm shit and everybody who looks at me knows I'm shit. Nixon! Nixon! That's who did it to me! That's what did it to me! Nixon sent me to Vietnam!"

Solemn as they are as they pile into the van, each bearing the weight of his remembrances, there is the relief of seeing Les, unlike the guy cracking up on the street, in a state of calm that never before existed for him. Though they are not men given to expressing transcendent sentiments, they feel, in Les's presence, the emotions that can accompany that kind of urge. During the course of the drive home, each of them—except for Les—apprehends to the greatest degree available to him the mystery of being alive and in flux.

He looked serene, but that was a fakeout. He'd made up his mind. Use his vehicle. Take them all out, including himself. Along the river, come right at them, in the same lane, in their lane, round the turn where the river bends.

He's made up his mind. Got nothin' to lose and everything to gain. It isn't a matter of if that happens or if I see this or if I think this I will do it and if I don't I won't. He's made up his mind to the extent that he's no longer thinking. He's on a suicide mission, and inside he is agitated big-time. No words. No thoughts. It's just seeing, hearing, tasting, smelling—it's anger, adrenaline, and it's resignation. We're not in Vietnam. We're beyond Vietnam.

(Taken again in restraints to the Northampton VA a year later, he tries putting into plain English for the psychologist this pure state of something that is nothing. It's all confidential anyway. She's a doc. Medical ethics. Strictly between the two of them. "What were you thinking?" "No thinking." "You had to be thinking something." "Nothing." "At what point did you get in your truck?" "After dark." "Had you had dinner?" "No dinner." "Why did you think you were getting into the truck?" "I knew why." "You knew where you were going." "To get him." "To get who?" "The Jew. The Jew professor." "Why were you going to do that?" "To get him." "Because you had to?" "Because I had to." "Why did you have to?" "Kenny." "You were going to kill him." "Oh yes. All of us." "There was planning, then." "No planning." "You knew what you were doing." "Yes." "But you did not plan it." "No." "Did you think you were back in Vietnam?" "No Vietnam." "Were you having a flashback?" "No flashbacks." "Did you think you were in the jungle?" "No jungle." "Did you think you would feel better?" "No feelings." "Were you thinking about the kids? Was this payback?" "No payback." "Are you sure?" "No payback." "This woman, you tell me, killed your children, 'a blow job,' you told me, 'killed my kids'—weren't you trying to get back at her, to take revenge for that?" "No revenge." "Were you depressed?" "No, no depression." "You were out to kill two people and yourself and you were not angry?" "No, no more anger." "Sir, you got in your truck, you knew where they would be, and you drove into their headlights. And you're trying to tell me you weren't trying to kill them." "I didn't kill them." "Who killed them?" "They killed themselves.")

Just driving. That's all he's doing. Planning and not planning.

Knowing and not knowing. The other headlights are coming at him, and then they're gone. No collision? Okay, no collision. Once they swerve off the road, he changes lanes and keeps going. He just keeps driving. Next morning, waiting with the road crew to go out for the day, he hears about it at the town garage. The other guys already know.

There's no collision so, though he has some sense of it, he's got no details, and when he gets home from driving and gets out of the truck he's not sure what happened. Big day for him. November the eleventh. Veterans Day. That morning he goes with Louie—that morning he goes to the Wall, that afternoon he comes home from the Wall, that night he goes out to kill everybody. Did he? Can't know because there's no collision, but still quite a day from a therapeutic point of view. Second half being more therapeutic than the first. Achieves a true serenity now. Now Kenny can speak to him. Firing side by side with Kenny, both of them opened up on fully automatic, when Hector, the team leader, gives the screaming order "Get your stuff and let's get out of here!" and suddenly Kenny is dead. Quick as that. Up on some hill. Under attack, pulling back— and Kenny's dead. Can't be. His buddy, another farm boy, same background except from Missouri, they were going to do dairy farming together, guy who as a kid of six watched his father die and as a kid of nine watched his mother die, raised after that by an uncle he loved and was always talking about, a successful dairy farmer with a good-sized spread—180 milking cows, twelve machines milking six cows a side in the parlor at a time—and Kenny's head is gone and he's dead.

Looks like Les is communicating with his buddy now. Showed Kenny that Kenny's not forgotten. Kenny wanted him to do it, and he did it. Now he knows that whatever he did—even if he's not sure what it was—he did it for Kenny. Even if he did kill someone and he goes to jail, it doesn't matter—it can't matter because he's dead. This was just one last thing to do for Kenny. Squared it with him. Knows everything is now all right with Kenny.

("I went to the Wall and there was his name and it was silence.

Waited and waited and waited. I looked at him, he looked at me. I didn't hear anything, didn't feel anything, and that's the point I knew it wasn't okay with Kenny. That there was more to be done. Didn't know what it was. But he wouldn't have just left me like that. That's why there was no message for me. Because I still had more to do for Kenny. Now? Now it's okay with Kenny. Now he can rest." "And are you still dead?" "What are you, an asswipe? Oh, I can't talk to you, you asswipe! I did it because I *am* dead!")

Next morning, first thing, he hears at the garage that she was with the Jew in a car crash. Everybody figures that she was blowing him and he lost control and they went off the road and through the barrier and over the embankment and front-end-first into the shallows of the river. The Jew lost control of the car.

No, he does not associate this with what happened the night before. He was just out driving, in a different state of mind entirely.

He says, "Yeah? What happened? Who killed her?"

"The Jew killed her. Went off the road."

"She was probably going down on him."

"That's what they say."

That's it. Doesn't feel anything about that either. Still feels nothing. Except his suffering. Why is he suffering so much for what happened to him when she can go on giving blow jobs to old Jews? He's the one who does the suffering, and now she just up and walks away from it all.

Anyway, as he sips his morning coffee at the town garage, looks that way to him.

When everybody gets up to start for the trucks, Les says, "Guess that music won't be coming from that house on Saturday nights anymore."

Though, as sometimes happens, nobody knows what he's talking about, they laugh anyway, and with that, the workday begins.

If she located herself in western Massachusetts, the ad could be traced back to her by colleagues who subscribed to the *New York Review of Books*, particularly if she went on to describe her appearance and list her credentials. Yet if she didn't specify her place of residence, she could wind up with not a single response from anyone within a radius of a hundred, two, even three hundred miles. And since in every ad she'd studied in the *New York Review,* the age given by women exceeded her own by from fifteen to thirty years, how could she go ahead to reveal her correct age—to portray herself correctly altogether—without arousing the suspicion that there was something significant undisclosed by her and wrong with her, a woman claiming to be so young, so attractive, so accomplished who found it necessary to look for a man through a personal ad? If she described herself as "passionate," this might readily be interpreted by the lascivious-minded to be an intentional provocation, to mean "loose" or worse, and letters would come pouring in to her *NYRB* box from the men she wanted nothing to do with. But if she appeared to be a bluestocking for whom sex was of decidedly less importance than her academic, scholarly, and intellectual pursuits, she would be sure to encourage a response from a type who would be all too maidenly for someone as excitable as she could be with an erotic counterpart she could trust. If she presented herself as "pretty," she would be associating herself with a vague catchall category of women, and yet if she described herself, straight out, as "beautiful," if she dared to be truthful enough to evoke the word that had never seemed extravagant to her lovers—who had called her *éblouissante* (as in "*Éblouissante! Tu as un visage de chat*"); dazzling, stunning—or if, for the sake of precision in a text of only thirty or so words, she invoked the resemblance noted by her elders to Leslie Caron who her father always enjoyed making too much of, then anyone other than a megalomaniac might be too intimidated to approach her or refuse to take her seriously as an intellectual. If she wrote, "A photo accompanying the letter would be welcome," or, simply, "Photo, please," it could be misunderstood to imply that she esteemed good looks above intelligence, erudition, and cultural refinement; moreover, any photos she received might be touched up, years old, or altogether spurious. Asking for a photo might even discourage a response from the very men whose interest she was hoping to elicit. Yet if she didn't request a photo, she could wind up traveling all the way to Boston, to New York, or farther, to find herself the dinner companion of someone wholly inappropriate and even distasteful. And distasteful not necessarily because of looks alone. What if he was a liar? What if he was a charlatan? What if he was a psychopath? What if he had AIDS? What if he was violent, vicious, married, or on Medicare? What if he was a weirdo, someone she couldn't get rid of? What if she gave her name and her place of employment to a stalker? Yet, on their first meeting, how could she *withhold* her name? In search of a serious, impassioned love affair leading to marriage and a family, how could an open, honest person start off by lying about something as fundamental as her name? And what about race? Oughtn't she to include the kindly solicitation "Race unimportant"? But it wasn't unimportant; it should be, it ought to be, it well might have been but for the fiasco back in Paris when she was seventeen that convinced her that a man of another race was an unfeasible—because an unknowable—partner.

She was young and adventurous, she didn't *want* to be cautious, and he was from a good family in Brazzaville, the son of a supreme court judge—or so he said—in Paris as an exchange student for a year at Nanterre. Dominique was his name, and she thought of him as a fellow spiritual lover of literature. She'd met him at one of the Milan Kundera lectures. He picked her up there, and outside they were still basking in Kundera's observations on *Madame Bovary,* infected, the both of them, with what Delphine excitedly thought of as "the Kundera disease." Kundera was legitimatized for them by being persecuted as a Czech writer, by being someone who had lost out in Czechoslovakia's great historical struggle to be free. Kundera's playfulness did not appear to be frivolous, not at all. *The Book of Laughter and Forgetting* they loved. There was something trustworthy about him. His Eastern Europeanness. The restless nature of the intellectual. That everything appeared to be difficult for him. Both were won over by Kundera's modesty, the very opposite of superstar demeanor, and both believed in his ethos of thinking and suffering. All that intellectual tribulation—and then there were

his looks. Delphine was very taken by the writer's poetically prize-
fighterish looks, to her an outward sign of everything colliding
within.

After the pickup at the Kundera lecture, it was completely a physical experience with Dominique, and she had never had that before.
It was completely about her body. She had just connected so much
with the Kundera lecture and she had mistaken that connection for
the connection she had to Dominique, and it happened all very
fast. There was nothing except her body. Dominique didn't understand that she didn't want just sex. She wanted to be something
more than a piece of meat on a spit, turned and basted. That's what
he did—those were even his words: turning her and basting her. He
was interested in nothing else, least of all in literature. Loosen up
and shut up—that's his attitude with her, and she somehow gets
locked in, and then comes the terrible night she shows up at his
room and he is waiting there for her with his friend. It's not that
she's now prejudiced, it's just that she realizes she would not have
so misjudged a man of her own race. This was her worst failure,
and she could never forget it. Redemption had only come with
the professor who'd given her his Roman ring. Sex, yes, wonderful
sex, but sex with metaphysics. Sex with metaphysics with a man
with gravitas who is not vain. Someone like Kundera. That is the
plan.

The problem confronting her as she sat alone at the computer
long after dark, the only person left in Barton Hall, unable to leave
her office, unable to face one more night in her apartment without
even a cat for company—the problem was how to include in her
ad, no matter how subtly coded, something that essentially said,
"Whites only need apply." If it were discovered at Athena that it was
she who had specified such an exclusion—no, that would not do
for a person ascending so rapidly through the Athena academic hi-
erarchy. Yet she had no choice but to ask for a photograph, even
though she knew—knew from trying as hard as she could to think
of everything, to be naive about nothing, on the basis of just her
brief life as a woman on her own to take into account how men

could behave—that there was nothing to stop someone sufficiently sadistic or perverse from sending a photograph designed to mislead *specifically* in the matter of race.

No, it was too risky altogether—as well as beneath her dignity— to place an ad to help her meet a man of the caliber that she'd never find anywhere among the faculty of as dreadfully provincial a place as Athena. She could not do it and she should not do it, and yet all the while she thought of the uncertainties, the outright dangers, of advertising oneself to strangers as a woman in search of a suitable mate, all the while she thought of the reasons why it was inadvisable, as chair of the Department of Languages and Literature, to risk revealing herself to colleagues as something other than a serious teacher and scholar—exposing herself as someone with needs and desires that, though altogether human, could be deliberately misconstrued so as to trivialize her—she was doing it: fresh from e-mailing every member of her department her latest thoughts on the subject of senior theses, trying to compose an ad that adhered to the banal linguistic formula of the standard *New York Review* personal but one that managed as well to present a truthful appraisal of *her* caliber. At it now for over an hour and she was still unable to settle on anything unhumiliating enough to e-mail to the paper even pseudonymously.

Western Mass. 29 yr. old petite, passionate, Parisian professor, equally at home teaching Molière as

Brainy, beautiful Berkshire academic, equally at home cooking médaillons de veau as chairing a humanities dept., seeks

Serious SWF scholar seeks

SWF Yale Ph.D. Parisian-born academic. Petite, scholarly, literature-loving, fashion-conscious brunette seeks

Attractive, serious scholar seeks

SWF Ph.D., French, Mass.-based, seeks

Seeks what? *Anything,* anything other than these Athena men—
the wisecracking boys, the feminized old ladies, the timorous, tedious family freaks, the professional dads, all of them so earnest
and so emasculated. She is revolted by the fact that they pride
themselves on doing half the domestic work. Intolerable. "Yes, I
have to go, I have to relieve my wife. I have to do as much diaper
changing as she does, you know." She cringes when they brag about
their helpfulness. Do it, fine, but don't have the vulgarity to mention it. Why make such a spectacle of yourself as the fifty-fifty husband? Just do it and shut up about it. In this revulsion she is very
different from her women colleagues who value these men for their
"sensitivity." Is that what overpraising their wives is, "sensitivity"?
"Oh, Sara Lee is such an extraordinary this-and-that. She's already
published four and a half articles . . ." Mr. Sensitivity always has to
mention her glory. Mr. Sensitivity can't talk about some great show
at the Metropolitan without having to be sure to preface it, "Sara
Lee says . . ." Either they overpraise their wives or they fall dead silent. The husband falls silent and grows more and more depressed,
and she has never encountered this in any other country. If Sara Lee
is an academic who can't find a job while he, say, is barely holding
on to his job, he would rather lose his job than have her think she is
getting the bad end of the deal. There would even be a certain pride
if the situation were reversed and he was the one who had to stay
home while she didn't. A French woman, even a French feminist,
would find such a man disgusting. The Frenchwoman is intelligent,
she's sexy, she's *truly* independent, and if he talks more than she
does, so what, where's the issue? What's the fiery contention all
about? Not "Oh, did you notice, she's so dominated by her rude,
power-hungry husband." No, the more of a woman she is, the
more the Frenchwoman *wants* the man to project his power. Oh,
how she had prayed, on arriving at Athena five years back, that she
might meet some marvelous man who projected his power, and instead the bulk of younger male faculty are these domestic, emasculated types, intellectually unstimulating, pedestrian, the overprais-

ing husbands of Sara Lee whom she has deliciously categorized for her correspondents in Paris as "The Diapers."

Then there are "The Hats." The Hats are the "writers in residence," America's incredibly pretentious writers in residence. Probably, at little Athena, she hasn't seen the worst of them, but these two are bad enough. They show up to teach once a week, and they are married and they come on to her, and they are impossible. When can we have lunch, Delphine? Sorry, she thinks, but I am not impressed. The thing she liked about Kundera at his lectures was that he was always slightly shadowy, even slightly shabby sometimes, a great writer *malgré lui*. At least she perceived it that way and that's what she liked in him. But she certainly does not like, cannot *stand*, the American I-am-the-writer type who, when he looks at her, she knows is thinking, With your French confidence and your French fashions and your elitist French education, you are very French indeed, but you are nonetheless the academic and I am the writer—we are not equals.

These writers in residence, as far as she can surmise, spend an enormous amount of time worrying about their headwear. Yes, both the poet *and* the prose writer have an extraordinary hat fetish, and so she categorizes them in her letters as The Hats. One of them is always dressed as Charles Lindbergh, wearing his antique pilot gear, and she cannot understand the relationship between pilot gear and writing, particularly writing in residence. She muses about this in her humorous correspondence to her Paris friends. The other is the floppy-hat type, the unassuming type—which is, of course, so recherché—who spends eight hours at the mirror dressing carelessly. Vain, unreadable, married by now a hundred and eighty-six times, and incredibly self-important. It's not so much hatred she feels for this one as contempt. And yet, deep in the Berkshires starving for romance, she sometimes feels ambivalent about The Hats and wonders if she shouldn't take them seriously as erotic candidates, at least. No, she couldn't, not after what she has written to Paris. She must resist them if only because they try to talk to her with her own vocabulary. Because one of them, the younger, minimally less self-important one, has read Bataille, because he knows just enough Bataille and has read just enough Hegel, she's gone out with him a few times, and never has a man so rapidly de-eroticized himself before her eyes; with every word he spoke—using, as he did, that language of hers that she herself is now somewhat uncertain about—he read himself right out of her life.

Whereas the older types, who are uncool and tweedy, "The Humanists" . . . Well, obliging as she must be at conferences and in publications to write and speak as the profession requires, the humanist is the very part of her own self that she sometimes feels herself betraying, and so she is attracted to them: because they are what they are and always have been and because she knows they think of her as a traitor. Her classes have a following, but they think of that following contemptuously, as a fashionable phenomenon. These older men, The Humanists, the old-fashioned traditionalist humanists who have read everything, the born-again teachers (as *she* thinks of *them*), make her sometimes feel shallow. Her following they laugh at and her scholarship they despise. At faculty meetings they're not afraid to say what they say, and you would think they should be; in class they're not afraid to say what they feel, and, again, you would think they should be; and, as a result, in front of them she crumbles. Since she doesn't herself have that much conviction about all the so-called discourse she picked up in Paris and New Haven, inwardly she crumbles. Only she needs that language to succeed. On her own in America, she needs so much to succeed! And yet everything that it takes to succeed is somehow compromising, and it makes her feel less and less genuine, and dramatizing her predicament as a "Faustian bargain" helps only a little.

At moments she even feels herself betraying Milan Kundera, and so, silently, when she is alone, she will picture him in her mind's eye and speak to him and ask his forgiveness. Kundera's intention in his lectures was to free the intelligence from the French sophistication, to talk about the novel as having something to do with human beings and the *comédie humaine;* his intention was to free his students from the tempting traps of structuralism and formalism and the obsession with modernity, to purge them of the French theory that they had been fed, and listening to him had been an enormous relief, for despite her publications and a growing scholarly reputation, it was always difficult for her to deal with literature through literary theory. There could be such a gigantic gap between what she liked and what she was supposed to admire—between how she was supposed to speak about what she was supposed to admire and how she spoke to herself about the writers she treasured—that her sense of betraying Kundera, though not the most serious problem in her life, would become at times like the shame of betraying a kindly, trusting, absent lover.

The only man she's been out with frequently is, oddly enough, the most conservative person on campus, a divorced man of sixty-five, Arthur Sussman, the Boston University economist who was to have been secretary of the treasury in the second Ford administration. He is a bit stout, a bit stiff, always wearing a suit; he hates affirmative action, he hates Clinton, he comes in from Boston once a week, is paid a fortune, and is thought to make the place, to put little Athena on the academic map. The women in particular are sure she has slept with him, just because he was once powerful. They see them occasionally having lunch together in the cafeteria. He comes to the cafeteria and he looks so excruciatingly bored, until he sees Delphine, and when he asks if he may join her, she says, "How generous of you to endow us with your presence today," or something along those lines. He likes that she mocks him, to a point. Over lunch, they have what Delphine calls "a real conversation." With a thirty-nine-billion-dollar budget surplus, he tells her, the government is giving nothing back to the taxpayer. The people earned it and they should spend it, and they shouldn't have bureaucrats deciding what to do with their money. Over lunch, he explains in detail why Social Security should be given over to private investment analysts. Everybody should invest in their own future, he tells her. Why should anyone trust the government to provide for people's futures when Social Security has been giving you x returns while anybody who had invested in the stock market over the same period of time would now have twice as much, if not more? The backbone of his argument is always personal sovereignty, personal freedom, and what he never understands, Delphine dares to tell the treasury-secretary-who-never-was, is that for most people there isn't enough money to make choices and there isn't enough education to make educated guesses—there isn't enough mastery of the market. His model, as she interprets it for him, is based on a notion of radical personal liberty that, in his thinking, is reduced to a radical sovereignty in the market. The surplus and Social Security—those are the two issues that are bugging him, and they talk about them all the time. He seems to hate Clinton most for proposing the Democratic version of everything he wanted. "Good thing," he tells her, "that little squirt Bob Reich is out of there. He'd have Clinton spending billions of dollars retraining people for jobs they could never occupy. Good thing he left the cabinet. At least they have Bob Rubin there, at least they have one sane guy who knows where the bodies are buried. At least he and Alan kept the interest rates where they had to be. At least he and Alan kept this recovery going . . ."

The one thing she likes about him is that, aside from his gruff insider's take on economic issues, he happens also to know all of Engels and Marx really well. More impressive, he knows intimately their *The German Ideology,* a text she has always found fascinating and loves. When he takes her out to dinner down in Great Barrington, things turn both more romantic and more intellectual than they do at lunch in the cafeteria. Over dinner he likes to speak French with her. One of his conquests years ago was Parisian, and he goes on endlessly about this woman. Delphine does not, however, open her mouth like a fish when he talks about his Parisian affair or about his manifold sentimental attachments before and after. About women he brags constantly, in a very suave way that she doesn't, after a while, find suave at all. She cannot stand the fact that he thinks she's impressed by all his conquests, but she puts up with it, only slightly bored, because otherwise she's glad to be having dinner with an intelligent, assertive, well-read man of the world. When at dinner he takes her hand, she says something to let him know, however subtly, that if he thinks he is going to sleep with her, he is crazy. Sometimes in the parking lot, he pulls her to him by cupping her behind and holding her against him. He says, "I cannot be with you time after time like this without some passion. I can't take out a woman as beautiful as you, talk to her and talk to her and talk to her, and have it end there." "We have a saying in France," she tells him, "which is . . ." "Which is what?" he asks, thinking he may pick up a new *bon mot* in the bargain. Smiling, she says, "I don't know. It'll come to me later," and in this way gently disentangles herself from his surprisingly strong arms. She is gentle with him because it works, and she is gentle with him because she knows he thinks it is a question of age, when in fact it is a question, as she explains to him driving back in his car, of nothing so banal: it is a question of "a frame of mind." "It's about who I am," she tells him, and, if nothing else has done it, that sends him away for two or three months, until he next turns up in the cafeteria, looking to see if she is there. Sometimes he telephones her late at night or in the early hours of the morning. From his Back Bay bed, he wants to talk with her about sex. She says she prefers to talk about Marx, and it takes no more, with this conservative economist, to put a stop to that stuff. And yet the women who don't like her are all sure that because he's powerful she has slept with him. It is incomprehensible to them that, bleak and lonely as her life is, she has no interest in becoming Arthur Sussman's little badge of a mistress. It has also gotten back to her that one of them has called her "so passé, such a parody of Simone de Beauvoir." By which she means that it is her judgment that Beauvoir sold out to Sartre—a very intelligent woman but in the end his slave. For these women, who observe her at lunch with Arthur Sussman and get it all wrong, everything is an issue, everything is an ideological stance, everything is a betrayal— everything's a selling out. Beauvoir sold out, Delphine sold out, et cetera, et cetera. Something about Delphine makes them go green in the face.

Another of her problems. She does not want to alienate these women. Yet she is no less philosophically isolated from them than from the men. Though it would not be prudent for her to tell them so, the women are far more feminist, in the American sense, than she is. It would not be prudent because they are dismissive enough and seem always to know where she stands anyway, always suspecting her motives and aims: she is attractive, young, thin, effortlessly stylish, she has climbed so high so fast she already has the beginnings of a reputation beyond the college, and, like her Paris friends, she doesn't use or need to use all their clichés (the very clichés by which The Diapers are so eagerly emasculated). Only in the anonymous note to Coleman Silk did she adopt their rhetoric, and that was not only accidental, because she was so overwrought, but, in the end, deliberate, to hide her identity. In truth, she is no less emancipated than these Athena feminists are and perhaps even more: she left her own country, daringly left France, she works hard at her job, she works hard at her publications, and she wants to make it; on her own as she is, she *has* to make it. She is utterly alone, unsupported, homeless, decountried—*dépaysée*. In a free state but oftentimes so forlornly *dépaysée*. Ambitious? She happens to be more ambitious than all those staunch go-it-alone feminists put together, but because men are drawn to her, and among them is a man as eminent as Arthur Sussman, and because, for the fun of it, she wears a vintage Chanel jacket with tight jeans, or a slip dress in summer, and because she likes cashmere and leather, the women are resentful. She makes it a point not to be concerned with *their* ghastly clothing, so by what right do they dwell on what they consider recidivist about hers? She knows everything they say in their annoyance with her. They say what the men she begrudgingly respects are saying—that she's a charlatan and illegitimate—and that makes it hurt more. They say, "She is fooling the students." They say, "How can the students not see through this woman?" They say, "Don't they see that she is one of those French male chauvinists in drag?" They say that she got to be the department chair *faute de mieux*. And they make fun of her language. "Well, of course, it's her intertextual charm that's gotten her her following. It's her relation-ship to phenomenology. She's *such* a phenomenologist ha-ha-ha!" She knows what they are saying to ridicule her, and yet she remem-bers being in France and being at Yale and *living* for this vocabu-lary; she believes that to be a good literary critic she *has* to have this vocabulary. She *needs* to know about intertextuality. Does that mean she's a phony? No! It means that she's unclassifiable. In some circles that might be thought of as her mystique! But just be the least bit unclassifiable at a backwoods hellhole like this place, and that annoys everyone. Her being unclassifiable even annoys Arthur Sussman. Why the hell won't she at least have phone sex? Be unclas-sifiable here, be something they cannot reconcile, and they torment you for it. That being unclassifiable is a part of her *bildungsroman,* that she has always *thrived* on being unclassifiable, nobody at Athena understands.

There is a cabal of three women—a philosophy professor, a soci-ology professor, and a history professor—who particularly drive her crazy. Full of animosity toward her simply because she is not ploddingly plugged in the way they are. Because she has an air of chic, they feel she hasn't read enough learned journals. Because their American notions of independence differ from her French notions of independence, she is dismissed by them as pandering to powerful males. But what has she ever actually done to arouse their distrust, except perhaps handle the men on the faculty as well as she does? Yes, she'd been at dinner in Great Barrington with Arthur Sussman. Does that mean she didn't consider herself his intellec-tual equal? There's no question in her mind that she is his equal. She isn't flattered to be out with him—she wants to hear what he has to say about *The German Ideology.* And hadn't she first tried to have lunch with the three of *them,* and could they have been any more condescending? Of course, they don't bother to read her scholarship. None of them reads anything she's written. It's all about perception. All they see is Delphine using what she under-stands they sarcastically call "her little French aura" on all the ten-ured men. Yet she is strongly tempted to court the cabal, to tell them in so many words that she doesn't *like* the French aura—if she did, she'd be living in France! And she doesn't own the tenured men—she doesn't own anyone. Why else would she be by herself, the only person at the desk of a Barton Hall office at ten o'clock at night? Hardly a week goes by when she doesn't try and fail with the three who drive her nuts, who baffle her most, but whom she cannot charm, finesse, or engage in any way. "*Les Trois Grâces*" she calls them in her letters to Paris, spelling "*grâces*" maliciously "*grasses*." The Three Greaseballs. At certain parties—parties that Delphine doesn't really want to be at—*Les Trois Grasses* are invariably present. When some big feminist intellectual comes along, Delphine would at least like to be invited, but she never is. She can go to the lecture but she's never asked to the dinner. But the infernal trio who call the shots, they are always there.

In imperfect revolt against her Frenchness (as well as being obsessed with her Frenchness), lifted voluntarily out of her country (if not out of herself), so ensnared by the disapproval of *Les Trois Grasses* as to be endlessly calculating what response might gain her their esteem without further obfuscating her sense of herself and misrepresenting totally the inclinations of the woman she once naturally was, at times destabilized to the point of shame by the discrepancy between how she must deal with literature in order to succeed professionally and why she first came to literature, Delphine, to her astonishment, is all but isolated in America. Decountried, isolated, estranged, confused about everything essential to a life, in a desperate state of bewildered longing and surrounded on all sides by admonishing forces defining her as the enemy. And all because she'd gone eagerly in search of an existence of her own. All because she'd been courageous and refused to take the prescribed view of herself. She seemed to herself to have subverted herself in the altogether admirable effort to *make* herself. There is something very mean about life that it should have done this to her. At its heart, very mean and very vengeful, ordering a fate not according to the laws of logic but to the antagonistic whim of perversity. Dare to give yourself over to your own vitality, and you might as well be in the hands of a hardened criminal. I will go to America and be the author of my life, she says; I will construct myself outside the orthodoxy of my family's given, I will fight *against* the given, impassioned subjectivity carried to the limit, individualism at its best—and she winds up instead in a drama beyond her control. She winds up as the author of nothing. There is the drive to master things, and the thing that is mastered is oneself.

Why should it be so impossible just to know what to do?

Delphine would be entirely isolated if not for the department secretary, Margo Luzzi, a mousy divorcée in her thirties, also lonely, wonderfully competent, shy as can be, who will do anything for Delphine and sometimes eats her sandwich in Delphine's office and who has wound up as the chairperson's only adult woman friend at Athena. Then there are the writers in residence. They appear to like in her exactly what the others hate. But she cannot stand *them*. How did she get *in the middle* like this? And how does she get out? As it does not offer any solace to dramatize her compromises as a Faustian bargain, so it isn't all that helpful to think of her in-the-middleness, as she tries to, as a "Kunderian inner exile."

Seeks. All right then, *seeks*. Do as the students say—Go for it! Youthful, petite, womanly, attractive, academically successful SWF French-born scholar, Parisian background, Yale Ph.D., Mass.-based, seeks . . . ? And now just lay it on the line. Do not hide from the truth of what you are and do not hide from the truth of what you seek. A stunning, brilliant, hyperorgasmic woman seeks . . . seeks . . . seeks specifically and uncompromisingly *what*?

She wrote now in a rush.

Mature man with backbone. Unattached. Independent. Witty. Lively. Defiant. Forthright. Well educated. Satirical spirit. Charm. Knowledge and love of great books. Well spoken and straight-speaking. Trimly built. Five eight or nine. Mediterranean complexion. Green eyes preferred. Age unimportant. But must be intellectual. Graying hair acceptable, even desirable . . .

And then, and only then, did the mythical man being summoned forth in all earnestness on the screen condense into a portrait of someone she already knew. Abruptly she stopped writing. The exercise had been undertaken only as an experiment, to try loosening the grip of inhibition just a little before she renewed her effort to compose an ad not too diluted by circumspection. Nonetheless, she was astonished by what she'd come up with, by *whom* she'd come up with, in her distress wanting nothing more than to delete those forty-odd useless words as quickly as possible. And thinking, too, of the many reasons, including her shame, for her to accept defeat as a blessing and forgo hope of solving her in-the-middleness by participating in such an impossibly compromising scheme . . . Thinking that if she had stayed in France she wouldn't need this ad, wouldn't need an ad for anything, least of all to find a man . . . Thinking that coming to America was the bravest thing she had ever done, but that how brave she couldn't have known at the time. She just did it as the next step of her ambition, and not a crude ambition either, a dignified ambition, the ambition to be independent, but now she's left with the consequences. Ambition. Adventure. Glamour. The glamour of going to America. The superiority. The superiority of leaving. Left for the pleasure of one day coming home, having done it, of returning home triumphant. Left because I wanted to come home one day and have them say—what is it that I wanted them to say? "She did it. She did that. And if she did that, she can do anything. A girl who weighs a hundred and four pounds, barely five foot two, twenty years old, on her own, went there on her own with a name that didn't mean anything to anybody, and she did it. Self-made. Nobody knew her. Made herself." And who was it that I wanted to have said it? And if they had, what difference would it make? "Our daughter in America . . ." I wanted them to say, to *have* to say, "She made it on her own in America." Because I could not make a French success, a real success, not with my mother and her shadow over everything—the shadow of her accomplishments but, even worse, of her family, the shadow of the Walincourts, named for the place given to them in the thirteenth century by the king Saint Louis and conforming still to the family ideals as they were *set* in the thirteenth century. How Delphine hated all those families, the pure and ancient aristocracy of the provinces, all of them thinking the same, looking the same, sharing the same stifling values and the same stifling religious obedience. However much ambition they have, however much they push their children, they bring their children up to the same litany of charity, selflessness, discipline, faith, and respect—respect not for the individual (*down* with the individual!) but for the traditions of the family. Superior to intelligence, to creativity, to a deep development of oneself apart from them, superior to *everything*, were the traditions of the stupid Walincourts! It was Delphine's mother who embodied those values, who imposed them on the household, who would have enchained her only daughter to those values from birth to the grave had her daughter been without the strength, from adolescence on, to run from her as far as she could. The Walincourt children of Delphine's generation either fell into absolute conformity or rebelled so gruesomely they were incomprehensible, and Delphine's success was to have done neither. From a background few ever even begin to recover from, Delphine had managed a unique escape. By coming to America, to Yale, to Athena, she had, in fact, *surpassed* her mother, who couldn't herself have dreamed of leaving France—without Delphine's father and his money, Catherine de Walincourt could hardly dream, at twenty-two, of leaving Picardy for Paris. Because if she left Picardy and the fortress of her family, who would she be? What would her *name* mean? I left because I wanted to have an accomplishment that nobody could mistake, that had nothing to do with them, that was my own . . . Thinking that the reason she can't get an American man isn't that she can't get an American man, it's that she can't understand these men and that she will never understand these men, and the reason she can't understand these men is because she is not fluent. With all her pride in her fluency, with all her *fluency,* she is not fluent! I think I understand them, and I do understand; what I don't understand isn't what they say, it's everything they don't say, everything they're *not* saying. Here she operates at fifty percent of

her intelligence, and in Paris she understood every nuance. What's
the point of being smart here when, because I am not from here, I
am de facto dumb . . . Thinking that the only English she really understands—no, the only *American* she understands—is academic
American, which is hardly American, which is why she can't make
it *in,* will never make it in, which is why there'll never be a man,
why this will never be her home, why her intuitions are wrong and
always will be, why the cozy intellectual life she had in Paris as a
student will never be hers again, why for the rest of her life she is
going to understand eleven percent of this country and zero percent of these men . . . Thinking that all her intellectual advantages
have been muted by her being *dépaysée* . . . Thinking that she has
lost her peripheral vision, that she sees things that are in front of
her but nothing out of the corner of her eye, that what she has here
is not the vision of a woman of her intelligence but a flat, a totally
frontal vision, the vision of an immigrant or a displaced person, a
misplaced person . . . Thinking, Why did I leave? Because of my
mother's shadow? This is why I gave up everything that was mine,
everything that was familiar, everything that had made me a subtle
being and not this mess of uncertainty that I've become. Everything
that I loved I gave up. People do that when their countries are impossible to live in because the fascists have taken change but not because of their mother's shadow . . . Thinking, Why did I leave, what
have I done, this is impossible. My friends, our talk, my city, the
men, all the intelligent men. Confident men I could converse with.
Mature men who could understand. Stable, passionate, masculine
men. Strong, unintimidated men. Men legitimately and unambigu-
ously men . . . Thinking, Why didn't somebody *stop* me, why didn't
somebody *say* something to me? Away from home for less than ten
years and it feels like two lifetimes already . . . Thinking that she's
Catherine de Walincourt Roux's little daughter still, that she has
not changed that by one iota . . . Thinking that being French in
Athena may have made her exotic to the natives, but it hasn't made
her anything more extraordinary to her mother and it never will . . .
Thinking, yes, that's why she left, to elude her mother's fixed-

forever overshadowing shadow, and that's what blocks her return, and now she's exactly nowhere, in the middle, neither there nor here . . . Thinking that under her exotic Frenchness she is to herself who she always was, that all the exotic Frenchness has achieved in America is to make of her the consummate miserable, misunderstood foreigner . . . Thinking that she's worse even than in the middle—that she's in *exile*, in, of all things, a stupid-making, self-imposed anguishing exile from her mother—Delphine neglects to observe that earlier, at the outset, instead of addressing the ad to the *New York Review of Books,* she had automatically addressed it to the recipients of her previous communication, the recipients of most of her communications—to the ten staff members of the Athena Department of Languages and Literature. She neglects first to observe that mistake and then, in her distracted, turbulent, emotionally taxing state, neglects also to observe that instead of hitting the delete button, she is adding one common-enough tiny error to another common-enough tiny error by hitting the send button instead. And so off, irretrievably off goes the ad in quest of a Coleman Silk duplicate or facsimile, and not to the classified section of the *New York Review of Books* but to every member of her department.

It was past 1 A.M. when the phone rang. She had long ago fled her office—run from her office thinking only to get her passport and flee the country—and it was already several hours after her regular bedtime, when the phone rang with the news. So anguished was she by the ad's inadvertently going out as e-mail that she was still awake and roaming her apartment, tearing at her hair, sneering in the mirror at her face, bending her head to the kitchen table to weep into her hands, and, as though startled out of sleep—the sleep of a heretofore meticulously defended adult life—jumping up to cry aloud, "It did not happen! I did not do it!" But who had then? In the past there seemed always to be people trying their best to trample her down, to dispose somehow of the nuisance she was to them, callous people against whom she had learned the hard way to protect herself. But tonight there was no one to reproach: her own hand had delivered the ruinous blow.

Frantic, in a frenzy, she tried to figure out some way, any way, to prevent the worst from happening, but in her state of incredulous despair she could envision the inevitability of only the most cataclysmic trajectory: the hours passing, the dawn breaking, the doors to Barton Hall opening, her departmental colleagues each entering his or her office, booting up the computer, and finding there, to savor with their morning coffee, the e-mail ad for a Coleman Silk duplicate that she'd had no intention of ever sending. To be read once, twice, three times over by all the members of her department and then to be e-mailed down the line to every last instructor, professor, administrator, office clerk, and student.

Everyone in her classes will read it. Her secretary will read it. Before the day is out, the president of the college will have read it, and the college trustees. And even if she were to claim that the ad had been meant as a joke, nothing more than an insider's joke, why would the trustees allow the joke's perpetrator to remain at Athena? Especially after her joke is written up in the student paper, as it will be. And in the local paper. After it is picked up by the *French* papers.

Her mother! The humiliation for her mother! And her father! The disappointment to *him!* All the conformist Walincourt cousins—the pleasure they will take in her defeat! All the ridiculously conservative uncles and the ridiculously pious aunts, together keeping intact the narrowness of the past—how this will please them as they sit snobbishly side by side in church! But suppose she explained that she had merely been experimenting with the ad as a literary form, alone at the office disinterestedly toying with the personal ad as . . . as utilitarian haiku. Won't help. Too ridiculous. *Nothing* will help. Her mother, her father, her brothers, her friends, her teachers. Yale. *Yale!* News of the scandal will reach everyone she's ever known, and the shame will follow her unflaggingly forever. Where can she even run with her passport? Montreal? Martinique? And earn her living how? No, not in the farthest

Francophone outpost will she be allowed to teach once they learn of her ad. The pure, prestigious professional life for which she had done all this planning, all this grueling work, the untainted, irreproachable life of the mind . . . She thought to phone Arthur Sussman. Arthur will figure a way out for her. He can pick up the phone and talk to anyone. He's tough, he's shrewd, in the ways of the world the smartest, most influential American she knows. Powerful people like Arthur, however upright, are not boxed in by the need to always be telling the truth. He'll come up with what it takes to explain everything. He'll figure out just what to do. But when she tells him what has happened, why will he think to help her? All he'll think is that she liked Coleman Silk more than she liked him. His vanity will do his thinking for him and lead him to the stupidest conclusion. He'll think what *everyone* will think: that she is pining for Coleman Silk, that she is dreaming not of Arthur Sussman, let alone of The Diapers or The Hats, but of Coleman Silk. Imagining her in love with Coleman Silk, he'll slam down the phone and never speak to her again.

To recapitulate. To go over what's happened. To try to gain sufficient perspective to do the rational thing. She didn't want to send it. She wrote it, yes, but she was embarrassed to send it and didn't want to send it and she *didn't* send it—yet it *went*. The same with the anonymous letter—she didn't want to send it, carried it to New York with no intention of ever sending it, and *it* went. But what's gone off this time is much, much worse. This time she's so desperate that by twenty after one in the morning the rational thing is to telephone Arthur Sussman regardless of what he thinks. Arthur has to help her. He has to tell her what she can do to undo what she's done. And then, at exactly twenty past one, the phone she holds in her hand to dial Arthur Sussman suddenly begins to ring. Arthur calling *her!*

But it is her secretary. "He's dead," Margo says, crying so hard that Delphine can't be quite sure what she's hearing. "Margo—are you all right?" "He's dead!" "Who is?" "I just heard. Delphine. It's terrible. I'm calling you, I have to, I have to call you. I have to tell

you something terrible. Oh, Delphine, it's late, I know it's late—"
"No! Not Arthur!" Delphine cries. "Dean Silk!" Margo says. "Is
dead?" "A terrible crash. It's too horrible." "What crash? Margo,
what has happened? Where? Speak slowly. Start again. What are
you telling me?" "In the river. With a woman. In his car. A crash."
Margo is by now unable to be at all coherent, while Delphine is so
stunned that, later, she does not remember putting down the receiver or rushing in tears to her bed or lying there howling his
name.

She put down the receiver, and then she spent the worst hours of
her life.

Because of the ad they'll think she liked him? They'll think she
loved him because of the ad? But what would they think if they saw
her now, carrying on like the widow herself? She cannot close her
eyes, because when she does she sees *his* eyes, those green staring
eyes of his, exploding. She sees the car plunge off the road, and his
head is shooting forward, and in the instant of the crash, his eyes
explode. "No! No!" But when she opens her eyes to stop seeing his
eyes, all she sees is what she's done and the mockery that will ensue.
She sees her disgrace with her eyes open and his disintegration with
her eyes shut, and throughout the night the pendulum of suffering
swings her from one to the other.

She wakes up in the same state of upheaval she was in when she
went to sleep. She can't remember why she is shaking. She thinks
she is shaking from a nightmare. The nightmare of his eyes exploding. But no, it happened, he's dead. And the ad—*it* happened. Everything has happened, and nothing's to be done. I wanted them to
say . . . and now they'll say, "Our daughter in America? We don't
talk about her. She no longer exists for us." When she tries to compose herself and settle on a plan of action, no thinking is possible:
only the derangement is possible, the spiraling obtuseness that is
terror. It is just after 5 A.M. She closes her eyes to try to sleep and
make it all go away, but the instant her eyes are shut, there are *his*
eyes. They are staring at her and then they explode.

She is dressing. She is screaming. She is walking out her door and it's barely dawn. No makeup. No jewelry. Just her horrified face. Coleman Silk is dead.

When she reaches the campus there's no one there. Only crows. It's so early the flag hasn't yet been raised. Every morning she looks for it atop North Hall, and every morning, upon seeing it, there is the moment of satisfaction. She left home, she dared to do it—she is in America! There is the contentment with her own courage and the knowledge that it hasn't been easy. But the American flag's not there, and she doesn't see that it's not. She sees nothing but what she must do.

She has a key to Barton Hall and she goes in. She gets to her office. She's done that much. She's hanging on. She's thinking now. Okay. But how does she get into their offices to get at their computers? It's what she should have done last night instead of running away in a panic. To regain her self-possession, to rescue her name, to forestall the disaster of ruining her career, she must continue to think. Thinking has been her whole life. What else has she been trained to do from the time she started school? She leaves her office and walks down the corridor. Her aim is clear now, her thinking decisive. She will just go in and delete it. It is her right to delete it— she sent it. And she did not even do that. It was not intentional. She's not responsible. It just went. But when she tries the handle of each of the doors, they are locked. Next she tries working her keys into the locks, first her key to the building, then the key to her office, but neither works. Of course they don't work. They wouldn't have worked last night and they don't work now. As for thinking, were she able to think like Einstein, thinking will not open these doors.

Back in her own office, she unlocks her files. Looking for what? Her c.v. Why look for her c.v.? It is the end of her c.v. It is the end of our daughter in America. And because it is the end, she pulls all the hanging files out of the drawer and hurls them on the floor. Empties the entire drawer. "We have no daughter in America. We have no daughter. We have only sons." Now she does not try to think that she should think. Instead, she begins throwing things.

Whatever is piled on her desk, whatever is decorating her walls—what difference does it make what breaks? She tried and she failed. It is the end of the impeccable résumé and of the veneration of the résumé. "Our daughter in America failed."

She is sobbing when she picks up the phone to call Arthur. He will jump out of bed and drive straight from Boston. In less than three hours he'll be in Athena. By nine o'clock Arthur will be here! But the number she dials is the emergency number on the decal pasted to the phone. And she had no more intention of dialing that number than of sending the two letters. All she had was the very human wish to be saved.

She cannot speak.

"Hello?" says the man at the other end. "Hello? Who is this?"

She barely gets it out. The most irreducible two words in any language. One's name. Irreducible and irreplaceable. All that is her. *Was* her. And now the two most ridiculous words in the world.

"Who? Professor who? I can't understand you, Professor."

"Security?"

"Speak louder, Professor. Yes, yes, this is Campus Security."

"Come here," she says pleadingly, and once again she is in tears. "Right away. Something terrible has happened."

"Professor? Where are you? Professor, what's happened?"

"Barton." She says it again so he can understand. "Barton 121," she tells him. "Professor Roux."

"What is it, Professor?

"Something terrible."

"Are you all right? What's wrong? What is it? Is somebody there?"

"*I'm* here."

"Is everything all right?"

"Someone broke in."

"Broke in where?"

"My office."

"When? Professor, when?"

"I don't know. In the night. I don't know."

"You okay? Professor? Professor Roux? Are you there? Barton Hall? You sure?"

The hesitation. Trying to think. Am I sure? Am I? "Absolutely," she says, sobbing uncontrollably now. "Hurry, please! Get here immediately, *please!* Someone broke into my office! It's a shambles! It's awful! It's horrible! My things! Someone broke into my computer! Hurry!"

"A break-in? Do you know who it was? Do you know *who* broke in? Was it a student?"

"Dean Silk broke in," she said. "Hurry!"

"Professor—Professor, are you there? Professor Roux, Dean Silk is dead."

"I've heard," she said, "I know, it's awful," and then she screamed, screamed at the horror of all that had happened, screamed at the thought of the very last thing he had ever done, and to her, to *her*— and after that, Delphine's day was a circus.

The astonishing news of Dean Silk's death in a car crash with an Athena college janitor had barely reached the last of the college's classrooms when word began to spread of the pillaging of Delphine Roux's office and the e-mail hoax Dean Silk had attempted to perpetrate only hours before the fatal crash. People were having trouble enough believing all of *this*, when another story, one about the circumstances of the crash, spread from town up to the college, further confounding just about everybody. For all its atrocious details, the story was said to have originated with a reliable source: the brother of the state trooper who had found the bodies. According to his story, the reason the dean lost control of his car was because, from the passenger seat beside him, the Athena woman janitor was satisfying him while he drove. This the police were able to infer from the disposition of his clothing and the position of her body and its location in the vehicle when the wreckage was discovered and pulled from the river.

Most of the faculty, particularly older professors who had known

Coleman Silk personally for many years, refused at first to believe this story, and were outraged by the gullibility with which it was being embraced as incontrovertible truth—the cruelty of the insult appalled them. Yet as the day progressed and additional facts emerged about the break-in, and still more came out about Silk's affair with the janitor—reports from numerous people who had seen them sneaking around together—it became increasingly difficult for the elders of the faculty "to remain"—as the local paper noted the next day in its human interest feature—"heartbreakingly in denial."

And when people began to remember how, a couple of years earlier, no one had wanted to believe that he had called two of his black students spooks; when they remembered how after resigning in disgrace he had isolated himself from his former colleagues, how on the rare occasions when he was seen in town he was abrupt to the point of rudeness with whoever happened to run into him; when they remembered that in his vociferous loathing of everything and everyone having to do with Athena he was said to have managed to estrange himself from his own children . . . well, even those who had begun the day dismissing any suggestion that Coleman Silk's life could have come to so hideous a conclusion, the old-timers who found it unendurable to think of a man of his intellectual stature, a charismatic teacher, a dynamic and influential dean, a charming, vigorous man still hale and hearty in his seventies and the father of four grown, wonderful kids, as forsaking everything he'd once valued and sliding so precipitously into the scandalous death of an alienated, bizarre outsider—even those people had to face up to the thoroughgoing transformation that had followed upon the spooks incident and that had not only brought Coleman Silk to his mortifying end but led as well—led inexcusably—to the gruesome death of Faunia Farley, the hapless thirty-four-year-old illiterate whom, as everyone now knew, he had taken in old age as his mistress.

5

The Purifying Ritual

TWO FUNERALS.

Faunia's first, up at the cemetery on Battle Mountain, always for me an unnerving place to drive by, creepy even in daylight, with its mysteries of ancient gravestone stillness and motionless time, and rendered all the more ominous by the state forest preserve that abuts what was originally an Indian burial ground—a vast, densely wooded, boulder-strewn wilderness veined with streams glassily cascading from ledge to ledge and inhabited by coyote, bobcat, even black bear, and by foraging deer herds said to abound in huge, precolonial numbers. The women from the dairy farm had purchased Faunia's plot at the very edge of the dark woods and organized the innocent, empty graveside ceremony. The more outgoing of the two, the one who identified herself as Sally, delivered the first of the eulogies, introducing her farming partner and their children, then saying, "We all lived with Faunia up at the farm, and why we're here this morning is why you're here: to celebrate a life."

She spoke in a bright, ringing voice, a smallish, hearty, round-faced woman in a long sack dress, buoyantly determined to keep to a perspective that would cause the least chagrin among the six farm-reared children, each neatly dressed in his or her best clothes, each holding a fistful of flowers to be strewn on the coffin before it was lowered into the ground.

"Which of us," Sally asked, "will ever forget that big, warm laugh of hers? Faunia could have us in stitches as much from the infectiousness of her laugh as from some of the things she could come out with. And she was also, as you know, a deeply spiritual person. A spiritual person," she repeated, "a spiritual seeker—the word to best describe her beliefs is pantheism. Her God was nature, and her worship of nature extended to her love for our little herd of cows, for all cows, really, for that most benevolent of creatures who is the foster mother of the human race. Faunia had an enormous respect for the institution of the family dairy farm. Along with Peg and me and the children, she helped to try to keep the family dairy farm alive in New England as a viable part of our cultural heritage. Her God was everything you see around you at our farm and everything you see around you on Battle Mountain. We chose this resting place for Faunia because it has been sacred ever since the aboriginal peoples bid farewell to their loved ones here. The wonderful stories that Faunia told our kids—about the swallows in the barn and the crows in the fields, about the red-tailed hawks that glide in the sky high above our fields—they were the same kind of stories you might have heard on this very mountaintop before the ecological balance of the Berkshires was first disturbed by the coming of . . ."

The coming of you-know-who. The environmentalist Rousseauism of the rest of the eulogy made it just about impossible for me to stay focused.

The second eulogist was Smoky Hollenbeck, the former Athena athletic star who was supervisor of the physical plant, Faunia's boss, and—as I knew from Coleman, who'd hired him—was for a time a bit more. It was into Smoky's Athena harem that Faunia had been conscripted practically from her first day on his custodial staff, and it was from his harem that she had been abruptly dismissed once Les Farley had somehow ferreted out what Smoky was up to with her.

Smoky didn't speak, like Sally, of Faunia's pantheistic purity as a natural being; in his capacity as representative of the college, he concentrated on her competence as a housekeeper, beginning with her influence on the undergraduates whose dormitories she cleaned.

"What changed about the students with Faunia being there," Smoky said, "was that they had a person who, whenever they saw her, greeted them with a smile and a hello and a How are you, and Did you get over your cold, and How are classes going. She would always spend a moment talking and becoming familiar with the students before she began her work. Over time, she was no longer invisible to the student, no longer just a housekeeper, but another person whom they'd developed respect for. They were always more cognizant, as a result of knowing Faunia, of not leaving a mess behind for her to have to pick up. In contrast to that, you may have another housekeeper who never makes eye contact, really keeps a distance from the students, really doesn't care about what the students are doing or want to know what they're doing. Well, that was not Faunia—never. The condition of the student dormitories, I find, is directly related to the relationship of the students and their housekeeper. The number of broken windows that we have to fix, the number of holes in the walls that we have to repair, that are made when students kick 'em, punch 'em, take their frustration out on them . . . whatever the case may be. Graffiti on walls. The full gamut. Well, if it was Faunia's building, you had none of this. You had instead a building that was conducive to good productivity, to learning and living and to feeling a part of the Athena community . . ."

Extremely brilliant performance by this tall, curly-haired, handsome young family man who had been Coleman's predecessor as Faunia's lover. Sensual contact with Smoky's perfect custodial worker was no more imaginable, from what he was telling us, than with Sally's storytelling pantheist. "In the mornings," Smoky said, "she took care of North Hall and the administrative offices there. Though her routine changed slightly from day to day, there were some basic things to be done every single morning, and she did them excellently. Wastepaper baskets were emptied, the rest rooms, of which there are three in that building, were tidied up and

cleaned. Damp mopping occurred wherever it was necessary. Vac-
uuming in high-traffic areas every day, in not-so-high-traffic areas
once a week. Dusting usually on a weekly basis. The windows in the
front and back door sash were cleaned by Faunia almost on a daily
basis, depending on the traffic. Faunia was always very proficient,
and she paid a lot of attention to details. There are certain times
you can run a vacuum cleaner and there's other times you can't—
and there was never once, not once, a complaint on that score
about Faunia Farley. Very quickly she figured out the best time for
each task to be done with the minimum inconvenience to the work
force."

Of the fourteen people, aside from the children, that I counted
around the grave, the college contingent appeared to consist only of
Smoky and a cluster of Faunia's coworkers, four men from mainte-
nance who were dressed in coats and ties and who stood silently listening to the praise for her work. From what I could make out, the
remaining mourners were either friends of Peg and Sally or local
people who bought their milk up at the farm and who'd come to
know Faunia through visiting there. Cyril Foster, our postmaster
and chief of the volunteer fire department, was the only local person I recognized. Cyril knew Faunia from the little village post
office where she came twice a week to clean up and where Coleman
first saw her.

And there was Faunia's father, a large, elderly man whose presence had been acknowledged by Sally in her eulogy. He was seated
in a wheelchair only feet from the coffin, attended by a youngish
woman, a Filipino nurse or companion, who stood directly behind
him and whose face remained expressionless throughout the service, though he could be seen lowering his forehead into his hands
and intermittently succumbing to tears.

There was no one there whom I could identify as the person responsible for the on-line eulogy for Faunia that I'd found the evening before, posted on the Athena fac.discuss news group. The
posting was headed:

From: clytemnestra@houseofatreus.com
To: fac.discuss
Subject: death of a faunia
Date: Thur 12 Nov 1998

I'd come upon it accidentally when, out of curiosity, I was checking the fac.discuss calendar to see if Dean Silk's funeral might show
up under coming events. Why this scurrilous posting? Intended as
a gag, as a lark? Did it signify no more (or less) than the perverse indulgence of a sadistic whim, or was it a calculated act of treachery?
Could it have been posted by Delphine Roux? Another of her un-
ascribable indictments? I didn't think so. There was nothing to be
gained by her going any further with her ingenuity than the break-
in story, and much to be lost if "clytemnestra@houseofatreus.com"
were somehow discovered to be her brainchild. Besides, from the
evidence at hand, there was nothing so crafty or contrived about a
typical Delphinian intrigue—hers smacked of hasty improvisation,
of hysterical pettiness, of the overexcited unthinking of the amateur that produces the kind of wacky act that seems improbable afterward even to its perpetrator: the counterattack that lacks both
provocation and the refined calculation of the acidic master, however nasty its consequences may be.

No, this was mischief, more than likely, *prompted* by Delphine's
mischief, but more artful, more confident, more professionally demonic by far—a major upgrade of the venom. And what would *it*
now inspire? Where would this public stoning stop? Where would
the gullibility stop? How can these people be repeating to one another this story told to Security by Delphine Roux—so transpar-
ently phony, so obviously a lie, how can any of them believe this
thing? And how can any connection to Coleman be proved? It can't
be. But they believe it anyway. Screwy as it is—that he broke in
there, that he broke open the files, that he broke into her computer,
e-mailed her colleagues—they believe it, they want to believe it,
they can't wait to repeat it. A story that makes no sense, that is im-

plausible, and yet nobody—certainly not publicly—raises the simplest questions. Why would the man tear apart her office and call attention to the fact that he'd broken in if he wanted to perpetrate a hoax? Why would he compose that particular ad when ninety percent of the people who saw it couldn't possibly think of it as having anything to do with him? Who, other than Delphine Roux, would read that ad and think of him? To do what she claimed he'd done, he would have had to be crazy. But where is the evidence that he was crazy? Where is the history of crazy behavior? Coleman Silk, who single-handedly turned this college around—that man is crazy? Embittered, angry, isolated, yes—but crazy? People in Athena know perfectly well that this is not the case and yet, as in the spooks incident, they willingly act as if they don't. Simply to make the accusation is to prove it. To hear the allegation is to believe it. No motive for the perpetrator is necessary, no logic or rationale is required. Only a label is required. The label is the motive. The label is the evidence. The label is the logic. Why did Coleman Silk do this? Because he is an x, because he is a y, because he is both. First a racist and now a misogynist. It is too late in the century to call him a Communist, though that is the way it used to be done. A misogynistic act committed by a man who already proved himself capable of a vicious racist comment at the expense of a vulnerable student. That explains everything. That and the craziness.

The Devil of the Little Place—the gossip, the jealousy, the acrimony, the boredom, the lies. No, the provincial poisons do not help. People are bored here, they are envious, their life is as it is and as it will be, and so, without seriously questioning the story, they repeat it—on the phone, in the street, in the cafeteria, in the classroom. They repeat it at home to their husbands and wives. It isn't just that because of the accident there isn't time to prove it's a ridiculous lie—if it weren't for the accident, she wouldn't have been able to tell the lie in the first place. But his death is her good fortune. His death is her salvation. Death intervenes to simplify everything. Every doubt, every misgiving, every uncertainty is swept aside by the greatest belittler of them all, which is death.

Walking alone to my car after Faunia's funeral, I still had no way
of knowing who at the college might have had the turn of mind to
conjure up the clytemnestra posting—the most diabolical of art
forms, the on-line art form, because of its anonymity—nor could I
have any idea of what somebody, anybody, might next come up
with to disseminate anonymously. All I knew for sure was that the
germs of malice were unleashed, and where Coleman's conduct was
concerned, there was no absurdity out of which someone wasn't
going to try to make indignant sense. An epidemic had broken out
in Athena—that's how my thinking went in the immediate after-
math of his death—and what was to contain the epidemic's spread-
ing? It was there. The pathogens were out there. In the ether. In the
universal hard drive, everlasting and undeletable, the sign of the viciousness of the human creature.

Everybody was writing *Spooks* now—everybody, as yet, except me.

> I am going to ask you to think [the fac.discuss posting
> began] about things that are not pleasant to think about.
> Not just about the violent death of an innocent woman
> of thirty-four, which is awful enough, but of the circum-
> stances particular to the horror and of the man who, al-
> most artistically, contrived those circumstances to com-
> plete his cycle of revenge against Athena College and his
> former colleagues.
> Some of you may know that in the hours before Cole-
> man Silk staged this murder-suicide—for that is what this
> man enacted on the highway by driving off the road and
> through the guardrail and into the river that night—he had
> forcefully broken into a faculty office in Barton Hall, ran-
> sacked the papers, and sent out as e-mail a communication
> written purportedly by a faculty member and designed to
> jeopardize her position. The harm he did to her and to the
> college was negligible. But informing that childishly spite-
> ful act of burglary and forgery was the same resolve, the
> same animus, which later in the evening—having been

monstrously intensified—inspired him simultaneously to kill himself while murdering in cold blood a college custodial worker whom he had cynically enticed, some months earlier, to service him sexually.

Imagine, if you will, the plight of this woman, a runaway at the age of fourteen, whose education had ended in the second year of high school and who, for the rest of her brief life, was functionally illiterate. Imagine her contending with the wiles of a retired university professor who, in his sixteen years as the most autocratic of faculty deans, wielded more power at Athena than the president of the college. What chance did she have to resist his superior force? And having yielded to him, having found herself enslaved by a perverse manly strength far exceeding her own, what chance could she possibly have had to fathom the vengeful purposes for which her hard-worked body was to be utilized by him, first in life and then in death?

Of all the ruthless men by whom she was successively tyrannized, of all the violent, reckless, ruthless, insatiable men who had tormented, battered, and broken her, there was none whose purpose could have been so twisted by the enmity of the unforgiving as the man who had a score to settle with Athena College and so took one of the college's own upon whom to wreak his vengeance, and in the most palpable manner he could devise. On her flesh. On her limbs. On her genitals. On her womb. The violating abortion into which she was forced by him earlier this year— and which precipitated her attempt at suicide—is only one of who knows how many assaults perpetrated upon the ravaged terrain of her physical being. We know by now of the awful tableau at the murder scene, of the pornographic posture in which he had arranged for Faunia to meet her death, the better to register, in a single, indelible image, her bondage, her subservience (by extension, the bondage and subservience of the college community) to his enraged contempt. We know—we are beginning to know, as the horrifying facts trickle out from the police investigation—that not all the bruise marks on Faunia's mangled body resulted from damage inflicted in the fatal accident, cataclysmic as that was. There were patches of discoloration discovered by the coroner on her buttocks and thighs that had nothing to do with the impact of the crash, contusions that had been administered, some time before the accident, by very different means: either by a blunt instrument or a human fist.

Why? A word so small, and yet large enough to drive us insane. But then a mind as pathologically sinister as Faunia's murderer's is not easy to probe. At the root of the cravings that drove this man, there is an impenetrable darkness that those who are not violent by nature or vengeful by design—those who have made their peace with the restraints imposed by civilization on what is raw and untrammeled in us all—can never know. The heart of human darkness is inexplicable. But that their car accident was no accident, that I do know, as sure as I know that I am united in grief with all who mourn the death of Athena's Faunia Farley, whose oppression began in the earliest days of her innocence and lasted to the instant of her death. That accident was no accident: it was what Coleman Silk yearned to do with all his might. Why? This "why" I can answer and I will answer. So as to annihilate not only the two of them, but, with them, all trace of his history as her ultimate tormentor. It was to prevent Faunia from exposing him for what he was that Coleman Silk took her with him to the bottom of the river.

One is left to imagine just how heinous were the crimes that he was determined to hide.

The next day Coleman was buried beside his wife in the orderly garden of a cemetery across from the level green sea of the college athletic fields, at the foot of the oak grove behind North Hall and its landmark hexagonal clock tower. I couldn't sleep the night before, and when I got up that morning, I was still so agitated over how the accident and its meaning was being systematically distorted and broadcast to the world that I was unable to sit quietly long enough even to drink my coffee. How can one possibly roll back all these lies? Even if you demonstrate something's a lie, in a place like Athena, once it's out there, it stays. Instead of pacing restlessly around the house until it was time to head for the cemetery, I dressed in a tie and jacket and went down to Town Street to hang around there—down to where I could nurse the illusion that there was something to be done with my disgust.

And with my shock. I was not prepared to think of him as dead, let alone to see him buried. Everything else aside, the death in a freak accident of a strong, healthy man already into his seventies had its own awful poignancy—there would at least have been a higher degree of rationality had he been carried off by a heart attack or cancer or a stroke. What's more, I was convinced by then—I was convinced as soon as I heard the news—that it was impossible for the accident to have occurred without the presence somewhere nearby of Les Farley and his pickup truck. Of course nothing that befalls anyone is ever too senseless to have happened, and yet with Les Farley in the picture, with Farley as primary *cause*, wasn't there more than just the wisp of an explanation for the violent extinction, in a single convenient catastrophe, of Farley's despised ex-wife and the enraging lover whom Farley had obsessively staked out?

To me, reaching this conclusion didn't seem at all motivated by a disinclination to accept the inexplicable for what it is—though it seemed precisely that to the state police the morning after Coleman's funeral, when I went to talk to the two officers who'd been first at the scene of the accident and who'd found the bodies. Their examination of the crash vehicle revealed nothing that could corroborate in any way the scenario I was imagining. The information I gave them—about Farley's stalking of Faunia, about his spying on Coleman, about the near-violent confrontation, just beyond the kitchen door, when Farley came roaring at the two of them out of the dark—was all patiently taken down, as were my name, address, and telephone number. I was then thanked for my cooperation, assured that everything would be held in strictest confidence, and told that if it seemed warranted they would be back in touch with me.

They never were.

On the way out, I turned and said, "Can I ask one question? Can I ask about the disposition of the bodies in the car?"

"What do you want to know, sir?" said Officer Balich, the senior of the two young men, a poker-faced, quietly officious fellow whose Croatian family, I remembered, used to own the Madamaska Inn.

"What exactly did you find when you found them? Their placement. Their posture. The rumor in Athena—"

"No, sir," Balich said, shaking his head, "that was not the case. None of that's true, sir."

"You know what I'm referring to?"

"I do, sir. This was clearly a case of speeding. You can't take that curve at that speed. Jeff Gordon couldn't have taken that curve at that speed. For an old guy with a couple glasses of wine playing tricks on his brain to drive round that bend like a hot-rodder—"

"I don't think Coleman Silk ever in his life drove like a hot-rodder, Officer."

"Well . . . ," Balich said, and put his hands up in the air, the palms to me, suggesting that, with all due respect, neither he nor I could possibly know that. "It was the professor who was behind the wheel, sir."

The moment had arrived when I was expected by Officer Balich not to insert myself foolishly as an amateur detective, not to press my contention further, but politely to take my leave. He had called me sir more than enough times for me to have no hallucinations about who was running the show, and so I did leave, and, as I say, that was the end of it.

The day Coleman was to be buried was another unseasonably warm, crisply lit November day. With the last of the leaves having fallen from the trees during the previous week, the hard bedrock contour of the mountain landscape was now nakedly exposed by the sunlight, its joints and striations etched in the fine hatched lines of an old engraving, and as I headed to Athena for the funeral that morning, a sense of reemergence, of renewed possibility, was inappropriately aroused in me by the illuminated roughness of a distant view obscured by foliage since last spring. The no-nonsense organization of the earth's surface, to be admired and deferred to now for the first time in months, was a reminder of the terrific abrasive force of the glacier onslaught that had scoured these mountains on the far edge of its booming southward slide. Passing just miles from Coleman's house, it had spat out boulders the size of restaurant refrigerators the way an automatic pitching machine throws fastball strikes, and when I passed the steep wooded slope that is known locally as "the rock garden" and saw, starkly, undappled by the summer leaves and their gliding shadows, those mammoth rocks all tumbled sideways like a ravaged Stonehenge, crushed together and yet hugely intact, I was once again horrified by the thought of the moment of impact that had separated Coleman and Faunia from their lives in time and catapulted them into the earth's past. They were now as remote as the glaciers. As the creation of the planet. As creation itself.

This was when I decided to go to the state police. That I didn't get out there that day, that very morning, even before the funeral, was in part because, while parking my car across from the green in town, I saw in the window of Pauline's Place, eating his breakfast, Faunia's father—saw him seated at a table with the woman who'd been steering his wheelchair up at the mountain cemetery the day before. I immediately went inside, took the empty table beside theirs, ordered, and, while pretending to read the *Madamaska Weekly Gazette* that someone had left by my chair, caught all I could of their conversation.

They were talking about a diary. Among the things of hers that Sally and Peg had turned over to Faunia's father, there had been Faunia's diary.

"You don't want to read it, Harry. You just don't want to."

"I have to," he said.

"You don't have to," the woman said. "Believe me you don't."

"It can't be more awful than everything else."

"You don't want to read it."

Most people inflate themselves and lie about accomplishments they have only dreamed of achieving; Faunia had lied about failing to reach proficiency at a skill so fundamental that, in a matter of a year or two, it is acquired at least crudely by nearly every schoolchild in the world.

And this I learned before even finishing my juice. The illiteracy had been an act, something she decided her situation demanded. But why? A source of power? Her one and only source of power? But a power purchased at what price? Think about it. Afflicts herself with illiteracy too. Takes it on voluntarily. Not to infantilize herself, however, not to present herself as a dependent kid, but just the opposite: to spotlight the barbaric self befitting the world. Not rejecting learning as a stifling form of propriety but trumping learning by a knowledge that is stronger and prior. She has nothing against reading per se—it's that pretending not to be able to feels right to her. It spices things up. She just cannot get enough of the toxins: of all that you're not supposed to be, to show, to say, to think but that you are and show and say and think whether you like it or not.

"I can't burn it," Faunia's father said. "It's hers. I can't just throw it in the trash."

"Well, I can," the woman said.

"It's not right."

"You have been walking through this mine field all your life. You don't need more."

"It's all that's left of her."

"There's the revolver. That's left of her. There's the bullets, Harry. She left that."

"The way she lived," he said, sounding suddenly at the edge of tears.

"The way she lived is the way she died. It's why she died."

"You've got to give me the diary," he said.

"No. It's bad enough we even came here."

"Destroy it, destroy it, and I just don't know what."

"I'm only doing what is best for you."

"What does she say?"

"It doesn't bear repeating."

"Oh, God," he said.

"Eat. You have to eat something. Those pancakes look good."

"My daughter," he said.

"You did all you could."

"I should have taken her away when she was six years old."

"You didn't know. How could you know what was going to be?"

"I should never have left her with that woman."

"And we should never have come up here," his companion said. "All you have to do now is get sick up here. Then the thing will be complete."

"I want the ashes."

"They should have buried the ashes. In there. With her. I don't know why they didn't."

"I want the ashes, Syl. Those are my grandkids. That's all I've got left to show for everything."

"I've taken care of the ashes."

"No!"

"You didn't need those ashes. You've been through enough. I will not have something happening to you. Those ashes are not coming on the plane."

"What did you *do?*"

"I took care of them," she said. "I was respectful. But they're gone."

"Oh, my God."

"That's over," she told him. "It's all over. You did your duty. You did more than your duty. You don't need any more. Now let's you eat something. I packed the room up. I paid. Now there's just getting you home."

"Oh, you are the best, Sylvia, the very best."

"I don't want you hurt anymore. I will not let them hurt you."

"You are the best."

"Try and eat. Those look real good."

"Want some?"

"No," she said, "I want *you* to eat."

"I can't eat it all."

"Use the syrup. Here, I'll do it, I'll pour it."

I waited for them outside, on the green, and then when I saw the wheelchair coming through the restaurant door, I crossed the street and, as she was wheeling him away from Pauline's Place, I introduced myself, walking alongside him as I spoke. "I live here. I knew your daughter. Only slightly, but I met her several times. I was at the funeral yesterday. I saw you there. I want to express my condolences."

He was a large man with a large frame, much larger than he'd seemed slumped over in the chair at the funeral. He was probably well over six feet, but with the look on his stern, strongly boned face (Faunia's inexpressive face, hers exactly—the thin lips, the steep chin, the sharp aquiline nose, the same blue, deep-set eyes, and above them, framing the pale lashes, that same puff of flesh, that same fullness that had struck me out at the dairy farm as her one exotic marking, her face's only emblem of allure)—with the look of a man sentenced not just to imprisonment in that chair but condemned to some even greater anguish for the rest of his days. Big as he was, or once had been, there was nothing left of him but his fear. I saw that fear at the back of his gaze the instant he looked up to thank me. "You're very kind," he said.

He was probably about my age, but there was evidence of a privileged New England childhood in his speech that dated back to long before either of us was born. I'd recognized it earlier in the restaurant—tethered, by that speech alone, by the patterns of moneyed, quasi-Anglified speech, to the decorous conventions of an entirely other America.

"Are you Faunia's stepmother?" That seemed as good a way as

any to get her attention—and to get her perhaps to slow down. I assumed they were on their way back to the College Arms, around the corner from the green.

"This is Sylvia," he said.

"I wonder if you could stop," I said to Sylvia, "so I could talk to him."

"We're catching a plane," she told me.

Since she was so clearly determined to rid him of me then and there, I said—while still keeping pace with the wheelchair—"Coleman Silk was my friend. He did not drive his car off the road. He couldn't have. Not like that. His car was forced off the road. I know who is responsible for the death of your daughter. It wasn't Coleman Silk."

"Stop pushing me. Sylvia, stop pushing a minute."

"No," she said. "This is insane. This is enough."

"It was her ex-husband," I said to him. "It was Farley."

"No," he said weakly, as though I'd shot him. "No—no."

"Sir!" She had stopped, all right, but the hand that wasn't holding tight to the wheelchair had reached up to take me by the lapel. She was short and slight, a young Filipino woman with a small, implacable, pale brown face, and I could see from the dark determination of her fearless eyes that the disorder of human affairs was not allowed to intrude anywhere near what was hers to protect.

"Can't you stop for one moment?" I asked her. "Can't we go over to the green and sit there and talk?"

"The man is not well. You are taxing the strength of a man who is seriously ill."

"But you have a diary belonging to Faunia."

"We do not."

"You have a revolver belonging to Faunia."

"Sir, go away. Sir, leave him alone, I am warning you!" And here she pushed at me—with the hand that had been holding my jacket, she shoved me away.

"She got that gun," I said, "to protect herself against Farley."

Sharply, she replied, "The poor thing."

I didn't know what to do then except to follow them around the corner until they reached the porch of the inn. Faunia's father was weeping openly now.

When she turned to find me still there, she said, "You have done enough damage. Go or I will call the police." There was great ferocity in this tiny person. I understood it: keeping him alive appeared to require no less.

"Don't destroy that diary," I said to her. "There is a record there—"

"Filth! There is a record there of filth!"

"Syl, *Sylvia*—"

"All of them, her, the brother, the mother, the stepfather—the whole bunch of them, trampling on this man his whole life. They have robbed him. They have deceived him. They have humiliated him. His daughter was a criminal. Got pregnant and had a child at sixteen—a child she abandoned to an orphan asylum. A child her father would have raised. She was a common whore. Guns and men and drugs and filth and sex. The money he gave her—what did she do with that money?"

"I don't know. I don't know anything about an orphan asylum. I don't know anything about any money."

"Drugs! She stole it for drugs!"

"I don't know anything about that."

"That whole family—filth! Have some pity, *please!*"

I turned to him. "I want the person responsible for these deaths to be held legally accountable. Coleman Silk did her no harm. He did not kill her. I ask to talk to you for only a minute."

"Let him, Sylvia—"

"*No!* No more letting anyone! You have let them long enough!"

People were collected now on the porch of the inn watching us, and others were watching from the upper windows. Perhaps they were the last of the leafers, out to catch the little left of the autumn blaze. Perhaps they were Athena alumni. There were always a handful visiting the town, middle-aged and elderly graduates checking to see what had disappeared and what remained, thinking the best, the very best, of every last thing that had ever befallen them on these streets in nineteen hundred and whatever. Perhaps they were visitors in town to look at the restored colonial houses, a stretch of them running nearly a mile down both sides of Ward Street and considered by the Athena Historical Society to be, if not so grand as those in Salem, as important as any in the state west of the House of the Seven Gables. These people had not come to sleep in the carefully decorated period bedrooms of the College Arms so as to awaken to a shouting match beneath their windows. In a place as picturesque as South Ward Street and on a day as fine as this, the eruption of such a struggle—a crippled man crying, a tiny Asian woman shouting, a man who, from his appearance, might well have been a college professor seemingly terrifying both of them with what he was saying—was bound to seem both more stupendous and more disgusting than it would have at a big city intersection.

"If I could see the diary—"

"*There is no diary,*" she said, and there was nothing more to be done than to watch her push him up the ramp beside the stairway and through the main door and into the inn.

Back around at Pauline's, I ordered a cup of coffee and, on writing paper the waitress found for me in a drawer beneath the cash register, I wrote this letter:

> I am the man who approached you near the restaurant on Town Street in Athena on the morning after Faunia's funeral. I live on a rural road outside Athena, a few miles from the home of the late Coleman Silk, who, as I explained, was my friend. Through Coleman I met your daughter several times. I sometimes heard him speak about her. Their affair was passionate, but there was no cruelty in it. He mainly played the part of lover with her, but he also knew how to be a friend and a teacher. If she asked for care, I can't believe it was ever withheld. Whatever of Coleman's

spirit she may have absorbed could never, never have poisoned her life.

I don't know how much of the malicious gossip surrounding them and the crash you heard in Athena. I hope none. There is, however, a matter of justice to be settled which dwarfs all that stupidity. Two people have been murdered. I know who murdered them. I did not witness the murder but I know it took place. I am absolutely sure of it. But evidence is necessary if I am to be taken seriously by the police or by an attorney. If you possess anything that reveals Faunia's state of mind in recent months or even extending back to her marriage to Farley, I ask you not to destroy it. I am thinking of letters you may have received from her over the years as well as the belongings found in her room after her death that were passed on to you by Sally and Peg.

My telephone number and address are as follows—

That was as far as I got. I intended to wait until they were gone, to phone the College Arms to extract from the desk clerk, with some story or other, the man's name and address, and to send off my letter by overnight mail. I'd go to Sally and Peg for the address if I couldn't get it from the inn. But I would, in fact, do neither the one thing nor the other. Whatever Faunia had left behind in her room had already been discarded or destroyed by Sylvia—the same way my letter would be destroyed when it arrived at its destination. This tiny being whose whole purpose was to keep the past from tormenting him further was never going to allow inside the walls of his home what she would not permit when she'd found herself up against me face to face. Moreover, her course was one that I couldn't dispute. If suffering was passed around in that family like a disease, there was nothing to do but post a sign of the kind they used to hang in the doorways of the contagiously ill when I was a kid, a sign that read QUARANTINE or that presented to the eyes of the uninfected nothing more than a big black capital Q. Little Sylvia was that ominous Q, and there was no way that I was going to get past it.

I tore up what I'd written and walked across town to the funeral.

The service for Coleman had been arranged by his children, and the four of them were there at the door to Rishanger Chapel to greet the mourners as they filed in. The idea to bury him out of Rishanger, the college chapel, was a family decision, the key component of what I realized was a well-planned coup, an attempt to undo their father's self-imposed banishment and to integrate him, in death if not in life, back into the community where he had made his distinguished career.

When I introduced myself, I was instantly taken aside by Lisa, Coleman's daughter, who put her arms around me and in a tearful, whispering voice said, "You were his friend. You were the one friend he had left. You probably saw him last."

"We were friends for a while," I said, but explained nothing about having seen him last several months back, on that August Saturday morning at Tanglewood, and that by then he had deliberately let the brief friendship lapse.

"We lost him," she said.

"I know."

"We lost him," she repeated, and then she cried without attempting to speak.

After a while I said, "I enjoyed him and I admired him. I wish I could have known him longer."

"Why did this happen?"

"I don't know."

"Did he go mad? Was he insane?"

"Absolutely not. No."

"Then how could all this happen?"

When I didn't answer (and how could I, other than by beginning to write this book?), her arms dropped slowly away from me, and while we stood together for a few seconds more, I saw how strong was her resemblance to her father—strong as Faunia's to *her* father. There were the same carved puppetlike features, the same green eyes, the same tawny skin, even a less broad-shouldered version of Coleman's slight athletic build. The visible genetic legacy of the mother, Iris Silk, seemed to reside solely in Lisa's prodigious tangle of dark bushy hair. In photograph after photograph of Iris— photographs I'd seen in family albums Coleman had showed me— the facial features hardly seemed to matter, so strongly did her importance as a person, if not her entire meaning, appear to be concentrated in that assertive, theatrical endowment of hair. With Lisa, the hair appeared to stand more in contrast to her character than— as with her mother—to be issuing from it.

I had the definite impression, in just our few moments together, that the link, now broken, between Lisa and her father would not be gone from her mind for a single day throughout the remainder of her life. One way or another, the idea of him would be fused to every last thing she would ever think about or do or fail to do. The consequences of having loved him so fully as a beloved girl-child, and of having been estranged from him at the time of his death, would never let this woman be.

The three Silk men—Lisa's twin brother, Mark, and the two eldest, Jeffrey and Michael—were not so emotional in greeting me. I saw nothing of Mark's angry intensity as an affronted son, and when, an hour or so later, his sober demeanor gave way at the graveside, it was with the severity of one bereft beyond redemption. Jeff and Michael were obviously the sturdiest Silk children, and in them you clearly saw the physical imprint of the robust mother: if not her hair (both men were by now bald), her height, her solid core of confidence, her open-hearted authority. These were not people who muddled through. That was apparent in just the greeting they extended and the few words they said. When you met Jeff and Michael, especially if they were standing side by side, you'd met your match. Back before I got to know Coleman—back in his heyday, before he began to spin out of control within the ever-narrowing prison of his rage, before the achievements that once particularized him, that *were* him, vanished from his life—you would surely have met your match in him too, which probably explains why a general willingness to compromise the dean was so quick to materialize once he was accused of uttering aloud something racially vicious.

Despite all the rumors circulating in town, the turnout for Coleman far exceeded what I'd been imagining it would be; it certainly exceeded what Coleman could have imagined. The first six or seven rows of pews were already full, and people were still streaming in behind me when I found an empty place midway up from the altar beside someone whom I recognized—from having seen him for the first time the day before—to be Smoky Hollenbeck. Did Smoky understand how close he might have come, only a year earlier, to having a funeral service of his own held here in Rishanger Chapel? Maybe he was attending the service more in gratitude for his own good luck than out of regard for the man who'd been his erotic successor.

On Smoky's other side was a woman I took to be his wife, a pretty blonde of about forty and, if I remembered correctly, an Athena classmate Smoky had married back in the seventies and the mother now of their five children. The Hollenbecks were among the youngest people, aside from Coleman's family, whom I saw in the chapel when I began to look around me. Largely there were Athena elders, college faculty and staff whom Coleman had known for close to forty years before Iris's death and his resignation. What would he think about these old-timers showing up at Rishanger to see him off could he observe them seated before his coffin? Probably something like, "What a wonderful occasion for self-approval. How virtuous they all must feel for not holding against me my contempt for them."

It was strange to think, while seated there with all his colleagues, that people so well educated and professionally civil should have fallen so willingly for the venerable human dream of a situation in which one man can embody evil. Yet there is this need, and it is undying and it is profound.

When the outside door was pulled shut and the Silks took their seats in the front row, I saw that the chapel was almost two-thirds full, three hundred people, maybe more, waiting for this ancient and natural human event to absorb their terror about the end of life. I saw, too, that Mark Silk, alone among his brothers, was wearing a skullcap.

Probably like most everyone else, I was expecting one of Coleman's children to mount the pulpit and speak first. But there was to be only one speaker that morning, and that was Herb Keble, the political scientist hired by Dean Silk as Athena's first black professor. Obviously Keble had been chosen by the family for the reason the family had chosen Rishanger for the service: to rehabilitate their father's name, to push back the Athena calendar and restore to Coleman his former status and prestige. When I recalled the severity with which Jeff and Michael had each taken my hand and acknowledged me by name and told me, "Thank you for coming—it means everything to the family that you're here," and when I imagined that they must have repeated something like that to each individual mourner, among whom there were many people they had known since childhood, I thought, And they don't intend to quit, not until the administration building is rededicated as Coleman Silk Hall.

That the place was nearly full was probably no chance occurrence. They must have been on the phone ever since the crash, mourners being rounded up the way voters used to be herded to the polls when the old Mayor Daley was running Chicago. And how they must have worked over Keble, whom Coleman had especially despised, to induce him voluntarily to proffer himself as the scapegoat for Athena's sins. The more I thought about these Silk boys twisting Keble's arm, intimidating him, shouting at him, denouncing him, perhaps even outright threatening him because of the way he had betrayed their father two years back, the more I liked them—and the more I liked Coleman for having sired two big, firm, smart fellows who were not reluctant to do what had to be done to turn his reputation right side out. These two were going to help put Les Farley away for the rest of his life.

Or so I was able to believe until the next afternoon, just before they left town, when—no less bluntly persuasive with me than I'd imagined them to have been with Keble—they let me know that I was to knock it off: to forget about Les Farley and the circumstances of the accident and about urging any further investigation by the police. They could not have made clearer that their disapproval would be boundless if their father's affair with Faunia Farley were to become the focal point of a courtroom trial instigated by my importuning. Faunia Farley's was a name they never wanted to hear again, least of all in a scandalous trial that would be written up sensationally in the local papers and lodged indelibly in local memory and that would leave Coleman Silk Hall forever a dream.

"She is not the ideal woman to have linked with our father's legacy," Jeffrey told me. "Our mother is," said Michael. "This cheap little cunt has nothing to do with anything." "Nothing," Jeffrey reiterated. It was hard to believe, given the ardor and the resolve, that out in California they were college science professors. You would have thought they ran Twentieth Century Fox.

Herb Keble was a slender, very dark man, elderly now, a bit stiff-gaited, though seemingly in no way stooped or hobbled by illness, and with something of the earnestness of the black preacher in both the stern bearing and the ominous, hanging-judge voice. He had only to say "My name is Herbert Keble" to cast his spell; he had only, from behind the podium, to stare silently at Coleman's coffin and then to turn to the congregation and announce who he was to invoke that realm of feeling associated with the declamation of the holy psalms. He was austere in the way the edge of a blade is austere—menacing to you if you don't handle it with the utmost care. Altogether the man was impressive, in demeanor and appearance both, and one could see where Coleman might have hired him to break the color barrier at Athena for something like the same reasons that Branch Rickey had hired Jackie Robinson to be organized baseball's first black. Imagining the Silk boys browbeating Herb Keble into doing their bidding wasn't that easy, at first, not until you took into account the appeal of self-drama to a personality marked so clearly by the vanity of those authorized to administer the sacraments. He very much displayed the authority of the second in power to the sovereign.

"My name is Herbert Keble," he began. "I am chairman of the Political Science Department. In 1996, I was among those who did not see fit to rise to Coleman's defense when he was accused of racism—I, who had come to Athena sixteen years earlier, the very year that Coleman Silk was appointed dean of faculty; I, who was Dean Silk's first academic appointment. Much too tardily, I stand before you to censure myself for having failed my friend and patron, and to do what I can—again, much too tardily—to begin to attempt to right the wrong, the grievous, the contemptible wrong, that was done to him by Athena College.

"At the time of the alleged racist incident, I told Coleman, 'I can't be with you on this.' I said it to him deliberately, though perhaps not entirely for the opportunistic, careerist, or cowardly reasons that he was so quick to assume to be mine. I thought then that I could do more for Coleman's cause by working behind the scenes to defuse the opposition than by openly allying myself with him in public, and being rendered impotent, as I surely would have been, by that all-purpose, know-nothing weapon of a sobriquet, 'Uncle Tom.' I thought that I could be the voice of reason from within—rather than without—the ranks of those whose outrage over Coleman's alleged racist remark provoked them into unfairly defaming him and the college for what were the failures of two students. I thought that if I was shrewd enough and patient enough I could cool the passions, if not of the most extreme of his adversaries, then of those thoughtful, level-headed members of our local African American community and their white sympathizers, whose antagonism was never really more than reflexive and ephemeral. I thought that, in time—and, I hoped, in less time rather than more—I could initiate a dialogue between Coleman and his accusers that would lead to the promulgation of a statement identifying the nature of the misunderstanding that had given rise to the conflict, and thereby bring this regrettable incident to something like a just conclusion.

"I was wrong. I should never have said to my friend, 'I can't be with you on this.' I should have said, 'I *must* be with you.' I should have worked to oppose his enemies not insidiously and misguidedly from within but forthrightly and honestly from without— from where he could have taken heart at the expression of support instead of being left to nurse the crushing sense of abandonment that festered into the wound that led to his alienation from his colleagues, to his resignation from the college, and from there to the self-destructive isolation which, I am convinced—horrible as believing this is for me—led not too circuitously to his dying as tragically, wastefully, and unnecessarily as he did in that car the other night. I should have spoken up to say what I want to say now in the presence of his former colleagues, associates, and staff, and to say, especially, in the presence of his children, Jeff and Mike, who are here from California, and Mark and Lisa, who are here from New York—and to say, as the senior African American member of the Athena faculty:

"Coleman Silk never once deviated in any way from totally fair conduct in his dealings with each and every one of his students for as long as he served Athena College. Never.

"The alleged misconduct never took place. Never.

"What he was forced to undergo—the accusations, the interviews, the inquiry—remains a blight on the integrity of this institution to this day, and on this day, more than ever. Here, in the New England most identified, historically, with the American individualist's resistance to the coercions of a censorious community— Hawthorne, Melville, and Thoreau come to mind—an American individualist who did not think that the weightiest thing in life were the rules, an American individualist who refused to leave un-examined the orthodoxies of the customary and of the established truth, an American individualist who did not always live in compli-ance with majority standards of decorum and taste—an American individualist *par excellence* was once again so savagely traduced by friends and neighbors that he lived estranged from them until his death, robbed of his moral authority by their moral stupidity. Yes, it is we, the morally stupid censorious community, who have abased ourselves in having so shamefully besmirched Coleman Silk's good name. I speak particularly of those like myself, who knew from close contact the depth of his commitment to Athena and the pu-rity of his dedication as an educator, and who, out of whatever de-luded motive, betrayed him nonetheless. I say it again: we betrayed him. Betrayed Coleman and betrayed Iris.

"Iris's death, the death of Iris Silk, coming in the midst of . . ."

Two seats to my left, Smoky Hollenbeck's wife was in tears, as were several other of the women nearby. Smoky was himself lean-ing forward, his forehead resting lightly on his two hands, which were entwined at the top of the pew in front of us in a vaguely ec-clesiastical manner. I suppose he wanted me or his wife or whoever else might be watching him to believe that the injustice done to Coleman Silk was unendurable to think about. I supposed he was meant to appear to be overcome by compassion, yet knowing what I did about all that he concealed, as a model family man, of the Dio-nysian substrata of his life, it was an inference hard to swallow.

But, Smoky aside, the attention, the concentration, the *acuity* of the concentration focused on Herb Keble's every word seemed gen-uine enough for me to imagine that any number of people present would be finding it difficult not to lament what Coleman Silk had unfairly endured. I wondered, of course, if Keble's rationalization for why he hadn't stood beside Coleman at the time of the spooks incident was of his own devising or one that the Silk boys had come up with so as to enable him to do as they demanded while still sav-ing face. I wondered whether the rationalization could be an accurate description of his motives when he'd said the words that Coleman bitterly repeated to me so many times: "I can't be with you on this."

Why was I unwilling to believe this man? Because, by a certain age, one's mistrust is so exquisitely refined that one is unwilling to believe anybody? Surely, two years back, when he was silent and didn't rise to Coleman's defense, it was for the reason that people are always silent: because it is in their interest to be silent. Expediency is not a motive that is steeped in darkness. Herb Keble was just another one out trying to kosher the record, albeit in a bold, even an interesting way, by taking the guilt upon himself, but the fact remained that he couldn't act when it mattered, and so I thought, on Coleman's behalf, Fuck him.

When Keble came down from the podium and, before returning to his seat, stopped to shake the hands of each of Coleman's children, that simple gesture served only to intensify the almost violent passion aroused by his speech. What would happen next? For a moment there was nothing. Just the silence and the coffin and the emotional intoxication of the crowd. Then Lisa stood up, mounted the few steps to the podium, and, from the lectern, said, "The last movement of Mahler's Third Symphony." That was it. They pulled out all the stops. They played Mahler.

Well, you can't listen to Mahler sometimes. When he picks you up to shake you, he doesn't stop. By the end of it, we were all crying.

Speaking only for myself, I don't think anything could have torn me apart like that other than hearing Steena Palsson's rendition of "The Man I Love" as she'd sung it from the foot of Coleman's Sullivan Street bed in 1948.

The three-block walk to the cemetery was memorable largely for its seemingly not having taken place. One moment we were immobilized by the infinite vulnerability of Mahler's adagio movement, by that simplicity that is not artifice, that is not a strategy, that unfolds, it almost seems, with the accumulated pace of life and with all of life's unwillingness to end . . . one moment we were immobilized by that exquisite juxtaposition of grandeur and intimacy that begins in the quiet, singing, restrained intensity of the strings and then rises in surges through the massive false ending that leads to the true, the extended, the monumental ending . . . one moment we were immobilized by the swelling, soaring, climaxing, and subsiding of an elegiac orgy that rolls on and on and on with a determined pace that never changes, giving way, then coming back like pain or longing that won't disappear . . . one moment we were, at Mahler's mounting insistence, inside the coffin with Coleman, attuned to all the terror of endlessness and to the passionate desire to escape death, and then somehow or other sixty or seventy of us had got ourselves over to the cemetery to watch as he was buried, a simple enough ritual, as sensible a solution to the problem as any ever devised but one that is never entirely comprehensible. You have to see it to believe it each time.

I doubted that most people had been planning to accompany the body all the way to the grave. But the Silk children had a flair for drawing out and sustaining pathos, and this, I assumed, was why there were so many of us crowding around as close as we could to the hole that was to be Coleman's eternal home, as though eager almost to crawl in there and take his place, to offer ourselves up as surrogates, as substitutes, as sacrificial offerings, if that would magically allow for the resumption of the exemplary life that, by Herb Keble's own admission, had been as good as stolen from Coleman two years back.

Coleman was to be buried beside Iris. The dates on her headstone read 1932–1996. His would read 1926–1998. How direct those numbers are. And how little they connote of what went on.

I heard the Kaddish begin before I realized that somebody there was chanting it. Momentarily I imagined that it must be drifting in from another part of the cemetery, when it was coming from the other side of the grave, where Mark Silk—the youngest son, the angry son, the son who, like his twin sister, bore the strongest resemblance to his father—was standing alone, with the book in his hand and the yarmulke on his head, and chanting in a soft, tear-filled voice the familiar Hebrew prayer.

Yisgadal, v'yiskadash . . .

Most people in America, including myself and probably Mark's siblings, don't know what these words mean, but nearly everyone recognizes the sobering message they bring: a Jew is dead. Another Jew is dead. As though death were not a consequence of life but a consequence of having been a Jew.

When Mark had finished, he shut the book and then, having induced a grim serenity in everyone else, was himself overcome by hysteria. That was how Coleman's funeral ended—with all of us immobilized this time by watching Mark go to pieces, helplessly flailing his arms in the air and, through a wide-open mouth, wailing away. That wild sound of lamentation, older even than the prayer he'd uttered, rose in intensity until, when he saw his sister rushing toward him with arms outstretched, he turned to her his contorted Silk face, and in sheer childlike astonishment cried, "We're never going to see him again!"

I did not think my most generous thought. Generous thoughts were hard to come by that day. I thought, What difference should that make? You weren't that keen on seeing him when he was here.

Mark Silk apparently had imagined that he was going to have his father around to hate forever. To hate and hate and hate and hate, and then perhaps, in his own good time, after the scenes of accusation had reached their crescendo and he had flogged Coleman to within an inch of his life with his knot of filial grievance, to forgive. He thought Coleman was going to stay here till the whole play could be performed, as though he and Coleman had been set down not in life but on the southern hillside of the Athenian acropolis, in an outdoor theater sacred to Dionysus, where, before the eyes of ten thousand spectators, the dramatic unities were once rigorously observed and the great cathartic cycle was enacted annually. The human desire for a beginning, a middle, and an end—and an end appropriate in magnitude to that beginning and middle—is realized nowhere so thoroughly as in the plays that Coleman taught at Athena College. But outside the classical tragedy of the fifth century B.C., the expectation of completion, let alone of a just and perfect consummation, is a foolish illusion for an adult to hold.

People began to drift away. I saw the Hollenbecks move along the path between the gravestones and head toward the nearby street, the husband's arm around his wife's shoulder, shepherding her protectively away. I saw the young lawyer, Nelson Primus, who had represented Coleman during the spooks incident, and with him a pregnant young woman, a woman weeping, who must have been his wife. I saw Mark with his sister, still having to be consoled by her, and I saw Jeff and Michael, who had run this whole operation so expertly, talking quietly to Herb Keble a few yards from where I was standing. I couldn't myself go because of Les Farley. Away from this cemetery he muscled on undisturbed, uncharged with any crime, manufacturing that crude reality all his own, a brute of a being colliding with whomever he liked however he liked for all the inner reasons that justified anything he wanted to do.

Sure, I know there's no completion, no just and perfect consummation, but that didn't mean that, standing just feet from where the coffin rested in its freshly dug pit, I wasn't obstinately thinking that this ending, even if it were construed as having permanently reestablished Coleman's place as an admired figure in the college's history, would not suffice. Too much truth was still concealed.

I meant by this the truth about his death and not the truth that was to come to light a moment or two later. There is truth and then again there is truth. For all that the world is full of people who go around believing they've got you or your neighbor figured out, there really is no bottom to what is not known. The truth about us is endless. As are the lies. Caught between, I thought. Denounced by the high-minded, reviled by the righteous—then exterminated by the criminally crazed. Excommunicated by the saved, the elect, the ever-present evangelists of the mores of the moment, then polished off by a demon of ruthlessness. Both human exigencies found their conjunction in him. The pure and the impure, in all their vehemence, on the move, akin in their common need of the enemy. Whipsawed, I thought. Whipsawed by the inimical teeth of this world. By the antagonism that *is* the world.

One woman, by herself, had remained as close to the open grave as I was. She was silent and did not look to be crying. She didn't even appear to be quite there—that is to say, in the cemetery, at a funeral. She could have been on a street corner, waiting patiently for the next bus. It was the way she was holding her handbag primly in front of her that made me think of someone who was already prepared to pay her fare, and then to be carried off to wherever she was going. I could tell she wasn't white only by the thrust of her jaw and the cast of her mouth—by something suggestively protrusive shaping the lower half of her face—and, too, by the stiff texture of her hairdo. Her complexion was no darker than a Greek's or a Moroccan's, and perhaps I might not have added one clue to another to matter-of-factly register her as black, if it wasn't that Herb Keble was among the very few who hadn't yet headed for home. Because of her age—sixty-five, maybe seventy—I thought she must be Keble's wife. No wonder, then, that she looked so strangely transfixed. It could not have been easy to listen to her husband publicly cast himself (under the sway of whatever motive) as Athena's scapegoat. I could understand how she would have a lot to think about, and how assimilating it might take more time than the funeral had allowed. Her thoughts had still to be with what he had said back in Rishanger Chapel. *That's* where she was.

I was wrong.

As I turned to leave, she happened to turn too, and so, with only a foot or two between us, we were facing each other.

"My name's Nathan Zuckerman," I said. "I was a friend of Coleman's near the end of his life."

"How do you do," she replied.

"I believe your husband changed everything today."

She did not look at me as if I were mistaken, though I was. Nor did she ignore me, decide to be rid of me, and proceed on her way.

Nor did she look as if she didn't know what to do, though that she was in a quandary had to have been so. A friend of Coleman's at the end of his life? Given her true identity, how could she have said nothing more than "I'm not Mrs. Keble" and walked off?

But all she did was to stand there, opposite me, expressionless, so profoundly struck dumb by the day's events and its revelations that *not* to understand who she was to Coleman would, at that moment, have been impossible. It wasn't a resemblance to Coleman that registered, and registered quickly, in rapid increments, as with a distant star seen through a lens that you've steadily magnified to the correct intensity. What I saw—when, at long last, I did see, see all the way, clear to Coleman's secret—was the facial resemblance to Lisa, who was even more her aunt's niece than she was her father's daughter.

It was from Ernestine—back at my house in the hours after the funeral—that I learned most of what I know about Coleman's growing up in East Orange: about Dr. Fensterman trying to get Coleman to take a dive on his final exams so as to let Bert Fensterman slip in ahead of him as valedictorian; about how Mr. Silk found the East Orange house in 1926, the small frame house that Ernestine still occupied and that was sold to her father "by a couple," Ernestine explained to me, "who were mad at the people next door and so were determined to sell it to colored to spite them." ("See, you can tell the generation I am," she said to me later that day. "I say 'colored' and 'Negro.'") She told me about how her father had lost the optician shop during the Depression, how it took time for him to get over the loss—"I'm not sure," she said, "he ever did"—and how he got a job as a waiter on the dining car and worked for the railroad for the rest of his life. She talked about how Mr. Silk called English "the language of Chaucer, Shakespeare, and Dickens," and saw to it that the children learned not just to speak properly but to think logically, to classify, to analyze, to describe, to enumerate, to learn not only English but Latin and Greek; how he took them to the New

York museums and to see Broadway plays; and how, when he found out about Coleman's secret career as an amateur boxer for the Newark Boys Club, he had told him, in that voice that radiated authority without ever having to be raised, "If I were your father I would say, 'You won last night? Good. Now you can retire undefeated.'" From Ernestine I learned how Doc Chizner, my own boxing instructor during the year I took his after-school class down in Newark, had, earlier, in East Orange, laid claim to young Coleman's talent after Coleman left the Boys Club, how Doc had wanted him to box for the University of Pittsburgh, could have gotten him a scholarship to Pitt as a white boxer, but how Coleman had enrolled at Howard because that was their father's plan. How their father dropped dead while serving dinner on the train one night, and how Coleman had immediately quit Howard to join the navy, and to join as a white man. How after the navy he moved to Greenwich Village to go to NYU. How he brought that white girl home one Sunday, the pretty girl from Minnesota. How the biscuits burned that day, so preoccupied were they all with not saying the wrong thing. How, luckily for everyone, Walt, who'd begun teaching down in Asbury Park, hadn't been able to drive up for dinner, how things just went along so wonderfully that Coleman could have had nothing to complain about. Ernestine told me how gracious Coleman's mother had been to the girl. Steena. How thoughtful and kind they'd been to Steena—and Steena to them. How hardworking their mother was always, how, after their father died, she had risen, by virtue of merit alone, to become the first colored head nurse on the surgical floor of a Newark hospital. And how she had adored her Coleman, how there was nothing Coleman could do to destroy his mother's love. Even the decision to spend the rest of his life pretending his mother had been somebody else, a mother he'd never had and who had never existed, even that couldn't free Mrs. Silk of him. And after Coleman had come home to tell his mother he was marrying Iris Gittelman and that she would never be mother-in-law to her daughter-in-law or grandmother to her grandchildren, when Walt forbade Coleman from ever contacting the family again, how Walt then made it clear to their mother—and employing the same steely authority by which his father had governed them—that she was not to contact Coleman either.

"I know he meant the best," Ernestine said. "Walt thought this was the only way to protect Mother from being hurt. From being hurt by Coleman every time there was a birthday, every time there was a holiday, every time it was Christmas. He believed that if the line of communication remained open, Coleman was going to break Mother's heart a thousand times over, exactly the way he did it that day. Walt was enraged at Coleman for coming over to East Orange without any preparation, without warning any of us, and to tell an elderly woman, a widow like that, just what the law was going to be. Fletcher, my husband, always had a psychological reason for Walt's doing what he did. But I don't think Fletcher was right. I don't think Walt was ever truly jealous of Coleman's place in Mother's heart. I don't accept that. I think he was insulted and flared up—not just for Mother but for all of us. Walt was the political member of the family; of course he was going to get mad. I myself wasn't mad that way and I never have been, but I can understand Walter. Every year, on Coleman's birthday, I phoned Athena to talk to him. Right down to three days ago. That was his birthday. His seventy-second birthday. I would think that when he got killed, he was driving home from his birthday dinner. I phoned to wish him a happy birthday. There was no answer and so I called the next day. And that's how I found out he was dead. Somebody there at the house picked up the phone and told me. I realize now that it was one of my nephews. I only began calling the house after Coleman's wife died and he left the college and was living alone. Before that, I phoned the office. Never told anybody about it. Didn't see any reason to. Phoned on his birthdays. Phoned when Mother died. Phoned when I got married. Phoned when I had my son. I phoned him when my husband died. We always had a good talk together. He always wanted to hear the news, even about Walter and his promotions. And then each of the times that Iris gave birth, with Jeffrey, with Michael, then with the twins, I got a call from Coleman. He'd call me at school. That was always a great trial for him. He was testing fate with so many kids. Because they were genetically linked to the past he had repudiated, there was always the chance, you see, that they might be a throwback in some distinguishing way. He worried a lot about that. It could have happened—it sometimes does happen. But he went ahead and had them anyway. That was a part of the plan too. The plan to lead a full and regular and productive life. Still, I believe that, in those first years especially, and certainly whenever a new child came along, Coleman suffered for his decision. Nothing ever escaped Coleman's attention, and that held true for his own feelings. He could cut himself away from us, but not from his feelings. And that was most true where the children were concerned. I think he himself came to believe that there was something awful about withholding something so crucial to what a person is, that it was their birthright to know their genealogy. And there was something dangerous too. Think of the havoc he could create in their lives if their children were born recognizably Negro. So far he has been lucky, and that goes for the two grandchildren out in California. But think of his daughter, who isn't married yet. Suppose one day she has a white husband, as more than likely she will, and she gives birth to a Negroid child, as she can—as she may. How does she explain this? And what will her husband assume? He will assume that another man fathered her child. A black man at that. Mr. Zuckerman, it was frighteningly cruel for Coleman not to tell his children. That is not Walter's judgment—that is mine. If Coleman was intent on keeping his race his secret, then the price he should have paid was not to have children. And he knew that. He had to know that. Instead, he has planted an unexploded bomb. And that bomb seemed to me always in the background when he talked about them. Especially when he talked about, not the twin girl, but the twin boy, Mark, the boy he had all the trouble with. He said to me that Markie probably hated him for his own reasons, yet it was as though he had figured out the truth. 'I got there what I produced,' he said, 'even if for the wrong reason. Markie doesn't even have the luxury of hating his father for the real thing. I robbed him,' Coleman said, 'of that part of his birthright, too.' And I said, 'But he might not have hated you at all for that, Coleman.' And he said, 'You don't follow me. Not that he would have hated me for being black. That's not what I mean by the real thing. I mean that he would have hated me for never telling him and because he had a right to know.' And then, because there was so much there to be misunderstood, we just let the subject drop. But it was clear that he could never forget that there was a lie at the foundation of his relationship to his children, a terrible lie, and that Markie had intuited it, somehow understood that the children, who carried their father's identity in their genes and who would pass that identity on to their children, at least genetically, and perhaps even physically, tangibly, never had the complete knowledge of who they are and who they were. This is somewhat in the nature of speculation, but I sometimes think that Coleman saw Markie as the punishment for what he had done to his own mother. Though that," Ernestine added, scrupulously, "is not something *he* ever said. As for Walter, what I was getting at about Walter is that all he was trying to do was to fill our father's shoes by making sure that Mother's heart would not be broken time and again."

"And was it?" I asked.

"Mr. Zuckerman, there was no repairing it—ever. When she died in the hospital, when she was delirious, do you know what she was saying? She kept calling for the nurse the way the sick patients used to call for her. 'Oh, nurse,' she said, 'oh, nurse—get me to the train. I got a sick baby at home.' Over and over, 'I got a sick baby at home.' Sitting there beside her bed, holding her hand and watching her die, I knew who that sick baby was. So did Walter know. It was Coleman. Whether she would have been better off had Walt not interfered the way he did by banishing Coleman forever like that . . . well, I still hesitate to say. But Walter's special talent as a man is his decisiveness. That was Coleman's as well. Ours is a family of decisive men. Daddy had it, and so did his father, who was a Methodist minister down in Georgia. These men make up their minds, and that's it. Well, there was a price to pay for their decisiveness. One thing is clear, however. And I realized that today. And I wish my parents could know it. We are a family of educators. Beginning with my paternal grandmother. As a young slave girl, taught to read by her mistress, then, after Emancipation, went to what was then called Georgia State Normal and Industrial School for Colored. That's how it began, and that's what we have turned out to be. And that is what I realized when I saw Coleman's children. All but one of them teachers. And all of us—Walt, Coleman, me, all of us teachers as well. My own son is another story. He did not finish college. We had some disagreements, and now he has a significant other, as the expression goes, and we have our disagreement about that. I should tell you that there were no colored teachers in the white Asbury Park school system when Walter arrived there in '47. You have to re-member, he was the first. And subsequently their first Negro princi-pal. And subsequently their first Negro superintendent of schools. That tells you something about Walt. There was already a well-es-tablished colored community, but it was not till Walter got there in '47 that things began to change. And that decisiveness of his had a lot to do with it. Even though you're a Newark product, I'm not sure you know that up until 1947, legally, constitutionally separate, segregated education was approved in New Jersey. You had, in most communities, schools for colored children and schools for white children. There was a distinct separation of the races in elemen-tary education in south Jersey. From Trenton, New Brunswick, on down, you had separate schools. And in Princeton. And in Asbury Park. In Asbury Park, when Walter arrived there, there was a school called Bangs Avenue, East or West—one of them was for colored children who lived in that Bangs Avenue neighborhood and the other one was for white children who lived in that neighborhood. Now that was one building, but it was divided into two parts. There was a fence between the two sides of the building, and one side was colored kids and on the other was white kids. Likewise, the teachers on one side were white and the teachers on the other side were colored. The principal was white. In Trenton, in Princeton—

and Princeton is not considered south Jersey—there were separate schools up until 1948. Not in East Orange and not in Newark, though at one time, even in Newark there was an elementary school for colored children. That was the early 1900s. But in 1947—and I'm getting to Walter's place in all this, because I want you to understand my brother Walter, I want you to see his relationship to Coleman within the wider picture of what was going on back then. This is years before the civil rights movement. Even what Coleman did, the decision that he made, despite his Negro ancestry, to live as a member of another racial group—that was by no means an uncommon decision before the civil rights movement. There were movies about it. Remember them? One was called *Pinky*, and there was another, with Mel Ferrer, though I can't remember the name of it, but it was popular too. Changing your racial group—there was no civil rights to speak of, no equality, so that was on people's minds, white as well as colored. Maybe more in their minds than happening in reality, but still, it fascinated people in the way they are fascinated by a fairy tale. But then in 1947, the governor called for a constitutional convention to revise the constitution of the state of New Jersey. And that was the beginning of something. One of the constitutional revisions was that there would no longer be separated or segregated National Guard units in New Jersey. The second part, the second change in the new constitution, said that no longer shall children be forced to pass one school to get to another school in their neighborhood. The wording was something like that. Walter could tell it to you verbatim. Those amendments eliminated segregation in the public schools and in the National Guard. The governor and the boards of education were told to implement that. The state board advised all the local boards of education to set into operation plans to integrate the schools. They suggested first integrating the faculties of the schools and then slowly integrating the schools insofar as pupils were concerned. Now, even before Walt went to Asbury Park, even as a student at Montclair State when he came home from the war, he was one of those who were politically concerned—one of those ex-GIs who were already actively fighting for integration of the schools in New Jersey. Even before the constitutional revision, and after it was revised, certainly, Walter remained among the most active in the fight to integrate the schools."

Her point was that Coleman was *not* one of those ex-GIs fighting for integration and equality and civil rights; in Walt's opinion, he was never fighting for anything other than himself. Silky Silk. That's who he fought as, who he fought for, and that's why Walt could never stand Coleman, even when Coleman was a boy. In it for himself, Walt used to say. In it always for Coleman alone. All he ever wanted was out.

We had finished lunch at my house several hours earlier, but Ernestine's energy showed no signs of abating. Everything whirling inside her brain—and not just as a consequence of Coleman's death but everything about the mystery of him that she had been trying to fathom for the last fifty years—was causing her to speak in a rush that was not necessarily characteristic of the serious small-town schoolteacher she'd been for the whole of her life. She was a very proper-looking woman, seemingly healthy if a bit drawn in the face, whose appetites you couldn't have imagined to be in any way excessive; from her dress and her posture, from the meticulous way she ate her lunch, even from the way she occupied her chair, it was clear that hers was a personality that had no difficulty subjugating itself to social convention and that her inmost reflex in any conflict would be to act automatically as the mediator—entirely the master of the sensible response, by choice more of a listener than a maker of speeches, and yet the aura of excitement surrounding the death of her self-declared white brother, the special significance of the end of a life that to her family had seemed like one long, perverse, willfully arrogant defection, could hardly be reckoned with by ordinary means.

"Mother went to her grave wondering why Coleman did it. 'Lost himself to his own people.' That's how she put it. He wasn't the first in Mother's family. There'd been others. But they were *others*. They weren't Coleman. Coleman never in his life chafed under being a

Negro. Not for as long as we knew him. This is true. Being a Negro was just never an issue with him. You'd see Mother sitting in her chair at night, sitting there stock-still, and you knew what she was wondering: could it be this, could it be that? Was it to get away from Daddy? But by the time he did it, Daddy was dead. Mother would propose reasons, but none was ever adequate. Was it because he thought white people were better than us? They had more money than we did, sure—but better? Is that what he believed? We never saw the slightest evidence of that. Now, people grow up and go away and have nothing to do with their families ever again, and they don't have to be colored to act like that. It happens every day all over the world. They hate everything so much they just disappear. But Coleman as a kid was not a hater. The breeziest, most optimistic child you ever wanted to see. Growing up, *I* was more unhappy than Coleman. *Walt* was more unhappy than Coleman. What with all the success he had, with the attention people gave him . . . no, it just never made sense to Mother. The pining never stopped. His photos. His report cards. His track medals. His yearbook. The certificate he got as valedictorian. There were even toys of Coleman's around, toys he'd loved as a small child, and she had all these things and she stared at them the way a mind reader stares into a crystal ball, as if they would unravel everything. Did he ever acknowledge to anyone what he'd done? Did he, Mr. Zuckerman? Did he ever acknowledge it to his wife? To his children?"

"I don't think so," I said. "I'm sure he didn't."

"So he was Coleman all the way. Set out to do it and did it. That was the extraordinary thing about him from the time he was a boy—that he stuck to a plan completely. There was a dogged commitment he could make to his every decision. All the lying that was necessitated by the big lie, to his family, to his colleagues, and he stuck to it right to the end. Even to be buried as a Jew. Oh, Coleman," she said sadly, "*so* determined. Mr. Determined," and in that moment, she was closer to laughter than to tears.

Buried as a Jew, I thought, and, if I was speculating correctly, killed as a Jew. Another of the problems of impersonation.

"If he acknowledged it to anyone," I said, "maybe it was to the woman he died with. To Faunia Farley."

She clearly didn't want to hear about that woman. But because of her sensibleness, she had to ask, "How do you know that?"

"I don't. I don't know anything. It's a thought I have," I said. "It ties into the pact that I sensed was between them—his telling her." By "the pact between them" I meant their mutual recognition that there was no clean way out, but I didn't go on to explain myself, not to Ernestine. "Look, learning this from you today, there's nothing about Coleman I don't have to rethink. I don't know what to think about anything."

"Well then, you're now an honorary member of the Silk family. Aside from Walter, in matters pertaining to Coleman none of us has ever known what to think. Why he did it, why he stuck to it, why Mother had to die the way she did. If Walt hadn't laid down the law," she said, "who knows what would have evolved? Who knows if Coleman wouldn't have told his wife as the years passed and he got further from the decision? Maybe even told his children one day. Maybe have told the world. But Walt froze everything in time. And that is never a good idea. Coleman did this when he was still in his twenties. A firecracker of twenty-seven. But he wasn't going to be twenty-seven forever. It wasn't going to be 1953 forever. People age. Nations age. *Problems* age. Sometimes they age right out of existence. Yet Walt froze it. Of course, if you look at it narrowly, from the point of view simply of social advantage, of course it was advantageous in the well-spoken Negro middle class to do it Coleman's way, as it's advantageous today not to dream of doing it that way. Today, if you're a middle-class intelligent Negro and you want your kids to go to the best schools, and on full scholarship if you need it, you wouldn't dream of saying that you're not colored. That would be the last thing you'd do. White as your skin might be, now it's advantageous *not* to do it, just as then it was advantageous *to* do it. So what is the difference? But can I tell that to Walter? Can I say to him, 'So what really is the difference?' First because of what Coleman did to Mother, and second because in Walter's eyes there was a fight to fight then, and Coleman didn't want to fight it—for those reasons alone, I most certainly cannot. Though don't think that over the years I haven't tried. Because Walter, in fact, is not a harsh man. You want to hear about my brother Walter? In 1944 Walter was a twenty-one-year-old rifleman with a colored infantry company. He was with another soldier from his outfit. They were on a ridge in Belgium overlooking a valley that was cut through by railroad tracks. They saw a German soldier walking east along the tracks. He had a small bag slung over his soldier and he was whistling. The other soldier with Walter took aim. 'What the hell are you doing?' Walter said to him. 'I'm going to kill him.' '*Why?* Stop! What's he doing? He's walking. He's probably walking home.' Walter had to wrestle the rifle away from this fellow. A kid from South Carolina. They went down the ridge and they stopped the German and they took him prisoner. Turned out he *was* walking home. He had a leave, and the only way he knew to get back to Germany was to follow the railroad tracks east. And it was Walter who saved his life. How many soldiers ever did that? My brother Walter is a determined man who can be hard if he has to be, but he is also a human being. It's *because* he's a human being that he believes that what you do, you do to advance the race. And so I have tried with him, tried sometimes by saying things to Walter that I only half believe myself. Coleman was a part of his time, I tell him. Coleman couldn't wait to go through civil rights to get to his human rights, and so he skipped a step. 'See him historically,' I say to Walt. 'You're a history teacher—see him as a part of something larger.' I've told him, 'Neither of you just submitted to what you were given. *Both* of you are fighters and *both* of you fought. You did battle your way and Coleman did battle his.' But that is a line of reasoning that has never worked with Walter. Nothing has ever worked. That was Coleman's way of becoming a man, I tell him—but he will not buy that. To Walt, that was Coleman's way of *not* becoming a man. 'Sure,' he says to me, 'sure. Your brother is more or less as he would have been, except he would have been black. Except? *Except?* That except would have changed everything.' Walt cannot see Coleman other than the way he always has. And what can I do about that, Mr. Zuckerman? Hate my brother Walt for what he did to Coleman by freezing our family in time like that? Hate my brother Coleman for what he did to Mother, for how he made the poor woman suffer down to the very last day of her life? Because if I'm going to hate my two brothers, why stop there? Why not hate my father for all the things that he did wrong? Why not hate my late husband? I was not married to a saint, I can assure you. I loved my husband, but I have clear vision. And what about my son? There's a boy it would not be at all hard to hate. He goes out of his way to make it easy for you. But the danger with hatred is, once you start in on it, you get a hundred times more than you bargained for. Once you start, you can't stop. I don't know anything harder to control than hating. Easier to kick drinking than to master hate. And that is saying something."

"Did you know before today," I asked her, "why it was that Coleman had resigned from the college?"

"I did not. I thought he'd reached a retirement age."

"He never told you."

"No."

"So you couldn't know what Keble was talking about."

"Not entirely."

So I told her about the spooks business, told her that whole story then, and when I was finished she shook her head and said, straight out, "I don't believe I've ever heard of anything more foolish being perpetrated by an institution of higher learning. It sounds to me more like a hotbed of ignorance. To persecute a college professor, whoever he is, whatever color he might be, to insult him, to dishonor him, to rob him of his authority and his dignity and his prestige for something as stupid and trivial as that. I am my father's daughter, Mr. Zuckerman, the daughter of a father who was a stickler for words, and with every passing day, the words that I hear spoken strike me as less and less of a description of what things really are. Sounds from what you've told me that anything is possible in a college today. Sounds like the people there forgot what it is to teach. Sounds like what they do is something closer to buffoonery. Every time has its reactionary authorities, and here at Athena they are apparently riding high. One has to be so terribly frightened of every word one uses? What ever happened to the First Amendment of the Constitution of the United States of America? In my childhood, as in yours, it was recommended that each student who graduated from high school in New Jersey get at graduation two things: a diploma and a copy of the Constitution. Do you recall that? You had to take a year of American history and a semester of economics—as, of course, you have to no longer: 'have to' is just gone out of the curriculum. At graduation it was traditional in many of our schools in those days for the principal to hand you your diploma and somebody else to give you a copy of the Constitution of the United States. So few people today have a reasonably clear understanding of the Constitution of the United States. But here in America, as far as I can see, it's just getting more foolish by the hour. All these colleges starting these remedial programs to teach kids what they should have learned in the ninth grade. In East Orange High they stopped long ago reading the old classics. They haven't even heard of *Moby-Dick,* much less read it. Youngsters were coming to me the year I retired, telling me that for Black History Month they would only read a biography of a black by a black. What difference, I would ask them, if it's a black author or it's a white author? I'm impatient with Black History Month altogether. I liken having a Black History Month in February and concentrating study on that to milk that's just about to go sour. You can still drink it, but it just doesn't taste right. If you're going to study and find out about Matthew Henson, then it seems to me that you do Matthew Henson when you do other explorers."

"I don't know who Matthew Henson is," I said to Ernestine, wondering if Coleman had known, if he had wanted to know, if not wanting to know was one of the reasons he had made his decision.

"Mr. Zuckerman . . . ," she said, gently enough, but to shame me nonetheless.

"Mr. Zuckerman was not exposed to Black History Month as a youngster," I said.

"Who discovered the North Pole?" she asked me.

I suddenly liked her enormously, and the more so the more pedantically teacherish she became. Though for different reasons, I was beginning to like her as much as I had liked her brother. And I saw now that if you'd put them side by side, it wouldn't have been at all difficult to tell what Coleman was. *Everyone knows* . . . Oh, stupid, stupid, stupid Delphine Roux. One's truth is known to no one, and frequently—as in Delphine's very own case—to oneself least of all. "I forget whether it was Peary or Cook," I said. "I forget which one got to the North Pole first."

"Well, Henson got there *before* him. When it was reported in the *New York Times,* he was given full credit. But now when they write the history, all you hear about is Peary. It would have been the same sort of thing if Sir Edmund Hillary were said to have gotten to the top of Mount Everest and you didn't hear a word about Tenzing Norkay. My point," said Ernestine, in her element now, all professional correctitude and instruction—and, unlike Coleman, everything her father ever wanted her to be—"my point is, if you have a course on health and whatever, then you do Dr. Charles Drew. You've heard of him?"

"No."

"Shame on you, Mr. Zuckerman. I'll tell you in a minute. But you do Dr. Drew when you have health. You don't put him in February. You understand what I mean?"

"Yes."

"You learn about them when you study explorers and health people and all the other people. But everything there now is black this and black that. I let it wash over me the best I could, but it wasn't easy. Years ago, East Orange High was excellent. Kids coming out of East Orange High, especially out of the honors program, would have their choice of colleges. Oh, don't get me started on this subject. What happened to Coleman with that word 'spooks' is all a part of the same enormous failure. In my parents' day and well into yours and mine, it used to be the person who fell short. Now it's the discipline. Reading the classics is too difficult, therefore it's the classics that are to blame. Today the student asserts his incapacity as a privilege. I can't learn it, so there is something wrong with it. And there is something especially wrong with the bad teacher who wants to teach it. There are no more criteria, Mr. Zuckerman, only opinions. I often wrestle with this question of what everything used to be. What education used to be. What East Orange High used to be. What East Orange used to be. Urban renewal destroyed East Orange, there's no doubt in my mind. They—the city fathers—talked about all the great things that were going to happen because of this urban renewal. It scared the merchants to death and the merchants left, and the more the merchants left, the less business there was. Then 280 and the parkway cut our little town in quarters. The parkway eliminated Jones Street—the center of our colored community the parkway eliminated altogether. Then 280. A devastating intrusion. What that did to that community! Because the highway had to come through, the nice houses along Oraton Parkway, Elmwood Avenue, Maple Avenue, the state just bought them up and they disappeared overnight. I used to be able to do all my Christmas shopping on Main Street. Well, Main Street and Central Avenue. Central Avenue was called the Fifth Avenue of the Oranges then. You know what we've got today? We've got a ShopRite. And we've got a Dunkin' Donuts. And there was a Domino's Pizza, but they closed. Now they've got another food place. And there's a cleaners. But you can't compare quality. It's not the same. In all honesty, I drive up the hill to West Orange to shop. But I didn't then. There was no reason to. Every night when we went out to walk the dog, I'd go with my husband, unless the weather was real bad—walk to Central Avenue, which is two blocks, then down Central Avenue for four blocks, cross over, then window-shop back, and home. There was a B. Altman. A Russek's. There was a Black, Starr, and Gorham. There was a Bachrach, the photographer. A very nice men's store, Minks, that was Jewish, that was over on Main Street. Two theaters. There was the Hollywood Theater on Central Avenue. There was the Palace Theater on Main Street. All of life was there in little East Orange . . ."

All of life was there in East Orange. And when? Before. Before urban renewal. Before the classics were abandoned. Before they stopped giving out the Constitution to high school graduates. Before there were remedial classes in the colleges teaching kids what they should have learned in ninth grade. Before Black History Month. Before they built the parkway and brought in 280. Before they persecuted a college professor for saying "spooks" to his class. Before she drove up the hill to West Orange to shop. Before everything changed, including Coleman Silk. That's when it all was different—before. And, she lamented, it will never be the same again, not in East Orange or anywhere else in America.

At four, when I started out of my drive for the College Arms, where she was staying, the afternoon light was ratcheting rapidly down and the day, heavy now with fearsome clouds, had turned into gusty November. That morning they'd buried Coleman—and the morning before buried Faunia—in springlike weather, but now everything was intent on announcing winter. And winter twelve hundred feet up. Here it comes.

The impulse I had then, to tell Ernestine about the summer day a mere four months earlier when Coleman had driven me out to the dairy farm to watch Faunia do the five o'clock milking in the late afternoon heat—that is, to watch him watching Faunia do the milking—did not require much wisdom to suppress. Whatever was missing from Ernestine's sense of Coleman's life, she was not driven to discover. Intelligent as she was, she hadn't asked a single question about how he had lived out his last months, let alone about what might have caused him to die in the circumstance he did; good and virtuous woman that she was, she preferred not to contemplate the specific details of his destruction. Nor did she wish to inquire into any biographical connection between the injunction to revolt that had severed him from his family in his twenties and the furious determination, some forty years on, with which he had disassociated himself from Athena, as its pariah and renegade. Not that I was sure there was any connection, any circuitry looping the one decision to the other, but we could try to look and see, couldn't we? How did such a man as Coleman come to exist? What is it that he was? Was the idea he had for himself of lesser validity or of greater validity than someone else's idea of what he was supposed to be? Can such things even be known? But the concept of life as something whose purpose is concealed, of custom as something that may not allow for thought, of society as dedicated to a picture of itself that may be badly flawed, of an individual as real apart and beyond the social determinants defining him, which may indeed be what to him seem most *unreal*—in short, every perplexity pumping the human imagination seemed to lie somewhat outside her own unswerving allegiance to a canon of time-honored rules.

"I have not read any of your books," she told me in the car. "I tend to lean toward mysteries these days, and English mysteries. But when I get home, I plan to take out something of yours."

"You haven't told me who Dr. Charles Drew was."

"Dr. Charles Drew," she told me, "discovered how to prevent blood from clotting so it could be banked. Then he was injured in an automobile accident, and the hospital that was nearest would not take colored, and he died by bleeding to death."

That was the whole of our conversation during the twenty minutes it took to drive down the mountain and into town. The torrent of disclosure was over. Ernestine had said all there was to say. With the result that the harshly ironic fate of Dr. Drew took on a significance—a seemingly special relevance to Coleman and *his* harshly ironic fate—that was no less disturbing for being imponderable.

I couldn't imagine anything that could have made Coleman more of a mystery to me than this unmasking. Now that I knew everything, it was as though I knew nothing, and instead of what I'd learned from Ernestine unifying my idea of him, he became not just an unknown but an uncohesive person. In what proportion, to what degree, had his secret determined his daily life and permeated his everyday thinking? Did it alter over the years from being a hot

secret to being a cool secret to being a forgotten secret of no importance, something having to do with a dare he'd taken, a wager made
to himself way back when? Did he get, from his decision, the adventure he was after, or was the decision in itself the adventure? Was it
the misleading that provided his pleasure, the carrying off of the
stunt that he liked best, the traveling through life incognito, or had
he simply been closing the door to a past, to people, to a whole race
that he wanted nothing intimate or official to do with? Was it the
social obstruction that he wished to sidestep? Was he merely being
another American and, in the great frontier tradition, accepting the
democratic invitation to throw your origins overboard if to do so
contributes to the pursuit of happiness? Or was it more than that?
Or was it less? How petty were his motives? How pathological? And
suppose they were both—what of it? And suppose they weren't—
what of *that*? By the time I met him, was the secret merely the tincture barely tinting the coloration of the man's total being or was the
totality of his being nothing but a tincture in the shoreless sea of a
lifelong secret? Did he ever relax his vigilance, or was it like being a
fugitive forever? Did he ever get over the fact that he couldn't get
over the fact that he was pulling it off—that he could meet the
world with his strength intact after doing what he had done, that he
could appear to everyone, as he did appear, to be so easily at home
in his own skin? Assume that, yes, at a certain point the balance
shifted toward the new life and the other one receded, but did he
ever completely get over the fear of exposure and the sense that he
was going to be found out? When he had come to me first, crazed
with the sudden loss of his wife, the *murder* of his wife as he conceived it, the formidable wife with whom he'd always struggled
but to whom his devotion once again became profound in the instant of her death, when he came barging through my door in the
clutches of the mad idea that because of her death I should write
his book for him, was his lunacy not itself in the nature of a coded
confession? Spooks! To be undone by a word that no one even
speaks anymore. To hang him on that was, for Coleman, to banalize
everything—the elaborate clockwork of his lie, the beautiful cali-

bration of his deceit, *everything*. Spooks! The ridiculous trivial-
ization of this masterly performance that had been his seemingly
conventional, singularly subtle life—a life of little, if anything excessive on the surface because all the excess goes into the secret. No
wonder the accusation of racism blew him sky high. As though his
accomplishment were rooted in nothing but shame. No wonder *all*
the accusations blew him sky high. His crime exceeded anything
and everything they wanted to lay on him. He said "spooks," he
has a girlfriend half his age—it's all kid stuff. Such pathetic, such
petty, such ridiculous transgressions, so much high school yam-
mering to a man who, on his trajectory outward, had, among other
things, done what he'd had to do to his mother, to go there and,
in behalf of his heroic conception of his life, to tell her, "It's over.
This love affair is over. You're no longer my mother and never
were." Anybody who has the audacity to do that doesn't just want
to be white. He wants to be able to do that. It has to do with more
than just being blissfully free. It's like the savagery in *The Iliad*,
Coleman's favorite book about the ravening spirit of man. Each
murder there has its own quality, each a more brutal slaughter than
the last.

And yet, after that, he had the system beat. After that, he'd done
it: never again lived outside the protection of the walled city that is
convention. Or, rather, lived, at the same moment, entirely within
and, surreptitiously, entirely beyond, entirely shut out—that was
the fullness of his particular life as a created self. Yes, he'd had it
beat for so very long, right down to all the kids being born white—
and then he didn't. Blindsided by the uncontrollability of something else entirely. The man who decides to forge a distinct historical destiny, who sets out to spring the historical lock, and who does
so, brilliantly succeeds at altering his personal lot, only to be ensnared by the history he hadn't quite counted on: the history that
isn't yet history, the history that the clock is now ticking off, the
history proliferating as I write, accruing a minute at a time and
grasped better by the future than it will ever be by us. The we that is
inescapable: the present moment, the common lot, the current

mood, the mind of one's country, the stranglehold of history that is one's own time. Blindsided by the terrifyingly provisional nature of everything.

When we reached South Ward Street and I parked the car outside the College Arms, I said, "I'd like to meet Walter sometime. I'd like to talk to Walter about Coleman."

"Walter hasn't mentioned Coleman's name since nineteen hundred and fifty-six. He won't talk about Coleman. As white a college as there was in New England, and that's where Coleman made his career. As white a subject as there was in the curriculum, and that's what Coleman chose to teach. To Walter, Coleman is more white than the whites. There is nothing beyond that for him to say."

"Will you tell him Coleman's dead? Will you tell him where you've been?"

"No. Not unless he asks."

"Will you contact Coleman's children?"

"Why would I?" she asked. "It was for Coleman to tell them. It's not up to me."

"Why did you tell me, then?"

"I didn't tell you. You introduced yourself at the cemetery. You said to me, 'You're Coleman's sister.' I said yes. I simply spoke the truth. I'm not the one with something to hide." This was as severe as she had been with me all afternoon—and with Coleman. Till that moment she had balanced herself scrupulously between the ruination of the mother and the outrage of the brother.

Here she drew a wallet out of her handbag. She unfolded the wallet to show me one of the snapshots that were tucked into a plastic sleeve. "My parents," she said. "After World War I. He'd just come back from France."

Two young people in front of a brick stoop, the petite young woman in a large hat and a long summer dress and the tall young man in his full-dress army uniform, with visored cap, leather bandoleer, leather gloves, and high sleek leather boots. They were pale but they were Negroes. How could you tell they were Negroes? By little more than that they had nothing to hide.

"Handsome young fellow. Especially in that outfit," I said. "Could be a cavalry uniform."

"Straight infantry," she said.

"Your mother I can't see as well. Your mother's a bit shaded by the hat."

"One can do only so much to control one's life," Ernestine said, and with that, a summary statement as philosophically potent as any she cared to make, she returned the wallet to her handbag, thanked me for lunch, and, gathering herself almost visibly back into that orderly, ordinary existence that rigorously distanced itself from delusionary thinking, whether white or black or in between, she left the car. Instead of my then heading home, I drove cross-town to the cemetery and, after parking on the street, walked in through the gate, and not quite knowing what was happening, standing in the falling darkness beside the uneven earth mound roughly heaped over Coleman's coffin, I was completely seized by his story, by its end and by its beginning, and, then and there, I began this book.

I began by wondering what it had been like when Coleman had told Faunia the truth about that beginning—assuming that he ever had; assuming, that is, that he *had* to have. Assuming that what he could not outright say to me on the day he burst in all but shouting, "Write my story, damn you!" and what he could not say to me when he had to abandon (*because* of the secret, I now realized) writing the story himself, he could not in the end resist confessing to her, to the college cleaning woman who'd become his comrade-in-arms, the first and last person since Ellie Magee for whom he could strip down and turn around so as to expose, protruding from his naked back, the mechanical key by which he had wound himself up to set off on his great escapade. Ellie, before her Steena, and finally Faunia. The only woman never to know his secret is the woman he spent his life with, his wife. Why Faunia? As it is a human thing to have a secret, it is also a human thing, sooner or later, to reveal it. Even, as in this case, to a woman who doesn't ask questions, who, you would think, would be quite a gift to a man in possession of just such a secret. But even to her—especially to her. Because her not asking questions isn't because she's dumb or doesn't want to face things; her not asking him questions is, in Coleman's eyes, at one with her devastated dignity.

"I admit that may not be at all correct," I said to my utterly transformed friend, "I admit that none of it may be. But here goes anyway: when you were trying to find out if she'd been a hooker . . . when you were trying to uncover *her* secret . . ." Out there at his grave, where everything he ever was would appear to have been canceled out by the weight and mass of all that dirt if by nothing else, I waited and I waited for him to speak until at last I heard him asking Faunia what was the worst job she'd ever had. Then I waited again, waited some more, until little by little I picked up the sassy vibrations of that straight-out talk that was hers. And that is how all this began: by my standing alone in a darkening graveyard and entering into professional competition with death.

"After the kids, after the fire," I heard her telling him, "I was taking any job I could. I didn't know what I was doing back then. I was in a fog. Well, there was this suicide," Faunia said. "This was up in the woods outside of Blackwell. With a shotgun. Bird shot. Body was gone. A woman I knew, this boozer, Sissie, called me to come up and help her. She was going up there to clean the place out. 'I know this is going to sound odd,' Sissie says to me, 'but I know you have a strong stomach and you can handle things. Can you help me do this?' There was a man and woman living there, and their children, and they had an argument, and he went in the other room and blew his brains out. 'I'm going up there to clean it out,' Sissie says, so I went up there with her. I needed the money, and I didn't know what I was doing anyway, so I went. The smell of death. That's what I remember. Metallic. Blood. The smell. It came out only when we started cleaning. You couldn't get the full effect until the warm water hit the blood. This place is a log cabin. Blood on the walls everywhere. Ba-boom, he's all over the walls, all over everything. Once the warm water and disinfectant hit it . . . whew. I had rubber gloves, I had to put on a mask, because even *I* couldn't take this anymore. Also chunks of bone on the wall, stuck in with the blood. Put the gun in his mouth. Ba-boom. Tendency to get bone and teeth out there too. Seeing it. There it all was. I remember looking at Sissie. I looked at her and she was shaking her head. 'Why the fuck are we doing this for *any* amount of money?' We finished the job as best we could. A hundred dollars an hour. Which I still don't think was enough."

"What would have been the right price?" I heard Coleman asking Faunia.

"A thousand. Burn the fucking place down. There was no right price. Sissie went outside. She couldn't handle it anymore. But me, two little kids dead, maniac Lester following me everywhere, on my case day and night, who cares? I started snooping. Because I can be that way. I wanted to know why the hell this guy had done it. It's always fascinated me. Why people kill themselves. Why there are mass murderers. Death in general. Just fascinating. Looked at the pictures. Looked if there was any happiness there. Looked at the whole place. Until I got to the medicine cabinet. The drugs. The bottles. No happiness *there*. His own little pharmacy. I figure psychiatric drugs. Stuff that should have been taken and hadn't. It was clear that he was trying to get help, but he couldn't do it. He couldn't take the medication."

"How do you know this?" Coleman asked.

"I'm assuming. I don't know. This is my own story. This is my story."

"Maybe he took the stuff and he killed himself anyway."

"Could be," she said. "The blood. Blood sticks. You could not possibly get the blood off the floor. Towel after towel after towel. Still had that color. Eventually it turned more and more a salmon color, but you still couldn't get it out. Like something still alive. Heavy-duty disinfectant—didn't help. Metallic. Sweet. Sickening. I don't gag. Put my mind above it. But I came close."

"How long did it take?" he asked her.

"We were there for about five hours. I was playing amateur detective. He was in his mid-thirties. I don't know what he did. Salesman or something. He was a woodsy-type personality. Mountain type. Big beard. Bushy hair. She was petite. Sweet face. Light skin. Dark hair. Dark eyes. Very mousy. Intimidated. This is only what I'm getting from the pictures. He was the big strong mountain type and she's this little mousy person. I don't know. But I want to know. I was an emancipated minor. Dropped out of school. I could not go to school. Aside from everything else, it was boring. All this real stuff was happening in people's houses. Sure as shit happening in *my* house. How could I go to school and learn what the capital of Nebraska was? I wanted to *know*. I wanted to get out and look around. That's why I went to Florida, and that's how I wound up all over, and that's why I snooped about that house. Just to look around. I wanted to know the worst. What is the worst? You know? She was there at the time he did it. By the time we got there, she was under psychiatric care."

"Is that the worst thing you've ever had to do? The worst work you've ever had to do?"

"Grotesque. Yes. I've seen a lot of stuff. But that thing—it wasn't that it was only grotesque. On the other hand, it was fascinating. I wanted to know why."

She wanted to know what is the worst. Not the best, the worst. By which she meant the truth. What is the truth? So he told it to her. First woman since Ellie to find out. First anyone since Ellie. Because he loved her at that moment, imagining her scrubbing the blood. It was the closest he ever felt to her. Could it be? It was the closest Coleman ever felt to anyone! He loved her. Because that is when you love somebody—when you see them being game in the face of the worst. Not courageous. Not heroic. Just game. He had no reservations about her. None. It was beyond thinking or calculating. It was instinctive. A few hours later it might turn out to be a very bad idea, but at that moment, no. He trusts her—that's what it is. He trusts her: she scrubbed the blood off the floor. She's not religious, she's not sanctimonious, she is not deformed by the fairy tale of purity, whatever other perversions may have disfigured her. She's not interested in judging—she's seen too much for all that shit. She's not going to run away like Steena, whatever I say. "What would you think," he asked her, "if I told you I wasn't a white man?"

At first she just looked at him, if stupefied, stupefied for a split second and no more. Then she started laughing, burst into the laughter that was her trademark. "What would I think? I would think you were telling me something that I figured out a long time ago."

"That isn't so."

"Oh, isn't it? I know what you are. I lived down south. I met 'em all. Sure, I know. Why else could I possibly like you so much? Because you're a college professor? I'd go out of my mind if that was you."

"I don't believe you, Faunia."

"Suit yourself," she said. "You done with your inquiry?"

"What inquiry?"

"About the worst job I ever had."

"Sure," he said. And then waited for her inquiry about his not being white. But it never came. She didn't really seem to care. And she didn't run away. When he told her the whole story, she listened all right, but not because she found it incredible or unbelievable or even strange—it certainly wasn't reprehensible. No. It sounded just like life to her.

In February, I got a call from Ernestine, maybe because it was Black History Month and she remembered having to identify for me Matthew Henson and Dr. Charles Drew. Maybe she was thinking that it was time for her to take up again my education in race, touching particularly on everything that Coleman had cut himself off from, a full-to-the-brimming ready-made East Orange world, four square miles rich in the most clinging creaturely detail, the solid, lyrical bedrock of a successful boyhood, all the safeguards, the allegiances, the battles, the legitimacy simply taken for granted, nothing theoretical about it, nothing specious or illusory about it—all the blissful stuff of a happy beginning throbbing with excitement and common sense that her brother Coleman had blotted out.

To my surprise, after telling me that Walter Silk and his wife would be up from Asbury Park on Sunday, she said that, if I didn't mind driving to Jersey, I was welcome to come for Sunday dinner. "You wanted to meet Walt. And I thought you might like to see the house. There are photograph albums. There's Coleman's room, where Coleman and Walter slept. The twin beds are still there. It was my boy's room after them, but the same maple frames are still right there."

I was being invited to see the Family Silk plenty that Coleman jettisoned, as though it were his bondage, in order to live within a sphere commensurate with his sense of his scale—in order to become somebody other, somebody who suited him, and make his destiny by being subjugated by something else. Jettisoned it all, the whole ramified Negro thing, thinking that he could not displace it by any other means. So much yearning, so much plotting and passion and subtlety and dissembling, all of it feeding the hunger to leave the house and be transformed.

To become a new being. To bifurcate. The drama that underlies America's story, the high drama that is upping and leaving—and the energy and cruelty that rapturous drive demands.

"I'd like to come," I said.

"I can't guarantee anything," she said. "But you're a grown man. You can look after yourself."

I laughed. "What are you telling me?"

"Walter may be getting up on eighty, but he is still a large and roaring furnace. What he says you're not going to like."

"About whites?"

"About Coleman. About the calculating liar. About the heartless son. About the traitor to his race."

"You told him he was dead."

"I decided to. Yes, I told Walter. We're a family. I told him every-thing."

A few days later, a photograph arrived in the mail with a note from Ernestine: "I came upon this and thought of our visit. Please keep it, if you like, as a memento of your friend Coleman Silk." It was a faded black-and-white photograph measuring about four by five inches, a blown-up snapshot, more than likely taken originally in somebody's backyard with a Brownie box camera, of Coleman as the fighting machine that his opponent will find facing him when the bell sounds. He couldn't have been more than fifteen, though with those small carved features that in the man had been so engag-ingly boyish looking mannishly adult in the boy. He sports, like a pro, the whammy glare, the unwavering gaze of the prowling carni-vore, everything eradicated but the appetite for victory and the finesse to destroy. That look is level, issuing straight out of him like a command, even while the sharp little chin is steeply tucked into the skinny shoulder. His gloves are at the ready in the classic posi-tion—out in front as though loaded not merely with fists but with all the momentum of his one and a half decades—and each is larger in circumference than his face. One gets the subliminal sense of a kid with three heads. *I am a boxer,* the menacing pose cockily announces, *I don't knock 'em out—I cut 'em up. I outclass 'em till they stop the fight.* Unmistakably the brother she had christened Mr. Determined; indeed, "Mr. Determined," in what must have been Ernestine's girlhood hand, was inscribed in faint blue fountain-pen ink across the back of the picture.

She's something too, I thought, and found a clear plastic frame for the boy boxer and set him on my writing desk. The audacity of that family did not begin and end with Coleman. It's a bold gift, I thought, from a deceptively bold woman. I wondered what she had in mind by inviting me to the house. I wondered what I might have in mind by accepting the invitation. Strange to think that Cole-man's sister and I had been taken so by each other's company—though strange only if you remembered that everything about Coleman was ten, twenty, a hundred thousand times stranger.

Ernestine's invitation, Coleman's photograph—this was how I came to set out for East Orange on the first February Sunday after the Senate had voted not to remove Bill Clinton from office, and how I came to be on a remote mountain road that ordinarily I never take on my local back-and-forth driving but that serves as a shortcut from my house to Route 7. And that was how I came to notice, parked at the edge of a wide field I would otherwise have shot right by, the dilapidated gray pickup truck with the POW/MIA bumper sticker that, I was sure, had to be Les Farley's. I saw that pickup, somehow knew it was his, and unable just to keep on going, incapable of recording its presence and continuing on, I braked to a halt. I backed up until my car was in front of his, and, at the side of the road, I parked.

I suppose I was never altogether convinced that I was doing what I was doing—otherwise how could I have done it?—but it was by then nearly three months during which time Coleman Silk's life had become closer to me than my own, and so it was unthinkable that I should be anywhere other than there in the cold, atop that mountain, standing with my gloved hand on the hood of the very vehicle that had come barreling down the wrong side of the road and sent Coleman swerving through the guardrail and, with Faunia beside him, into the river on the evening before his seventy-second birthday. If this was the murder weapon, the murderer couldn't be far away.

When I realized where I was headed—and thought again of how surprising it was to hear from Ernestine, to be asked to meet Walter, to be thinking all day and often into the night about someone I'd known for less than a year and never as the closest of friends—the course of events seemed logical enough. This is what happens when you write books. There's not just something that drives you to find out everything—something begins putting everything in your path. There is suddenly no such thing as a back road that doesn't lead headlong into your obsession.

And so you do what I was doing. Coleman, Coleman, Coleman, you who are now no one now run my existence. Of course you could not write the book. You'd written the book—the book was your life. Writing personally is exposing and concealing at the same time, but with you it could only be concealment and so it would never work. Your book was your life—and your art? Once you set the thing in motion, your art was being a white man. Being, in your brother's words, "more white than the whites." That was your singular act of invention: every day you woke up to be what you had made yourself.

There was hardly any snow left on the ground, only patches of it cobwebbing the stubble of the open field, no trail to follow, so I started bang across to the other side, where there was a thin wall of trees, and through the trees I could see another field, so I kept going until I reached the second field, and I crossed that, and through another, a deeper wall of trees, thick with high evergreens, and there at the other side was the shining eye of a frozen lake, oval and pointed at either end, with snow-freckled brownish hills rising all around it and the mountains, caressable-looking, curving away in the distance. Having walked some five hundred yards from the road, I'd intruded upon—no, trespassed upon; it was almost an unlawful sense that I had . . . I'd trespassed upon a setting as pristine, I would think, as unviolated, as serenely unspoiled, as envelops any inland body of water in New England. It gave you an idea, as such places do—as they're cherished for doing—of what the world was like before the advent of man. The power of nature is sometimes very calming, and this was a calming place, calling a halt to your trivial thinking without, at the same time, overawing you with reminders of the nothingness of a life span and the vastness of extinction. It was all on a scale safely this side of the sublime. A man could absorb the beauty into his being without feeling belittled or permeated by fear.

Almost midway out on the ice there was a solitary figure in brown coveralls and a black cap seated on a low yellow bucket, bending over an ice hole with an abbreviated fishing rod in his gloved hands. I didn't step onto the ice until I saw that he'd looked up and spotted me. I didn't want to come upon him unawares, or in any way look as though I intended to, not if the fisherman really was Les Farley. If this was Les Farley, he wasn't someone you wanted to take by surprise.

Of course I thought about turning back. I thought about heading back to the road, about getting into my car, about proceeding on to Route 7 South and down through Connecticut to 684 and from there onto the Garden State Parkway. I thought about getting a look at Coleman's bedroom. I thought about getting a look at Coleman's brother, who, for what Coleman did, could not stop hating him even after his death. I thought about that and nothing else all the way across the ice to get my look at Coleman's killer. Right up to the point where I said, "Hi. How's it goin'?" I thought: Steal up on him or don't steal up on him, it makes no difference. You're the enemy either way. On this empty, ice-whitened stage, the *only* enemy.

"The fish biting?" I said.

"Oh, not too good, not too bad." He did no more than glance my way before focusing his attention back on the ice hole, one of twelve or fifteen identical holes cut into rock-hard ice and spread randomly across some forty or so square feet of lake. Most likely the holes had been drilled by the device that was lying just a few steps away from his yellow bucket, which was itself really a seven-gallon detergent pail. The drilling device consisted of a metal shaft about four feet long ending in a wide, cylindrical length of corkscrew blade, a strong, serious boring tool whose imposing bit—rotated by turning the cranked handle at the top—glittered like new in the sunlight. An auger.

"It serves its purpose," he mumbled. "Passes the time."

It was as though I weren't the first but more like the fiftieth person who'd happened out on the ice midway across a lake five hundred yards from a backcountry road in the rural highlands to ask about the fishing. As he wore a black wool watch cap pulled low on his forehead and down over his ears, and as he sported a dark, graying chin beard and a thickish mustache, there was only a narrow band of face on display. If it was remarkable in any way, that was because of its broadness—on the horizontal axis, an open oblong plain of a face. His dark eyebrows were long and thick, his eyes were blue and noticeably widely spaced, while centered above the mustache was the unsprouted, bridgeless nose of a kid. In just this band of himself Farley exposed between the whiskered muzzle and the woolen cap, all kinds of principles were at work, geometric and psychological both, and none seemed congruent with the others.

"Beautiful spot," I said.

"Why I'm here."

"Peaceful."

"Close to God," he said.

"Yes? You feel that?"

Now he shed the outer edge, the coating of his inwardness, shed something of the mood in which I'd caught him, and looked as if he were ready to link up with me as more than just a meaningless distraction. His posture didn't change—still very much fishing rather than gabbing—but at least a little of the antisocial aura was dissipated by a richer, more ruminative voice than I would have expected. Thoughtful, you might even call it, though in a drastically impersonal way.

"It's way up on top of a mountain," he said. "There's no houses anywhere. No dwellings. There's no cottages on the lake." After each declaration, a brooding pause—declarative observation, supercharged silence. It was anybody's guess, at the end of a sentence, whether or not he was finished with you. "Don't have a lot of activity out here. Don't have a lot of noise. Thirty acres of lake about. None of those guys with their power augers. None of their noise and the stink of their gasoline. Seven hundred acres of just open good land and woods. It's just a beautiful area. Just peace and quiet. And clean. It's a clean place. Away from all the hustle and bustle and craziness that goes on." Finally the upward glance to take me in. To assess me. A quick look that was ninety percent opaque and unreadable and ten percent alarmingly transparent. I couldn't see where there was any humor in this man.

"As long as I can keep it secret," he said, "it'll stay the way it is."

"True enough," I said.

"They live in cities. They live in the hustle and bustle of the work routine. The craziness goin' to work. The craziness *at* work. The craziness comin' home from work. The traffic. The congestion. They're caught up in that. I'm out of it."

I hadn't to ask who "they" were. I might live far from any city, I might not own a power auger, but I was they, we all were they, everyone but the man hunkered down on this lake jiggling the shortish fishing rod in his hand and talking into a hole in the ice, by choice communicating less with me—as they—than to the frigid water beneath us.

"Maybe a hiker'll come through here, or a cross-country skier, or someone like you. Spots my vehicle, somehow they spot me out here, so they'll come my way, and seems like when you're out on the ice—people like you who don't fish—" and here he looked up to take in again, to divine, gnostically, my unpardonable theyness. "I'm guessin' you don't fish."

"I don't. No. Saw your truck. Just driving around on a beautiful day."

"Well, they're like you," he told me, as though there'd been no uncertainty about me from the time I'd appeared on the shore. "They'll always come over if they see a fisherman, and they're curious, and they'll ask what he caught, you know. So what I'll do . . ." But here the mind appeared to come to a halt, stopped by his thinking, *What am I doing? What the hell am I going on about?* When he started up again, my heart all at once started racing with fear. Now that his fishing has been ruined, I thought, he's decided to have some fun with me. He's into his act now. He's out of the fishing and into being Les and all the many things that is and is not.

"So what I'll do," he resumed, "if I have fish layin' on the ice, I'll do what I did when I saw you. I'll pick all the fish up right away that I caught and I'll put 'em in a plastic bag and put 'em in my bucket, the bucket I'm sittin' on. So now the fish are concealed. And when the people come over and say, 'How are they bitin',' I say, 'Nothin'. I don't think there's anything in here.' I caught maybe thirty fish already. Excellent day. But I'll tell 'em, 'Naw, I'm gettin' ready to leave. I been here two hours and I haven't gotten a bite yet.' Every time they'll just turn around and leave. They'll go somewhere else. And they'll spread the word that that pond up there is no good. That's how secret it is. Maybe I end up tending to be a little dishonest. But this place is like the best-kept secret in the whole world."

"And now I know," I said. I saw that there was no possible way to get him to laugh along conspiratorially at his dissembling with interlopers like myself, no way I was going to get him to ease up by smiling at what he'd said, and so I didn't try. I realized that though nothing may have passed between us of a truly personal nature, by his decision, if not mine, we two were further along than smiling could help. I was in a conversation that, out in this remote, secluded, frozen place, seemed suddenly to be of the greatest importance. "I also know you're sitting on a slew of fish," I said. "In that bucket. How many today?"

"Well, you look like a man who can keep a secret. About thirty, thirty-five fish. Yeah, you look like an upright man. I think I recognize you anyway. Aren't you the author?"

"That I am."

"Sure. I know where you live. Across from the swamp where the heron is. Dumouchel's place. Dumouchel's cabin there."

"Dumouchel's who I bought it from. So tell me, since I'm a man who can keep a secret, why are you sitting right here and not over there? This whole big frozen lake. How'd you choose this one spot to fish?" Even if he really wasn't doing everything he could to keep me there, I seemed on my own to be doing everything I could not to leave.

"Well, you never know," he told me. "You start out where you got 'em the last time. If you caught fish the last time, you always start out at that spot."

"So that solves that. I always wondered." Go now, I thought. That's all the conversation necessary. More than is necessary. But the thought of who he was drew me on. The *fact* of him drew me on. This was not speculation. This was not meditation. This was not that way of thinking that is fiction writing. This was the thing itself. The laws of caution that, outside my work, had ruled my life so strictly for the last five years were suddenly suspended. I couldn't turn back while crossing the ice and now I couldn't turn and flee. It had nothing to do with courage. It had nothing to do with reason or logic. Here he is. That's all it had to do with. That and my fear. In his heavy brown coveralls and his black watch cap and his thick-soled black rubber boots, with his two big hands in a hunter's (or a soldier's) camouflage-colored fingertipless gloves, here is the man who murdered Coleman and Faunia. I'm sure of it. They didn't drive off the road and into the river. Here is the killer. He is the one. How can I go?

"Fish always there?" I asked him. "When you return to your spot from the time before?"

"No, sir. The fish move in schools. Underneath the ice. One day they'll be at the north end of the pond, the next day they might be at the south end of the pond. Maybe sometimes two times in a row they'll be at that same spot. They'll still be there. What they tend to do, the fish tend to school up and they don't move very much, because the water's so cold. They're able to adjust to water temperature, and the water being so cold, they don't move so much and they don't require as much food. But if you get in an area where the fish are schooled up, you will catch a lot of fish. But some days you can go out in the same pond—you can never cover the entire thing—so you might try about five or six different places, drill holes, and never get a hit. Never catch a fish. You just didn't locate the school. And so you just sit here."

"Close to God," I said.

"You got it."

His fluency—because it was the last thing I was expecting—fascinated me, as did the thoroughness with which he was willing to explain the life in a pond when the water's cold. How did he know I was "the author"? Did he also know I was Coleman's friend? Did he also know I was at Faunia's funeral? I supposed there were now as many questions in his mind about me—and my mission here—as there were in mine about him. This great bright arched space, this cold aboveground vault of a mountaintop cradling at its peak a largish oval of fresh water frozen hard as rock, the ancient activity that is the life of a lake, that is the formation of ice, that is the metabolism of fish, all the soundless, ageless forces unyieldingly working away—it is as though we have encountered each other at the top of the world, two hidden brains mistrustfully ticking, mutual hatred and paranoia the only introspection there is anywhere.

"And so what do you think about," I asked, "if you don't get a fish? What do you think about when they're not biting?"

"Tell you what I was just thinking about. I was thinking a lot of things. I was thinking about Slick Willie. I was thinking about our president—his freakin' luck. I was thinkin' about this guy who gets off everything, and I was thinkin' about the guys who didn't get off nothin'. Who didn't dodge the draft and didn't get off. It doesn't seem right."

"Vietnam," I said.

"Yeah. We'd go up in the freakin' helicopters—in my second tour I was a door gunner—and what I was thinking about was this one time we went into North Vietnam to pick up these two pilots. I was sitting out here thinking about that time. Slick Willie. That son of a bitch. Thinkin' about that scumbag son of a bitch gettin' his dick sucked in the Oval Office on the taxpayer's money, and then thinkin' about these two pilots, they were on an air strike over Hanoi harbor, these guys were hit real bad, and we picked up the signal on the radio. We weren't even a rescue helicopter, but we were in the vicinity, and they were giving a mayday that they were goin' to bail out, because they were at the altitude point where if they didn't bail out they were goin' to crash. We weren't even a rescue helicopter—we were a gunship—we were just taking a chance that we could save a couple of lives. We didn't even get permission to get up there, we just went. You act on instinct like that. We just all agreed, two door gunners, the pilot, the copilot, though the chances weren't that good because we had no cover. But we went in anyway—to try to pick 'em up."

He's telling me a war story, I thought. He knows he's doing it. There's a point here that he's going to make. Something he wants me to carry away with me, to the shore, to my car, to the house whose location he knows and wishes me to understand that he knows. To carry away as "the author"? Or as somebody else—somebody who knows a secret of his that is even bigger than the secret of this pond. He wants me to know that not many people have seen what he's seen, been where he's been, done what he's done and, if required to, can do again. He's murdered in Vietnam and he's brought the murderer back with him to the Berkshires, back with him from the country of war, the country of horror, to this completely uncomprehending other place.

The auger out on the ice. The candor of the auger. There could be no more solid embodiment of our hatred than the merciless steel look of that auger out in the middle of nowhere.

"We figure, okay, we're gonna die, we're gonna die. So we went up there and we homed in on their signals, we saw one parachute, and we went down in the clearing, and we picked that guy up with no trouble at all. He jumped right in, we dragged him right in and took off, no opposition whatsoever. So we said to him, 'You have any idea?' and he said, 'Well, he drifted off that way.' So we went up in the air, but by then they knew we were there. We went over a little farther looking for the other parachute, and all freakin' hell broke loose. I'm telling you, it was unbelievable. We never picked up the other guy. The helicopter was gettin' hit like you wouldn't believe it. Ting ping ping boom. Machine guns. Ground fire. We just had to turn around and get the hell out of there as fast as we could. And I remember the guy we picked up started to cry. This is what I'm getting at. He was a navy pilot. They were off the *Forrestal*. And he knew the other guy was either killed or captured, and he started to bawl. It was horrible for him. His buddy. But we couldn't go back. We couldn't risk the chopper and five guys. We were lucky we got one. So we got back to our base and we got out and we looked at the chopper and there were a hundred and fifty-one bullet holes in it. Never hit a hydraulic line, a fuel line, but the rotors were all pinged up, a lot of bullets hit the rotors. Bent them a little bit. If they hit the tail rotor, you go right down, but they didn't. You know they shot down five thousand helicopters during that war? Twenty-eight hundred jet fighters we lost. They lost two hundred fifty B-52s in high-altitude bombing over North Vietnam. But the government'll never tell you that. Not that. They tell you what they want to tell you. Never Slick Willie who gets caught. It's the guy who served who gets caught. Over and over. Nope, doesn't seem right. You know what I was thinking? I was thinking that if I had a son he'd be out here with me now. Ice fishin'. That's what I was thinking when you walked out here. I looked up and I saw someone comin', and I'm sort of daydreamin', and I thought, That could be my son. Not you, not a man like you, but my son."

"Don't you have a son?"

"No."

"Never married?" I asked.

This time he didn't answer me right off. He looked at me, homed in on me as though I had a signal that was going off like the two pilots bailing out, but he didn't answer me. Because he knows, I thought. He knows I was at Faunia's funeral. Somebody told him that "the author" was there. What kind of author does he think I am? An author who writes books about crimes like his? An author who writes books about murderers and murder?

"Doomed," he said finally, staring back into the hole and jiggling his rod, jerking it with a flick of his wrist a dozen or so times. "Marriage was doomed. Came back from Vietnam with too much anger and resentment. Had PTSD. I had what they call post-traumatic stress disorder. That's what they told me. When I come back, I didn't want to know anybody. I come back, I couldn't relate to anything that was going on around here, as far as civilized living. It's like I was there so long, it was totally insane. Wearing clean clothes, and people saying hello, and people smiling, and people going to

THE HUMAN STAIN

parties, and people driving cars—I couldn't relate to it anymore. I didn't know how to talk to anybody, I didn't know how to say hello to anybody. I withdrew for a long time. I used to get in my car, drive around, go in the woods, walk in the woods—it was the weirdest thing. I withdrew from *myself*. I had no idea what I was going through. My buddies would call me, I wouldn't call back. They were afraid I was going to die in a car accident, they were afraid I was—"

I interrupted. "Why were they afraid you were going to die in a car accident?"

"I was drinking. I was driving around and drinking."

"Did you ever get into a car accident?"

He smiled. Didn't take a pause and stare me down. Didn't give me an especially threatening look. Didn't jump up and go for my throat. Just smiled a little, more good nature in the smile than I could have believed he had in him to show. In a deliberately light-hearted way, he shrugged and said, "Got *me*. I didn't know what I was going through, you *know?* Accident? In an accident? I wouldn't know if I did. I suppose I didn't. You're going through what they call post-traumatic stress disorder. Stuff keeps coming back into your subconscious mind that you're back in Vietnam, that you're back in the army again. I'm not an educated guy. I didn't even know that. People were so pissed at me for this and that, and they didn't even know what I was going through and *I* didn't even know—you know? I don't have educated friends who know these things. I got assholes for friends. Oh, man, I mean real guaranteed hundred percent assholes or double your money back." Again the shrug. Comical? Intended to be comical? No, more a happy-go-lucky strain of sinisterness. "So what can I do?" he asked helplessly.

Conning me. Playing with me. Because he knows I know. Here we are alone up where we are, and I know, and he knows I know. And the auger knows. All ye know and all ye need to know, all inscribed in the spiral of its curving steel blade.

"How'd you find out you had PTSD?"

"A colored girl at the VA. Excuse me. An African American. A

· 354 ·

very intelligent African American. She's got a master's degree. You got a master's degree?"

"No," I said.

"Well, she's got one, and that's how I found out what I had. Otherwise I still wouldn't know. That's how I started learning about myself, what I was going through. They told me. And not just me. Don't think it was just me. Thousands and thousands of guys were going through what I was going through. Thousands and thousands of guys waking up in the middle of the night back in Vietnam. Thousands and thousands of guys people are calling up and they don't call them back. Thousands and thousands of guys having these real bad dreams. And so I told that to this African American and she understood what it was. Because she had that master's degree, she told me how it was going through my subconscious mind, and that it was the same with thousands and thousands of other guys. The subconscious mind. You can't control it. It's like the government. It *is* the government. It's the government all over again. It gets you to do what you don't want to do. Thousands and thousands of guys getting married and it's doomed, because they have this anger and this resentment about Vietnam in their subconscious mind. She explained all this to me. They just popped me from Vietnam onto a C-41 air force jet to the Philippines, then on a World Airways jet to Travis Air Force Base, then they gave me two hundred dollars to go home. So it took me, like, from the time I left Vietnam to go home, it took about three days. You're back in civilization. And you're doomed. And your wife, even if it's ten years later, she's doomed. She's doomed, and what the hell did she do? Nothin'."

"Still have the PTSD?"

"Well, I still tend to isolate, don't I? What do you think I'm doin' out here?"

"But no more drinking and driving," I heard myself saying. "No more accidents."

"There were never accidents. Don't you listen? I already told you that. Not that I know of."

"And the marriage was doomed."

"Oh yeah. My fault. Hundred percent. She was a lovely woman. Entirely blameless. All me. Always all me. She deserved a helluva lot better than me."

"What happened to her?" I asked.

He shook his head. A sad shrug, a sigh—complete bullshit, deliberately *transparent* bullshit. "No idea. Ran away, I scared her so. Scared the woman shitless. My heart goes out to her, wherever she may be. Completely blameless person."

"No kids."

"Nope. No kids. You?" he asked me.

"No."

"Married?"

"No more," I said.

"So, you and me in the same boat. Free as the wind. What kind of books do you write? Whodunits?"

"I wouldn't say that."

"True stories?"

"Sometimes."

"What? Romance?" he asked, smiling. "Not pornography, I hope." He pretended that that was an unwanted idea it vexed him even to entertain. "I sure hope our local author is not up there in Mike Dumouchel's place writing and publishing pornography."

"I write about people like you," I said.

"Is that right?"

"Yes. People like you. Their problems."

"What's the name of one of your books?"

"*The Human Stain.*"

"Yeah? Can I get it?"

"It's not out yet. It's not finished yet."

"I'll buy it."

"I'll send you one. What's your name?"

"Les Farley. Yeah, send it. When you finish it, send it care of the town garage. Town Garage. Route 6. Les Farley." Needling me again, sort of needling everyone—himself, his friends, "our local author"—he said, even as he began laughing at the idea, "Me and the guys'll read it." He didn't so much laugh aloud as nibble at the bait of an out-loud laugh, work up to and around the laugh without quite sinking his teeth in. Close to the hook of dangerous merriment, but not close enough to swallow it.

"I hope you will," I said.

I couldn't just turn and go then. Not on that note, not with him shedding ever so slightly a bit more of the emotional incognito, not with the possibility raised of peering a little further into his mind. "What were you like before you went into the service?" I asked him.

"Is this for your book?"

"Yes. Yes." *I* laughed out loud. Without even intending to, with a ridiculous, robust burst of defiance, I said, foolishly, "It's *all* for my book."

And he now laughed with more abandon too. On this loony bin of a lake.

"Were you a gregarious guy, Les?"

"Yeah," he said. "I was."

"With people?"

"Yeah."

"Like to have a good time with them?"

"Yeah. Tons of friends. Fast cars. You know, all that stuff. I worked all the time. But when I wasn't working, yeah."

"And all you Vietnam veterans ice fish?"

"I don't know." The nibbling laughter once again. I thought, It's easier for him to kill somebody than to cut loose with real amusement.

"I started ice fishing," he told me, "not that long ago. After my wife ran away. I rented a little shack, back in the woods, on Dragonfly. Back in the woods, right on the water, Dragonfly Pond, and I always summer fished, all my life, but I was never too interested in ice fishing. I always figure it's too cold out there, you know? So the first winter I lived on the pond, and I wasn't myself that winter—goddamn PTSD—I was watching this ice fisherman walk out there and go out fishing. So I watched this a couple of times, so one day I put on my clothes and took a walk out there and this guy was catching a lot of fish, yellow perch and trout and everything. So I figure, this fishin' is just as good as the summertime, if not better. All you have to do is get the right amount of clothing on and get the right equipment. So I did. I went down and bought an auger, a nice auger"—he points—"jiggin' rod, lures. Hundreds of different kinds of lures you can get. Hundreds of different manufacturers and makes. All various sizes. You drill a hole through the ice, and you drop your favorite lure down there with the bait on it—it's just a hand movement, you just make that jig move up and down, you know. Because it's dark down underneath the ice. Oh, it is dark all right," he told me, and, for the first time in the conversation, he looked at me with not too much but too little opacity in his face, too little deceit, too little duplicity. In his voice there was a chilling resonance when he said, "It's *real* dark." A chilling and astonishing resonance that made everything about Coleman's accident clear. "So any kind of a flash down there," he added, "the fish are attracted to it. I guess they're adaptable to that dark environment."

No, he's not stupid. He's a brute and he's a killer but not so dumb as I thought. It isn't a brain that is missing. Beneath whatever the disguise, it rarely is.

"Because they have to eat," he's explaining to me, scientifically. "They find food down there. And their bodies are able to adapt to that extracold water and their eyes adapt to the dark. They're sensitive to movement. If they see any kind of flashes or they maybe feel the vibrations of your lure moving, they're attracted to it. They know that it's something alive and it might be edible. But if you don't jig it, you'll never get a hit. If I had a son, you see, which is what I was thinkin', I'd be teachin' him how to jig it. I'd be teachin' him how to bait the lure. There's different kinds of baits, you see, most of them are fly larvae or bee larvae that they raise for ice fishin'. And we'd go down to the store, me and Les Junior, and we'd buy 'em at the ice fishin' store. And they come in a little cup, you know. If I had Little Les right now, a son of my own, you know, if I wasn't doomed instead for life with this freakin' PTSD, I'd be out here with him teachin' him all this stuff. I'd teach him how to use the auger." He pointed to the tool, still just out of reach behind him on the ice. "I use a five-inch auger. They come from four inches up to eight inches. I prefer a five-inch hole. It's perfect. I never had a problem yet gettin' a fish through a five-inch hole. Six is a little too big. The reason six is too big, the blades are another inch wider, which doesn't seem like much, but if you look at the five-inch auger—here, let me show you." He got up and went over and he got the auger. Despite the padded coveralls and the boots that added to his bulk as a shortish, stocky man, he moved deftly across the ice, sweeping up the auger in one hand the way you might sweep the bat up off the field while jogging back to the bench after running out a fly ball. He came up to me and raised the auger's long bright bit right up to my face. "Here."

Here. Here was the origin. Here was the essence. Here.

"If you look at the five-inch auger compared to the six-inch auger," he said, "it's a big difference. When you're hand drilling through a foot to eighteen inches of ice, it takes a lot more effort to use a six-inch than a five-inch. With this here I can drill through a foot and a half of ice in about twenty seconds. If the blades are good and sharp. The sharpness is everything. You always gotta keep your blades sharp."

I nodded. "It's cold out here on the ice."

"You better believe it."

"Didn't notice till now. I'm getting cold. My face. It's getting to me. I should be going." And I took my first step backward and away from the thin slush surrounding him and the hole he was fishing.

"Good enough. And you know your ice fishing now, don't you? Maybe you want to write a book about that instead of a whodunit."

Shuffling backward a half-step at a time, I'd retreated toward the shore some four or five feet, but he was still holding the auger up in his one hand, the corkscrew blade raised still to the level where my eyes had been before. Completely bested, I'd begun backing away. "And now you know my secret spot. That too. You know everything," he said. "But you won't tell nobody, will you? It's nice to have a secret spot. You don't tell anybody about 'em. You learn not to say anything."

"It's safe with me," I said.

"There's a brook that comes in down off the mountain, it flows over ledges. Did I tell you that?" he said. "I never traced its source. It's a constant flow of water that comes down into the lake here from there. And there's a spillway on the south side of the lake, which is where the water flows out." He pointed, still with that auger. He was holding it tight in the fingertipless glove of one big hand. "And then there's numerous springs underneath the lake. The water comes up from underneath, so the water constantly turns over. It cleans itself. And fish have to have clean water to survive and get big and healthy. And this place has all of those ingredients. And they're all God-made. Nothing man had to do with it. That's why it's clean and that's why I come here. If man has to do with it, stay away from it. That's my motto. The motto of a guy with a subconscious mind full of PTSD. Away from man, close to God. So don't you forget to keep this my secret place. The only time a secret gets out, Mr. Zuckerman, is when you tell that secret."

"I hear ya."

"And, hey, Mr. Zuckerman—the book."

"What book?"

"Your book. Send the book."

"You got it," I said, "it's in the mail," and started back across the ice. He was behind me, still holding that auger as slowly I started away. It was a long way. If I even made it, I knew that my five years alone in my house here were over. I knew that if and when I finished the book, I was going to have to go elsewhere to live.

I turned from the shore, once I was safely there, to look back and see if he was going to follow me into the woods after all and to do me in before I ever got my chance to enter Coleman Silk's boyhood house and, like Steena Palsson before me, to sit with his East Orange family as the white guest at Sunday dinner. Just facing him, I could feel the terror of the auger—even with him already seated back on his bucket: the icy white of the lake encircling a tiny spot that was a man, the only human marker in all of nature, like the X of an illiterate's signature on a sheet of paper. There it was, if not the whole story, the whole picture. Only rarely, at the end of our century, does life offer up a vision as pure and peaceful as this one: a solitary man on a bucket, fishing through eighteen inches of ice in a lake that's constantly turning over its water atop an arcadian mountain in America.

Philip Roth

I MARRIED A COMMUNIST

'Knotted with energy, barely wasting a scene or a word in its
crackling velocity'
Mail on Sunday

Radio actor Iron Rinn is a big Newark roughneck blighted
by a brutal personal secret from which he is perpetually in
flight. An idealistic Communist, an uneducated ditchdigger
turned popular performer, a six-foot, six-inch Abe Lincoln
lookalike, he emerges from serving in WW2 passionately
committed to making the world a better place and winds up
instead blacklisted and unemployable, his life in ruins.

I Married a Communist is the story of Iron Rinn's denunciation and disgrace. It is also a story of cruelty, humiliation,
betrayal and revenge – an American tragedy as only Philip
Roth can conceive one – fierce and funny, eloquently
rendered and deadly accurate.

'Roth remains as edgy, as furious, as funny, and as dangerous as he was forty years ago'
New York Review of Books

VINTAGE

Philip Roth

PORTNOY'S COMPLAINT

'The most outrageously funny book about sex yet written'
Guardian

The famous confession of Alexander Portnoy, who is thrust
through life by his unappeasable sexuality, yet held back
at the same time by the iron grip of his unforgettable
childhood.

'Roth's gift for fantasy, his superb dialogue, his ability to
evoke places and atmospheres, make *Portnoy's Complaint*
at once hilariously, scabrously funny and deeply moving'
Financial Times

'A hysterically funny monologue which has already added a
new prototype to American literature...Anyone who can
recall anything of the awesome mystery and humiliating
farce of growing up will find this book compulsive reading.
And it is blessedly, extremely funny'
Spectator

Philip Roth

OUR GANG

'The uncontested master of comic irony'
Time

In the character of Tricky – self-promoted legal whiz, peace-loving Quaker – and, somehow, President of the United States – Philip Roth has created one of contemporary literature's greatest hypocritical opportunists.

An unprincipled self-seeker who hides his heartlessness behind the anaesthetising clichés of high office, Tricky's public language is a merciless parody of that 'candid' Presidential prose which is merely double-talk.

Though steeped in fantasy and slapstick, *Our Gang* is conceived in indignation, a satirical vision of a debased national leadership speaking a language that, in Orwell's words, 'is designed to make lies sound truthful and murder respectable, and give an appearance of solidity to pure wind'.

'A bitter yet hilarious lampoon...a remarkable display of satiric vehemence. An extremely (in every sense) funny, nail-bitingly anxious work'
Financial Times

VINTAGE

Philip Roth

OPERATION SHYLOCK
A Confession

'Subtle, funny and furious'
Observer

What if a lookalike stranger stole your name, usurped your biography, and went about the world pretending to be you?

In this *tour de force* of fact and fiction, Philip Roth meets a man who may or may not be Philip Roth. Because someone with that name has been touring Israel, promoting a bizarre exodus in reverse, Roth decides to stop him – even if that means impersonating his impersonator.

Suspenseful, hilarious, hugely impassioned, pulsing with intelligence and narrative energy, *Operation Shylock* is at once a spy story, a political thriller, a meditation on identity, and a confession.

'A very buoyant book, part truth, part fiction, combining sophistication with an equally beguiling vulgarity...it does leave one relishing it and wanting to read more'
Spectator

VINTAGE

BY PHILIP ROTH
ALSO AVAILABLE IN VINTAGE

☐	The Ghost Writer	0099477572	£7.99
☐	The Anatomy Lesson	0099476614	£7.99
☐	The Prague Orgy	0099476517	£6.99
☐	Zuckerman Bound	0099515113	£9.99
☐	American Pastoral	0099771810	£7.99
☐	I Married a Communist	0099287838	£7.99
☐	Operation Shylock	009930791X	£6.99
☐	Patrimony	0099914301	£7.99
☐	The Professor of Desire	0099389010	£6.99
☐	The Dying Animal	0099422697	£6.99
☐	Shop Talk	0099428431	£7.99
☐	Portnoy's Complaint	0099399016	£6.99
☐	Our Gang	0099389118	£6.99

FREE POST AND PACKING
Overseas customers allow £2.00 per paperback

BY PHONE: 01624 677237

BY POST: Random House Books
C/o Bookpost, PO Box 29, Douglas
Isle of Man, IM99 1BQ

BY FAX: 01624 670923

BY EMAIL: bookshop@enterprise.net

Cheques (payable to Bookpost) and credit cards accepted

Prices and availability subject to change without notice.
Allow 28 days for delivery.
When placing your order, please mention if you do not wish to receive
any additional information.

www.randomhouse.co.uk/vintage